ESSENTIALS OF
PSYCHIATRY

ESSENTIALS OF PSYCHIATRY

Sandeep Kumar Goyal
MD (Psychiatry), ACME
Senior Consultant
SPS Hospitals
Ludhiana
and
Formerly, Professor and Head Department of Psychiatry
Christian Medical College and Hospital
Ludhiana

Wolters Kluwer

Sr Publishing Manager: P Sangeetha
Development Editor: Dr Vallika Devi Katragadda
Production Editor: K Annie Devi
Assistant Manager-Manufacturing: Sumit Johry

ISBN: 978-93-89859-03-4

Published by Wolters Kluwer (India) Pvt. Ltd., New Delhi
Compositor: B2K - Bytes 2 Knowledge
Printed and bound at Sterling Graphics Pvt. Ltd., Manesar

For product enquiry, please contact–Marketing Department (marketing@wolterskluwerindia.co.in) or log on to our website www.wolterskluwerindia.co.in.

Foreword

Mental health problems, both worldwide and in India, pose a major challenge for the health administrators and healthcare providers. Lifetime prevalence of mental disorders in India is estimated to be 13.7%. However, there is a tremendous and worrying treatment gap that hovers around 80% for different mental disorders. The problem is further compounded by the lack of sufficient number of psychiatrists and other trained mental health professionals. Therefore, there is a need for adequate training of graduate doctors for identification and management of common mental disorders. There are more than 60,000 medical graduates who pass out annually from different medical colleges of India in contrast to only 800 or so qualified psychiatrists available afresh each year to the healthcare system in India. It thus becomes imperative for medical educators to strengthen the MBBS curriculum with adequate knowledge and skills in dealing with mental health problems. Recently, MCI has taken steps in the right direction by increasing the teaching hours allotted to Psychiatry from 20 to 40, and clinical posting from 2 to 4 weeks.

The above scenario calls for comprehensive teaching and learning material in this field of medicine. The present title, *Essentials of Psychiatry*, by Dr Sandeep Goyal as its Editor should prove to be a useful textbook for MBBS students. This book covers all the major psychiatric disorders as well as special topics such as psychopharmacology, psychotherapy, neuro-stimulation and psychosurgery, forensic psychiatry, community psychiatry, and emergency psychiatry. Each chapter is written by renowned experts in the field in succinct and lucid style in order to achieve easy comprehension by the reader. This publication will certainly fill the vacuum in the availability of authentic educational material and, in turn enhance the treatment availability to the sufferers with mental health problems.

Dr Ajit Avasthi, MD
Formerly, Professor & Head
Department of Psychiatry
PGIMER
Chandigarh

Preface

In recent years, Psychiatry as a branch of Medicine has become increasingly relevant and important. There is a change in the mindset of the medical graduates in India and they now see psychiatry as a rewarding career option. The social stigma attached to psychiatric illness is fast disappearing and the number of people visiting psychiatry clinics is increasing by the day.

It is not surprising that the new MBBS curriculum has increased the number of hours allotted to Psychiatry. It is not only a welcome step but a much-needed one. Medical Council of India (presently called National Medical Commission) has recently introduced competency-based medical education (CBME), which brought in several changes in learning objectives, teaching/learning instructions as well as assessment methods. This book is CBME compliant and covers the MBBS syllabus completely. The book covers almost all the competencies listed in the psychiatry curriculum.

The content is based on DSM-5, which will help the students preparing for the USMLE examination. However, most chapters include comparative nosology wherein differences between ICD-10 and DSM-5 are mentioned. The chapter *Communication Skills and Doctor–Patient Relationship* is added to sensitize the reader about the importance of the same. The chapter *Investigations in Psychiatry* will help the students to use investigations judiciously. The chapters on clinical disorders covers the etiology, clinical features, and diagnosis and management. Differential diagnosis is given a special emphasis to help the student understand the disorder better. Key points that summarize the chapter and self-assessment including case-based questions are added at the end of each chapter.

The book will help the undergraduate medical students immensely to understand the subject and perform well in their examinations. It will also be useful to interns, postgraduate students of Psychiatry, and nursing students. Students of physiotherapy and psychology can also benefit by understanding the subject better.

Dr Sandeep K Goyal

Acknowledgments

At first, I am thankful to *The Almighty* for the blessings showered on me without which I could not have reached the place where I am now.

I am obliged to my Teachers, Dr Paramjit Singh and Dr P.D. Gargi, for teaching me the *ABC* of Psychiatry. I am beholden to my teachers of Advance Course in Medical Education, Dr T. Singh and Dr Dinesh K. Badyal, who taught me the recent advances in medical education.

I acknowledge the constant support provided by my friends Dr Gaurav Rajender, Dr Manish Bathla, Dr Naresh Nebhinani, Dr Purav Midha, Dr Ravi Gupta, Dr Sandeep Grover, Dr Savinder Singh, Dr Tushar Jagawat and Dr Vaibhav Dubey.

I am thankful to all the authors for their earnest efforts in writing the chapters and giving me the liberty to edit the chapters freely to maintain uniformity throughout the book. I recognize the contribution of all the reviewers who spared time to give valuable suggestions.

I am grateful to Wolters Kluwer for entrusting me with the writing of this book and bringing out a high-quality product. I appreciate Dr Vallika Devi Katragadda and her team for their commendable work and contribution in ensuring that the book upholds high standards in terms of content as well as presentation.

I am forever indebted to my parents for their constant support at every point of life. This journey would not have been possible without the unconditional support and advice of my wife Dr Samta Goyal. I am thankful to my kids Parth Goyal and Namish Goyal for moral and emotional support.

Dr Sandeep K Goyal

Contributors

Abdul Majid
Associate Professor
Department of Psychiatry
Sher-i-Kashmir Institute of Medical Sciences
Srinagar, J&K

Adarsh Tripathi
Additional Professor
Department of Psychiatry
King George's Medical University
Lucknow, Uttar Pradesh

Amrit Pattojoshi
Professor and Head
Department of Psychiatry
Hi-Tech Medical College and Hospital
Bhubaneshwar, Odisha

Ankit Mangla
Consultant
Department of Pediatric Nephrology
Surya Hospital
Jaipur, Rajasthan

Arshad Hussain
Professor
Department of Psychiatry
GMC
Srinagar, J&K

Arvind Sharma
Professor and Head
Department of Psychiatry
GGS Medical College and Hospital
Faridkot, Punjab

AW Khan
Professor
Department of Psychiatry
Sher-i-Kashmir Institute of Medical Sciences
Srinagar, J&K

Darpan Kaur
Associate Professor
Department of Psychiatry
MGM Medical College and Hospital
Navi Mumbai, Maharashtra

Dinesh Kumar Badyal
Professor and Head
Department of Pharmacology
CMC
Ludhiana, Punjab

Himanshu Singla
Consultant Psychiatrist
Manodisha Hospital
Barnala, Punjab

Jitendra Jeenger
Professor
Department of Psychiatry
Geetanjali Medical Sciences and Hospital
Udaipur, Rajasthan

KS Shaji
Professor
Department of Psychiatry
GMCH
Thrissur, Kerala

Mamta Singla
Professor and Head
Department of Psychiatry
CMC
Ludhiana, Punjab

Manish Bathla
Professor and Head
Department of Psychiatry
MMIMSR, Mullana
Ambala, Haryana

Mitali Soni Loya
Assistant Professor
Department of Psychiatry
People's College of Medical Sciences and Research Centre
Bhopal, Madhya Pardesh

Mohd Aleem Siddiqui
Professor
Department of Psychiatry
Era's Lucknow Medical College and Hospital
Lucknow, Uttar Pradesh

Mukesh Kumar Swami
Assistant Professor
Department of Psychiatry
AIIMS
Jodhpur, Rajasthan

Nand Kumar
Professor
Department of Psychiatry
AIIMS
New Delhi

Naresh Nebhinani
Additional Professor
Department of Psychiatry
AIIMS
Jodhpur, Rajasthan

Navratan Suthar
Assistant Professor
Department of Psychiatry
AIIMS
Jodhpur, Rajasthan

Nidhi Aggarwal
Assistant Professor (Clinical Psychology)
Department of Psychiatry
CMC
Ludhiana, Punjab

Nidhi Chauhan
Assistant Professor
Department of Psychiatry
GMCH, Chandigarh

Nimmi A Jose
Assistant Professor
Department of Psychiatry
SGT Medical College Hospital and Research Institute
Gurugram, Haryana

Nimmy Chandran
Assistant Professor
Department of Psychiatry
GMCH
Palakkad, Kerala

Nitin Gupta
Senior Consultant
Gupta Mind Healing and Counselling Centre
Chandigarh

Nizam Ud Din
Assistant Professor
Department of Psychiatry
Sher-i-Kashmir Institute of Medical Sciences
Srinagar, J&K

Om Prakash Singh
Consultant Psychiatrist
AMRI Hospital
Kolkata, West Bengal

Pratap Sharan
Professor
Department of Psychiatry
AIIMS
New Delhi

Pooja Patnaik Kuppili
Assistant Professor
Department of Psychiatry
Sri Venkateshwaraa Medical College Hospital and Research Centre
Puducherry, India

Praveen Pandey
Junior Resident
Department of Psychiatry
King George's Medical University
Lucknow, Uttar Pradesh

Prithpal Singh
Professor and Head
Department of Pharmacology
Teerthanker Mahaveer Medical College and Research Centre
Moradabad, UP

Priti Arun
Professor
Department of Psychiatry
GMCH, Chandigarh

Rajeev Gupta
Senior Consultant Psychiatrist
Manas Hospital
Ludhiana, Punjab

Ravi Gupta
Additional Professor
Department of Psychiatry
AIIMS
Rishikesh, Uttarakhand

Ruchita Shah
Assistant Professor
Department of Psychiatry
PGIMER, Chandigarh

Rupesh Chaudhary
Professor
Department of Psychiatry
DMCH
Ludhiana, Punjab

Samta Goyal
Consultant
Department of Critical Care
SPS Hospitals
Ludhiana, Punjab

Sandeep Grover
Professor
Department of Psychiatry
PGIMER, Chandigarh

Sandeep Kumar Goyal
Senior Consultant
SPS Hospitals
Ludhiana, Punjab

Sathya Prakash
Consultant
Institute of Brain and Spine
New Delhi

Shashidhara HN
Psychiatrist (Specialist Grade)
NIMHANS
Bangalore, Karnataka

Shazia Veqar Siddiqui
Consultant Clinical Psychologist
HealthyMinds
Lucknow, Uttar Pradesh

Shazia Anjum
Medical Officer (Psychiatrist)
Civil Hospital
Malerkotla, Punjab

SK Kar
Assistant Professor
Department of Psychiatry
King George's Medical University
Lucknow, Uttar Pradesh

Suresh Bada Math
Professor
Department of Psychiatry
NIMHANS
Bangalore, Karnataka

Sushmita Bhattacharya
Senior Resident
Department of Psychiatry
Kalpana Chawla Government Medical College and Hospital
Karnal, Haryana

Swapnajeet Sahoo
Assistant Professor
Department of Psychiatry
PGIMER, Chandigarh

Swarndeep Singh
Senior Resident
Department of Psychiatry
AIIMS
New Delhi

Vaibhav Dubey
Professor and Head
Department of Psychiatry
People's College of Medical Sciences and Research Centre
Bhopal, Madhya Pardesh

Vinay B
Psychiatrist (Specialist Grade)
NIMHANS
Bangalore, Karnataka

Yuman Kawoos
Consultant Psychiatrist
Directorate of Health Services
Kashmir

Reviewers

Archish Khivsara
Senior Resident
Department of Psychiatry
AIIMS
Jodhpur, Rajasthan

Dheeraj Goya
Senior Resident
Department of Psychiatry
AIIMS
Jodhpur, Rajasthan

Gurvinder Pal Singh
Associate Professor
Department of Psychiatry
GMCH
Chandigarh

Nand Kumar
Professor
Department of Psychiatry
AIIMS
New Delhi

Naresh Nebhinani
Additional Professor
Department of Psychiatry
AIIMS
Jodhpur, Rajasthan

Neetu Gupta
Assistant Professor
Department of Laws
Panjab University
Chandigarh

Nitin Gupta
Senior Consultant
Gupta Mind Healing and Counselling Centre
Chandigarh

Ruchita Shah
Assistant Professor
Department of Psychiatry
PGIMER
Chandigarh

Sandeep Grover
Professor
Department of Psychiatry
PGIMER
Chandigarh

Contents

Chapter 1

History Taking and Mental Status Examination

Sandeep Kumar Goyal · Swapnajeet Sahoo · Naresh Nebhinani

Health is "a state of complete physical, mental, and social well-being and not merely the absence of disease or infirmity" as defined by the World Health Organization (WHO). Hence, mental health is an essential component of health. **Mental health** is a state of well-being in which every individual realizes her/his own potential, can cope with the normal stresses of life, can work productively and fruitfully, and is able to contribute to her or his community (WHO).

Mental illness is characterized by a disturbance in thinking, emotion, or behavior (or a combination of these) and is associated with distress and/or problems functioning in social, work, or family activities.

The term **psychiatry** (means the "medical treatment of the soul") was first coined by the German physician Johann Christian Reil in 1808. It is a medical specialty devoted to the diagnosis, prevention, and treatment of mental disorders. Psychiatry has several subspecialties such as addiction psychiatry, child and adolescent psychiatry, community psychiatry, consultation-liaison psychiatry, emergency psychiatry, forensic psychiatry, geriatric psychiatry, and social psychiatry.

Normality Normality is the pattern of behavior or personality that conforms to certain standard of proper and acceptable way of behaving and being. It may, however, be noted that the words proper and acceptable are ambiguous and involve value judgments and vary from culture to culture.

Daniel Offer and Melvin Sabshin described four perspectives of normality:

1. **Normality as health:** Behavior is assumed to be within normal limits when no manifest psychopathology is present. This perspective is the traditional medical approach to health and illness according to which a lack of signs and symptoms constitutes health.
2. **Normality as utopia:** This perspective defines normality as a harmonious and optimal blending of the diverse elements of mental apparatus that culminates in optimal functioning. This approach is used by psychoanalysts when they discuss their criteria for a successful treatment.
3. **Normality as average:** This perspective is based on mathematical principle of bell-shaped curve and considers middle range normal and both extremes deviant. It is commonly used in normative studies of behavior.
4. **Normality as process:** As per this perspective, normal behavior is the end result of interacting systems. This perspective stresses on changes or processes rather than a cross-sectional

definition of normality. An example of this perspective is epigenesis of personality development.

Most psychoanalysts view capacity for work and enjoyment as normality indicator or as Sigmund Freud described the ability "to love and to work."

CLASSIFICATION OF PSYCHIATRIC ILLNESS

For psychiatric disorders, there are two major classification systems: ICD-10 *(International Classification of Diseases, 10th edition)* and DSM-5 (*Diagnostic and Statistical Manual of Mental Disorders,* 5th edition).

ICD is the WHO's classification system. The *ICD-10 Classification of Mental and Behavioral Disorders: Clinical Descriptions and Diagnostic Guidelines* was published in 1992. The classification is divided into 22 chapters. Chapter V deals with mental and behavioral disorders and it is represented by letter "F." ICD-11 will come into effect on January 1, 2022.

DSM is the American Psychiatric Society's classification. DSM-5 was released in 2013. DSM-5 is a nonaxial system whereas DSM-IV had five axes—I—Psychiatric diagnosis, II: Mental retardation and personality disorders, III: General medical conditions, IV: Psychosocial and environmental problems, and V: Global assessment of functioning.

PSYCHIATRIC HISTORY TAKING

History taking in psychiatry is a skill that is learned by regular practice and by observing experts. One needs to have a few basic communication skills to take a good history. A good history can be taken only if one has adequate knowledge about the subject. Additionally, one must be well aware of the cultural background of the patient and be able to understand the language of the patient. Basic requirements for history taking are given in Box 1.1.

Psychiatric history taking is different in certain aspects from history taking of other medical and surgical specialties. In psychiatric history taking, an informant (family member/caregiver) is required for adequate history as the patient may not have insight and may altogether deny having psychiatric symptoms or otherwise also even if the patient has insight he/she may not give correct history pertaining to substance abuse, relational problems, etc. Psychiatric history taking not only focuses on the patient's current problems but also focuses on how the patient's problems have evolved over a specific duration (years/months/days), on past similar or other types of mental health issues with the patient or his/her family members and on significant childhood, developmental, marital history, etc. Therefore, psychiatric history taking is a holistic approach to understand the psyche of the individual along with various other factors that can affect the individual's mental health. Box 1.2 enumerates various subheadings of psychiatric history.

History taking should be done in a proper format as given below.

1. **Personal data/identification data:** It typically includes the patient's name, age, gender, educational, occupational, and marital status, race/religion, family background (nuclear/extended/joint family), and socio-economic status, area of residence (urban/rural), and distance of the

Box 1.1 Basic prerequisites for psychiatric history taking

1. **Interview room:** Psychiatric interview should be carried out in a room with adequate provisions for privacy and personal and patient safety.
2. **Safety:** The doctor should sit nearest to the door and neither the patient nor any object should block the doctor's way to exit. There can be provisions of an alarm buzzer system to inform the security personals in case of violence and risk to self or others.
3. **Privacy and confidentiality:** These are essential prerequisites of psychiatric history taking.
    - ***Privacy*:** Privacy is a necessary prerequisite to get a reliable history. Sometimes it is difficult to establish privacy, for example, in a medical or surgical ward.
    - ***Confidentiality*:** Boundaries of confidentiality should be decided at the start of the interview. The patient should be reassured that the details would not be discussed with her/his significant other without her/his consent unless there are some emergency situations (e.g., the risk of suicide or violence). The patient should also be informed that if required her/his problems may be discussed with other mental health professionals for her/his benefit.
4. **Communication skills:**
    - Use language which patient can understand.
    - Establish and maintain rapport.
    - Listen actively using nonverbal (eye contact) and verbal (e.g., words of encouragement) techniques.
    - Allow the patient to complete the statements and elicit all of his or her concerns using open- and close-ended questions appropriately.
    - Have an open, empathetic, and nonjudgmental approach.

Box 1.2 Format of psychiatric history taking

1. Identification/personal data
2. Source of information—informant(s) details and nature of information
3. Chief complaints
4. History of present illness
5. Past history—medical and psychiatric
6. Family history of mental illness
7. Personal history
    a. Developmental history
    b. Educational history
    c. Occupational history
    d. Sexual and marital history
    e. Substance abuse history
8. Premorbid personality

patient's home to the hospital/treatment center. The referral source/department can also be mentioned. All these variables have specific importance and identification data many a time help in taking the patient management decisions.

2. **Source of information and its nature:** The details of informants accompanying the patient should be noted down in terms of their names, age, occupation, education, relationship with the patient, and duration since when they have been staying with the patient. Sources other than family members can be police officers/hospital authority/office staff/colleagues/classmates/school authority who can also bring the patient to the healthcare setup. It should be mentioned that how much reliable the information provided is. The provided information is said to be "**reliable**" if the given information is consistent amongst different informants and over different times.
3. **Chief complaints:** Chief complaints are the main problems for which the patient has come for seeking consultation. It should be noted in the patient's language (verbatim) with their duration in chronological order. Chief complaints should be separately noted down for both patients and caregivers/informants. Examples include *"I am tensed"* or *"People are after my life."*
    a. ***Onset*:** The time between the appearance of the first symptom to full-blown syndrome of a diagnosable disorder is defined as the onset. The onset is abrupt when it occurs within 48 hours and it is called acute when it occurs within more than 48 hours but less than 2 weeks. When the symptoms develop so gradually that it is difficult to ascertain when the onset exactly occurred, it is known as insidious onset.
    b. ***Course*:** The course of illness is the manner of evolution and progression of the symptoms. It can be continuous, fluctuating, steady, progressive, or episodic.
    c. ***Precipitating factors*:** Precipitating factors are the risk factors that have a temporal relationship with the onset of illness and without these factors, illness might not have occurred.
4. **History of presenting illness:** This segment includes a description of the symptoms and their duration. The onset and progression of every symptom should be described along with their relationship with specific life events/stressors and the effect of treatment on the symptom profile if the patient has undergone treatment earlier. Any change in biological functions like sleep, appetite, and the impact of the illness on the patient's socio-occupational domains should be mentioned. Predominant mood symptoms, behavioral problems, and cognitive disturbances should also be mentioned. A specific inquiry of death wish, suicidal ideations, and previous suicide attempts should be mentioned. Any substance use history if present should be elaborated along which a description of its relationship with the patient's symptomology. Treatment history should be ascertained with medication details (dose, duration of treatment, effects, side effects, and compliance) and details of psychotherapy.

    Important negative information obtained during history taking should also be mentioned.
5. **Past history:** The past history should include both significant medical and

psychiatric history. Details of past major medical and surgical illnesses should be enlisted as these can help in deciding psychotropic medications. If the psychiatric condition has an episodic course, the details of each episode should be provided along with treatment received. Any past incident of self-harm, suicidal ideations, or violence should be mentioned.

6. **Family history of mental illness:** A careful review of family history is an essential part of the psychiatric assessment. It should include psychiatric diagnoses, medications, hospitalizations, substance use disorders, and lethality history. Any family member (blood relative) having symptoms suggestive of intellectual disability, epilepsy, alcohol and/or drug dependence, suicide, psychosis, mood disorders, etc. should be explored and noted. A pedigree chart is an ideal way of representing family history.
7. **Personal history**
   a. ***Developmental history*:** Information concerning prenatal or birth history and developmental milestones are to be explored. Neurotic traits if any should be noted. Any problems related to delay in developmental milestones and childhood behavioral problems should be noted. Specific inquiry into childhood physical and sexual abuse should also be done.
   b. ***Educational history*:** A detailed school history including any specific requirement for special education, behavioral issues at school, problems in learning, grade of performance in exams, and extracurricular activities should be documented. The highest degree of educational qualifications along with problems in academics as well as peer relationships should be enquired too.
   c. ***Occupational history*:** Current occupational status along with all past occupational posts held and reasons for changing jobs should be mentioned.
   d. ***Sexual and marital history*:** Age of onset of menarche/menopause, type of menstrual cycles, masturbation, and associated guilt feelings should be documented. Marital and relationship history including sexual history should be explored.
   e. ***Substance abuse history*:** A careful review of substance abuse and its relation to psychiatric symptoms should be done. History of initiation, progression, and current status of all the substances should be noted. Any use of intravenous drug should also be enquired. The exact duration of use and periods of abstinence should be enquired.

   The personal history should also include any physical disability, food habits, sleep habits, and bowel and bladder habits.
8. **Premorbid personality (PMP):** The PMP of an individual helps in providing important understandings into individual symptomatology, diagnosis, and management. PMP includes social relations, intellectual activities, hobbies, predominant mood, character, attitude toward work and responsibility, attitude to self and others, religious beliefs and moral attitudes, interpersonal relationships, energy, habits, and fantasy life. Personality traits (assertive, introvert vs. extrovert, sociable, anxious and worrisome, compulsive, suspicious)

are to be noted from reliable informants knowing the patient before the onset of the illness.

A detailed general physical examination (GPE), systemic examination, and a complete neurological examination should be done in every patient. It should be noted that patients with psychiatric illnesses have a high rate of physical comorbidities, which are often neglected by patients. A psychiatrist must note all the physical findings, vitals, and anthropometric data (such as height, weight, waist circumference, body mass index).

MENTAL STATUS EXAMINATION

The mental status examination (MSE) is the detailed account of the present state of mind of an individual and is based upon a series of observations and interview conducted in a standardized format. It is the cornerstone of the psychiatric assessment. Therefore, MSE should be carried out on every patient, and all relevant findings should be documented appropriately. Box 1.3 lists down the components of MSE.

1. General Appearance, Attitude, and Behavior (GAAB)

Many times, various important findings can be found in the GAAB (like catatonic symptoms—staring, smiling to self, hallucinatory behavior). Broadly one should note and describe the following things:

- Physical health condition
- Attire, manner of dress worn, hygiene, signs of self-neglect, grooming, odor
- Facial expression—verbal and nonverbal cues
- Any signs of physical illness, drug withdrawal, tremors, scar marks, self-harm scars/cut marks
- Eye-to-eye contact—initiated or not, able to maintain during interview or not
- Attitude toward examiner—cooperative, indifferent, disinterested, etc.
- Motor movements such as dyskinesias, akathisia, stereotype movements (repetitive non-goal directed movements, e.g., rocking to and fro in a chair), mannerisms (idiosyncratic goal-directed movements, e.g., style of walking, frequently raising the eyebrows), echopraxia, and catatonic signs

Box 1.3 Mental status examination

1. General appearance, attitude, and behavior (GAAB)
2. Psychomotor activity (PMA)
3. Speech
4. Mood and affect
5. Thought: Form, flow, content, and possession
6. Perceptual disturbances
7. Cognitive functions: Orientation, attention, concentration, and memory—immediate, recent and remote, intelligence, abstract thinking
8. Insight
9. Judgment

- Gait and posture maintained during the interview
- Rapport—defined as the instantaneous reciprocal emotional resonance between the patient and the interviewer, whether it was established or not, needs to be mentioned

2. Psychomotor Activity (PMA)

It refers to how the psychic component affect the motor activity. It is usually a goal-directed response involving both motor and psychological components. It is usually described as normal/average, increased, and decreased. PMA is usually increased in cases of agitation, mania, or hypomania and decreased in cases of depression. Generalized slowing or bradykinesia due to any medical/neurological/drug-related side effects can also be seen and documented. Thus, mere giving specific attention to PMA can also provide hints to adverse reactions or side effects of medications such as extrapyramidal symptoms.

3. Speech

It is described under various subheadings. The rate of speech is described as slowed/rapid. The tone of speech is labeled as "normal" with normal tonal inflections or "monotonous" in the absence of tonal inflections. Additionally, the amount and volume of speech should be noted. If the rate of speech is more than 150 words per minute, then it is denoted as "pressure of speech" (often occurs in mania and agitated psychosis). One should also note if the speech was spontaneous or not. Further, the relevance and coherence (i.e., understandability) should be examined and documented. An important aspect of the interpretation of speech is that the examiner should always compare the patient's current speech with premorbid level by taking the help of patient's family members/caregivers and interpret accordingly.

4. Mood and Affect

The mood of the individual is defined as the person's internal and *sustained emotional state* while affect is an immediate external expression of mood.

The predominant mood should be noted. The affect is described in terms of quality, quantity, range, appropriateness, and congruence.

Quality of mood and affect are described as happy, cheerful, angry, dysphoric, euthymic, euphoric, etc. The quantity of affect is a measure of its intensity. The range can be restricted, normal, labile, blunted, or flat. Appropriateness refers to how the affect correlates to the setting. A patient laughing at a funeral service is an example of inappropriateness of the affect. Affect can be congruent or incongruent with the described mood and thought content, for example, a patient reporting sadness with smiling is an example of incongruent affect.

5. Thought

Form of thought refers to the disturbance in the arrangement of thoughts or the logical connections between ideas. Disorders of the form of thought are usually recognized from speech and writing. Disorders of the form of thought are known as "formal thought disorder." Common abnormal thought processes are flight of ideas, tangentiality, circumstantiality, perseveration, thought block, neologism, and poverty of speech. Box 1.4 lists down various common formal thought disorders.

Content of thought Thought content is essentially what thoughts are occurring to the patient. Disorders of the content of thought include an abnormality in content or material of thought. It is explored from the spontaneous expression of the patient as well as responses of the patient to the various questions asked. Depressive cognitions (hopelessness, worthlessness), self-harm/suicidal thoughts or plans, and delusions are some common thought content abnormalities.

Delusion is a false, unshakeable belief that is out of keeping with the patient's social and cultural background.

Possession of thought Normally a person feels that his/her thoughts are under his control, but sometimes a person loses control of his sense of possession of thinking. Disorders of possession can be obsessions (recurrent, irrational, intrusive, ego-dystonic thoughts which the patient is unable to control). Another type of thought possession is thought alienation which includes thought insertion (thoughts are being inserted by someone from outside), thought withdrawal (thoughts are being taken out by someone), and thought broadcasting (thoughts are being escaped to the surrounding or being diffused to others due to some mechanism and other persons can hear the thoughts). In thought alienation, the patient has an experience that others are participating in his/her thinking.

Box 1.4 Formal thought disorders

- **Derailment:** A pattern of spontaneous speech in which the ideas slip off the track onto another one that is clearly but obliquely related, or onto one that is completely unrelated.
- **Flight of ideas:** The patient rapidly moves from one thought to another, at a pace that is difficult for the listener to keep up with, but all of the ideas are logically connected.
- **Circumstantiality:** When in response to a question, the patient gives very unnecessary trivial details before actually answering the question. The patient answers the question by elaborating on many minor details.
- **Tangentiality:** Mild form of derailment in which there is a breakdown in associations. It refers to a disturbance in which a person replies to a question in the oblique, digressive manner and the central idea is not communicated. Failure to communicate central idea distinguishes tangentiality from circumstantiality.
- **Perseveration:** The persistent repetition of the same idea in response to a new question.
- **Thought blocking:** Sudden arrest of the train of thought leaving a "blank." The patient may stop mid-sentence and leave the interviewer waiting for the completion.
- **Neologisms:** Refers to the invention of a new word or condensed combination of several words that is not a valid word and is not readily understandable.

6. Perceptual Disturbances

Perceptual disturbances include hallucinations and illusions, depersonalization, and derealization. **Hallucination** is a perception without external stimuli whereas the **illusion** is a misinterpretation of a real external stimulus. While describing a hallucination, the presenter should take into account the type of hallucination one is experiencing, how frequently it occurs and when it occurs (e.g., auditory hallucination occurring while falling asleep is a hypnogogic hallucination and may be normal).

Types of the auditory hallucinations, for example, command hallucinations, third person hallucinations, etc. should be noted.

Depersonalization is a feeling of unfamiliarity with the self and derealization is feeling that one's environment is changed.

7. Cognitive Functions

The elements of cognitive functioning that should be assessed are orientation, attention and concentration, memory (both short- and long-term), intelligence, and abstract reasoning. A major point to note is that the interviewer should describe in detail the exact procedure of how the cognitive tests will be carried out before asking questions to test cognitive functions. This is necessary as patients often feel that they are being subjected to silly questions that are unrelated to their problems. So it is of utmost importance to explain to them that it is part of their evaluation process.

- **Orientation:** The person's orientation to time, place, and person is assessed by direct questioning about the same (i.e., by asking the time, date, day, month, year, season, and the time spent in hospital, the present location/area, his own name, and whether he can identify people around him). Disorientation in time usually precedes disorientation in place and person. First, ask orientation to time, then place and then person, finally check if he can name himself/herself.
- **Attention and concentration: Attention** is the patient's ability to attend to a specific stimulus without being distracted by extraneous, internal, or environmental stimuli, and **concentration** is the sustained attention or the ability to maintain attention to a specific stimulus over an extended period. A basic and simple test of attention and concentration is asking the patient to repeat the days of the week backward and note how long it takes. Similarly, attention can also be tested by asking the patient to repeat digit forwards and backward, and concentration can be tested by asking serial subtraction of 7 from 100 or 3 from 40 and noting the time taken and mistakes done.
- **Memory:** Memory in clinical practice is usually assessed as immediate registration and recall, which is short-term memory (within minutes); and recent memory is assessed by asking about the things/events occurred within last few days and remote memory assessed by asking facts that had occurred years before.
  - ***Registration*** of the patient is tested by asking the patient to repeat three words (e.g., *"school, sky, horse"*) after the interviewer. The **recall** is tested by asking the patient to recollect the three words given 3 minutes earlier. Digit forwards and backward also tests the immediate registration and recall.

- *Recent memory* is the patient's capacity to remember current, day-to-day events (e.g., the current date, the doctor's name, breakfast, or asking how the patient came to the hospital).
- *Remote memory* is the recall of facts or events that occurred years earlier (e.g., names of old school/college, birth dates, and anniversary dates).

- **Intelligence:** Intelligence is defined as the ability to think logically, act rationally, and deal effectively with others. It is assessed under the following headings:
  - ***General fund of knowledge*:** General fund of knowledge should be asked keeping in mind the patient's socio-economic and educational background as well as his experiences and interests (e.g., the current and the past prime ministers, sarpanch/head of the village, the capital of India, naming any five rivers of the country, naming any five cities of the country, and how to prepare a cup of tea, etc.).
  - ***Calculations*:** The test is done by asking the patient to answer verbally (simple calculations), and by writing/calculating on paper (complex calculations). It should start with addition and then moving to subtraction, multiplication, and division and sequentially verbal simple and complex and then written simple and complex.
  - ***Comprehension*:** Comprehension is the ability to understand and get meaning from spoken and written language. It is assessed by asking the patient to follow a command with a motor response, for example, "Squeeze my fingers."
- **Abstract thinking:** Abstract reasoning is the ability to conceptualize or break the whole into its parts and to construct the whole from its parts. It is assessed by asking the similarities and differences between different objects such as apple and banana/car and airplane. Cultural and educational factors and limitations should be kept in mind when assessing the ability to abstract. **Proverb interpretation** is another method of testing abstraction. The patient is asked to tell the meaning of common proverbs in the local language. Based on the answers given, the response could be concrete, semi-abstract, or abstract.

For example, when asked "A stitch on time saves nine," if the patient replies as:

- Stitches can save nine persons—it is concrete thinking.
- Appropriate action done at the appropriate time can save us from many untoward events—it is abstract thinking.

8. Insight

It refers to the patient's understanding of whether he/she has an illness, the nature of the illness (i.e., physical or psychological), and if he/she requires any treatment or not. Depending on the assessment, the insight is divided into six grades. Insight is generally absent in acute psychosis. Box 1.5 lists the various grades of insight and how to ask questions for assessing insight.

Judgment

It is the ability of the person to take correct decisions and act effectively on them. It has two parts: social judgment and test judgment. The *social judgment* includes

Box 1.5 Insight assessment and grading

Questions to be asked to assess insight

- Do you think you have an illness or do you think there is anything wrong with you?
- If there is something wrong, is it of physical nature or psychological nature?
- How do you describe your problem and what do you think what caused it?
- Do you think you can be helped by treatment or do you need treatment?

Grades of insight

- Grade 1: Complete denial of illness.
- Grade 2: Slight awareness of being sick and needing help, but denying it at the same time.
- Grade 3: Awareness of being sick, but it is attributed to external or physical factors.
- Grade 4: Awareness of being sick, due to something unknown in self.
- Grade 5: **Intellectual insight—**awareness of being ill and that the symptoms are due to own particular irrational feelings/thoughts but do not apply this knowledge to the current/future experiences.
- Grade 6: **True emotional insight—**awareness of being ill and taking appropriate steps to bring about necessary changes in future behavior.

how the patient behaves during the interview, that is, if he/she has basic knowledge of the socially appropriate responses in social situations or not. The *test judgment* is assessed by asking the person how he/she would react if placed in a hypothetical/realistic situation like "What you would do if your house gets on fire?" or "What would you do if you find the tap is overflowing the bucket?" It is usually described as normal or impaired.

ENDING THE PSYCHIATRIC INTERVIEW

After a detailed history and mental state examination, the interviewer should not end the interview abruptly. The patient should be asked, "Is there any issues left which the patient wants to discuss?" The patient should be given a chance to ask questions. The patient should be informed about the summary of the diagnosis and treatment options available.

CONCEPT OF PSYCHOSIS AND NEUROSIS

The conceptual framework of psychiatric disorders has been broadly divided into two groups of disorders, that is, psychotic and neurotic disorders. Although obsolete, this classification is still useful in understanding the concept.

Psychosis is a term that is used when there is a loss of contact with the reality. The person's thought process and perceptions are largely affected. The classic clinical presentation includes delusions and hallucinations. Insight is absent in psychotic disorders. The groups of disorders in which all the above symptoms are present are classified under "psychotic disorders."

These include schizophrenia, persistent delusional disorder, acute and transient psychotic disorders/brief psychotic disorder, schizoaffective disorder, etc.

Neurosis is a term that is generally used to describe nonpsychotic mental illness in which contact with reality and some degree of insight is usually retained by the patient. The main disturbances occur in a person's emotional, occupational, and social life. The groups of disorders with neurosis are classified as "neurotic disorders." These include anxiety disorders (panic disorder, generalized anxiety disorder, phobias), depression, obsessive-compulsive disorder, post-traumatic stress disorder, somatoform, and dissociative disorders.

KEY POINTS

- **Health** is "a state of complete physical, mental, and social well-being and not merely the absence of disease or infirmity" as defined by the WHO. Hence, mental health is an essential component of health.
- **Mental health** is a state of well-being in which every individual realizes her/his own potential, can cope with the normal stresses of life, can work productively and fruitfully, and is able to contribute to her or his community (WHO).
- **Mental illness** is characterized by a disturbance in thinking, emotion, or behavior (or a combination of these) and associated with distress and/or problems functioning in social, work, or family activities.
- The term **psychiatry** (means the "medical treatment of the soul") was first coined by the German physician Johann Christian Reil in 1808.
- Psychiatry is a medical specialty devoted to the diagnosis, prevention, and treatment of mental disorders.
- Normality is the pattern of behavior or personality that conforms to certain standard of proper and acceptable way of behaving and being.
- For psychiatric disorders, there are two major classification systems ICD-10 and DSM-5.
- History taking in psychiatry is a skill that is learned by regular practice and by observing experts.
- **Privacy and confidentiality** are essential prerequisites of psychiatric history taking.
- In psychiatric history taking, an informant (family member/caregiver) is required for adequate history.
- The mental status examination (MSE) is the detailed account of the present state of mind of an individual and is based upon a series of observations and interviews conducted in a standardized format. It is the cornerstone of the psychiatric assessment.
- **Psychosis** is a term that is used when there is a loss of contact with reality. The classic clinical presentation includes delusions and hallucinations. Insight is absent in psychotic disorders.
- **Neurosis** is a term that is generally used to describe mental illness in which contact with reality and some degree of insight is usually retained by the patient. The groups of disorders with neurosis are classified as "neurotic disorders."

SELF-ASSESSMENT

1. Define insight and discuss the various grades of insight.
2. Write short notes on:
   a. Normality
   b. Formal thought disorder
   c. Psychosis and neurosis

Chapter 2

Communication Skills and Doctor–Patient Relationship

Sandeep Kumar Goyal

Good communication skills are extremely important for doctors. They help in creating an interpersonal relationship and facilitate the exchange of information, thus helping in establishing the correct diagnosis. Good communication skills also help in counseling the patients and giving therapeutic instructions.

Doctors may or may not be possessing excellent communication skills. However, they can learn and practice good communication.

COMPONENTS OF COMMUNICATION

Verbal, nonverbal, and paraverbal are the three basic components of effective communication. The *verbal component* includes content and selection of the words whereas the *paraverbal component* includes tone, pitch, pacing, and volume of the voice. The *nonverbal component* includes body language (e.g., posture, gesture, facial expression, and spatial distance).

Verbal component (content) conveys information about the various aspects of the disease, for example, nature, course, prognosis of the disease, and various treatment options available, etc. Nonverbal component significantly influences important outcomes like patient's satisfaction, adherence to advice, and clinical outcome.

Paraverbal communication adds more meaning to the words. Even if one has the right words, how he delivers them can change the impact of the verbal component. Appropriate use of the paraverbal component helps in making the desired impact.

Attentive listening skills, empathy, and use of open-ended questions are some examples of skillful communication. Some of the characteristics of good communication are as follows:

1. Maintaining eye contact: Eye contact is considered an important component of effective communication. Maintaining eye contact doesn't mean staring at the person.
2. Being attentive: Attentive means ignoring external distractions like background activity and noise as well as internal distractions like one's own thoughts or feelings.
3. Show interest in what the patient is saying with your mannerism (e.g., head nodding), body language, and active involvement (e.g., leaning toward the patient).
4. Mannerism like patting patient's shoulder may convince the patient that you care for them.
5. Don't interrupt the patient and wait for him/her to complete the conversation.
6. Pay attention to both the verbal and nonverbal components of the communication

of the patient and observe if there is any discrepancy between the two.

7. The doctor should be aware of his/her nonverbal clues like body language and gestures.
8. Never have discussions with patients or relatives while walking in the corridors.

DIFFERENT MODELS OF COMMUNICATION

Several models of communication during clinical consultations (BIHC Communication E4 Model, Three Function Model, The Calgary–Cambridge Observation Guide, Patient-centered clinical method, and SEGUE Framework for Teaching and Assessing Communication Skills) were in use. A group of representatives developed a consensus model of the five models mentioned earlier describing the essential steps in clinical consultation. This model is called the **Kalamazoo Consensus Statement**, which identifies seven essential sets of communication tasks.

1. Building the Doctor–Patient Relationship

A strong, therapeutic and effective relationship is the sine qua non of physician–patient communication.

2. Opening the Discussion

It includes allowing the patient to complete his or her opening statement and eliciting the patient's full set of concerns and establishing a personal connection.

3. Gathering Information

It includes using open-ended and closed-ended questions appropriately and by active listening using nonverbal (e.g., eye contact) and verbal (e.g., words of encouragement) communication followed by structuring, clarifying, and summarizing information.

4. Understanding the Patient's Perspective

It includes exploring contextual factors (e.g., family, culture, gender, age, socio economic status, and spirituality), beliefs, concerns, expectations about health and illness, and acknowledging and responding to the patient's ideas, feelings, and values.

5. Sharing the Information

It includes using the language the patient can understand, checking for understanding, and encouraging the patients to ask questions.

6. Reaching Agreement on Problems and Plans

This can be achieved by encouraging the patient to participate in decisions to the extent he or she desires and by checking the patient's willingness and ability to follow the plan.

7. Providing Closure

It includes asking whether the patient has any other issues or concerns. At the end summarize and discuss the follow-up (e.g., next visit, plan for unexpected outcomes).

TRAINING IN COMMUNICATION SKILLS

Teaching communication skills requires educators who themselves are excellent communicators. A communication skills training (CST) program should be multi-session and multi-disciplinary; should use multiple methods; and include opportunities for demonstration, discussion, reflection, practice, and feedback.

Experiential methods supplemented with feedback (e.g., role-plays or interaction with simulated or real patients) are more effective than instructional methods (e.g., lectures and seminars). Experiential methods help students in identifying their strengths and weaknesses in communication and are preferred by students. Closed-circuit television (CCTV) video-recording can be used to provide feedback to trainees during CST.

In a role-play, a student performs a given role and the facilitator and peers give feedback after the session. To be effective, educators utilizing role-play should provide feedback in a way which does not make the learner anxious. Students reflect and learn the significance of voice, tone, or body language through role-plays.

Training in verbal and nonverbal communication goes hand-in-hand. Students also learn by observing clinicians working in a clinical setting in addition to learning during training sessions. The faculty members should be sensitized that they are the role models and are knowingly or unknowingly imparting training in communication skills while providing clinical care.

Communication skills should be assessed in examination settings throughout the medical curriculum.

BREAKING BAD NEWS

Breaking bad news (BBN) is an important clinical skill for doctors and nurses. Bad news is defined as any information which adversely affects an individual's view of his or her future. While the most common perception of bad news is terminal illness, it can be any life-altering diagnoses ranging from fetal demise to degenerative conditions to debilitating infections. BBN can be about diagnosis, treatment, prognosis, cost or impact of the disease on an individual or family.

BBN skills do not make the bad news good, but soften the impact of the same. BBN allows the patients and relatives to deal with the impact of bad news, and encourages them to express their feelings. Most of the clinicians and nurses are not trained in BBN.

The bearer of bad news often experiences strong emotions such as anxiety. This stress creates a reluctance to deliver bad news, which is named as the "*mum effect*."

There are several strategies that can be used to deliver bad news.

SPIKES model This is the most well-known model for delivering the bad news proposed by Buckman. The steps in this model are as follows:

- **S - Setting:** Ensure privacy and appropriate setting and environment for the discussion
- **P - Perception:** Understand the patient's perception of the illness
- **I - Invitation:** Explore how much information the patient needs. In other words, obtain the patient's invitation for details regarding the illness
- **K - Knowledge:** Warn the patient about the imminent bad news before breaking it and provide the information in chunks, all the while ensuring that he/she understands what is being conveyed
- **E - Empathy:** Listen to the patient, identify the emotions, and address the patient's emotions with empathic responses

- **S - Strategy and summary:** Summarize the information you have provided and formulate a clear plan with the next steps neatly chalked out

ABCDE Another practical model suggested by Rabow and McPhee uses the mnemonic **ABCDE**.

- **A**dvance preparation
- **B**uild a therapeutic environment/relationship
- **C**ommunicate well
- **D**eal with patient and family reactions
- **E**ncourage and validate emotions

BREAKS protocol It includes another systematic and easy strategy for BBN.

- **B**ackground information about the illness
- **R**apport building
- **E**xploring the patient's knowledge about the illness
- **A**nnounce the bad news with a warning
- **K**indling the patient's emotions
- **S**ummarize the information and plan of action

The underlying concepts across all the above strategies are:

1. Deciding the amount of bad news to be delivered or the extent of truth to be divulged
2. Managing psychological reactions

Challenges

The following are challenges in implementation of the above models for BBN in the Indian setting:

1. **Poor literacy and lack of information about illnesses:** Patients and family members are not equipped with sufficient prior knowledge about the illness to process the news given to them.
2. **Cultural and social norms related to terminal illness and death:** Family members do not wish the physician to discuss end-of-life care with the patient.
3. Discussing psychological stress and issues openly is still not a norm in rural India, and patients and their family members do not engage with the physician in such discussions.
4. **Inadequate preparation to deliver bad news:** Residents and physicians are not equipped to deliver bad news.

Recommendations

Recommendations to address specific challenges are as follows:

1. Identify the literacy level of the patient and tailor the information in the native language of the patient such that he comprehends it. Generously use pictures to explain what cannot be put across in words.
2. Discuss patient autonomy and medical proxy in the first consultation. If the patient chooses not to know about her/his diagnosis, ensure that a responsible medical proxy is identified who is acceptable to the patient. Assure the patient that anytime during the process, he/she can choose to know his/her diagnosis or change his/her medical proxy. This helps maintain the trust the patient reposes in the physician and does not make him/her feel abandoned.
3. Try to understand family dynamics before broaching sensitive subjects. Assure the patient about absolute confidentiality before discussing emotional and psychosocial stress. Offer appropriate counseling to the patient and caregivers as they play a crucial role in the entire decision-making process.

4. It is essential to train undergraduate medical students in the art of listening and speaking to patients, providing information effectively and showing empathy, which forms the basis of BBN.

DOCTOR–PATIENT RELATIONSHIP

The quality of the doctor–patient relationship is very crucial to the practice of psychiatry. The good doctor–patient relationship helps in better data collection, improves compliance, helps in achieving better therapeutic results, and prevents unnecessary legal hassles.

The doctor–patient relationship can be discussed under the following headings:

1. Patient-related factors
2. Treating physician-related factors
3. The approach toward the patient
4. Models of interaction between doctor and patients

Patient-Related Factors

The personality of the individual, past experiences, coping mechanisms, and transference are common patient factors.

Transference is defined as the patient's feelings toward the doctor. This is determined by psychodynamic conflicts. The patient may perceive the doctor as good/bad/caring/hostile/brother/sister/father/mother. Transference is not based on how the doctor actually behaves but is a repetition of the attitude of the patient toward the authority figures.

Treating Physician-Related Factors

The personality of the doctor, his preconceived notions, and countertransference are common factors.

Doctor's feelings toward the patient are known as "**countertransference**" and it has several psychodynamic components. Countertransference can be negative, positive, idealizing, or even eroticized reactions to the patients.

The Approach Toward the Patient

The doctor should have a nonjudgmental and empathic approach toward the patient. The patient should be given a patient hearing and assured of confidentiality.

Models of Interaction Between Doctor and Patients

An experienced physician uses different approaches with different patients or at times different approaches with the same patients at different times as per need.

Paternalistic Model

In this model, it is assumed that the doctor knows the best. A patient is supposed to obey the prescribed treatment without asking questions. The doctor can withhold information if it is in the best interest of the patient. Paternalistic model is desired in emergencies where the doctor needs to make lifesaving decisions.

Informative Model

In the informative model, the doctor dispenses information and choice is left wholly up to the patient. In the informative model, the patient may think that the doctor is cold and uncaring. This model may be appropriate for certain one-time consultations where the patient will return to the regular care of his/her known physician.

Interpretive Model

In this model, shared decision-making is done. The role of the doctor is to discuss alternatives with the patient and to find the best alternative for a particular patient with his participation.

Deliberative Model

In the deliberative model, the doctor presents the information and actively advocates a particular course of action. This approach is used when convincing patients to stop smoking or lose weight. In this model, the doctor acts as a counselor to the patient.

An effective doctor–patient relationship is characterized by good rapport. Empathy increases rapport.

Rapport **Rapport** is the spontaneous and conscious feeling of harmonious responsiveness that promotes the development of a constructive therapeutic alliance. It is an understanding and trust between the doctor and the patient.

Empathy Empathy means "feel into" an object. **Carl Rogers** defined empathy as "To perceive the internal frame of reference of another with accuracy, and with emotional components which pertain thereto, as if one were the other person, but without ever losing the 'as if' condition." Empathy is an essential characteristic of a psychiatrist.

Barrett–Lennard described an **empathy cycle** in which a therapist listens openly to the patient; the therapist resonates with that experience; the therapist expresses the resonance back and then the patient becomes aware of being understood and continues to express her or himself with a heightened level of comfort.

Empathy correlates with better patient satisfaction and outcomes.

Confidentiality Confidentiality involves the ethical duty of the clinician not to disclose information about a patient without his/her authorization. Medical professionals are bound to protect the confidentiality of the patients. Confidentiality helps to build and develop trust in the doctor–patient relationship. It also helps the patient to be truthful during a healthcare visit. If the confidentiality of the information provided by the patient is not protected, trust in the physician-patient relationship would be diminished.

The following are recognized exceptions to the duty of confidentiality:

1. Consent of the patient or a legally authorized surrogate decision-maker, such as a parent, guardian, or other surrogate designated by an advance directive.
2. Court order.
3. Comply with the law, for example, mandatory reporting of child abuse.
4. Communication of a threat is a well-known Tarasoff exception to confidentiality that involves the clinician's duty to protect others from violence by a patient.

KEY POINTS

- Good communication skills help in creating an interpersonal relationship and facilitate the exchange of information, thus helping in establishing the correct diagnosis.
- Effective communication has three basic components, that is, verbal, nonverbal, and paraverbal.
- The *verbal component* includes content and selection of the words whereas *the paraverbal component* includes tone, pitch, pacing, and volume of the voice.
- The *nonverbal component* includes body language (e.g., posture, gesture, facial expression, and spatial distance).
- Kalamazoo Consensus Statement identifies seven essential sets of communication tasks in clinical consultation.
- A communication skills training (CST) program should be multi-session and multi-disciplinary; should use multiple methods; and include opportunities for demonstration, discussion, reflection, practice, and feedback.
- Experiential methods supplemented with feedback (e.g., role-plays or interaction with simulated or real patients) are more effective than instructional methods (e.g., lectures and seminars).
- Breaking bad news (BBN) is an important clinical skill for doctors and nurses. BBN skills do not make the bad news good, but soften the impact of the same, allow dealing with the impact of bad news, and encourage the expression of feelings by the patients and relatives.
- Various models for BBN are **BREAKS** model, **ABCDE** model, and **SPIKES** protocol.
- **Rapport** is the spontaneous and conscious feeling of harmonious responsiveness that promotes the development of a constructive therapeutic alliance.
- **Empathy** means "feel into" an object. **Carl Rogers** defined empathy as "To perceive the internal frame of reference of another with accuracy, and with emotional components which pertain thereto, as if one were the other person, but without ever losing the 'as if' condition." Empathy is an essential characteristic of a psychiatrist.
- Medical professionals are bound to protect the confidentiality of the patients. Confidentiality helps to build and develop trust in the doctor-patient relationship.

SELF-ASSESSMENT

1. Describe the components of communication and their importance.
2. Describe essential sets of communication tasks in Kalamazoo Consensus Statement.
3. Describe the various models of breaking bad news.
4. Describe the various models of the doctor-patient interaction.
5. Write short notes on:
   a. Transference and countertransference
   b. Rapport
   c. Empathy
   d. Confidentiality

Chapter 3

Signs and Symptoms in Psychiatry

Mukesh Kumar Swami · Naresh Nebhinani

Understanding of signs and symptoms is the backbone of any clinical specialty and becomes essential in psychiatric practice due to the lack of confirmatory laboratory investigations. **Symptoms** are complaints or subjective experiences reported by a patient and indicate the presence of a disease. **Signs**, on the other hand, are objective evidence of any symptom, observed by the clinician. Though there is an overlap between signs and symptoms, they are labeled as per perspective, for example, sad mood is a symptom when reported by the patient; however, when observed by the clinician it is recorded as depressed affect (a sign).

PSYCHIATRIC SYMPTOMATOLOGY

Significance of a symptom Certain symptoms can be experienced by healthy individuals for a short period. Everyone can become suspicious, angry, anxious, depressed, or may have unusual experience at some point but it is not pathological all the time. A symptom can be labeled as significant or pathological if it is persistent, severe, frequent, and causes distress to an individual or other persons.

Psychiatric signs and symptoms are elaborated under the following domains:

- Disorders of mood
- Disorders of perception
- Disorders of thought
- Disorders of self-awareness
- Disorders of motor function

DISORDERS OF MOOD

The ***mood*** is defined as *"pervasive and sustained emotion that colors the person's perception of the world."* It is subjective and reflects the experience of the individual. ***Affect*** is a cross-sectional outward expression of mood, which is visible to others and interpreted with facial expressions, posture, gestures, and overall way of communication.

The normal mood is termed as "***euthymic***." Affect is described under the following dimensions: quality, quantity, range, appropriateness, and congruence.

Quality (Type)

Examples of various affect types include the following:

- **Depressed:** Sadness which is often accompanied by depressed facies (downward gaze, lowered corner of the mouth, increased wrinkling in forehead).
- **Anxious:** An expression of inner restlessness often accompanied by visible restlessness, sitting on the edge, and fidgeting.
- **Euphoric:** Unusually cheerful and an increased sense of well-being.

- **Apathetic:** Individual appears indifferent, disinterested, and unaffected by surroundings.
- **Irritable/angry:** This usually reflects the discomfort of an individual with a particular situation. Though it has limited diagnostic value, it helps in risk assessment.
- **Perplexed:** Individual appears confused and anxious.

Quantity, range, appropriateness, and congruence of affect are discussed in Chapter 1, *History Taking and Mental Status Examination.*

DISORDERS OF PERCEPTION

Perceptual abnormalities include illusions, hallucinations, depersonalization, and derealization.

Illusions

Illusion is defined as "*misinterpretations of a sensory stimulus.*" They occur in conditions of inattention, low sensory stimuli, and lower level of consciousness or anxious state. Illusions lack diagnostic significance and are different from hallucination by the presence of a stimulus.

Hallucinations

Hallucination is defined as "*a false perception which is not a sensory distortion or a misinterpretation, but which occurs at the same time as real perceptions.*" Individual believes and reacts to hallucinations as a real perception.

Hallucinations are described according to the involved sensory modality.

Auditory hallucinations These are the most common type of hallucinations seen in psychiatric patients. The patient may hear clear voices communicating to the patient *(second person hallucination)*, talking among themselves about the patient *(third person hallucination)*, commenting about the patient's activities *(running commentary type hallucination)*, or instructing the patient *(commanding hallucination).*

Visual hallucinations These are less common than auditory hallucinations. The patient may see people, objects, or animals and sometimes as a complete scene like a movie (*scenic hallucination*). Their presence in the absence of auditory hallucination should raise suspicion of some organic brain disorder.

Olfactory and gustatory hallucinations Olfactory and gustatory hallucinations involve smell and taste, respectively. Their presence in isolation should raise suspicion of temporal lobe epilepsy or other organic brain disease. They may be present in schizophrenia.

Tactile hallucinations These can be a superficial sensation over or under the skin *(tactile or haptic hallucination)* or a feeling of sensations like pressure, tearing or twisting in deep visceral organs *(visceral hallucination).*

Special types of hallucinations are given in Box 3.1.

Depersonalization and Derealization

Depersonalization is characterized by a feeling of unreality or unfamiliarity with oneself whereas **derealization** is unfamiliarity with surroundings.

DISORDERS OF THOUGHT

Disturbances of thinking are reflected through the speech of the patient.

Box 3.1 Special types of hallucinations

- **Reflex hallucination:** Stimulation in one sensory modality induces hallucination in other sensory modality
- **Autoscopic hallucination:** Seeing own body in external space
- **Extracampine hallucination:** Hallucinatory experiences beyond the normal sensory range
- **Lilliputian hallucination:** A type of visual hallucination seen in delirium where the patient sees dwarf figures

Box 3.2 Types of delusions

- **Delusion of persecution:** Delusion that he/she is being conspired against, spied on or followed, poisoned by someone
- **Delusion of reference:** Delusion that the behavior of others refers to the patient, for example, patient has a delusion that people are talking about him/her
- **Delusion of grandiosity:** Delusion of exaggeration of self-worth, power, knowledge, or special relationship with the God
- **Delusion of infidelity:** Delusion that spouse is unfaithful
- **Delusion of control:** Delusion that the patient's thought and actions are controlled by some external agency
- **Nihilistic delusion:** Delusion that things do not exist, for example, the patient denies the existence of their body, mind, or the world
- **Hypochondriacal delusion:** Delusion of having some illness or functional/structural bodily changes

The thought is a *"goal-directed flow of idea"* so its disorders can be either in the idea itself or the process of ideas (flow, connection, and goal-directedness). Though there are several classifications of thought disorders, broadly they can be divided into disorders of the content of thinking, disorders of the form of thinking, and disorder of the possession of the thought.

Disorders of Content

They include delusions, hopelessness, worthlessness, and suicidal thoughts.

Delusion is defined as "*a false, unshakeable belief that is out of keeping with the patient's social and cultural background.*" Delusion does not get affected by rational argument or showing contrary evidence.

Delusions can be either *primary* (*autochthonous*) or *secondary*. Contrary to primary, secondary delusions can be derived from another psychological phenomenon. An autochthonous delusion takes form instantly without identifiable preceding events. Delusion needs to be differentiated from an *overvalued idea*, which is similar to quality in delusion except that it is less fixed and firm.

Different types of delusions are presented in Box 3.2.

Disorders of possession and disorders of the form of thinking are described in Chapter 1, *History Taking and Mental Status Examination.*

DISORDERS OF MOTOR FUNCTION

Motor functions reflect the degree and quality of activities. There can be an increase in the activity level in the form of restlessness, increased goal-directed activities, and agitation or decrease in the activity level in the form of slowness or motor retardation. In these situations, motor activity reflects the mood and thought state of an individual. Disorders of motor functions in psychiatry are usually subsumed under the term *catatonia.* Common catatonic signs are described in Box 3.3.

Finally, as stated earlier, all these psychopathological findings are not diagnostic on their own but require corroboration with other findings and history. Table 3.1 summarizes associations of symptom, MSE findings, and probable diagnosis for better understanding.

Box 3.3 Catatonic signs

- **Automatic obedience:** Obedience of commands without critical judgment
- **Command automatism:** Automatic compliance with instructions
- **Echolalia:** Mimicking other person's speech
- **Echopraxia:** Mimicking other person's movement
- **Excitement:** Apparently purposeless motor activity, not influenced by external stimuli
- **Mannerisms:** Ingrained habitual involuntary movement
- **Mutism:** Lack of speech
- **Negativism:** Motiveless resistance to commands or attempt to be moved (passive) or movement in the opposite direction
- **Perseveration:** Pathological repetition of the same response to different stimuli (different questions)
- **Posturing:** Voluntary assumption and maintenance of the awkward posture for long
- **Rigidity:** Maintenance of a rigid posture against efforts to be moved
- **Stereotypies:** Continuous mechanical repetition of speech or physical activities
- **Stupor:** Marked decrease in reactivity to the environment and in spontaneous movements
- **Waxy flexibility:** Maintenance of limbs in externally imposed positions

Table 3.1 Common psychiatric symptoms, associated findings, and probable diagnoses

Symptoms	Associated findings including MSE findings	Probable diagnosis
Decreased interaction and remaining aloof	• Apathetic affect, suspicious or indifferent attitude	Psychotic disorders
	• Depressed affect • Help-seeking attitude • Reduced psychomotor activity	Depressive disorders

(*Continued*)

Table 3.1 (*Continued*)

Symptoms	Associated findings including MSE findings	Probable diagnosis
Muttering/ self-talking	• Auditory hallucination • Hallucinatory behavior	• Schizophrenia • Depression or mania with psychotic feature
Poor self-care	• Appearance: Poorly clad and kept • Preoccupied (self-absorbed) inattention • Catatonia • Apathetic affect	Schizophrenia
	• Depressed affect • Hopelessness • Delusion of guilt	Severe depression
Restlessness	• Sitting on edge • Fidgeting • Anxious mood	Anxiety disorders
	• Perplexed affect • Delusion of persecution/reference	Psychotic disorder

KEY POINTS

- The **mood** is defined as *"pervasive and sustained emotion that colors the person's perception of the world."* It is subjective and reflects the experience of the individual.
- **Affect** is a cross-sectional expression of mood and is interpreted with facial expressions, posture, gestures, and overall way of communication.
- Perceptual abnormalities include illusions, hallucinations, depersonalization, and derealization.
- **Hallucination** is defined as *"a false perception which is not a sensory distortion or a misinterpretation, but which occurs at the same time as real perceptions."*
- **Illusion** is misinterpretation of a sensory stimulus.
- Auditory hallucination is the most common type of hallucination seen in psychiatric patients.
- **Depersonalization** is characterized by a feeling of unreality or unfamiliarity with oneself whereas **derealization** is unfamiliarity with surroundings.
- **Delusion** is defined as *"a false, unshakeable belief that is out of keeping with the patient's social and cultural background."*
- Mutism, rigidity, negativism, posturing, stupor, echolalia, echopraxia, waxy flexibility, mannerisms, stereotypies, and automatic obedience are various **catatonic symptoms**.

SELF-ASSESSMENT

1. Define delusion and enumerate various delusions.
2. Define hallucination. What are different types of hallucinations?
3. Enumerate various catatonic signs and elaborate any four.

Chapter 4

Investigations in Psychiatry

Mukesh Kumar Swami · Sandeep Kumar Goyal · Naresh Nebhinani

In medical sciences, laboratory investigations have an important role in diagnosis and evidence-based management of the patient, though their role in psychiatric practice is limited. Psychiatric diagnosis is mainly based on phenomenology so laboratory investigations are of little use for diagnosing most of the psychiatric conditions. However, there are some conditions where laboratory investigations and imaging studies become essential in the diagnosis and management of the patient as described next:

- Presence of signs and symptoms suggesting the possibility of underlying medical disorder, for example, when a patient presenting with palpitations, chest pain, dryness of mouth, difficulty in breathing, impending doom, confirmatory diagnosis of the panic disorder can be made only after ruling out the medical causes like anemia, thyroid dysfunction and cardiac illness.
- For patients presenting with delirium, investigations are needed to find out the cause of delirium.
- To monitor the side effects of various medications, for example, a thyroid function test of a patient who is on lithium.
- Monitoring plasma levels of a drug, for example, serum lithium levels.
- Nonresponse after standard management, for example, thyroid functions, vitamin B_{12} and vitamin D levels in patients of depression not responding to treatment.

However, routine testing among every psychiatric patient is not recommended. It should be individualized based on history, physical examination and assessment of individual needs and risks. This chapter intends to describe the role of investigations when dealing with a psychiatric patient to promote rational use of laboratory investigation in practice.

BASELINE INVESTIGATIONS

Psychotropic medications are linked with various adverse effects and to identify these adverse effects as well as to rule out pre-existing medical conditions, if any, certain investigations are recommended (Table 4.1). Many medications are not suitable for patients suffering from certain conditions; for example, in a patient with diabetes mellitus, olanzapine should be avoided. In such cases, baseline investigations help the clinician in the selection of medication as some drugs are likely to worsen pre-existing medical conditions.

The investigations provide a baseline to which subsequent drug-induced changes can be compared.

Plasma Levels of Medications

Plasma levels of medications are used in the following conditions:

- To guide treatment**:** Lithium levels are essential due to its narrow therapeutic index. With the help of serum lithium levels, the dose of lithium is titrated to

Table 4.1 Suggested monitoring for patients receiving various psychiatric medications

Medication	Investigation	Frequency	Rationale
Antipsychotics	ECG	Baseline, when the target dose is reached and yearly after that	QTc prolongation
	• Fasting blood sugar • HbA1C (if available)	Baseline, at 4–6 months, yearly after that	Impaired glucose metabolism
	Complete blood count	• Baseline and yearly • For clozapine (see Chapter 31, *Psychopharmacology II: Antipsychotics*)	Neutropenia, bone marrow suppression
	Lipid profile	Baseline, at 3 months and then yearly	Dyslipidemia
	Urea and creatinine	Baseline and yearly	Dose adjustment in case of deranged renal function
	Prolactin	Baseline, 6 months and then yearly	Hyperprolactinemia
	Liver function test	Baseline and yearly	Risk of hepatitis, stop the suspected drug if transaminase elevation is more than three times normal
Mood stabilizers			
Lithium	eGFR	Baseline and every 6 months	Deranged renal function
	Thyroid function test	Baseline and every 6 months	Hypothyroidism
	Serum lithium	7 days after initiation, then 7 days after every dose change until the desired level is achieved, after that every 3 months in the first year and then every 6 months or suspicion of toxicity	Dose adjustment

(*Continued*)

Table 4.1 *(Continued)*

Medication	Investigation	Frequency	Rationale
	ECG	Baseline and every 6 months	Indicated for patients who have risk factors for or existing cardiovascular disease
Valproate	Liver function test	Baseline and every 6 months	Risk of hepatitis, stop the suspected drug if transaminase elevation is more than three times normal
	Complete blood count	Baseline and every 6 months	Leukopenia, thrombocytopenia
Antidepressants (SSRIs)	Sodium level for those at high risk, for example, elderly patients, those with medical comorbidity (hypothyroidism, diabetes, COPD) or are already on drugs causing hyponatremia	Baseline, at 2 and 4 weeks and then every 3 months	Hyponatremia
Antidepressants (TCAs)	ECG	Baseline	TCAs are avoided in patients at serious risk of arrhythmia

keep the plasma levels of lithium in the therapeutic range.

- To check the lack of effectiveness, poor adherence or toxicity, for example, valproate and carbamazepine.

DRUG SCREENING IN SUBSTANCE USE DISORDERS

Drug screening is important among patients with substance use disorder during initial workup when history provided is contradictory or dubious. It also helps in ensuring abstinence and treatment compliance. Though both blood and urine-based testing are available, urine-based screening is more commonly used.

ROLE OF NEUROIMAGING IN PSYCHIATRY

Computed tomography (CT) scan and magnetic resonance imaging (MRI) are used to identify structural abnormalities that may be associated with patient's behavioral changes. Neuroimaging is indicated for patients with new-onset psychosis and acute changes in mental status. Tumors of frontal or temporal lobes can present as psychosis. Neuroimaging is also indicated in patients diagnosed with dementia. Neuroimaging helps by showing different patterns, for example, frontotemporal dementia, normal pressure hydrocephalus, and Lewy body disease. MRI scan can differentiate gray and white matter better than CT scan and can visualize smaller brain lesions and white matter abnormalities.

ROLE OF ELECTROENCEPHALOGRAM

Electroencephalogram (EEG) is useful in the following conditions:

- To localize seizure foci.
- To evaluate delirium: EEG in delirium shows diffuse bilateral slowing of the background rhythm along with moderate-to-high wave amplitude. **Triphasic waves** are found in hepatic encephalopathy and **periodic sharp wave complex** are seen in Creutzfeldt–Jakob disease.
- To establish the diagnosis of pseudoseizures, video of EEG is helpful.
- To analyze sleep-related abnormalities, sleep EEG (polysomnography) is used.
- To monitor seizure during electroconvulsive therapy (ECT).

KEY POINTS

Laboratory Investigations

- Laboratory investigations become essential to **monitor the side effects** of various medications (e.g., thyroid function test of a patient who is on lithium), to **find out the cause of delirium, monitor plasma level of drugs**, and **rule out medical illnesses**.
- Plasma levels of medications are used to check lack of effectiveness, poor adherence or toxicity, for example, valproate and carbamazepine.
- Serum lithium levels are essential due to its narrow therapeutic index. With the help of serum lithium levels, the dose of lithium is titrated to keep the plasma levels of lithium in the therapeutic range.

Neuroimaging

- Neuroimaging is indicated for patients with new-onset psychosis and acute changes in mental status. Tumors of frontal or temporal lobes can present as psychosis.
- Neuroimaging is also indicated in patients diagnosed with dementia. It helps by showing different patterns, for example, frontotemporal dementia, normal pressure hydrocephalus, and Lewy body disease.

Electroencephalogram (EEG)

- EEG is useful to localize seizure foci, evaluate delirium, establish the diagnosis of pseudoseizures (video EEG), analyze sleep-related abnormalities (polysomnography), and monitor seizure during electroconvulsive therapy (ECT).

- EEG in delirium shows diffuse bilateral slowing of the background rhythm along with moderate-to-high wave amplitude. **Triphasic waves** are found in hepatic encephalopathy, and **periodic sharp wave complex** is seen in Creutzfeldt-Jakob disease.

SELF-ASSESSMENT

1. Case-based Questions

   A 40-year-old male presented to psychiatry OPD and after a detailed history and mental status examination a diagnosis of bipolar affective disorder was made. It was planned to start him on lithium.

   a. What baseline investigations will you order before starting him on lithium?
2. Describe the role of investigations in psychiatry.
3. Describe the baseline investigations required before the start of various psychotropic drugs and also investigations required during the use of psychotropic drugs.
4. Describe the role of neuroimaging in psychiatry.
5. Describe the role of plasma levels of medications in psychiatry.
6. What are the indications of electroencephalogram (EEG) in psychiatry?

Chapter 5

Psychoanalysis

Sandeep Kumar Goyal · Nidhi Aggarwal · Mamta Singla

Psychoanalysis is the child of Sigmund Freud (1856–1939). Although psychoanalysis has advanced far beyond him, still his strong and pervasive impact is evident. Psychoanalysis serves as the fundamental theoretical frame of reference for a variety of forms of therapeutic interventions, including psychoanalysis itself and various other forms of psychoanalytically oriented psychotherapies. It enables an extensive understanding of unconscious conflicts, character, and personality development.

BASIC CONCEPTS

The Topographical Model

In 1900, Freud published *The Interpretation of Dreams* in which he divided the mind into conscious, preconscious, and unconscious.

Conscious This part of the mind is involved in the continual processing of perceptions, both from the outside world and from within the body as well as mind, and brings them into consciousness. Consciousness is a subjective phenomenon and its content can be communicated by language or behavior.

Preconscious It consists of all mental events, contents, and processes that are capable of being easily brought back to consciousness by focusing attention. Preconscious has an interface with both the conscious and the unconscious. To reach conscious awareness, the content of the unconscious must become attached to words and thus become preconscious. Preconscious maintains the repressive barrier and censors unacceptable desires.

Unconscious The unconscious is characterized by *primary process thinking* to facilitate wish fulfillment and instinctual discharge. Its contents are kept from conscious awareness by repression. It is governed by the *pleasure principle* and disregards logical connections. It allows contradictions to exist simultaneously, denies the existence of negatives. Memories in the unconscious are detached from verbal symbols. In psychoanalytic treatment, words are reapplied to these memories and the memories reach consciousness.

The Structural Model

In 1923, Freud propounded the structural model of the psychic apparatus. The structural perspective advocates that the mental apparatus is tripartite, constituted by three independent, interacting, and often conflicting functional units: the Id, the Ego, and the Superego.

Id Id contains unorganized, instinctual drives and operates under the domination of the primary process and the *pleasure principle* (the psychic force that motivates immediate gratification of impulses). It is not synonymous with the unconscious, as ego and superego also have unconscious components.

Ego Ego has all the three topographical components: conscious, preconscious, and unconscious. Logical and abstract thinking resides in the conscious and preconscious domain and defense mechanisms in the unconscious domain. The ego mediates between instincts and the outer world and works to avoid unpleasure by regulating the discharge of instinctual drives to conform to the demands of the external world. It operates on the *reality principle* (the regulating mechanism which enables the delay in the gratification of immediate needs).

Superego Superego is the last component to develop. It reflects the internalization of the moral values, prohibitions, and standards of parental images. Superego regulates our social behavior. It operates on *the morality principle.* **Ego ideal** is a component of superego and it prescribes what a person should do as per internalized values, whereas superego proscribes what a person should not do.

THEORY OF ANXIETY

Freud initially defined anxiety as dammed-up libido. Neuroses are caused by this build-up. After the structural theory, Freud introduced the concept of signal anxiety. As per this hypothesis, anxiety operates at an unconscious level and mobilizes ego resources to prevent danger. Danger can be external or internal. This theory explains neurotic symptoms as ego's partial failure to cope with distressing stimuli.

INTERPRETATION OF DREAMS

Freud described dreams experience as a conscious expression of unconscious fantasies or wishes not acceptable to conscious experience. The dream images represent unconscious wishes or thoughts disguised by symbolization and other distorting mechanisms. In his landmark publication *"The Interpretation of Dreams,"* Freud maintained that every dream represents a wish-fulfillment.

Dream analysis elicits repressed material. These unconscious thoughts include nocturnal sensory stimuli (pain, hunger, and urinary urgency), the day residues (thoughts and preoccupations of current daily life), and repressed unacceptable impulses. Dream enables partial gratification of the repressed impulse.

Freud described two layers of dream content—manifest and latent. The manifest content is recalled by the person and latent content threatens to awaken the person. Freud described the unconscious process by which latent content is converted to manifest content as the dream work. Repressed impulses must attach to neutral images to pass the dream censor. Dream work consists of condensation, displacement, symbolic representation, projection, and secondary revision. Condensation, displacement, projection, and symbolic representation are termed as the primary process. The primary process makes illogical, bizarre, and absurd images, whereas secondary revision makes dreams more rational.

EGO DEFENSE MECHANISMS

The cornerstone of psychodynamic thinking is the "theory of defense." Freud in 1894 explained defense mechanisms as counterforce acting against the expression of impulses and drives. They are "involuntary, unconscious mental mechanisms directed against both, the internal drives and external demands, particularly imposing threats to the integration of self-identity and self-esteem." They protect the integration of the self and reduce excessive anxiety in everyday living.

Defenses can be grouped hierarchically according to the relative degree of maturity. Narcissistic defenses are the most primitive. George Valliant classified defenses into four types:

1. **Narcissistic—psychotic defenses** are usually found in psychosis, but may occur in young children or dreams and fantasies. They work in avoiding or distorting reality (e.g., projection, denial, and distortion).
2. **Immature defenses** are usually common in preadolescents. They are usually regarded as undesirable (e.g., acting out, blocking, hypochondriasis, introjection, regression, passive-aggressive behavior, schizoid fantasy, and somatization).
3. **Neurotic defenses** are common in apparently normal and healthy objects as well as neurotic disorders. They help in removing distressing affects and may be expressed in neurotic behavior. Examples are controlling, displacement, dissociation, externalization, intellectualization, isolation, rationalization, reaction formation, repression, sexualization, and inhibition.
4. **Mature defenses** are healthy and adaptive throughout the life cycle. They are socially adaptive and help in the integration of personal needs and motives, social demands, and interpersonal relations. Examples are altruism, anticipation, asceticism, humor, sublimation, and suppression. Suppression is the only defense mechanism at a conscious level.

THE PSYCHOSEXUAL THEORY

Earlier, bodily functions were considered as nonsexual such as feeding and development of bowel and bladder control. However, Freud hypothesized that these functions involved sensual pleasure which he termed as psychosexual stimulation. He classified developmental phases, each of which was thought to build on accomplishments of previous phases. He classified oral, anal, and phallic phases, and urethral, latency, and genital phases were added later. The urethral stage is a transitional stage between anal and phallic stages.

Karl Abraham further subdivided the oral phase into the sucking and biting phase and anal phase into a destructive expulsive (anal-sadistic) and a mastering retaining (anal erotic) phase.

At each psychosexual developmental stage, a distinct bodily region, erotogenic zone, dominates the child's subjective experience and gives rise to erotic gratification.

Oral Stage

It occurs during the first 12–18 months of life, and the major site of gratification is the mouth and the dominant erotic activity of the oral stage is chewing, biting, and sucking. The early oral phase is oral erotic (sucking) and the later phase is oral sadistic (biting and chewing). Schizophrenia occurs due to oral fixation or regression to this stage of psychosexual development. Pathological traits of oral fixation include excessive optimism, narcissism, pessimism, and demandingness.

Anal Stage

The dominant erotic activity of the anal stage is bowel function and control, and the anal stage lasts from 18 to 36 months of age. The anal stage is also divided into anal-sadistic and anal erotic phases. Obsessive compulsive disorder occurs due to anal fixation or regression to this stage of psychosexual development. Orderliness, stubbornness, willfulness, frugality, and parsimony are features of anal character.

Phallic Phase

In the phallic stage (3–5 years), urination is the main erotic activity. The penis is the organ of interest to children of both sexes. It is associated with an increase in genital masturbation, accompanied by unconscious fantasies of sexual involvement with the opposite sex parent.

Boys have castration anxiety and aggressive feelings toward father, and these are called an *Oedipus complex*. *Electra complex* derives from penis envy. Electra complex is a girl's psychosexual competition with her mother for possession of her father. The resolution of these complexes occurs by identification with father and mother, respectively.

Latent Phase

The latent phase is the stage of relative instinctual quiescence or inactivity of the sexual drive during the period of resolution of the Oedipus and Electra complex to puberty (from about 5 years to 11–13 years). In the latent stage, the superego is formed, and ego functions further mature which allows greater control of instinctual impulses. Gender and sex-role identity is formed in the latent stage.

Genital Phase

The genital phase occurs from the onset of puberty (11–13 years) to young adulthood. Penis and vagina are the erotogenic zones in males and females. The objective of the genital phase is separation from dependence on parents and the establishment of mature, nonincestuous, and heterosexual object relations.

To conclude, psychoanalysis was introduced by Sigmund Freud. Dreams were explained in Psychoanalysis as material which a person cannot express in one's awareness. Freud's other seminal contributions were proposing the stages of psychosexual development, topographical and structural models. However, the most critical aspect of understanding psychoanalysis and utilizing it in treatment has been the subject of defense mechanisms.

KEY POINTS

- Psychoanalysis is the child of Sigmund Freud. Psychoanalysis serves as the fundamental theoretical frame of reference for a variety of forms of therapeutic interventions, including psychoanalysis itself and various other forms of psychoanalytically oriented psychotherapies. It enables an extensive understanding of unconscious conflicts, character, and personality development.
- Topographical model classified mental operations and contents into conscious, preconscious, and unconscious.

- In 1923, Freud propounded the structural model of the psychic apparatus. The structural perspective advocates that the mental apparatus is tripartite, constituted by three independent, interacting, and often conflicting functional units: the Id, the Ego, and the Superego.
- After the structural theory, Freud introduced the concept of signal anxiety. As per this hypothesis, anxiety operates at an unconscious level and mobilizes ego resources to prevent danger.
- In his landmark publication *The Interpretation of Dreams,* Freud maintained that every dream represents a wish-fulfillment.
- Dream analysis elicits repressed material. These unconscious thoughts include nocturnal sensory stimuli (pain, hunger, and urinary urgency), the day residues (thoughts and preoccupations of current daily life), and repressed unacceptable impulses.
- Dream enables partial gratification of the repressed impulse.
- Freud described two layers of dream content: manifest and latent. The manifest content is recalled by the person and latent content threatens to awaken the person.
- Freud in 1894 explained defense mechanisms as counterforce acting against the expression of impulses and drives.
- George Valliant classified defenses into four types: narcissistic–psychotic, immature, neurotic, and mature defenses.
- In psychosexual theory, Freud classified the oral, anal, and phallic phases. Urethral, latency, and genital phases were added later.
- Schizophrenia occurs due to oral fixation or regression to this stage of psychosexual development.
- Obsessive compulsive disorder occurs due to anal fixation or regression to this stage of psychosexual development.
- The phallic phase is characterized by the *Oedipus complex in boys* (castration anxiety and aggressive feelings toward father) and *Electra complex in girls* (psychosexual competition with her mother for possession of her father).

SELF-ASSESSMENT

1. Write short notes on:
    a. Topographical model
    b. Structural model
    c. Interpretation of dreams
    d. Defense mechanisms
    e. Psychosexual theory

Chapter 6

Neurodevelopmental Disorders I: Autism Spectrum Disorders

Ruchita Shah · Nidhi Chauhan

The neurodevelopmental disorders have their onset in the developmental period and are characterized by developmental deficits that produce impairment of personal, social, academic, or occupational functioning. The neurodevelopmental disorders frequently co-occur, for example, individuals with autism spectrum disorders (ASDs) often have an intellectual disability (ID). Neurodevelopmental disorders include ASD, attention-deficit/hyperactivity disorder (ADHD), intellectual disabilities, communication disorders, specific learning disorders, and motor disorders.

ASDs are dealt in this chapter while ADHD and intellectual disability are discussed in the next two chapters (Chapter 7, *Neurodevelopmental Disorders II: Attention-Deficit/Hyperactivity Disorder and Chapter 8, Neurodevelopmental Disorders III: Intellectual Disability*).

AUTISM SPECTRUM DISORDERS

ASD refer to a range of neurodevelopmental conditions characterized by early-onset delays and deviances in the development of speech and communication, nonverbal communicative behaviors along with a tendency to engage in repetitive or stereotyped patterns of behavior, activities, and interests.

Comparative nosology ASD is covered in ICD-10 under the diagnostic category of "Pervasive Developmental Disorders" (PDD). ICD-10 PDD include childhood autism, atypical autism, Rett syndrome, childhood disintegrative disorder, and Asperger syndrome. However, certain conditions such as Rett syndrome and Asperger syndrome do not find a place in DSM-5.

EPIDEMIOLOGY

Prevalence Present estimates place prevalence rates at around 1 per 100 children in the developed nations, while rates in developing countries are comparatively lower. Epidemiological studies from India report prevalence rates ranging from 9 to 23.3 per 10,000 children. Some variability may be attributed to methodological differences across studies.

Sex ratio and social class Like other neurodevelopmental disorders, ASD is more common in boys with a gender ratio of 3.5 or 4 males to 1 female.

ETIOLOGY

In the 1950s and 1960s, ASD was thought to be due to the defective upbringing of children by cold and rejecting parents, especially "refrigerator mothers," thus leaving no alternative with the child, but seeking solace in solitude. However, with time, it became clear that ASD has a biological basis given the high heritability estimates to the tune of ~90%, high rates of comorbid intellectual disability and epilepsy, and presence of genetic syndromes associated with ASD. Overall, risk factors for ASD can be categorized as biological and environmental.

Biological Factors

Genetic factors Family and twin studies have proven without a doubt that genetics is central to the etiology of ASD. The concordance rates for strictly defined autism is around 60% for monozygotic twin pairs.

In around 5%–15% of individuals with ASD, it has been associated with single-gene disorders such as Fragile X syndrome, neurofibromatosis type 1, and certain chromosomal abnormalities.

Neurotransmitters Around 25%–50% of individuals with ASD have elevated blood and platelet serotonin levels. Dopamine is also implicated in the causation of ASD and is said to be responsible for the overactivity and stereotyped movements seen in autism. Endogenous opioids, namely, enkephalins and endorphins, may have a role to play in the social withdrawal and unusual sensitivities to the environment displayed by individuals with ASD.

Immunological factors These have also been implicated in ASD due to the observations of association of ASD with viral infections and the presence of fetal protein reactive IgG antibodies in maternal plasma.

Neuroimaging findings Increased brain volume in frontal and anterior temporal regions is the most commonly replicated finding in neuroimaging studies in ASD. Aberrant or reduced connectivity patterns between the "social brain" and other cortical areas are seen in functional imaging studies.

Perinatal factors Prenatal, perinatal, and postnatal obstetric complications are the most studied risk factors in ASD. Obstetric complications associated with ASD include prematurity, birth hypoxia, neonatal encephalopathy, bleeding during pregnancy, gestational diabetes, breech presentation, and medication use during pregnancy (e.g., valproate, ethanol, and thalidomide).

Environmental Factors

Exposure to environmental toxins such as pesticides and the occurrence of ASD has a positive relationship. Parental age, especially paternal age, is considered as a potential risk factor.

CLINICAL FEATURES AND DIAGNOSIS

Clinical presentation of ASD is heterogeneous depending on the chronological age, developmental level, and presence of speech. It can change over time due to the presence of associated comorbid disorders. To make a diagnosis of ASD, DSM-5 requires persistent deficits in social communication and social interaction across multiple contexts and restrictive, repetitive patterns of behavior, interests, or activities in the early developmental period. Diagnosis is made if symptoms cause clinically significant impairment in social, occupational, or other important areas of functioning.

Qualitative impairment in social interaction There is a deficit in socio-emotional reciprocity; these deficits may range from no sharing of emotions to a failure to initiate or respond to social interactions. Thus, social behaviors may not be absent, but there is a qualitative impairment in social interaction. The earliest behaviors seen in an infant suggestive of the high risk of ASD are: not lifting arms or changing position in anticipation of being held, poor eye contact, and impaired joint attention (i.e., ability to share focus on an object or area with another person). Young children may show a lack of interest in peers, love solitary play, have no meaningful play with toys, and no imaginative play (pretend play). On the other hand, some children may seek friendships based on shared special interests only.

Qualitative impairment in communication This includes both verbal and nonverbal communication. Deficits may vary from speech delay to complete absence of speech, monotonous speech, inability to modulate conversational style according to context, not responding to name being called (at times mistaken to be severely hearing impaired), putting/lifting others' hands toward the object of interest (**hand-on-hand pointing**), inability to initiate and sustain conversation, use of neologisms, echolalia (i.e., repeating words/phrases heard), and **pronoun reversals** (calling "me" as "you").

Repetitive, stereotyped patterns of behavior, interests, or activities These children may exhibit stereotyped or repetitive behaviors that may include stereotyped use of objects such as lining up blocks or toy cars and spinning of wheels; motor stereotypies such as finger flicking or hand flapping, repetitive speech (early and delayed echolalia), and stereotyped use of words. There may be an excessive adherence to routines and resistance to change. Hyper or hyposensitivity to sensory stimuli is often seen, for example, apparent indifference to pain or heat/cold. Children may appear fascinated with sensory aspects of their inanimate environments (e.g., smelling or touching objects such as toys and blocks). Children or adults with ASD have restricted and, fixated interests, for example, preoccupation with unusual objects like vacuum cleaner.

Associated symptoms in ASD Intellectual and/or language impairment is present in almost 70% of the children with ASD. To make diagnosis of comorbid ASD and ID, the social communication should be below the expected level in general development. Motor deficits such as clumsiness and odd gait may be present. Some children may walk tiptoes. Some children show self-injurious behaviors such as headbanging.

Rating Scales

Some of the most used diagnostic and observational instruments include the Autism Diagnostic Interview-Revised; Autism Diagnostic Observation Schedule; and Diagnostic Interview for Social and Communication Disorders. Indian instruments for ASD include the INCLEN Diagnostic Tool for Autism and the Indian Scale for Assessment of Autism (ISAA).

Differential Diagnosis

Certain conditions should be considered as a differential diagnosis while evaluating for ASD as these can have some features in common with ASD as well as some of these may be present comorbidly. These are:

- Intellectual disability
- Language disorder

- Attention-deficit/hyperactivity disorder
- Rett syndrome
- Childhood onset schizophrenia
- Selective mutism
- Severe hearing and/or visual impairment

COURSE AND PROGNOSIS

ASD is a chronic condition and the diagnosis remains stable in a majority of individuals. A wide variation in the outcome is reported with less than one-fourth of individuals diagnosed with ASD having a very good outcome. It is seen that with age autistic symptoms may decrease in intensity and severity, and adaptive functions may improve. Higher cognitive abilities and the presence of useful speech by 5–6 years of age are predictors for a better outcome in ASD. Challenges in the form of occurrence of comorbid disorders (e.g., seizures, mood disorders, anxiety disorders) are common during ASD.

MANAGEMENT

Management of ASD involves a multipronged, multidisciplinary approach involving psychiatry, pediatrics, speech therapy, physiotherapy, clinical psychology, rehabilitation psychology, and occupational therapy services. Keeping into account the earlier mentioned deficits in ASD, an individualized plan needs to be tailored for the child with ASD and its family. Plans need to be modified according to the age and needs of the individual. The goals of intervention should include:

1. Reduction of core symptoms/behaviors of ASD.
2. Treatment of comorbid illness and associated problems that impede the overall development of the individual.
3. Addressing family burden and providing support for the family.
4. Enabling the individual to achieve his/her potential.

Psychosocial and Behavioral Interventions

Overall, psychosocial and behavioral interventions targeting the core symptoms or behaviors of ASD should be intensive and structured. The earlier the intervention and more sustained the efforts, the better are the results. The interventions may be therapist mediated or parent mediated. Most of the interventions use evidence-based strategies to promote communication (e.g., using visual supports), enhance attention and learning, and reduce challenging behaviors (e.g., interventions based on the Applied Behavioral Analysis Model).

Sensory integration therapy, music therapy, auditory integration therapy, pet therapy, occupational therapy, restriction diets (a diet free of casein and gluten), and supplementation with omega-3 fatty acids have also been used in individuals with ASD.

Parent training programs form an essential component of the management plan for individuals with ASD.

Pharmacological Interventions

There is no specific drug to date for the core symptoms of ASD. Many drugs have been tried, for example, risperidone, methylphenidate, fluoxetine, citalopram, oxytocin, vasopressin, GABA agonist, and glutamate antagonist, but there is a paucity of evidence about their use in ASD. Management of associated symptoms and other comorbid disorders should be done as per need.

KEY POINTS

- Autism spectrum disorders (ASDs) are characterized by **qualitative impairment in social interaction, qualitative impairment in communication, and repetitive, stereotyped patterns of behavior, interests, or activities**.
- Family and twin studies have proven without a doubt that genetics is central to the etiology of ASD.
- Exposure to environmental toxins such as pesticides and the occurrence of ASD has a positive relationship.
- Parental age, especially paternal age, is considered as a potential risk factor.
- Not lifting arms or changing position in anticipation of being held, poor eye contact, and impaired joint attention are symptoms that point toward qualitative impairment in social interaction.
- **Qualitative impairment in communication** is characterized by speech delay to complete absence of speech, monotonous speech, not responding to name being called (at times mistaken to be severely hearing impaired), putting/lifting other's hands toward the object of interest (**hand-on-hand pointing**) and **pronoun reversals** (calling "me" as "you").
- These children may exhibit stereotyped or repetitive behaviors, motor stereotypies, repetitive speech (early and delayed echolalia), and stereotyped use of words.
- Intellectual and/or language impairment is present in almost 70% of individuals.
- Management of ASD involves a multipronged, multidisciplinary approach using structured psychosocial and behavioral interventions targeting the core symptoms. The earlier the intervention and more sustained the efforts; the better are the results.
- There is no specific drug to date for the core symptoms of ASD. Management of associated symptoms and other comorbid disorders should be done as per need.

SELF-ASSESSMENT

1. Case-based Questions

   A 28-month-old boy was brought to the psychiatry OPD with the complaint that he does not respond when he is called by his name and does not maintain eye-to-eye contact with anyone. His mother further reported that he does not play with his peers and does not indulge in imaginative play. His speech and social development were delayed. He used to speak in a monotonous voice with occasional pronoun reversal. He was found to resist changes in routine and would throw tantrums on any change. He used to play in repetitive and idiosyncratic ways and indulged in self-stimulatory behaviors, for example, waving his hands in front of his eyes.

   He was born as full-term normal delivery and cried immediately. Pregnancy was uneventful. His motor milestones were normal but his speech was delayed. His hearing test was normal. His IQ was relatively less on verbal subtests as compared to performance subtests.

   a. What is your provisional diagnosis and discuss the reasons for it?
2. Describe the etiology, clinical features, and treatment of ASD.

Chapter 7

Neurodevelopmental Disorders II: Attention-Deficit/Hyperactivity Disorder

Priti Arun · Nidhi Chauhan

Attention-deficit/hyperactivity disorder (ADHD) is a neurodevelopmental disorder, manifesting early in development, that is, preschool years. It manifests with a classical triad of hyperactivity, inattention, and impulsivity in varying combinations of severity.

COMPARATIVE NOSOLOGY

The equivalent of ADHD in International Classification of Diseases, 10th revision (ICD-10) is a hyperkinetic disorder.

EPIDEMIOLOGY

Prevalence The prevalence of ADHD varies greatly depending upon the part of the world from which it is reported, age group evaluated, and diagnostic scheme used. Despite variations in the rates, pooled estimates suggest that the worldwide prevalence of ADHD is around 5% in school-going children. The symptoms of ADHD tend to persist into adulthood with a prevalence during adulthood of around 2.5%.

ADHD tends to affect more boys than girls with a male:female ratio of 3:1. This variation could be a result of lesser disruptive symptoms and more inattentive symptoms in girls, thereby not being brought for evaluation and thus being under-diagnosed.

ETIOLOGY

The etiology of ADHD is largely genetic.

Genetics Family studies, adoption, and twin studies suggest that ADHD is familial and highly heritable. Siblings of the patient with ADHD have a two- to eight-fold increased risk of having ADHD. Data from twin and adoption studies report that ADHD is one of the most heritable conditions with the heritability estimates of around 70%–90%.

Neurobiology Children with ADHD have reduced intracranial volume by up to 5% and the reduction affects both the gray and white matter. Apart from the neuroanatomical changes, various regions of the prefrontal cortex are predominantly implicated in the causation of symptoms of hyperactivity, impulsivity, and inattention. The inattentive symptoms result due to inefficient processing in the dorsolateral prefrontal cortex. Hyperactivity and impulsivity occur due to abnormal processing in the supplementary motor area and orbitofrontal cortex, respectively. As mentioned earlier, neurotransmitters like dopamine, serotonin, and norepinephrine are primarily implicated in ADHD. There is decreased neurotransmission of dopamine in the **cortico-striatal-thalamic-cortical circuit** (CSTC circuit) along with an increased dopamine transporter density in the brain.

Environmental factors Substance abuse in mother especially alcohol and smoking cigarettes during pregnancy is implicated as one of the important preventable factors. The use of certain medications, for example, antiepileptic and anxiolytic agents, maternal stress, and maternal hypothyroidism during pregnancy are also implicated. Obstetric complications, low birth weight, and premature birth are some of the perinatal factors suggested having a role in ADHD. Family environment, especially depriving and neglectful families, are an added risk factor.

CLINICAL FEATURES AND DIAGNOSIS

The clinical features of ADHD vary depending upon the age of the individual at presentation, developmental level, and associated comorbid psychiatric and physical conditions.

Hyperactivity-impulsivity manifests as fidgeting or tapping hands, leaving the seat in the classroom, and the inability of the child to play quietly. Excessive talking, running and climbing inappropriately, difficulty waiting for a turn, and blurting out answers before a question is completed are common symptoms. Children with hyperactivity usually butt into others' conversations and games and are always "on the go" as if their feet have wheels that drive them continuously.

Inattention manifests as making careless mistakes in homework, inability to sustain attention in tasks (reading for long periods), not following through instructions and failing to finish schoolwork or duties in the workplace. Children with inattention often have difficulty in time management and fail to meet deadlines. They often dislike or avoid tasks requiring sustained mental effort, for example, homework or preparing reports (adults). They frequently lose things (e.g., school stationery, keys, spectacles) and are easily distractible and forgetful. For older adults, forgetfulness may include forgetting to pay bills and keep appointments.

In adults, residual symptoms include impulsivity and attention deficits, for example, inability to concentrate, distractibility, and abrupt decision making without thinking about the consequences.

To make a diagnosis of ADHD, symptoms in one or both domains (inattention or hyperactivity-impulsivity) should be present in a given individual, in more than one setting (i.e., home, school, outdoors) for at least 6 months to a degree that is inconsistent with developmental level and which causes impairment in social and academic/occupational activities. Inattentive or hyperactive-impulsive symptoms must be present before the age of 12.

ADHD can be predominant hyperactive-impulsive type, predominantly inattentive type, and combined inattentive and hyperactive type.

It is important to mention that children with ADHD usually present to mental health clinics following a referral from schools for various problems. To arrive at a diagnosis of ADHD, always obtain information from multiple sources (parents, caregivers, and teachers) and across different situations (home, school). Thus, gathering information from all possible sources helps in making or refuting the diagnosis of ADHD.

Rating Scales

Various rating scales available for use in individuals with ADHD are:

1. Conners' Parent Rating Scale
2. Vanderbilt ADHD Diagnostic Parent Rating Scale
3. Wender Utah Rating Scale for adults

Differential Diagnosis

Three main types of psychiatric conditions, that is, neurodevelopmental disorders, disorders of childhood-onset, and adult-type mental illnesses can either simulate symptoms of ADHD or coexist with ADHD.

Neurodevelopmental Disorders

Intellectual disability Attention problems can be secondary to intellectual disability, whereas problems in learning can be secondary to poor attention. Diagnosis of ADHD should be made only if the impairment of attention is out of proportion to developmental level. A useful clinical rule of thumb is to judge the patient's attentiveness with reference to that which would be expected in a child of chronological age equivalent to the patient's mental age.

Autism spectrum disorders Autism can produce a motor restlessness, to be distinguished from ADHD by its stereotyped nature. The distinction is made by the type of overactivity, which contrasts with the impulsive and frequently changing behaviors seen in ADHD.

Tourette disorder It can either simulate or be comorbid with ADHD. Sometimes, the presentation of overactivity is attributable to a large number of motor tics; therefore, a prolonged observation is required to delineate the two.

Childhood-Onset Problems

Oppositional defiant disorder (ODD) The diagnostic difficulty occurs when uncontrolled and impulsive behavior is considered to occur as a result of ODD. Clear delineation of symptomatology is required in these cases.

Adult-Type Mental Disorders

Bipolar affective disorder The goal-directed overactivity of mania can be distinguished from the disorganized and off-task activity of ADHD. Euphoria is an essential feature of mania and precludes ADHD. Moreover, the symptoms of overactivity and poor concentration in bipolar affective disorder are episodic.

COURSE AND OUTCOME

Hyperactivity is the predominant symptom during the preschool and school-going children; whereas inattentiveness predominates during the adolescence period and hyperactivity is decreased. About 40% of the cases diagnosed with ADHD during childhood may remit at puberty or in early adulthood. The risk of substance misuse is high in individuals with ADHD.

MANAGEMENT

Both pharmacological and nonpharmacological interventions are to be used for the best results. The severity of ADHD symptoms and dysfunction caused by these symptoms determines whether pharmacological treatment is to be used or not, whereas nonpharmacological interventions are mandatory in every case.

Nonpharmacological

Nonpharmacological management is an important adjunct in the treatment of ADHD. The **psychoeducation** of the parents about various aspects of ADHD is most common, for example, its presentation, how parental handling plays a vital role in the maintenance or resolution of symptoms, and different ways for its management. In addition to parental training, teaching self-control to children with ADHD also helps children manage their emotions and behaviors. Social skill training, family therapy, and individual therapy are other modalities found to be beneficial.

Behavioral therapy It includes the following:

1. A structured routine/timetable.
2. Clear rules should be formulated in consonance with the child with ADHD.
3. Good behaviors should be rewarded (praise, appreciation, or small rewards that are predecided) immediately and consistently. Material rewards should be gradually faded and replaced with verbal praise and appreciation.
4. Ignoring is a technique for not giving attention to unwanted behavior which is not serious.
5. Clear, crisp, short instructions should be used while communicating with children with ADHD. Complex and multiple instructions in one statement tend to confuse a child with ADHD.
6. The token system can be followed for increasing desired behaviors and reducing undesirable behaviors.

Pharmacological

Central nervous system stimulants (amphetamines, methylphenidate) remain the gold standard for the treatment of ADHD. These drugs help by reducing motor hyperactivity, impulsivity, and improve attention. Amphetamines are not available in India; however, various formulations of **methylphenidate** are available for use in India. It is given in the morning or afternoon after the meal and should not be given late in the evenings as it can cause sleep disturbances. Side effects are minor and can be managed symptomatically and tend to abate once the drug is stopped. The most common side effects include loss of appetite, growth reduction, irritability, tachycardia, sleep disturbances, raised blood pressure, and drug misuse. Arrhythmias are a rare side effect and warrant a cardiology consultation if it appears. It is always a good idea to evaluate for any history of current cardiac problems and family history of the same before putting an individual on stimulants. It is approved for use in children above 6 years of age.

The other drugs approved for use in ADHD are **Atomoxetine** (serotonin-norepinephrine reuptake inhibitor) and extended-release **Guanfacine** (not available in India). Atomoxetine is a good choice for use in ADHD comorbid with anxiety disorders. Clonidine (α_2 agonist), bupropion, and modafinil are other drugs used in ADHD but are not approved.

KEY POINTS

- ADHD is characterized by the "classical triad" of hyperactivity, inattention, and impulsivity in more than one setting that interferes with functioning and the symptoms must start before the age of 12.
- The equivalent of ADHD in ICD-10 is a hyperkinetic disorder.
- The worldwide prevalence of ADHD is around 5% in school-going children and around 2.5% in adults.
- Family studies, adoption, and twin studies suggest that ADHD is familial and highly heritable. Siblings of ADHD have an eight-fold increased risk of having ADHD.
- The inattentive symptoms result due to inefficient processing in the dorsolateral prefrontal cortex, hyperactivity, and impulsivity due to abnormal processing in the supplementary motor area and orbitofrontal cortex, respectively.
- Substance abuse by mother especially alcohol, smoking cigarettes during pregnancy is implicated as one of the important preventable factors.
- Hyperactivity-impulsivity manifests as fidgeting or tapping hands, leaving the seat in the classroom, excessive talking, running and climbing inappropriately, difficulty waiting for a turn, and blurting out answers before a question is completed.
- Inattention manifests as making careless mistakes in homework, inability to sustain attention in tasks, and failing to finish schoolwork or duties in the workplace. They often have difficulty in time management, losing things frequently, distractibility, and forgetfulness.
- In adults, residual symptoms include impulsivity and attention deficits, for example, inability to concentrate, distractibility, and abrupt decision making without thinking about the consequences.
- Psychoeducation of the parents about various aspects of ADHD is most important.
- Amphetamines are not available in India; however, various formulations of **methylphenidate** are available for use in India.

SELF-ASSESSMENT

1. Case-based Questions

   A 7-year-old male child was referred by his school for psychiatric evaluation. He was in second grade. The reasons for his referral were:

   He does not sit at his designated seat and keeps on roaming around in the class and while sitting in his seat he keeps on squirming in his seat. He does not seem to listen and gets distracted very easily. He is very noisy in routine talking. He answers the questions without waiting for his turn. Parents report similar complaints at home.

   a. What is your provisional diagnosis?
   b. Discuss the differential diagnosis of the disorder.
2. Describe the etiology, clinical features, and treatment of ADHD.

Chapter 8

Neurodevelopmental Disorders III: Intellectual Disability

Shazia Veqar Siddiqui · Nidhi Chauhan · Mohd Aleem Siddiqui · Amrit Pattojoshi

Intellectual disability (ID) (formerly known as mental retardation) is a neurodevelopmental disorder characterized by deficits in general mental abilities, such as reasoning, planning, problem-solving, academic learning, judgment, abstract thinking, and deficits in adaptive functioning. These deficits result in impairment of adaptive behaviors, as a result of which the individual is not able to meet age-appropriate standards of personal independence and social responsibility in one or more aspects of daily functioning, resulting in significant consequences for the individual as well as for the family. It typically manifests early in development, often before the child enters the school grade.

COMPARATIVE NOSOLOGY

Intellectual disability is the term used in DSM-5 (Diagnostic and Statistical Manual of Mental Disorders, 5th edition), whereas it is labeled as "Mental Retardation" in ICD-10 (International Classification of Diseases, 10th edition). DSM-5 lays more emphasis on assessment of adaptive functioning as compared to IQ score.

EPIDEMIOLOGY

The prevalence rate for ID in India is approximately 1%–3% for mild ID. The rates may vary according to age and severity of ID. The prevalence of severe ID is approximately 0.5%. ID is more common in boys than in girls with a ratio of 1.4:1.

ETIOLOGY

Children with ID have abnormal brain development. Any pathogenic process that hampers normal brain development can give rise to ID. There are more than 1000 known genetic causes of ID; however, still, 30%–40% cases of ID do not have an identifiable cause. ID occurs as a result of complex interaction of genetic factors, brain development, and environment. The severity of ID depends much on the timing (i.e., prenatal/perinatal/postnatal period), intensity (i.e., severity of pathologic process), and type (i.e., genetic cause/birth asphyxia/antenatal infections) of brain insult.

Major causes of ID are highlighted in Table 8.1.

Table 8.1 Known causes of intellectual disability

Time period	Type	Examples
Prenatal	Chromosomal disorders	Down syndrome, Turner syndrome, Klinefelter syndrome, Prader–Willi syndrome, Cri-du-chat syndrome, Angelman syndrome, William syndrome
	Single gene disorders	Inborn errors of metabolism: galactosemia, phenylketonuria, mucopolysaccharidosis (MPS), Tay–Sachs disease, Lesch–Nyhan syndrome, hypothyroidism
		Neurocutaneous: tuberous sclerosis, neurofibromatosis
		Brain malformations: autosomal recessive primary microcephaly, hydrocephalus, spina bifida
		Others: fragile X syndrome, Rett syndrome, Smith–Lemli–Opitz syndrome
	Other conditions of uncertain genetic origin	Rubinstein Taybi syndrome, De Lange syndrome
	Adverse maternal/ environmental influences	Iodine deficiency and folate deficiency
		Severe malnutrition in pregnancy
		Substance use: alcohol, nicotine, cocaine
		Exposure to harmful chemicals: lead, mercury, arsenic, pollutants, abortifacients, teratogenic medications
		Maternal infections: rubella, syphilis, toxoplasma, cytomegalovirus, herpes, HIV
		Others: exposure to radiation, Rh isoimmunization
Perinatal	Third trimester	Diabetes, eclampsia, placental dysfunction, maternal cardiac or renal disease
	Labor	Prematurity, birth trauma, low birth weight (LBW), birth asphyxia
	Neonatal	Septicemia, jaundice, hypoglycemia
Postnatal	Brain infections	Tuberculosis, Japanese encephalitis, bacterial meningoencephalitis
	Head injury	
	Chronic lead exposure	
	Severe and prolonged malnutrition	
	Gross understimulation and experiential deprivation	

CLINICAL FEATURES

As per DSM-5, ID is characterized by deficits in intellectual functioning along with deficits in social and adaptive functioning and the onset is during the developmental period or adolescence. The deficits in intellectual functioning imply that higher mental functions like reasoning, response-inhibition, planning, problem-solving, critical and abstract thinking, conceptual understanding, experiential, and academic learning are all below average. The onset is usually during the formative years, and it is not diagnosed if this condition occurs after the developmental period due to an accident or brain injury or infection.

DSM-5 specifies the severity of ID according to the level of adaptive functioning and not IQ scores, as adaptive functioning determines the degree of support required. Further, the deficits are categorized in three domains, namely conceptual domain (related to the formation of concepts, abstraction, reasoning), social domain (related to communication, interaction, emotional regulation), and practical domain (related to activities of daily living, recreational activities, employment). Table 8.2 highlights the manifestations in each domain according to the severity of ID.

ICD-10 classifies the severity of ID based on IQ scores. Table 8.3 shows the categorization of ID based on IQ scores as per ICD-10 and AAMR (American Association of Mental Retardation)/AAIDD (American Association on Intellectual and Developmental Disabilities).

Table 8.2 Manifestations of intellectual disability as per severity

Severity of ID → Skills ↓	**Mild ID**	**Moderate ID**	**Severe ID**	**Profound ID**
Conceptual domain	At the primary level, goes undetected, for school-age children and adults, learning academic skills could be challenging	Conceptual skills lag markedly behind those of peers. At the primary level, language, communication, and academic skills are delayed. In adult life, support required at work and personal life	Conceptual skills are severely compromised. Individual has little comprehension of the concepts of number, time, written language and money. Needs extensive support in problem solving.	Nil conceptual skills; some visuospatial skills like matching and sorting based on physical characteristics may be acquired.

(Continued)

Table 8.2 *(Continued)*

Severity of ID → Skills ↓	Mild ID	Moderate ID	Severe ID	Profound ID
Social domain	Immature handling, difficulty in the modulation of emotions, poor risk assessment	May not have meaningful social relationships, social judgment and decision-making skills are compromised	Language and communication skills are limited, simple gestures and speech are understood, may need life-long support	Limited understanding of social nuances, the expression is through nonverbal gestures
Practical domain	Capable of being vocationally rehabilitated; however, require support in making complex decisions	Maybe independent in activities of daily living, unskilled jobs can be taught, work best in protected environments, need supervision	Need supervision and guidance in almost all the activities, cannot take responsibility and decisions. Behavioral problems may be evident	Can learn minimal self-care skills, simple activities like carrying dishes may be the basis of participation and recreational activities like listening to music or watching movies with support may be carried out, maladaptive behaviors are present

Table 8.3 Categorization of ID based on IQ scores as per ICD-10 and AAMR/AAIDD

ICD-10	AAMR/AAIDD
Mild: 50–69	Mild: 51–75
Moderate: 35–49	Severe: <50
Severe: 20–34	
Profound: <20	

AAIDD, American Association on Intellectual and Developmental Disabilities; *AAMR*, American Association of Mental Retardation.

DIAGNOSIS

Good clinical history and detailed physical examination allow the physician to come to a close provisional diagnosis. The points in clinical history and physical examination are as follows:

- **Birth history:** It includes a detailed account of mother's health during pregnancy, record of drugs taken, antenatal check-up, mode of delivery, place of delivery, who conducted the delivery, details about birth cry, birth weight, any neonatal complications like metabolic disturbances (hypoglycemia, hypomagnesemia, etc.), neonatal jaundice, neonatal seizures, any need for neonatal ICU care, nursery care, ability to suck mother's milk, and type of feed given.

- **Developmental milestones:** Any delay or deviance in the attainment of milestones in fine motor, gross motor, social, emotional, speech, and language domains should be noted.
- Detailed general physical examination, measurement of height, weight, and head circumference, and detailed neurological examination should be done.
- **Look for neurocutaneous stigmata:** Café-au-lait spots are seen in neurofibromatosis, shagreen patches in tuberous sclerosis, and Mongoloid features in Down syndrome, etc.
- Certain genetic syndromes can be identified by a good and thorough general physical examination. A few examples of such clinically recognizable syndromes associated with ID are given in Table 8.4.
- Always try to look out for a medical cause, especially reversible cause, for example, hypothyroidism, nutritional deficiencies, hearing impairment, vision impairment, and social deprivation.
- Formulate a comprehensive diagnosis, which has management implications. The headings for a comprehensive diagnosis are:
  - Presence and degree of ID
  - Etiologic/syndromal diagnosis
  - Associated medical problem
  - Associated psychiatric problem
  - Family and psychosocial issues

Rating Scales

Most commonly used screening instruments and psychological tests in the Indian setting are as follows:

- Developmental Screening Test (1–15 years)
- Mental and Motor Growth of Indian Babies (1–2 years)

Table 8.4 Genetic syndromes associated with intellectual disability

Syndrome	Physical features
Down syndrome (most common genetic cause of ID)	Hypotonia, hyperflexible joints, flat facial profile, slanted palpebral fissures, poor Moro reflex, excess skin on the back of the neck, abnormal ears, dysplasia of mid phalanx of fifth finger, and single palmar crease
Fragile X syndrome (second most common cause of ID)	Long face, protruding ears, a large jaw, hyperextensible joints, enlarged testis in males
De Lange syndrome	Hirsutism, long eyelashes, synophrys (the fusion of eyebrows above the bridge of nose), bushy eyebrows, microcephaly
Tuberous sclerosis	Sebaceous adenomas, ash-leaf spots, shagreen patches, seizures
Congenital hypothyroidism	Lethargy, growth failure, coarse and dry skin, constipation, feeding problems, protuberant abdomen, bradycardia
Phenylketonuria	Light-colored hair, an abnormal smell of urine, microcephaly, seizures

- Vineland Social Maturity Scale (0–15 years)
- Behavioral Assessment Scale for Indian Children with M.R. (BASIC-MR)
- Malin's Intelligence Test for Indian children (6–15 years)
- Seguin Form Board Test (3–15 years)
- Ravens Progressive Matrices (5–11 years)
- Binet–Kamat Scale (3–22 years)

An IQ score of less than 70 is taken as a cut-off score for making a diagnosis of mental retardation as per ICD-10.

MANAGEMENT

A multidisciplinary team approach is required for the comprehensive management of an individual with ID. Various professionals, such as psychiatrists, pediatricians, psychologists, social workers, physiotherapists, speech therapists, occupational therapists, special educators, and geneticists, make up this team. Management in ID entails individual interventions (both pharmacological and nonpharmacological management) as well as nonpharmacological interventions with the family.

Interventions with the individual with ID include the following:

- Drug treatment of medical and psychiatric disorders
- Multisensory stimulation
- Physiotherapy, speech therapy, and occupational therapy
- Individualized training program depending upon the individual's assets and deficits
- Educational programs
- Vocational rehabilitation

Pharmacological Management

There is no evidence to suggest that "nootropics," that is, drugs that enhance cognition, are effective in ID. Pharmacological therapy is required to manage medical conditions, psychiatric disorders, and severe behavioral problems associated with the ID. Antiepileptic drugs are useful to control seizure disorder, and antipsychotic drugs in low dose help in managing behavior problems associated with the ID. **Risperidone** is the most researched drug in ID. Antidepressants, such as SSRIs (selective serotonin reuptake inhibitors), are useful in managing anxiety and depressive symptoms as well as repetitive behaviors and self-injurious behaviors associated with the ID. Benzodiazepines have no evidence for use in behavioral and emotional problems associated with the ID. Stimulants (methylphenidate and amphetamines), atomoxetine, and clonidine are beneficial in managing attention-deficit/hyperactivity disorder comorbid with ID.

Nonpharmacological Management

Nonpharmacological management remains an important strategy for handling behavior problems in individuals with ID. Behavioral techniques, such as ignoring, time out, response cost, and token economy, can be used for managing problem behaviors.

Family Interventions

- **Psycho-education and family counseling:** The main aim is to devise a realistic management plan to deal with their expectations and assist them with home-training programs. The role of the family in teaching adaptive skills, dealing with stigma, vocational rehabilitation, and reducing the problematic behavior needs to be highlighted.

- **Group counseling:** These sessions are conducted for the family members including the child/adult with the disability. The focus is on specific behavior problems. Insight is generated into the behavior and fear and insecurities are dealt with. Members gain confidence and support by sharing their experiences.
- **Behavior therapy:** The main aim is to increase adaptive behaviors and reduce problem behaviors. The principles of behavior therapy and reinforcement/reward contingencies are explained. The focus is on the family and their role in the management of the problem.
- **Supportive psychotherapy:** Supportive psychotherapy is done to instill confidence and improve self-esteem of the persons with ID. Help and guidance are given to minimize the problems they face in terms of stigmas, handicaps, and emotional and personal problems. Liaison is created with the family, and the best possible solution is generated.

DISABILITY ASSESSMENT

The degree of disability is ascertained according to the guidelines provided by the Director-General of Health Services, Government of India. Persons with 40% disability are eligible for social schemes given by the Government of India. Depending upon the IQ score, the degree of disability is as follows:

- Borderline ID (IQ 70–79) = 25% disability
- Mild ID (IQ 50–69) = 50% disability
- Moderate ID (IQ 35–49) = 75% disability
- Severe ID (IQ 20–34) = 90% disability
- Profound ID (IQ < 20) = 100% disability

A Medical Board is constituted by the Central and the State Governments for disability certification.

PREVENTION

Various preventive strategies that can be employed to minimize the risk of ID are antenatal vaccination for rubella to the pregnant mother, and prenatal screening of the mother for syphilis, newborn screening for congenital hypothyroidism, phenylketonuria, galactosemia, genetic counseling, and prenatal diagnostic tests (amniocentesis and chorionic villus sampling) if high fetal risk exists, for example, increased maternal age.

Sociocultural mental retardation is the term used to describe the lack of a stimulating environment particularly during infancy and early childhood leading to poor brain development and consequently diminished cognitive capacity. An enriching and stimulating environment can prevent the occurrence of such a condition.

KEY POINTS

- As per DSM-5, intellectual disability (ID) is characterized by deficits in intellectual functioning along with deficits in social and adaptive functioning and the onset is during the developmental period or adolescence.
- Intellectual disability is the term used in DSM-5, whereas it is labeled as "Mental Retardation" in ICD-10.
- ICD-10 and AAMR (American Association of Mental Retardation)/AAIDD (American Association on Intellectual and Developmental Disabilities) classify the severity of ID mainly based on IQ scores whereas DSM-5 specifies the severity of ID according to the level of adaptive functioning.
- Down syndrome is the most common genetic cause of ID.
- Long face, protruding ears, a large jaw, hyperextensible joints, and enlarged testis in males are common symptoms of Fragile X syndrome. It is the second most common cause of ID.
- Hypothyroidism, nutritional deficiencies, hearing impairment, vision impairment, and social deprivation are the reversible causes of ID.
- Antipsychotic drugs at low doses help in managing behavior problems associated with the ID.
- Behavioral techniques, such as ignoring, time out, response cost, token economy, can be used for managing problem behaviors in individuals with ID.
- Various preventive strategies that can be employed to minimize the risk of ID are antenatal vaccination to the pregnant mother, prenatal maternal screening for syphilis, newborn screening for congenital hypothyroidism, phenylketonuria, galactosemia, genetic counseling, diagnostic tests (amniocentesis and chorionic villus sampling), if high fetal risk exists, for example, increased maternal age.

SELF-ASSESSMENT

1. Write short notes on:
    a. Etiology of ID
    b. Clinical features of ID
    c. Genetic syndromes associated with ID
    d. Categories of ID as per ICD-10
    e. Disability assessment in a person with ID

Chapter 9
Schizophrenia

Sandeep Grover · Himanshu Singla

Schizophrenia is one of the most common disorders among serious mental disorders. Signs and symptoms of the disorder involve changes in perception, emotion, cognition, thinking, and behavior. The word "schizophrenia" comes from the Greek roots *schizo* (split) and *phrene* (mind) to describe the fragmented thinking of people with the disorder. As with other psychiatric disorders, the diagnosis of schizophrenia is based on a detailed history and mental status examination.

HISTORY

Emil Kraepelin was the first to make a distinction between what he called "dementia praecox" and "manic depressive psychosis." He named the disorder "dementia praecox" (early dementia) to distinguish it from other forms of dementia (such as Alzheimer's disease) which typically occur late in life. Patients with dementia praecox were considered to have a long-term deteriorating course, and the clinical picture was characterized by hallucinations and delusions.

Eugen Bleuler, a Swiss psychiatrist, coined the term, "**schizophrenia**," as he believed that the term "dementia praecox" was misleading and the illness was not dementia. Bleuler also described the specific fundamental symptoms of schizophrenia, which are described as 4 A's, that is, **associations disturbances** (loosening of associations), **affect disturbances** (inappropriate affect), **autism** (withdrawal into self), and **ambivalence** (inability to decide for or against). He also described accessory (secondary) symptoms in the form of hallucinations and delusions.

Kurt Schneider Historically Kurt Schneider described the first-rank symptoms of schizophrenia (Box 9.1), which were initially considered to be specific for schizophrenia.

EPIDEMIOLOGY

The lifetime prevalence of schizophrenia is reported to be 0.3%–0.7%; although, there is reported variation by race/ethnicity, across countries. Males are more commonly affected as compared to females, and the usual age of onset is 10–25 years for males and 25–35 years for females. Women display a bimodal distribution of age of onset, with a second peak occurring in middle age.

Season of the birth has been linked to the incidence of schizophrenia with late winter and early spring birth being more common in these patients.

ETIOLOGY

Various biological, psychological, and social factors have been reported to be associated with the development of schizophrenia.

Box 9.1 First-rank symptoms of schizophrenia

- **Audible thoughts:** The patient hears his/her thoughts being spoken aloud in his/her voice.
- **Voices arguing or discussing:** Auditory hallucinations in which two or more voices are usually heard arguing or discussing the patient in the third person.
- **Voices commenting on patient's actions:** The patient hears hallucinatory voices commenting on his/her actions.
- **Somatic passivity:** The patient is a passive recipient of external influence in the form of tactile or visceral hallucinations, which are imposed upon him/her.
- **Thought withdrawal:** The patient experiences that his/her thoughts are being actively removed from the mind by some external agency.
- **Thought insertion:** The patient experiences that the thoughts are being inserted into his/her mind by some external agency.
- **Thought broadcasting:** The patient experiences that his/her thoughts are escaping the mind and are available to others in the vicinity.
- **Made feelings impulses, and acts:** The patient feels that his/her feelings, impulses, or acts are imposed on him/her by an external agency and they are not his/her own.
- **Delusional perception:** The patient has a perception with delusional interpretation and has a unique and idiosyncratic meaning for him/herself.

Biological

- **Genetics:** Schizophrenia occurs at an increased frequency among the biological relatives of patients with schizophrenia with higher risk among first-degree relatives compared to second-degree relatives. Among monozygotic twin pairs, the approximate concordance rate for schizophrenia is 47% which is much higher than the concordance rate in dizygotic twin pairs (12%).
- **Neurotransmitters:** Among the various neurochemical hypotheses for schizophrenia, the most accepted hypothesis is that of dopamine hypothesis which suggests that the signs and symptoms of schizophrenia are a result of too much dopaminergic activity. The most commonly implicated dopaminergic tracts include mesocortical and mesolimbic tracts. It has been established that the severity of positive symptoms is linked with excessive dopamine release.

  Besides the dopamine hypothesis, other neurochemical hypotheses for schizophrenia include abnormalities in serotonin and norepinephrine. According to the serotonin hypothesis, serotonin excess causes both positive and negative symptoms in schizophrenia. Norepinephrine abnormalities have been linked to impaired capacity for emotional gratification and the decreased ability to experience pleasure.
- **Neuropathology:** Among the various neural structures of the brain, schizophrenia has been shown to be linked to abnormalities in the limbic system and the basal ganglia, along

with the abnormalities in the cerebral cortex, the thalamus, and the brainstem.

Psychoanalytic and Psychosocial Theories

Among the various psychoanalytic theories, schizophrenia has been reported to be an outcome of ego disintegration that represents a return to the time when the ego was not yet developed or had just begun to be established.

Among the various psychosocial factors, the risk of schizophrenia has been shown to be associated with poor mother-child relationship, hostile environment, and dysfunctional families.

CLINICAL FEATURES

No clinical sign or symptom is pathognomonic for schizophrenia, and the clinical picture of schizophrenia often changes during the course of illness. The patient may manifest with disorders of thought perception, affect, motor behavior, cognitive symptoms, and negative symptoms (Box 9.2).

SUBTYPES OF SCHIZOPHRENIA

ICD-10 describes paranoid, disorganized, catatonic, undifferentiated, residual, and simple and post-psychotic/schizophrenic depression as various subtypes (Box 9.3). However, the most recent classification,

Box 9.2 Clinical features of schizophrenia

- **General description:** The appearance of a patient with schizophrenia can vary, ranging from a completely disheveled, screaming, and agitated to a person who is obsessively groomed, completely silent, and immobile. Patients may be talkative and may exhibit bizarre postures or agitated or violent behavior.
- **Disorders of thought:** The patient can have delusions, loosening of associations, derailment, incoherence, circumstantiality, tangentiality, neologisms, word salad, flight of ideas, thought blocking, poverty of thought content, and perseveration.
- **Disorders of perception:** In schizophrenia, the most common hallucinations are auditory and are in the form of voices that are commenting on the patient's actions or life, or discussing among themselves about the patient. Visual hallucinations are common but tactile, olfactory, and gustatory hallucinations are unusual, and in their presence, clinicians should look for the possibility of an underlying medical or neurological disorder.
- **Disorders of affect:** Affective symptoms in schizophrenia are either reduced emotional responsiveness or overly active and *inappropriate emotions* (e.g., extremes of rage, happiness, and anxiety). A *flat or blunted affect* can be a symptom of the illness itself, of the extrapyramidal side effects of antipsychotic medications or depression.
- **Disorders of motor behavior:** These can be associated with decreased or increased psychomotor activity. Catatonic features (described in Box 3.3) are the common motor manifestations of schizophrenia.
- **Cognitive symptoms:** Cognitive dysfunction can be present in the domains of attention, executive function, working memory, and episodic memory.

(*Continued*)

Box 9.2 *(Continued)*

Cognitive impairment is a better predictor of functionality in schizophrenia than the severity of psychotic symptoms.

- **Negative symptoms:** These include *Alogia* (poverty of speech), *Affective blunting* (lack of emotional expression), *Avolition* (impairment of willful action), *Anhedonia* (loss of enjoyment in favored activities), *Asociality* (inability to undertake normal social activities), and *Amotivation* (lack of self-initiated purposeful activity).
- **Lack of insight:** A majority of individuals with schizophrenia have poor insight regarding the fact that they have a psychotic illness. It has an impact on treatment seeking, adherence, and prognosis of the patient.
- **Self-harm/suicidal behavior:** Suicide is the single most leading cause of premature death among persons with schizophrenia. It has been observed that the presence of a major depressive episode is the most important risk factor for suicidal behavior. Other possible contributors include command hallucinations and drug abuse.

Box 9.3 Subtypes of schizophrenia

- **Paranoid:** Delusions or hallucinations are predominant, and disturbance of affect, volition, speech, and catatonic symptoms are relatively inconspicuous. Delusions of control, influence, or passivity and persecutory beliefs are most characteristic. The age of onset is usually later, and the prognosis is better than other clinical subtypes.
- **Disorganized (Hebephrenic):** Patients have marked thought disorder and poor contact with reality and their behavior is unorganized and disinhibited. The onset is generally early before the age of 25 years. Appearance is usually disheveled, and they exhibit inappropriate social behavior and emotional responses. This subtype has one of the worst prognosis among the various subtypes of schizophrenia.
- **Catatonic:** Catatonic schizophrenia is characterized by marked disturbance in motor function. The important catatonic symptoms (Box 3.3) are stupor, excitement, posturing, negativism, rigidity, waxy flexibility, command automatism, and perseveration of words and phrases. Catatonic excitement can result in significant injury to self and others.
- **Undifferentiated:** Patients having symptoms of schizophrenia that do not fit into one type or another either due to lack of full features of one subtype or due to the presence of features of more than one subtype.
- **Residual:** In residual schizophrenia, the patients no longer have prominent psychotic symptoms but once met the criteria for schizophrenia and still have continuing evidence of illness. Commonly encountered features are social withdrawal,

(Continued)

Box 9.3 *(Continued)*

emotional blunting, eccentric behavior, illogical thinking, and mild loosening of associations. Delusions or hallucinations can occur but are usually less prominent.

- **Simple:** It is characterized by a gradual, insidious loss of drive and ambition. Patients have a primary symptom in the form of withdrawal from social and work-related situations and are not overtly psychotic with no persistent delusions or hallucinations. This subtype has a poor prognosis.
- **Post/schizophrenic depression:** After an acute schizophrenic episode, some patients become depressed. Post-schizophrenic depression is diagnosed when: the patient has had a schizophrenic illness meeting the general criteria for schizophrenia within the past 12 months; some schizophrenic symptoms are still present; and the depressive symptoms fulfill the criteria for a depressive episode.

Other subtypes

- **Oneiroid:** In the oneiroid state, patients may be deeply perplexed and not fully oriented in time and place. Engagement with their hallucinatory experience is to such an extent that the patient is cut-off from the real world.
- **Pseudoneurotic schizophrenia:** Occasionally, patients have initial symptoms of anxiety, phobias, obsessions, and compulsions and they develop symptoms of thought disorder and psychosis later on. These patients are characterized by symptoms of pananxiety, panneurosis, and pansexuality.
- **Very early and early-onset schizophrenia:** When the onset of illness is before 13 years of age it is known as very early onset, and when the onset is between 13 and 18 years of age, it is known as early onset schizophrenia.
- **Late-onset schizophrenia:** Age of onset of illness is after 45 years, and the disorder is clinically indistinguishable from schizophrenia. Women tend to suffer more frequently with a marked predominance of paranoid symptoms. The prognosis is favorable, and the response to antipsychotic medications is usually good.
- **Van Gogh syndrome:** Self-mutilation in schizophrenia is also called Van Gogh syndrome. Vincent Willem van Gogh was the famous painter who cut his own ear during the active phase of the illness.
- **Pfropf schizophrenia:** Schizophrenia in a person with mental retardation (IQ less than 70).

that is, DSM-5 has removed the various subtypes of schizophrenia due to the lack of validity of these subtypes. The subtypes are categorized after the patient fulfills the general criteria for the diagnosis of schizophrenia.

DIAGNOSIS

Diagnosis can be made according to either DSM-5 or ICD-10 (Box 9.4).

As per ICD-10, for the diagnosis of schizophrenia, a minimum of one very clear-cut symptom (and usually two or

Box 9.4 Diagnostic criteria for schizophrenia as per ICD-10

a. Thought echo, thought insertion or withdrawal, and thought broadcasting;
b. Delusions of control, influence, or passivity, clearly referred to body or limb movements or specific thoughts, actions, or sensations; delusional perception;
c. Hallucinatory voices giving a running commentary on the patient's behavior or discussing the patient among themselves, or other types of hallucinatory voices coming from some part of the body;
d. Persistent delusions of other kinds that are culturally inappropriate and completely impossible, such as religious or political identity, or superhuman powers and abilities (e.g., being able to control the weather, or being in communication with aliens from another world);
e. Persistent hallucinations in any modality, when accompanied either by fleeting or half-formed delusions without clear affective content, or by persistent over-valued ideas, or when occurring every day for weeks or months on end;
f. Breaks or interpolations in the train of thought, resulting in incoherence or irrelevant speech, or neologisms;
g. Catatonic behavior, such as excitement, posturing, or waxy flexibility, negativism, mutism, and stupor;
h. "Negative" symptoms such as marked apathy, the paucity of speech, and blunting or incongruity of emotional responses, usually resulting in social withdrawal and lowering of social performance; it must be clear that these are not due to depression or neuroleptic medication;
i. A significant and consistent change in the overall quality of some aspects of personal behavior, manifest as loss of interest, aimlessness, idleness, a self-absorbed attitude, and social withdrawal.

more if less clear-cut) belonging to any one of the groups listed as (a) to (d) or symptoms from at least two of the groups referred to as (e) and (h) should have been clearly present for most of the time during a period of 1 month or more. Symptom (i) in the list applies only to a diagnosis of simple schizophrenia and a duration of at least 1 year is required.

DIFFERENTIAL DIAGNOSIS

It is important to rule out organic causes of psychotic symptoms, before considering the diagnosis of schizophrenia (Box 9.5).

COURSE AND PROGNOSIS

The course can be continuous, episodic with progressive deficit, episodic with stable deficit, episodic remittent, incomplete remission, or complete remission.

Several factors have been associated with the prognosis of schizophrenia (Box 9.6).

MANAGEMENT

Various treatment options for the management of schizophrenia include the following:

- Antipsychotic medications
- Electroconvulsive therapy (ECT)
- Psychosocial interventions

Although antipsychotic medications form the mainstay of the treatment for schizophrenia, psychosocial interventions, including psychotherapy, have been shown to augment the clinical improvement. After the acute phase of illness has subsided, due importance must be given to the psychosocial interventions and rehabilitation of the patient.

Box 9.5 Differential diagnosis of schizophrenia

- **Secondary psychotic disorders:** Psychotic symptoms are due to various medical and neurological conditions or due to the use of a variety of substances.
- **Major depressive or bipolar disorder with psychotic symptoms:** In patients with mood disorders, usually the affective symptoms emerge before the onset of psychotic symptoms and the psychotic symptoms are mostly mood-congruent.
- **Schizoaffective disorder:** When both mood episode (major depressive or manic episode) and the active-phase symptoms of schizophrenia are present simultaneously, and mood symptoms are present for a majority of the total duration of the active periods of illness.
- **Schizophreniform disorder and brief psychotic disorder:** In schizophreniform disorder, symptoms are present for less than 6 months and in brief psychotic disorder, symptoms are present at least 1 day but less than 1 month.
- **Delusional disorder:** Clinical picture is marked by the presence of delusions in the absence of the other symptoms characteristic of schizophrenia for more than 3 months.
- **Schizotypal personality disorder:** Subthreshold symptoms associated with persistent personality features.

Box 9.6 Prognostic factors for schizophrenia

Good prognostic factors

- Late age of onset
- Presence of precipitating factors
- Acute onset
- Good premorbid adjustment
- Symptoms of mood disorder (especially depressive disorders)
- Married
- Family history of mood disorders
- Good social support
- Positive symptoms

Poor prognostic factors

- Young age of onset
- Absence of precipitating factors
- Insidious onset
- Poor premorbid adjustment
- Withdrawn, autistic behavior
- Single, divorced, or widowed
- A family history of schizophrenia
- Poor social support
- Negative symptoms
- Neurological signs and symptoms
- Lack of remissions in 3 years
- Multiple relapses

Antipsychotics medications used for the management of schizophrenia can be broadly classified as first-generation antipsychotic (FGAs) and second-generation antipsychotics (SGAs) (Table 9.1).

Various antipsychotic agents do not differ significantly in terms of efficacy except for clozapine, which is considered to have better efficacy than other antipsychotics, especially among patients with treatment-resistant schizophrenia. Hence, selection of antipsychotics among patients is mostly determined by patient-related factors (Box 9.7) and the medication-related factors, including side effect profile. Considering the metabolic side effects, when atypical antipsychotics are used for a longer duration, it is recommended to monitor the patient's blood glucose levels, serum lipids, body weight, waist circumference, and blood pressure.

Usually, antipsychotics should be started in a low dose, and the doses should be escalated slowly with close monitoring of the side effects.

Whenever an antipsychotic medication is prescribed to a patient with schizophrenia, the medication should be used in the highest tolerable therapeutic doses for a minimum duration of 6–8 weeks to consider it as an adequate trial. However, for clozapine, adequate trial duration

Table 9.1 Classification of antipsychotic medications

	Usual starting dose (mg/day)	**Usual therapeutic doses (mg/day)**
Typical antipsychotics		
• Chlorpromazine	• 30–70	• 75–300
• Fluphenazine	• 5–15	• 5–40
• Haloperidol	• 1–15	• 1–40
• Loxapine	• 15–30	• 30–50
• Prochlorperazine	• 5	• 15–125
• Thioridazine	• 30–80	• 5–100
• Trifluoperazine	• 2–5	• 5–20
Atypical antipsychotics		
• Amisulpride	• 200–800	• 400–800
• Aripiprazole	• 5–10	• 15–30
• Asenapine	• 5–10	• 10–20
• Clozapine	• 12.5–25	• 300–400
• Iloperidone	• 2	• 12–24
• Lurasidone	• 40–80	• 40–80
• Olanzapine	• 5	• 10–20
• Paliperidone	• 3–6	• 6
• Quetiapine	• 25–50	• 400–800
• Risperidone	• 0.5–1	• 2–6
• Ziprasidone	• 20	• 40–200

Box 9.7 Factors that influence the selection of antipsychotics

Patient-related factors

- Past treatment response
- Psychiatric comorbidity
- Medical comorbidity
- Preference of patient or family
- Preferred route of administration
- Concomitant medications
- Non-adherence
- Treatment resistance

Medication-related factors

- Side effects
- Cost of treatment, affordability

is defined as 6 months. Before considering any antipsychotic medication to be ineffective, it is important to evaluate the medication compliance of the patient.

Clozapine needs to be considered after the failure of two sequential trials of antipsychotics (at least one of which is an SGA).

Electroconvulsive therapy ECT is indicated in a subgroup of patients with schizophrenia (Box 9.8). There is evidence to suggest that ECT can be used for augmentation and acceleration of response to antipsychotic medications.

Psychosocial interventions Psychosocial interventions are considered to be an integral part of the management of schizophrenia. Different psychosocial interventions including family interventions, cognitive behavioral therapy, social skills training, cognitive remediation, individual supportive therapy, group therapy, vocational rehabilitation, case management, use of community mental-health teams, and crisis resolution teams have been proven to be useful in the management of schizophrenia.

Box 9.8 Indications for use of ECT in schizophrenia

- Catatonic symptoms
- Affective symptoms
- Need for rapid control of symptoms
- Presence of suicidal behavior which puts the life of the patient at risk
- Presence of severe agitation or violence which puts the lives of others at risk
- Refusal to eat which puts the life of the patient at risk
- History of good response in the past
- Patients not responding to an adequate trial of an antipsychotic medication
- Augmentation of partial response to antipsychotic medication
- Clozapine-resistant schizophrenia
- Not able to tolerate antipsychotic medications

KEY POINTS

- The word "schizophrenia" comes from the Greek roots, *schizo* (split) and *phrene* (mind) to describe the fragmented thinking of people with the disorder.
- Emil Kraepelin was the first to make a distinction between what he called "dementia praecox" and "manic depressive psychosis."
- Eugen Bleuler, a Swiss psychiatrist, coined the term, "schizophrenia."
- Bleuler also described the specific fundamental symptoms of schizophrenia, which are described as 4 A's, that is,
  - associations disturbances (loosening of associations),
  - affect disturbances (inappropriate affect),
  - autism (withdrawal into self), and
  - ambivalence (inability to decide for or against).
- Kurt Schneider described the first-rank symptoms of schizophrenia.
- The lifetime prevalence of schizophrenia is reported to be 0.3%–0.7%.
- Various biological, psychological, and social factors have been reported to be associated with the development of schizophrenia.
- Among monozygotic twin pairs, the approximate concordance rate for schizophrenia is 47% which is much higher than the concordance rate in dizygotic twin pairs (12%).
- As per dopamine hypothesis the signs and symptoms of schizophrenia are a result of too much dopaminergic activity.
- Besides the dopamine hypothesis, other neurochemical hypotheses for schizophrenia include abnormalities in serotonin and norepinephrine.
- No clinical sign or symptom is pathognomonic for schizophrenia, and the clinical picture of schizophrenia often changes during illness. The patient may manifest with disorders of thought perception, affect, motor behavior, cognitive symptoms, and negative symptoms.
- ICD-10 describes paranoid, disorganized, catatonic, undifferentiated, residual, simple, and post-psychotic/schizophrenic depression as various subtypes; whereas, DSM-5 has removed the various subtypes of schizophrenia due to lack of validity of these subtypes.
- Stupor, catalepsy, waxy flexibility, mutism, negativism, posturing, mannerisms, stereotypy, grimacing, echolalia, and echopraxia are various catatonic symptoms.
- Self-mutilation in schizophrenia is also called Van Gogh syndrome. Vincent Willem van Gogh was a famous painter who cut his ear during the active phase of the illness.
- Schizophrenia in a person with mental retardation (IQ less than 70) is known as Pfropf schizophrenia.
- When the onset of illness is before 13 years of age it is known as very early-onset, and when the onset is between 13 and 18 years of age, it is known as early-onset schizophrenia.
- Late age of onset, presence of precipitating factors, acute onset, good premorbid adjustment, symptoms of mood disorder, married, family history of mood disorders, good social support, and positive symptoms are good prognostic factors.
- Young age of onset, absence of precipitating factors, insidious onset, poor premorbid adjustment, withdrawn, autistic behavior, single, divorced or widowed, a family history of schizophrenia, poor social support, negative symptoms, neurological signs and symptoms, lack of remissions in 3 years, and multiple relapses are bad prognostic signs.
- Various treatment options for the management of schizophrenia include the following:

  - Antipsychotic medications
  - Electroconvulsive therapy
  - Psychosocial interventions
- Clozapine needs to be considered after the failure of two sequential trials of antipsychotics (at least one of which is an second-generation antipsychotic [SGA]).
- Electroconvulsive therapy (ECT) is indicated if schizophrenia is associated with catatonic symptoms, affective symptoms, need for rapid control of symptoms, suicidal behavior, refusal to eat which puts the life of the patient at risk, history of good response in the past, patients not responding to an adequate trial of an antipsychotic medication, clozapine-resistant schizophrenia, and not able to tolerate antipsychotic medication.
- Psychosocial interventions are considered to be an integral part of the management of schizophrenia.

SELF-ASSESSMENT

1. Case-based Questions

   A 28-year-old male presented with a history of hearing the voices of two people discussing ill about him, commenting on his day-to-day actions, commanding him to carry out certain actions for the last 5 years whereas family members deny hearing such voices. He believes that neighbors are conspiring against him and want to harm him and are talking ill about him. Since the onset of these symptoms, the patient has confined himself to his room, avoids meeting people, and does not take bath regularly. Over the years, he has been treated with multiple antipsychotics, with which there is some reduction in symptoms, but he discontinues the medications within a few months and then experiences a full-blown relapse.

   a. What is your provisional diagnosis and discuss the reasons for it?
   b. Discuss differential diagnosis.
2. Discuss the etiology, clinical features, and treatment of schizophrenia.
3. Discuss the diagnostic criteria of schizophrenia as per ICD-10.
4. Enumerate various subtypes of schizophrenia and describe any two.
5. Describe the various indications of ECT in schizophrenia.
6. Discuss the prognostic factors of schizophrenia.

Chapter 10

Other Psychotic Disorders

Sandeep Grover

Psychotic disorders are characterized by the presence of delusions, hallucinations, disorganized thinking (speech), grossly disorganized, or abnormal motor behavior including catatonia and negative symptoms. However, it is important to remember that these symptoms are not seen exclusively in schizophrenia. Many patients with these psychotic symptoms may not meet the diagnostic criteria of schizophrenia, and these disorders are classified as other psychotic disorders.

COMPARATIVE NOSOLOGY

Delusional disorder, brief psychotic disorder, schizophreniform disorder, and schizoaffective disorder are major disorders classified in DSM-5 as other psychotic disorders.

Some of the major differences between the two nosological systems (DSM-5 and ICD-10) include classification of schizotypal disorders with other psychotic disorders in the ICD-10, whereas DSM-5 categorizes the same along with personality disorders.

Short-lasting psychotic disorders in ICD-10 are categorized as acute and transient psychotic disorders (ATPD), whereas DSM-5 categorizes the same into two categories, that is, brief psychotic disorder and schizophreniform disorder (Table 10.1). ICD-10 categorizes persistent delusional disorders and induced delusional disorder separately, whereas DSM-5 includes a single category of delusional disorder.

DELUSIONAL DISORDER

Delusional disorder is characterized by the presence of well-formed delusions These patients lack other psychotic symptoms. Hallucinations, if present, are not prominent. The delusions in patients with delusional disorder may be either a single delusion or a set of related delusions, which are usually persistent, and sometimes, lifelong. The commonly seen delusions in patients with delusional disorder

Table 10.1 Classification of other psychotic disorders

ICD-10	DSM-5
• Schizotypal disorder • Persistent delusional disorders • Acute and transient psychotic disorders • Induced delusional disorder • Schizoaffective disorders	• Delusional disorder • Brief psychotic disorder • Schizophreniform disorder • Schizoaffective disorder • Substance/medication-induced disorder • Psychotic disorders due to another medical condition • Catatonia associated with another medical disorder

are categorized as persecutory, grandiose, jealousy, erotomanic, and somatic type. In delusional disorder, functioning of the patient is not markedly impaired and behavior is not odd.

DSM-5 requires these symptoms to be present at least for 1 month to make the diagnosis of delusional disorder, whereas the duration criterion in ICD-10 is that of 3 months.

BRIEF PSYCHOTIC DISORDER

Brief psychotic disorder is characterized by the presence of psychotic symptoms (delusions, hallucinations, disorganized speech, grossly disorganized, or catatonic behavior) and at least one of the symptom must be delusion, hallucination, or disorganized speech. Duration of the episode should be at least 1 day but less than 1 month. The diagnosis is made only when the symptoms cannot be attributed to major depressive or bipolar disorder with psychotic features, schizophrenia, catatonia, substance use, and another medical condition.

SCHIZOPHRENIFORM DISORDER

Schizophreniform disorder is characterized by psychotic symptoms (delusions, hallucinations, disorganized speech, grossly disorganized or catatonic behavior, negative symptoms) and at least one of the symptoms must be delusion, hallucination, or disorganized speech. Duration of the episode should be at least 1 month but less than 6 months. The diagnosis is made only when the symptoms cannot be attributed to schizoaffective disorder, depressive or bipolar disorder with psychotic features, substance use, and another medical condition.

SCHIZOAFFECTIVE DISORDER

According to DSM-5, for the diagnosis of schizoaffective disorder, the person must meet the criteria for major mood episode (major depressive or manic) concurrent with the criteria of schizophrenia. The mood symptoms should be present for the majority of the illness, and there should be a period of two or more weeks in which the person should have delusions and hallucinations without mood symptoms sometimes during the lifetime of the illness. DSM-5 describes depressive and manic subtypes of the schizoaffective disorder.

MANAGEMENT OF OTHER PSYCHOTIC DISORDERS

Management of various psychotic disorders includes thorough evaluation to rule out organic causes and psychotic disorders secondary to use of substances or drugs. Once the diagnosis is firmly established, the management can be broadly divided as pharmacological and nonpharmacological treatment.

The mainstay of pharmacological treatment of various "other psychotic disorders" includes the use of antipsychotic medications. For schizoaffective disorder in addition to the use of antipsychotics, use of mood stabilizers is necessary.

Nonpharmacological management involves psychoeducation and various psychotherapies. While using antipsychotics, the doses described in Chapter 9, *Schizophrenia,* must be followed.

KEY POINTS

- Delusional disorder, brief psychotic disorder, schizophreniform disorder, and schizoaffective disorders are major disorders classified in DSM-5.
- **Delusional disorder** is characterized by the presence of delusions and the lack of other psychotic symptoms. DSM-5 requires these symptoms to be present at least for 1 month to make the diagnosis of delusional disorder, whereas the duration criterion in ICD-10 is that of 3 months.
- **Brief psychotic disorder** is characterized by the presence of psychotic symptoms (delusions, hallucinations, disorganized speech, grossly disorganized, or catatonic behavior) and at least one of the symptom must be delusion, hallucination, or disorganized speech. The duration of the episode should be at least 1 day but less than 1 month.
- **Schizophreniform disorder** is characterized by the psychotic symptoms (delusions, hallucinations, disorganized speech, grossly disorganized or catatonic behavior, negative symptoms) and at least one of the symptoms must be delusion, hallucination, or disorganized speech. The duration of the episode should be at least 1 month but less than 6 months.
- According to DSM-5, for the diagnosis of **schizoaffective disorder**, the person must meet the criteria for major mood episodes (major depressive or manic) concurrent with the criteria of schizophrenia. The mood symptoms should be present for the majority of the illness, and there should be a period of two or more weeks in which the person should have delusions and hallucinations without mood symptoms.
- The mainstay of pharmacological treatment of various other psychotic disorders like that of schizophrenia includes the use of antipsychotic medications.
- For schizoaffective disorder in addition to the use of antipsychotics, the use of mood stabilizers is necessary.

SELF-ASSESSMENT

1. Write short notes on:
   a. Delusional disorder
   b. Brief psychotic disorder
   c. Schizophreniform disorder
   d. Schizoaffective disorder

Chapter 11

Mood Disorders

Manish Bathla · Shazia Anjum

Mood disorders include disorders in which pathological mood and related vegetative and psychomotor disturbance are the dominant symptoms. Previously these were known as affective disorders.

COMPARATIVE NOSOLOGY

In ICD-10, mood disorders include manic episode, bipolar affective disorder, depressive episode, recurrent depressive disorder, persistent mood (affective) disorders, whereas in DSM-5, bipolar and related disorders and depressive disorders are classified separately.

As per DSM-5 classification, disruptive mood dysregulation disorder, major depressive disorder (MDD), persistent depressive disorder (dysthymia), and premenstrual dysphoric disorder (PMDD) are major categories in depressive disorders and bipolar I disorder, bipolar II disorder, and cyclothymic disorder are major categories in bipolar disorders.

Although bipolar and related disorders and depressive disorders are separate as per DSM-5 but considering the undergraduate level we have described these two together.

Disruptive mood dysregulation disorder is found in children and adolescents and is discussed in detail in Chapter 21, *Psychiatric Disorders in Childhood and Adolescence*.

EPIDEMIOLOGY

The lifetime prevalence of major depressive disorders is 5%–17%. Bipolar I disorder has a lifetime prevalence of 0%–2.4% and bipolar II disorder has a lifetime prevalence of 0.3%–4.8%. The mean age of onset in major depressive disorders is 40 years, whereas in bipolar disorder mean age of onset is 30 years. A major depressive disorder is twice more prevalent in females than in males. Bipolar I disorder has equal prevalence among men and women. Depressive disorder and bipolar I disorder are more prevalent in single, divorced, or separated individuals.

ETIOLOGY

Biological Theories

- **Neurotransmitters:** Alteration in monoamines (norepinephrine, serotonin, and dopamine) in the central nervous system is the main hypothesis (**biogenic amine theory**). Depletion in the level of monoamines in the synaptic cleft leads to depressive disorders and a rise in the level of monoamines leads to mania.
  The increase in the level of biogenic amines in the brain by antidepressant medications further supports the biogenic amine theory. The involvement of gamma-aminobutyric acid (GABA) and acetylcholine in mood disorders is also hypothesized.

- **Neuroendocrine hypothesis:** Elevated hypothalamic pituitary adrenal (HPA) axis activity is the hallmark of the stress response and indicates the link between depression and chronic stress. Depression is associated with elevated cortisol level, nonsuppression with dexamethasone challenge (dexamethasone suppression test [DST]).
- **Genetics:** There is evidence of a significant role of genetics in the causation of depressive disorders and bipolar disorders which is supported by family, twin, adoption, and linkage studies.
  - **Family studies** show that if one of the parents has a mood disorder, then the chances of having mood disorders in children are 10%–25%, and this risk is doubled if both parents have mood disorders. Family studies reveal that the risk of major depression in first-degree relatives of a patient with depression is two to threefold over the general population.
  - **Twin studies** show that the involvement of genes in mood disorder is 50%–70% and the rest is explained by the contribution of the environmental factors. The concordance rate of mood disorders is 70%–90% in monozygotic twins while it is 16%–35% in same-sex dizygotic twins.
  - **Adoption studies** show that there is three times increased risk for bipolar disorders and two times for unipolar disorders in biological relatives of the bipolar proband.
  - **Linkage studies** have shown the involvement of chromosome 2q, 3q, 12q, 15q, and 18q for recurrent early-onset form of major depression. Chromosomes 13q and 22q are the two regions with the strongest evidence for linkage to bipolar disorder.
- **Altered sleep neurophysiology:** Studies have shown decreased rapid eye movement (REM) latency, increased REM density, and decreased sleep maintenance in depressive patients.
- **Neuroimaging:** Magnetic resonance imaging (MRI) and computed tomography (CT) scan show hyperintensities in subcortical areas such as periventricular regions, the basal ganglia, and the thalamus in depressive disorders. Positron emission tomography (PET) scans show decreased anterior brain metabolism in the left side of the brain in depressive disorders. The reversal of hypofrontality occurs after the shift from depression into mania.

Psychosocial Theories

- **Role of life events**: Studies show that stressful life events do play a role in the precipitation of the first episode of mood disorders, but not for subsequent episodes. This association has been reported for patients with major depressive disorder and patients with bipolar I disorder. Loss of parents at a younger age, loss of spouse, and unemployment are the major environmental factors that have been found to have a role in the development of depressive disorders.

Psychodynamic Theory

This theory proposed by Sigmund Freud and Karl Abraham states that depression is due to the disturbed infant–mother relationship in the oral phase, real or imagined loss of the object, introjection of the departed object, and internalization of the feeling of love and hate toward the lost object.

Klein defined mania as a defensive reaction to depression using the defense mechanism of omnipotence, in which a person develops delusion of grandeur.

Cognitive Theory

According to cognitive theory, depression occurs due to cognitive distortions in thinking. According to Beck, there is a cognitive triad of depression which includes a negative view of oneself, of the world, and about the future.

MAJOR DEPRESSIVE DISORDER

Clinical Features and Diagnosis

Major depressive disorder is associated with the following symptoms:

Mood Depressed mood (sadness, irritability, or anxiousness) and loss of interest in the activities which were pleasurable before the onset of illness are the cardinal symptoms of depression. The patient gives up previously enjoyed activities.

Psychomotor disturbance Psychomotor retardation is the primary pathology in major depressive disorder and presents as decreased spontaneous movements, downcast gaze, fatigue, reduced speech with increased latency, a subjective feeling that time has stopped, poor concentration, and indecisiveness.

Vegetative disturbance It includes a decrease in sleep, appetite, sexual functioning, and alterations in circadian rhythms such as morning worsening of mood. Sleep disturbance is the cardinal symptom of depression and is characterized by early morning awakening rather than the difficulty in the onset of sleep. Anorexia and weight loss are the most reliable indicators of depressive disorder. Decreased sexual desire is seen in men and women.

Some patients present with reversal of vegetative functions and circadian rhythms characterized by an increase in sleep and appetite and worsening of mood in the evening. These symptoms are labeled as atypical features.

Cognitive disturbance Cognitive disturbances include a cognitive triad of negative views of the self, the world, and the future. Other cognitive symptoms are low self-esteem and self-confidence, pathological guilt, hopelessness, worthlessness, helplessness, and suicidal thoughts. Depression is associated with forgetfulness (**pseudodementia**).

In depression, the patient may present with delusions which are usually mood-congruent. The patient can have the delusion of poverty, persecution, infidelity, and nihilistic delusions. Persecutory delusions are often prosecutory in which a person believes that he deserves punishment.

In DSM-5, the minimum duration of symptoms required to diagnose a major depressive episode is 2 weeks. A depressive episode is severe enough to cause clinically significant distress or impairment in social, occupational, or other important areas of functioning.

Specifiers

With melancholic features Melancholic features include loss of interest in almost all activities or lack of reactivity to usually pleasurable stimuli along with depressed mood characterized by profound despondency or empty mood, early morning awakening (at least 2 hours before usual time), depression worse in the morning, marked psychomotor agitation or retardation, significant loss of appetite or weight loss, and excessive guilt. This type is also known as an **endogenous type**.

With seasonal pattern This applies to recurrent major depressive disorder. Depression with a seasonal pattern is characterized by the regular temporal relationship between the onset and remission of major depressive episodes and a particular time of year (e.g., in the fall or winter) for at least 2-year period without any nonseasonal episode occurring during this period.

With psychotic features When a depressive episode is associated with delusions/hallucinations.

With catatonia When a depressive episode is associated with catatonic symptoms.

With peripartum onset If mood symptoms develop during pregnancy or in the 4 weeks after delivery.

Scales Used

Hamilton rating scale for depression (HAM-D), Beck Depression Inventory (BDI), Montgomery–Åsberg Depression Rating Scale (MADRS), and Amritsar Depression Inventory (ADI) are commonly used scales for assessment of depression.

Differential Diagnosis

- **Substance-induced depressive disorder:** Substance-induced depressive disorder is diagnosed if it is judged that mood disturbance developed during or soon after substance intoxication, or withdrawal, and the involved substance is capable of producing the mood disturbance.

  Primary depressive disorder is diagnosed if the depressive symptoms precede the onset of substance/medication use or symptoms persist for a substantial period (1 month) after cessation of substance or severe intoxication.
- **Mood disorder due to a medical condition:** Many medical and neurological diseases can produce symptoms of depression. Mood disorder due to a medical condition is diagnosed if mood disturbance is judged to be a direct pathophysiological consequence of another medical condition, for example, multiple sclerosis, hypothyroidism.
- **Adjustment disorder:** A major depressive episode in response to a stressor is distinguished from adjustment disorder by the fact that the full criteria for the major depressive episode are not met in adjustment disorder.

Course and Prognosis

Major depressive disorder episode lasts 6–12 months if untreated. A 5%–10% of the patients suffering from MDD have a manic episode 6–10 years after the first depressive episode. *Good prognostic factors* include the absence of comorbidity and personality disorder, and the advanced age of onset, while *poor prognostic factors* are coexisting dysthymia or anxiety disorder symptoms, alcohol and other substance abuse, and a history of more than one previous depressive episode.

Management of Major Depressive Disorder

The first important decision to make is whether to hospitalize a patient or treat as an outpatient.

Indications for Hospitalization

- Risk of suicide or homicide
- Need for diagnostic procedures
- Lack of capacity to cooperate with treatment
- Need of electroconvulsive therapy (ECT)
- Severe psychotic symptoms
- Need to address comorbid conditions
- Treatment-resistant depression

Treatment of mood disorders can be divided into the following categories:

- Psychological treatment
- Pharmacological treatment
- Neuromodulation

Psychological Treatment

Cognitive Therapy

This therapy is based on Beck's triad of depression and aims to correct the cognitive errors of thinking which include negative views of the self, the world, and the future. A combination of cognitive therapy and pharmacotherapy is more effective than either therapy alone. Cognitive therapy shows good results in depressive disorders, though it has some role in bipolar disorders too.

Interpersonal Therapy

This therapy focuses on the patient's interpersonal issues. It addresses interpersonal issues developed in an early dysfunctional relationship and the issues which are exaggerating and maintaining the illness. Interpersonal psychotherapy has a good role in major depressive disorders.

Behavior Therapy

Behavior therapy is based on the fact that maladaptive behavior results in the person receiving little positive feedback from society. It aims at correcting maladaptive patterns of behavior so that he receives positive feedback.

Family Therapy

Family therapy is indicated if family issues are helping to maintain the mood disorder or if the disorder threatens the marriage or family functioning. It mainly focuses on family dynamics and factors which are perpetuating the illness and address the same.

Pharmacological Treatment

Antidepressants

Selective serotonin reuptake inhibitors (**SSRIs**; citalopram, escitalopram, fluoxetine, fluvoxamine, sertraline, and paroxetine) and **serotonin–norepinephrine reuptake inhibitors** (**SNRIs;** venlafaxine, desvenlafaxine, and duloxetine) are preferred in the treatment of depression due to the better side effect profile as compared to the **tricyclic antidepressants (TCAs)**.

Vilazodone is a new antidepressant (serotonin partial agonist and reuptake inhibitor [SPARI]) which is supposed to have similar efficacy to that of SSRIs but with lesser sexual side effects and less weight gain.

TCAs (imipramine, amitriptyline, desipramine, and amoxapine) and **monoamine oxidase inhibitors** (**MAOIs**; tranylcypromine and moclobemide) are first-generation drugs to treat depression. Side effects of these drugs like postural hypotension, excessive sedation, weight gain, and anticholinergic and cardiac side effects make them less favorite.

Adjunctive Drugs

As antidepressant effect starts after 2–3 weeks, benzodiazepines can be effective at the beginning of the treatment to provide quick relief from anxiety or insomnia. Benzodiazepines can be stopped by tapering the dose once the antidepressant effect starts.

Augmenting Agents

Lithium, stimulants (methylphenidate), and thyroid hormones are used as augmenting agents.

Antipsychotics

Antipsychotics are used in depression with psychotic symptoms. Atypical antipsychotics, especially quetiapine, olanzapine, risperidone, and aripiprazole, are the drugs of choice in this indication.

General Guidelines

- Although SSRIs or SNRIs are the first-line antidepressants, the choice of antidepressant is based upon side effect profile of antidepressants, patient's sensitivity to side effects, response to a specific drug in past episode, the severity of the current episode, and any comorbidity associated with illness. The choice of antidepressants also depends upon the type of prominent symptoms in depression. For example, mirtazapine is sedative and often prescribed to the patients of depression with severe insomnia. Bupropion is an antidepressant and also helps in smoking cessation, so it can be preferred in a patient of depression with comorbid nicotine dependence. Atypical depression patients respond better to SSRIs and MAOIs.
- Antidepressants take 2–3 weeks for the onset of antidepressant action.
- The dose of all antidepressants should be adequate (until the maximum tolerable therapeutic dose is reached) for an adequate duration of time (6–8 weeks) to get the response.
- If there is a partial response, that is, less than 50% response, the treatment can be augmented by the addition of one more antidepressant/lithium/thyroid hormones (**augmentation**).
- If there is no response at 6–8 weeks, then **switching** from initial single antidepressant to another single antidepressant is preferred.
- When the treatment is stopped, it should be tapered down slowly over 1–2 weeks.

Neuromodulation

Electroconvulsive Therapy

ECT is indicated in the following conditions in a patient of severe depression with:

- Suicidal intent
- Depression refractory to treatment
- Severe side effects of drugs or drugs are contraindicated

- Stupor
- Psychotic features

Vagus nerve stimulation (VNS) and repetitive transcranial magnetic stimulation (rTMS) are FDA-approved neuromodulation treatment modalities for depression.

Phototherapy

Phototherapy is indicated in patients who suffer from the seasonal affective disorder. These patients are exposed to bright light in the range of 1,500–10,000 lx (lux) for 1–2 hours daily before dawn with a light box. The patient is instructed not to look directly at the light source. This therapy is also effective in shift workers and persons suffering from jet lag having sleep disturbances due to an altered circadian rhythm.

PERSISTENT DEPRESSIVE DISORDER (DYSTHYMIA IN ICD-10)

Persistent depressive disorder or dysthymia is a syndrome characterized by persistent but milder depressive symptoms lasting for a minimum of 2 years (1 year for children or adolescents). The symptoms of persistent depressive disorder include depressed mood, poor appetite or overeating, insomnia or hypersomnia, low energy or fatigue, low self-esteem, poor concentration or difficulty making decisions and feelings of hopelessness. A persistent depressive disorder is diagnosed if depressive symptoms do not meet criteria for a major depressive episode and the patient never had a manic/hypomanic episode and cyclothymic disorder. In persistent depressive disorder, the patient is never asymptomatic for more than 2 months at a time. If full criteria for a major depressive episode are met at any point during the current episode, diagnosis of major depressive disorder is made.

A 1-year prevalence of persistent mood disorder is 0.5%. Double depression is a syndrome when a major depressive episode adds to underlying dysthymia.

SSRIs, venlafaxine, and bupropion are effective in the treatment of persistent depressive disorders.

PREMENSTRUAL DYSPHORIC DISORDER

The PMDD presents as mood and associated symptoms during the majority of menstrual cycles. These symptoms start in the last week before the onset of menses, start improving after the onset of menses, and become minimal or absent in the week post menses. PMDD is associated with mood symptoms, affective lability, irritability, or anger, depressed mood, feelings of hopelessness, self-deprecating thoughts, anxiety, decreased interest in work and hobbies, difficulty in concentration, lack of energy, change in appetite, or specific food cravings, hypersomnia or insomnia, sense of being out of control, and physical symptoms such as breast tenderness or swelling, joint or muscle pain, a sensation of bloating or weight gain.

PMDD is diagnosed after ruling out other medical or surgical causes which can mimic the symptoms, for example, hyperthyroidism and endometriosis. It should not be merely an exacerbation of the symptoms of another disorder such as major depressive disorder, panic disorder, persistent depressive disorder.

A 1-year prevalence of the PMDD is 1.8%–5.8% in menstruating females. The PMDD can start at any age after the start of first menstruation, it may be worsened in perimenopausal phases, and it ends after menopause. SSRIs (fluoxetine, sertraline and paroxetine) and alprazolam are effective in the treatment of PMDD.

RECURRENT DEPRESSIVE DISORDER

This disorder is characterized by repeated episodes of depression without any manic or hypomanic episodes. If a major depressive disorder is followed by at least one episode of another major depressive disorder and two episodes are separated by at least 2 months of symptom-free period, then it is known as a recurrent depressive disorder.

BIPOLAR DISORDER

Bipolar I disorder is characterized by at least one manic episode which may have been preceded/followed by major depressive or hypomanic episodes. Major depressive and hypomanic episodes are common in bipolar I disorder but are not required for the diagnosis of bipolar I disorder.

Bipolar II disorder is characterized by at least one hypomanic episode preceded/followed by a depressive episode in a lifetime and there is no manic episode.

Clinical Features and diagnosis

Mania or hypomania is associated with the following symptoms:

Mood Manic patients can be **cheerful/euphoric** (feeling of happiness associated with the feeling of well-being)/**elated** (associated with the feeling of confidence)/**exalted** (associated with the delusion of grandiosity)/**ecstatic** (associated with the feeling of extreme blissful). Alternatively, the mood may be irritable (dysphoric mania). The mood in mania can be labile, that is, transient crying can be present without significant stimuli.

Cognitive distortions Manic patients have grandiosity (i.e., they have distinct abilities, powers, and wealth) and feeling of the heightened sense of inflated self-esteem and they often get involved in high-risk activities like reckless driving, buying sprees, and foolish business deals.

Psychomotor activity Increased psychomotor activity is a hallmark of mania which manifests as increased energy and activity, overtalkativeness, and pressure of speech. Mania is associated with flight of ideas with a subjective feeling that thoughts are racing. Manic patients are distractible, engage in multiple activities in which they display poor judgment, for example, dancing in the street. Overfamiliarity with strangers is an important symptom of mania.

Vegetative disturbances Decreased need for sleep is the cardinal sign. These patients feel energetic after a few hours' (2–3 hours) sleep only. The manic patient may have weight loss due to overactivity and inattention to nutrition. Hypersexuality is a cardinal symptom of mania which can lead to illegitimate relationships during this manic phase.

Psychotic symptoms Mania may be associated with psychotic symptoms (delusions and hallucinations), which are usually mood-congruent but may be incongruent. The patient may have the delusion of grandiosity or persecutory delusions.

Symptoms of hypomania are similar to mania with the difference that hypomania is not associated with a marked impairment in socio-occupational functioning and hospitalization is not required. If psychotic features are present, the episode is considered as manic.

In DSM-5, the minimum duration of symptoms required to diagnose a manic episode is 7 days, whereas for hypomanic episode duration criteria is 4 days.

Specifiers

With rapid cycling Presence of at least four mood episodes (manic, hypomanic, or depressive) in the past 12 months.

With psychotic features When a manic episode is associated with delusions/hallucinations.

With catatonia When a manic episode is associated with catatonic symptoms.

With peripartum onset If affective/mood symptoms develop during pregnancy or in the 4 weeks after delivery.

Scales Used

Young Mania Rating Scale (YMRS) is the most commonly used scale to assess manic symptoms.

Differential Diagnosis

Differential diagnosis for depression in a patient of bipolar I or II disorder is same as for MDD. For a **manic** or **hypomanic episode** differential diagnosis includes the following:

- **Bipolar I disorder:** Diagnosis of a manic episode currently or in the past confirms the diagnosis of bipolar I disorder.
- **Bipolar II disorder:** The presence of depressive and/or hypomanic episodes in the lifetime and absence of manic episodes currently or in the past is required for the diagnosis of bipolar II disorder.
- **Cyclothymic disorder:** In cyclothymic disorder, criteria for the depressive, manic, or hypomanic episodes are never met.
- **Attention-deficit/hyperactivity disorder (ADHD):** Rapid speech, racing thoughts, distractibility, and less need for sleep are overlapping symptoms; ADHD may be misdiagnosed as bipolar disorder. Bipolar disorder is diagnosed if symptoms represent distinct episodes.
- **Schizophrenia:** Psychotic symptoms are present in the absence of prominent mood symptoms in schizophrenia.
- **Substance-induced bipolar disorder:** Substance-induced bipolar disorder is diagnosed if it is judged that mood disturbance developed during or soon after substance intoxication, withdrawal, or after exposure to medicine and the involved substance is capable of producing the mood disturbance.

  Independent bipolar disorder can be diagnosed if symptoms precede the onset of substance/medication or symptoms persist for a substantial period (1 month) after cessation of acute withdrawal or severe intoxication.

Course and Prognosis

Bipolar I disorder usually starts with depression. An untreated manic episode usually lasts 3 months. After a single manic episode, 90% of the persons have another episode. Of the persons suffering from bipolar disorder, 5%–15% are rapid cyclers. Patients with bipolar I disorder have poorer prognosis as compared to patients suffering from a major depressive disorder.

Bipolar II disorder patients have a stable diagnosis of up to 5 years. Bipolar II disorder is a chronic disorder that requires long-term treatment.

Pharmacological Treatment

Treatment of bipolar disorder depends on the acute or maintenance phase of the disorder and it is also based on whether the patient is manic, hypomanic, or depressive. Treatment is aimed at control of symptoms of acute mania and depression and prevention of future episodes.

Treatment of Bipolar Depression

The most common treatment is antidepressants combined with mood stabilizers to prevent a manic switch. Antidepressant drugs are the same as used for unipolar depression, but they are used at lower doses for a shorter duration as a precaution. Some experts start with bupropion as the chance of manic switch is least with bupropion. Olanzapine and Fluoxetine fixed-dose combination and lurasidone are indicated for the treatment of bipolar depression. Quetiapine monotherapy is also effective for treatment for the depressive episode in bipolar disorder.

Treatment of Acute Mania

Mood Stabilizers

Lithium is the most widely used mood stabilizer in bipolar disorders. Lithium is more helpful in patients with euphoric mania and patients having few or infrequent episodes. Anticonvulsant mood stabilizers are more effective in dysphoric, mixed mania, and rapid cyclers and in patients who have had multiple episodes.

As mood stabilizers have a slower onset of action, they are supplemented with a low dose of antipsychotics or benzodiazepines till they start acting.

Antipsychotics

Haloperidol is effective in decreasing hyperactivity and treating hallucinations and delusions in psychotic mania. Atypical antipsychotics such as risperidone and olanzapine are also effective and have fewer side effects. Atypical antipsychotics are preferred over typical antipsychotics because of a better side effect profile.

Benzodiazepines

Benzodiazepines like clonazepam and lorazepam are used in acute mania as a sedative with or without antipsychotics. When the mood stabilizer's show effect, benzodiazepines should be tapered down and then stopped as these drugs have high addiction potential if used for long term.

Maintenance and Prophylactic Treatment

Mood stabilizers such as lithium, valproate, and carbamazepine are used for prophylaxis in bipolar disorders, while lamotrigine is more effective in the prophylaxis of depressive episodes than manic episodes.

CYCLOTHYMIC DISORDERS

In cyclothymia, for at least 2 years (at least 1 year in children and adolescents) there have been numerous periods with hypomanic symptoms that do not meet criteria for a hypomanic episode and numerous periods with depressive symptoms that do not meet criteria for a major depressive episode. In cyclothymia criteria for major depressive, manic or hypomanic episodes are never met.

The mood stabilizers and antimanic drugs are the first line of treatment for patients with cyclothymic disorder.

KEY POINTS

- Mood disorders include disorders in which pathological mood and related vegetative and psychomotor disturbance are the dominant symptoms. Previously these were known as affective disorders.
- As per DSM-5 classification, disruptive mood dysregulation disorder, major depressive disorder, persistent depressive disorder (dysthymia), and premenstrual dysphoric disorder (PMDD) are major categories in depressive disorders.
- As per DSM-5 classification, bipolar I disorder, bipolar II disorder, and cyclothymic disorders are major categories in bipolar disorders.
- Depletion in the level of monoamines in the synaptic cleft leads to depressive disorders and a rise in the level of monoamines leads to mania (**biogenic amine theory**).
- Stressful life events do play a role in the precipitation of the first episode of mood disorders, but not for subsequent episodes.
- According to cognitive theory, depression occurs due to cognitive distortions in thinking.
- According to Beck, there is a cognitive triad of depression which includes a negative view of oneself, of the world, and about the future.
- Depressed mood (sadness, irritable, or anxious) and loss of interest in the activities which were pleasurable before the onset of illness are the cardinal symptoms of depression.
- Psychomotor retardation is the primary pathology in major depressive disorder and presents as decreased spontaneous movements, downcast gaze, fatigue, reduced speech with increased latency, and a subjective feeling that time has stopped.
- Forgetfulness associated with depression is termed as pseudodementia.
- **Melancholia** is associated with loss of interest in almost all activities or lack of reactivity to usually pleasurable stimuli along with depressed mood characterized by profound despondency or empty mood, early morning awakening (at least 2 hours before usual time), depression worse in the morning, marked psychomotor agitation or retardation, significant loss of appetite or weight loss, and excessive guilt. This type is also known as an **endogenous type**.
- **Atypical depression** is characterized by an increase in sleep and appetite and worsening of mood in the evening.
- Hamilton rating scale for depression (HAM-D), Beck Depression Inventory (BDI), Montgomery-Åsberg Depression Rating Scale (MADRS), and Amritsar Depression Inventory (ADI) are commonly used scales for assessment of depression.
- A combination of cognitive therapy and pharmacotherapy is more effective than either therapy alone. Cognitive therapy has good results in depressive disorders.
- The choice of antidepressants is based upon side effects profile of antidepressants, patient's sensitivity to side effects, response to a specific drug in past episode, the severity of the current episode, and any comorbidity associated with illness.
- Antidepressants take 2–3 weeks for the onset of antidepressant action.

- Electroconvulsive therapy (ECT) is indicated in a patient of severe depression with suicidal intent, depression refractory to treatment, when drugs are not tolerated or are contraindicated or depression with psychotic features.
- Phototherapy is indicated in patients who suffer from the seasonal affective disorder.
- Persistent depressive disorder or dysthymia is a syndrome characterized by persistent but milder depressive symptoms lasting for a minimum of 2 years.
- The PMDD presents as mood and associated symptoms during the majority of menstrual cycles. These symptoms start in the last week before the onset of menses, start *improving* after the onset of menses, and become *minimal* or absent in the week post menses.
- SSRIs (fluoxetine, sertraline, and paroxetine) and alprazolam are effective in the treatment of PMDDs.
- Bipolar I disorder is characterized by at least one manic episode which may have been preceded/ followed by major depressive or hypomanic episodes. Major depressive and hypomanic episodes are common in bipolar I disorder but are not required for the diagnosis of bipolar I disorder.
- Bipolar II disorder is characterized by at least one hypomanic episode preceded/followed by a depressive episode in a lifetime and there is no manic episode.
- Manic patients can be cheerful, euphoric, elated, exalted, or ecstatic. Alternatively, the mood may be irritable (dysphoric mania). Manic patients have grandiosity and they often get involved in high-risk activities like reckless driving, buying sprees, and foolish business deals.
- Increased psychomotor activity is a hallmark of mania which manifests as increased energy and activity, overtalkativeness, pressure of speech, and flight of ideas. Overfamiliarity with strangers is an important symptom of mania. Decreased need for sleep is the cardinal sign.
- Mania may be associated with psychotic symptoms (delusions and hallucinations), which are usually mood-congruent but may be incongruent. The patient may have the delusion of grandiosity or persecutory delusions.
- Symptoms of hypomania are similar to mania with the difference that hypomania is not associated with the marked impairment in socio-occupational functioning and hospitalization is not required. If psychotic features are present, the episode is considered as manic.
- Young Mania Rating Scale (YMRS) is the most commonly used scale to assess manic symptoms.
- In cyclothymia, for at least 2 years (at least 1 year in children and adolescents) there have been numerous periods with hypomanic symptoms that do not meet criteria for a hypomanic episode and numerous periods with depressive symptoms that do not meet criteria for a major depressive episode.
- The most common treatment of bipolar depression is antidepressants combined with mood stabilizers to prevent a manic switch.
- For the treatment of acute mania, mood stabilizers are supplemented with a low dose of antipsychotics or benzodiazepines till mood stabilizers start acting.
- Lithium is more helpful in patients with euphoric mania and patients having few or infrequent episodes. Anticonvulsant mood stabilizers are more effective in dysphoric, mixed mania, and rapid cyclers and in patients who have had multiple episodes.
- Mood stabilizers such as lithium, valproate, and carbamazepine are used for prophylaxis in bipolar disorders, while lamotrigine is more effective in the prophylaxis of depressive episodes than manic episodes.

SELF-ASSESSMENT

1. Case-based Questions

   A 28-year-old married female presented with a 1-month history of sadness of mood, fatigue, and difficulty concentrating at work. She gives a history of eating less and a loss of 5 kg weight in the last month. She also admitted that now she does not enjoy making paintings which earlier she was fond of. She reports feelings of worthlessness and shame due to her inability to perform. She denies having suicidal thoughts, but she has frequent thoughts of wishing she was dead. The patient had no comorbid psychiatric or medical disorder and had no history of any substance abuse or addiction. She had no history of psychiatric illness in the past.
   a. What is your provisional diagnosis?
   b. Discuss the differential diagnosis of the disorder.
   c. How will you manage this patient?
2. Case-based Questions

   A 35-year-old male was brought to the OPD with 10 days history of elation, talking more, decreased sleep, and overspending. He purchased two new luxury cars on loan. He claimed to be the richest man in the world and boasted about his connections to the politicians across the globe. He reported that he sleeps only for 2 hours at night and feels energetic and fresh. On examination, he was overtalkative, distractible, had the pressure of speech, and insight was absent. The wife of the patient reported that he has increased libido. The patient had no comorbid psychiatric or medical disorder and had no history of any substance abuse or addiction. He had a history of two episodes of mania and one episode of depression in the last 3 years.
   a. What is your provisional diagnosis?
   b. Discuss the differential diagnosis of the disorder.
   c. How will you manage this patient?
3. Discuss the etiology of mood disorders.
4. Write short notes on:
   a. Clinical features of depression
   b. Clinical features of mania
   c. Persistent depressive disorder
   d. Premenstrual dysphoric disorder
   e. Cyclothymic disorder

Chapter 12

Anxiety Disorders

Adarsh Tripathi · Praveen Pandey · SK Kar

Anxiety is a normal human emotion. It is defined as a sustained, unpleasant vague sense of apprehension due to the anticipation of a future threat. Anxiety is a response to an unknown, internal, vague threat, whereas fear is a short-lasting emotional response to a known, external, definite, real threat.

When accounted as a group, anxiety disorders are the most common psychiatric disorders. Anxiety disorders are one of the key causes of absenteeism from school, offices, and other working places.

If anxiety is persistent and repetitive and if it causes significant distress and impairment, it is considered pathological.

The symptoms of anxiety are given in Box 12.1.

Box 12.1 Symptoms of anxiety

- Butterflies in the stomach
- Chest pain
- Diarrhea
- Dizziness
- Dyspnea
- Lightheadedness
- Nausea, vomiting
- Palpitation
- Poor concentration
- Restlessness
- Syncope
- Tachycardia
- Tingling and numbness
- Tremors

COMPARATIVE NOSOLOGY

The DSM-5 classifies anxiety disorders based on human development, with disorders sequenced according to their usual age of onset. Anxiety disorders differ from one another in types of objects or situations and associated cognitive ideas which induce anxiety. Anxiety disorders include the following:

- Separation anxiety disorder
- Selective mutism
- Specific phobia
- Social anxiety disorder (social phobia)
- Panic disorder
- Agoraphobia
- Generalized anxiety disorder (GAD)

In ICD-10, separation anxiety disorder and selective mutism are not grouped under the umbrella of anxiety disorders, whereas obsessive–compulsive disorder (OCD) is considered under the neurotic, stress-related, and somatoform disorders along with other anxiety disorders.

ETIOPATHOLOGY

Anxiety is a normal and adaptive response when it makes a person to take the steps imperative to avoid an expected danger or in dampening its outcomes.

The levels of arousal (stress) relate to the performance: too little arousal and excessive arousal are both associated with poor performance (**Yerkes–Dodson law**) (Fig. 12.1).

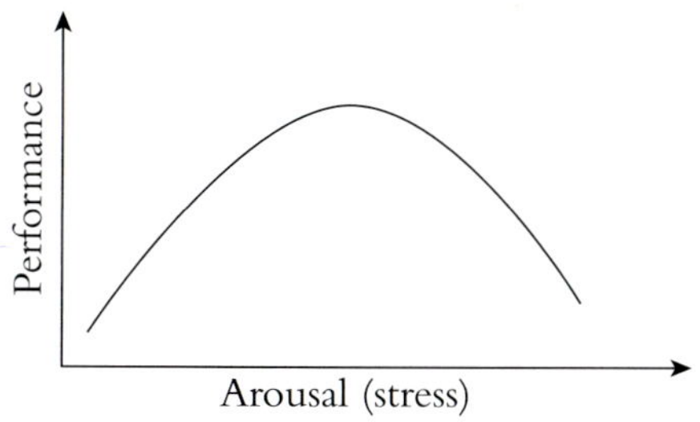

Figure 12.1 Yerkes–Dodson law.

Psychodynamic Theories

Anxiety arises when there is a conflict between unconscious sexual or aggressive impulses and corresponding threats from superego or external reality.

Behavioral Theories

According to the behavioral or learning theory, anxiety can be understood as a conditioned response developed over time to a specific environmental stimulus.

Neurobiological Aspects

Various neurotransmitters are implicated in anxiety disorders; gamma-aminobutyric acid (GABA), serotonin, and norepinephrine are the three major neurotransmitters associated with anxiety. Fear and anxiety have three essential elements, which are attributed to different brain structures (Fig. 12.2).

SEPARATION ANXIETY DISORDER

Separation from attachment figures gives rise to anxiety and is part of normal development in infants and toddlers. It is considered normal in children under 3 years of age.

Separation anxiety disorder is characterized by the presence of anxiety or distress on separation from significant attachment figures or when anticipating periods of separation.

Epidemiology

Separation anxiety disorder is the most prevalent anxiety disorder in children younger than 12 years. Its prevalence decreases from childhood to adulthood. Onset of separation anxiety disorder may be as early as preschool age and may occur at any time during childhood and rarely in adolescence.

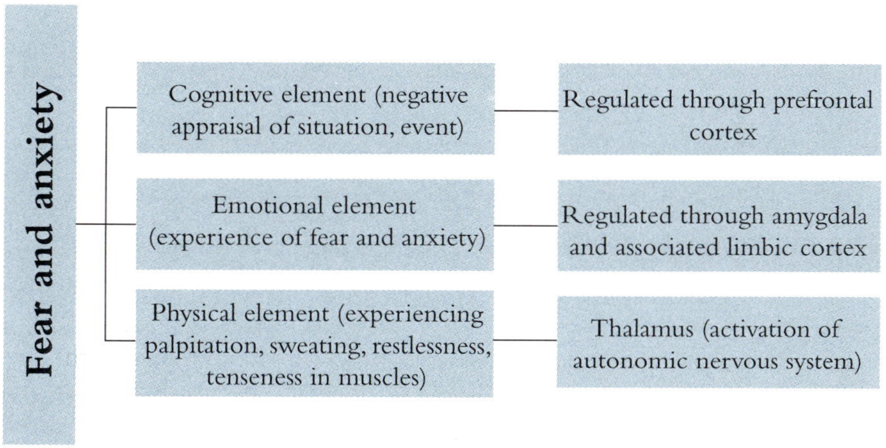

Figure 12.2 Neurobiology of anxiety disorders.

Etiology

Environmental

Life stress, especially following the death of a close relative, the divorce of parents, a change of school, and natural disasters can lead to the development of separation anxiety. Parental overprotection and intrusiveness may be associated with separation anxiety disorder.

Genetic

Female offspring may be more predisposed to inherit separation anxiety disorder as compared to male.

Clinical Features

Individuals suffering from separation anxiety disorder have persistent and excessive worry about experiencing an untoward event, like getting lost or being kidnapped, which can cause separation from major attachment figures. Individuals who have separation anxiety disorder are reluctant to go out, away from home, to school, to work, because of the fear of separation. They may be reluctant to sleep without major attachment figures. Patients have nightmares involving themes of separation. They can have somatic symptoms of anxiety (e.g., headache, nausea, and vomiting) when separation from major attachment figures occurs or is anticipated. Separation anxiety may lead to school refusal leading to academic difficulties.

Clinical presentation of separation anxiety disorder varies with age groups. In children up to ages of 8 years, it may manifest as undue worry about forthcoming harm to their parents or caregiver (significant attachment figures) and refusal to part with them or go to school. Whereas children aged 9–12 years commonly present with excessive distress at times of separation (e.g., sleepover at grandparent's place, overnight school trips) from attachment figures. Adolescents present with school refusal often owing to physical complaints such as headaches, lightheadedness, sweating, stomachache, nausea, cramps, vomiting, or body ache.

SELECTIVE MUTISM

Selective mutism is characterized by a child's inability to speak and communicate effectively in certain social settings. However, these children can speak in other situations. Selective mutism is diagnosed if the failure to speak is not due to lack of comfort with the spoken language required in that social situation.

Epidemiology

Selective mutism is a relatively rare disorder with prevalence less than 1%. The onset usually occurs before 5 years of age but may not be noticed until the child goes to attend school.

Etiology

Presence of traits such as social anxiety, shyness, and social isolation in parents is common.

Clinical Features

The settings where mutism is observed, the child is not refusing to speak but is, in fact, unable to speak. The child displays appropriate language skills when at home or in the presence of the individuals around whom he feels at ease. The child may at times use nonverbal communication like pointing or writing as a means of expression. Selective mutism is often disabling, in the sense that it restricts children suffering from it in making friends and children with the disorder are often misunderstood as rude or shy. Selective mutism is diagnosed after ruling out communication disorder, autism spectrum disorder (ASD), and schizophrenia.

SPECIFIC PHOBIA

The term specific phobia refers to an excessive fear of a specific situation or object. The patients of specific phobia when exposed to the feared object develop intense anxiety, even to the point of panic.

Epidemiology

Lifetime prevalence of specific phobia is about 10%. The peak age of onset of phobia for the natural environment and blood-injection-injury type is 5–9 years, whereas the peak age of onset for situational type (except fear of heights) is in the mid-20s. Animals, natural environment, and situational specific phobias are more prevalent in females, and blood-injection-injury phobia is equally prevalent among males and females.

Etiology

Psychoanalytic theories

Suggest that phobias are derived from an intrinsic source of anxiety. The actual intrinsic source is shunned by the consciousness by use of defense mechanisms of repression and attributed to the external source or object by means of displacement.

Conditioning theory

Suggests that association learning is at play in the genesis of specific phobias.

Cognitive factors

Contribute in the perpetuation of the fear, mainly by fearful anticipation of and selectively attending to the phobic stimuli.

Neurobiological mechanisms

Suggested by functional imaging studies have revealed hyperactivity of the amygdala upon presentation of the feared stimulus, which appears to diminish with successful treatment. The anticipation of a phobic stimulus activates the anterior cingulate cortex and the insular cortex.

Clinical Features

People with specific phobias experience unusual levels of anxiety when subjected to a specific situation or object. This fear is out of proportion to the actual risk posed on the individual. There is also a presence of anticipatory anxiety and the person tends to avoid the situation. Patients with specific phobia have clinically significant distress and socio-occupational or functional impairment. Young children may present with crying, tantrums, clinging, and freezing.

The various phobias are coded into the following groups based on phobic stimulus:

1. Animals
2. Natural environment
3. Blood-injection-injury
4. Situational (e.g., airplanes, lifts, enclosed spaces)

SOCIAL ANXIETY DISORDER (SOCIAL PHOBIA)

In the social anxiety disorder, a person experiences inappropriate anxiety when placed in social situations, where the person feels that he is being observed by others and may be criticized by them. There is a presence of an avoidance pattern for socially demanding situations. If they are unable to avoid the situation, they tend to avoid conversation with other people, or sit in a spot where people are less likely to spot them.

Epidemiology

Social anxiety disorder is more common in females as compared to males, and peak age of onset is early teenage years. Social anxiety disorder is associated with depression and alcoholism.

Etiology

Genetic factors Social anxiety disorder is three times more common in first-degree relatives. The risk of social anxiety disorder decreases as the degree of relatedness decreases. This view is also supported by twin studies.

Learning theory Social anxiety disorders, to start with, may arise as paroxysmal anxiety in a certain socially demanding situation. Further development and continuation of phobic symptoms are acquired by conditioning.

Cognitive theory The fear of negative evaluation, which is the apprehension of criticism from other people when present in a specific social situation, is considered the main cognitive factor in the genesis of social anxiety disorder.

Neurobiological mechanisms suggested by functional neuroimaging studies have shown increased amygdala responses to the presentation of faces with expressions of negative affect. The anticipation of public speaking leads to increased activation in limbic and associated regions, including the amygdala, hippocampus, and insula, while activation of cortical regulatory areas such as the prefrontal cortex was diminished.

Clinical Features

Some degree of social anxiety or self-consciousness is normal. Individuals with social anxiety disorder experience marked distress in situations which they perceive themselves exposed to possible scrutiny or negative evaluation by others. Such situations include opening a conversation, attending a party or delivering a speech in front of an audience or eating/drinking in front of others and so on. These persons often have a fear of embarrassing themselves in such situations and they fear rejection. As with all phobias, avoidance is frequently present and the social anxiety causes significant distress and impairment. The fear or anxiety is out of proportion to the actual threat posed by the social situations and to the sociocultural context. Obvious symptoms of anxiety, psychological as well as somatic may be experienced when persons with social anxiety disorder find themselves in one of the dreaded situations.

PANIC DISORDER

An acute discrete episode of severe anxiety characterized by feelings of impending doom or anticipation of a catastrophic outcome is known as a panic attack. In panic disorder, these episodes can vary from having multiple attacks over a day to only a few attacks occurring in a year.

Epidemiology

Though it can develop at any age, the mean age of onset is around 25 years of age. The lifetime prevalence is about 1%–4%. Women are affected two to three times more in comparison to men. Most patients with panic disorder have a comorbid psychiatric disorder, most commonly depression and agoraphobia.

Etiology

Biological factors The sympathetic tone is increased. The autonomic nervous system of patients with panic disorder tends to adapt slowly to repeated stimuli, and even a moderate stimulus can produce a disproportionate, excessive response.

The neurotransmitter systems, norepinephrine, serotonin, and GABA, are implicated in panic disorders.

The noradrenergic neurons of the locus ceruleus and the serotonergic neurons of the median raphe nucleus in the brainstem are associated with panic disorder. The generation of anticipatory anxiety is linked to the limbic system, whereas avoidance pattern seen in panic disorder is linked to the prefrontal cortex.

Structural brain imaging studies show an association of pathological changes in the temporal lobes with panic disorder, specifically in the amygdala and hippocampus.

Genetic factors Panic disorders run in families with four to eight times higher risk in first-degree relatives. No chromosomal loci or pattern of inheritance are known so far.

Psychosocial factors The cause of panic attacks possibly involves the unconscious meaning attributed to stressful events. It is believed that these psychological reactions may set off neurophysiological factors implicated in the genesis of panic attacks.

Clinical Features

Panic attacks are characterized by paroxysmal episodes of anxiety associated with an extreme sense of fear of the catastrophic outcome. The symptoms of anxiety during a panic attack may consist of palpitations, excessive sweating, tremulousness, breathlessness or a choking sensation, chest or abdominal discomfort or nausea, lightheadedness, tingling sensations or numbness, depersonalization, derealization, fear of going crazy, and most importantly fear of catastrophic outcome or death. Every individual may not have all of these symptoms when experiencing a panic attack, but the most characteristic features to consider are:

- The anxiety rises quickly.
- The symptoms are intense.
- There is a feeling of impending doom or a catastrophic outcome.

The panic attack causes the person to stop whatever activity he was engaged in before the onset of an episode. The person may lie on the floor, rush into the open air, run back into the house, or seek a visit to the hospital. The patient may have anticipatory anxiety about having another panic attack. The first panic attack is often spontaneous, although panic attacks occasionally follow excitement, physical exertion, sexual activity, or moderate emotional trauma.

Differential Diagnosis

Psychiatric disorders panic disorder, panic attacks are seen in social and specific phobia, post-traumatic stress disorder (PTSD), and OCD. Differentiation from GAD can also be difficult. These panic attacks can be distinguished from those of a panic disorder by the absence of concern about having future attacks, that is, anticipatory anxiety.

Medical disorders can be mimicked by a variety of illnesses that may produce similar symptoms. Cardiovascular diseases like angina, anemia; pulmonary diseases like asthma, hyperventilation; neurological diseases like cerebrovascular disease, epilepsy; endocrine diseases like carcinoid syndrome, Addison disease; hyperthyroidism; pheochromocytoma; drug intoxications; and drug withdrawal in alcohol.

AGORAPHOBIA

Fear of or anxiety arising in places from where escape is considered difficult by a person is the defining feature of agoraphobia. Agoraphobia is derived from the Greek words *agora* and *phobos* meaning fear of the marketplace.

Epidemiology

Agoraphobia has a lifetime prevalence of 2%–6%. The risk in women is two to three times higher than that of men. Agoraphobia frequently occurs with panic disorders.

Etiology

Theories of Onset

In a genetically predisposed individual, a chance stimuli from his immediate environment result in exaggerated anxiety. It usually starts with experiencing anxiety in a public place, most commonly a panic attack. Certain aspects of the situation or physical symptoms of the anxiety attack are feared unreasonably by the person.

Theories of Recurrence and Progression

A sort of conditioning occurs for the association of anxiety with an increasing number of situations, leading the person to avoid such situations consecutively.

Clinical Features

In agoraphobia, the patient has marked fear or anxiety in any of the following five situations:

- Using public transportation (e.g., buses, trains)
- Being in open spaces (e.g., parking lots, marketplaces)
- Being in enclosed places (e.g., shops, theaters)
- Standing in line or being in a crowd
- Being outside of the home alone

Patients tend to avoid such situations. They feel anxious when they anticipate them, and experience symptoms of anxiety when eventually placed in such a situation.

The symptoms of anxiety that are felt by patients of agoraphobia in these situations are same as those of other anxiety disorders, but specifically involve panic attacks.

As the illness progresses, the person becomes increasingly avoidant to these situations in which it would be difficult to obtain help. They prefer to be accompanied by a family member in these situations, and in worse cases they may continue to remain confined only to their home.

GENERALIZED ANXIETY DISORDER

GAD manifests as the so-called free-floating anxiety. There is increased anxiety and worry about many events and while performing most of the activities.

Epidemiology

GAD has a lifetime prevalence of 5%, which often begins in the late adolescents and is twice more common in females.

Etiology

A number of factors both genetic and environmental are at interplay. A genetically predisposed person under the influence of stresses from the environment in childhood seems to be causative for GAD. It may begin so and continue in the long term with persistence of stressful situations.

Biological factors Therapeutic efficacy of benzodiazepines and buspirone in patients suffering from GAD points toward the possible role of GABA and serotonin neurotransmitter systems in the etiology. Induction of anxiety by Flumazenil (benzodiazepine receptor antagonist) also points toward GABA. One positron emission tomography (PET) study showed lower metabolic rate in basal ganglia and white matter in patients suffering from GAD as compared to controls. Concordance rate is 50% in monozygotic twins as compared to 15% in dizygotic twins, indicating the role of genetics in the etiology of GAD.

Clinical Features

GAD is characterized by frequent and persistent worry and anxiety that is out of proportion to the impact of the event, that is, the focus of the worry. The anxiety is excessive in GAD when compared to that in healthy people and causes significant impairment or distress. The worry is nonspecific (free-floating anxiety)—means not focused on a special situation or object.

Psychological arousal is manifested as irritability, difficulty in concentration, restlessness, muscle tension, being easily fatigued, and/or sensitivity to noise. Patients with GAD often seek help for somatic symptoms. Autonomic overactivity can cause palpitations, sweating, dry mouth, gastric disturbance, and dizziness.

Sleep disturbances may be present. Some patients wake suddenly feeling intense anxiety and may have night terrors. Presence of early morning awakening, however, should raise suspicion of a depressive disorder.

MANAGEMENT OF ANXIETY DISORDERS

Broadly, the management of anxiety disorders is divided into pharmacological treatment, psychotherapy, and neuromodulation techniques.

Pharmacological

Antidepressants and benzodiazepines are commonly used medications for the management of anxiety disorders. Selective serotonin reuptake inhibitors (SSRIs) are most frequently prescribed drugs for the management of anxiety disorders, followed by serotonin−norepinephrine reuptake inhibitors (SNRIs).

Benzodiazepines

Benzodiazepines are potent anxiolytic agents; they often produce an immediate reduction of anxiety. The use of benzodiazepines for reduction of anxiety should be less than 4 weeks to avoid the risk of benzodiazepine dependence. Commonly used benzodiazepines for anxiolysis are alprazolam, lorazepam, clonazepam, diazepam, and chlordiazepoxide. The risk of dependence is more with short-acting benzodiazepines like alprazolam.

Selective Serotonin Reuptake Inhibitors

The SSRIs are most commonly used medications in the management of anxiety disorders. SSRIs may cause a rebound increase in anxiety in some patients, after initiation of therapy; hence it needs to be started in a lower dose with gradual increment in the dose. Among the SSRIs, escitalopram and sertraline have minimum drug-drug interaction and side effects, so commonly preferred across all ages as well as those with medical comorbidities. Most of the anxiety disorders can be managed with moderate doses of SSRIs; however, panic disorder needs a relatively higher dose of medication. Often, paroxetine (due to strong serotonergic property) is chosen over other SSRIs for management of panic disorder.

Serotonin-Norepinephrine Reuptake Inhibitor

Venlafaxine and duloxetine are effective in the management of anxiety disorder.

Tricyclic Antidepressants

The TCAs like clomipramine, imipramine, doxepin, and amitriptyline were commonly used in the management of anxiety disorders initially. However, their use is limited nowadays due to their side effects and the availability of more safe and efficacious medications like SSRIs.

Other Antidepressants

Similarly, other antidepressants like mirtazapine as well as monoamine oxidase inhibitors (MAOIs) may be useful in the management of anxiety disorders.

Other Agents

Buspirone is $5HT_{1A}$ partial agonist and is effective in patients suffering from GADs. The patients who had treatment with benzodiazepines are less likely to respond to treatment with buspirone.

β-adrenergic receptor antagonist (propranolol) is effective in performance anxiety seen in social anxiety disorder.

Psychotherapy

Cognitive behavior therapy (CBT) is a highly effective, evidence-based psychotherapy technique in the management of anxiety disorder.

The common behavior techniques used in the management of anxiety disorders are systematic desensitization or graded exposure and flooding (for phobic anxiety disorders). Various relaxation techniques used in the management of anxiety disorders are Jacobson's progressive muscular relaxation, deep breathing techniques, autogenic training, mindfulness relaxation techniques, yoga, meditation, and aerobic exercises.

KEY POINTS

- Anxiety is defined as a sustained, unpleasant vague sense of apprehension due to the anticipation of a future threat.
- Anxiety is a response to an unknown, internal, vague threat, whereas fear is a short-lasting emotional response to a known, external, definite, real threat.
- When accounted as a group, anxiety disorders are the most common psychiatric disorders.
- Dizziness, poor concentration, lightheadedness, restlessness, tingling and numbness, palpitation, tachycardia, chest pain, tremors, diarrhea, butterflies in the stomach, nausea, vomiting, and dyspnea are common anxiety symptoms.
- As per DSM-5 separation anxiety disorder, selective mutism, specific phobia, social anxiety disorder (social phobia), panic disorder, agoraphobia, and generalized anxiety disorder (GAD) are major categories in anxiety disorders.
- According to psychodynamic theory, anxiety arises when there is a conflict between unconscious sexual or aggressive impulses and corresponding threats from superego or external reality.
- According to the behavioral or learning theory, anxiety can be understood as a conditioned response developed over time to a specific environmental stimulus.
- Gamma-aminobutyric acid (GABA), serotonin, and norepinephrine are the three major neurotransmitters associated with anxiety.

Separation anxiety disorder

- Separation anxiety disorder is characterized by the presence of anxiety or distress on separation from significant attachment figures or when anticipating periods of separation.
- Separation anxiety disorder is the most prevalent anxiety disorder in children younger than 12 years. Its prevalence decreases from childhood to adulthood. Onset of separation anxiety disorder may be as early as preschool age and may occur at any time during childhood and rarely in adolescence.

Selective mutism

- Selective mutism is characterized by consistent failure to speak in specific social situations in which there is an expectation for speaking (e.g., at school) despite speaking in other situations.

Specific phobia

- The term specific phobia refers to an excessive fear of a specific situation or object.
- People with specific phobias experience unusual levels of anxiety when subjected to a specific situation or object. There is also a presence of anticipatory anxiety and the person tends to avoid the situation.
- **Psychoanalytic theories** suggest that phobias are derived from an intrinsic source of anxiety. The actual intrinsic source is shunned by the consciousness by use of defense mechanisms of repression and attributed to the external source or object by means of displacement.
- **Neurobiological mechanisms** suggested by functional imaging studies have revealed hyperactivity of the amygdala upon presentation of the feared stimulus, which appears to diminish with successful treatment.
- The types of specific phobia are coded based on phobic stimulus: animals, natural environment, blood-injection-injury, and situational (e.g., airplanes, lifts, enclosed spaces).

Social anxiety disorder

- In the social anxiety disorder, a person experiences inappropriate anxiety when placed in social situations, where the person feels that he is being observed by others and may be criticized by them. There is a presence of an avoidance pattern for socially demanding situations.

Panic attack

- An acute discrete episode of severe anxiety characterized by feelings of impending doom or anticipation of a catastrophic outcome is known as a panic attack.
- Most characteristic features of panic disorder are:
  - The anxiety rises quickly.
  - The symptoms are intense.
  - There is a feeling of impending doom or a catastrophic outcome.

Agoraphobia

- Fear of or anxiety arising in places from where escape is considered difficult by a person is the defining feature of agoraphobia.
- In agoraphobia, the patient has marked fear or anxiety in any of the following five situations:
  - Using public transportation (e.g., buses, trains)
  - Being in open spaces (e.g., parking lots, marketplaces)
  - Being in enclosed places (e.g., shops, theaters)
  - Standing in line or being in a crowd
  - Being outside of the home alone

Generalized anxiety disorder

- GAD manifests as the so-called free-floating anxiety. There is excessive anxiety and worry (apprehensive expectation) about a number of events or activities (such as work or school performance) for at least 6 months. The worry cannot be controlled easily and is associated with physical symptoms such as irritability, muscle tension, disturbed sleep, and restlessness.

Treatment

- Therapeutic efficacy of benzodiazepines and buspirone in patients suffering from GAD points toward the possible role of GABA and serotonin neurotransmitter systems in the etiology.
- Antidepressants and benzodiazepines are commonly used medications for the management of anxiety disorders. Selective serotonin reuptake inhibitors (SSRIs) are most frequently prescribed drugs for the management of anxiety disorders followed by serotonin-norepinephrine reuptake inhibitors (SNRIs).
- Cognitive behavior therapy (CBT) is a highly effective, evidence-based psychotherapy technique in the management of anxiety disorder.
- The common behavior techniques used in the management of anxiety disorders are systematic desensitization or graded exposure and flooding (for phobic anxiety disorders).

SELF-ASSESSMENT

1. Case-based Questions

   A 27-year-old female was brought to the casualty department with complaints of palpitations, sweating, trembling of body, dizziness, and a fear that she will die of a heart attack. She was evaluated clinically; relevant blood investigations and ECG were done which revealed no abnormality. She reported that she had one more such episode 2 months back. The patient reports that she remains preoccupied with the thought of having another episode. Previous such episode happened when she was driving a car and now she avoids driving a car fearing a panic attack. On detailed history, no stressful life event was reported by the patient. In between the episodes, other than a preoccupation of having an additional panic attack, she did not have any mood symptoms.

   a. What is your provisional diagnosis?
   b. Discuss the clinical features of the disorder.
   c. Discuss the differential disorder.
   d. How will you manage this patient?
2. Define anxiety, enumerate anxiety symptoms.
3. Enumerate various anxiety disorders and discuss clinical features, types, and treatment of specific phobia.
4. Write short notes on:
   a. Separation anxiety disorder
   b. Selective mutism
   c. Social anxiety disorder
   d. Diagnosis of agoraphobia
   e. Generalized anxiety disorder

Chapter 13

Obsessive–Compulsive and Related Disorders

Sandeep Kumar Goyal

Obsessive—compulsive and related disorders (OCRDs) include obsessive—compulsive disorder (OCD), body dysmorphic disorder (BDD), hoarding disorder (HD), trichotillomania (TTM), and excoriation disorder. These disorders share phenomenological and psycho-biological features.

OBSESSIVE–COMPULSIVE DISORDER

The OCD is characterized by the presence of obsessions and compulsions. **Obsessions** are recurrent thoughts (e.g., contamination), images (e.g., violent or sexual scenes), or urges (e.g., to hit someone). These obsessions are not pleasurable and provoke anxiety in an individual. Obsessions are recognized as intrusive and unwanted. An individual tries to ignore or suppress these obsessions or to neutralize them with another thought or action (i.e., by performing a compulsion).

Compulsions are repetitive behaviors (washing, checking) or mental acts (counting, prayers), which have to be performed by an individual to neutralize anxiety caused by obsessions or preventing some feared event.

Compulsions too are not pleasurable, but the individual feels better as compulsions reduce anxiety caused by obsessions.

Comparative Nosology

ICD-10 classifies the OCD in the neurotic, stress-related, and somatoform disorders along with other anxiety disorders. In DSM-IV, OCD was classified under anxiety disorders whereas in DSM-5, it is separated from anxiety disorders and clubbed with BDD, HD, TTM, and excoriation disorder and placed under the category of OCRDs.

Epidemiology

The 12-month prevalence internationally is 1.1–1.8%. In childhood males are affected more, whereas in adults females are affected slightly more than males. In the United States, the mean age at onset of OCD is 19.5 years. Males have an earlier age of onset. Females have more cleaning rituals and males have more symptoms in forbidden thoughts and symmetry dimension.

Etiology

Psychodynamic Theory

Freud linked OCD to the anal stage of psychosexual development. According to Freudian theory, OCD occurs due to anal fixation or regression to this stage of psychosexual development with the use of defense mechanisms of isolation, undoing, and reaction formation.

Isolation An obsession (idea) is associated with anxiety (affect). The defense mechanism of isolation separates affect and the idea. If isolation is successful, the patient is consciously aware of only the affectless idea.

Undoing Undoing is a compulsive act performed to undo the anxiety or distress caused by obsessions (e.g., washing hands result in a decrease of anxiety).

Reaction formation Reaction formation leads to the formation of personality traits.

Behavioral Theory

According to the behavioral theory, obsessions are conditioned stimuli and are produced by **classical conditioning** through which a neutral stimulus gets associated with anxiety by being paired with anxiety-producing events. Thus, previous neutral objects and thoughts become conditioned stimuli which can produce anxiety (e.g., patient associates shaking hands with contamination).

Formation of compulsions involves **operant conditioning**. When an individual discovers that the anxiety is reduced by a particular behavior, then that behavior becomes the compulsion.

Neurotransmitters

Abnormality of the serotonergic system, particularly hypersensitivity of the postsynaptic 5-HT receptor, is the main hypothesis. Most of the drugs used to treat OCD are serotonergic, which also supports the hypothesis. However, the potential role of dopamine is also emerging. The evidence for dopamine involvement comes from the presence of OCD symptoms in basal ganglia disorders like Tourette syndrome and Sydenham's chorea.

Neurobiology

The neurobiological explanation of OCD focuses on aberrant functioning of **cortico-striatal-thalamic-cortical (CSTC) circuits.** The CSTC circuits start from cortical areas and pass through the basal ganglia (striatum) via either direct or indirect pathways to the thalamus and the cortical areas receive feedback projections from the thalamus (Fig. 13.1). The direct and indirect basal ganglia pathways through glutamatergic and GABAergic neurotransmission appear to work antagonistically, and imbalance between these pathways is theorized as a contributing pathophysiological factor in OCD.

Clinical Features and Diagnosis

Most of the patients have both obsessions and compulsions. The patient may have a mental compulsion rather than behavioral compulsion (e.g., mental prayers after blasphemous thoughts). Some patients may have only obsessions without compulsions.

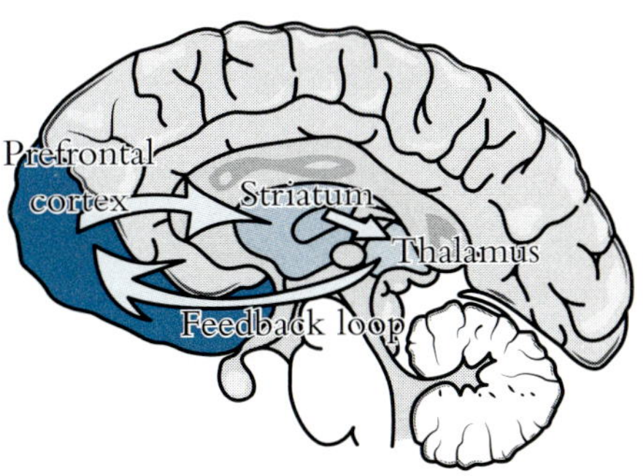

Figure 13.1 Diagrammatic representation of a cortico-striatal-thalamic-cortical circuit in a sagittal view of the human brain. Reprinted from ***Pathobiology of Human Disease***, A. Vahabzadeh, C.J. McDougle, 2512–21, 2014, with permission from Elsevier.

The obsessions and compulsions are ego alien, that is, they are perceived as foreign to person's experience of oneself.

Symptom Patterns

Contamination Contamination is the most common type of obsession followed by increased hand washing or other rituals like more time spent in taking a bath, washing the already washed clothes or utensils, washing of currency notes or avoidance of the object. The patient can have skin lesions due to excessive hand washing.

Pathological doubts The second most common type is obsession of doubt, followed by repeated checking behavior. For example, obsession includes forgetting to lock the door and compulsion is repeated checking of the door.

Intrusive thoughts These are intrusive obsessive thoughts without a compulsion (e.g., thoughts of an aggressive or sexual act).

Symmetry Obsession of symmetry or precision leads to slowness. Patients take hours to complete a simple task (e.g., dressing up). Obsessions of symmetry lead to the delayed completion of work.

Magical thinking The patients with obsessions about symmetry may also have magical thinking associated with their concerns. For example, "if my toys are not arranged symmetrically, my mom will die" and he arranges his toys in a symmetry to prevent harm to his/her mother.

Compulsions are not linked to feared consequences realistically (e.g., arranging items symmetrically will not prevent harm to family members).

Blasphemous thoughts Blasphemous thoughts are sexual thoughts about God and religious figures or evil thoughts or images during prayer or meditation.

In OCD, usually the patients have good insight and recognize that their OCD beliefs are not true, but some patients have poor insight and think that their OCD beliefs are probably true. Rarely patients have no insight and think that their OCD beliefs are true (delusional beliefs).

To make a diagnosis of OCD as per DSM-5, the obsessions and compulsions must consume more than 1 hour per day or cause impairment in the social, occupational, or other important areas of functioning.

Scales Used

Yale—Brown obsessive compulsive scale (Y-BOCS) is considered the gold standard for assessing the severity of obsessive—compulsive symptoms and is to be administered by a clinician (clinician administered). Obsessive—compulsive inventory-revised (OCI-R), Florida obsessive—compulsive inventory (FOCI), Leyton obsessional inventory survey form (LOI-SF), and schedule of compulsions, obsessions, and pathological impulses (SCOPI) are commonly used scales which a patient can self-administer (self-report).

Differential Diagnosis

Other OCD spectrum disorders OCD spectrum disorders should be differentiated from each other. In BDD, symptoms are limited only to concerns about physical appearance. In HD, there is difficulty discarding possessions and excessive accumulation of objects. If hoarding occurs in response to obsessions, then the diagnosis is OCD in place of HD. Skin picking (excoriation) and hair pulling (TTM) are not triggered by obsessions. Excoriation and TTM are preceded by increasing sense of tension and hair pulling, or skin picking may lead to a sense of relief.

Major depressive disorder Major depressive disorder and OCD can coexist, and OCD symptoms can be present in depression also. Obsessions associated with depression are present only during depressive episode, whereas true obsessions persist even when there is remission of depression.

Anxiety disorders In generalized anxiety disorder, recurrent thoughts are regarding real-life concerns. In phobias, anxiety is related to specific phobias, and there is avoidance of phobic object and rituals are not present. In social phobia, anxiety is related to social interactions.

Tics and stereotyped movements Tourette's syndrome is associated with recurrent motor and vocal tics which resemble OCD. Approximately two-thirds of the persons with Tourette's syndrome have comorbid OCD. Tics are associated with premonitory sensory urge, whereas compulsions are preceded by obsessions.

Psychotic disorders Sometimes it is difficult to distinguish OCD with poor insight from psychotic disorders. OCD patients acknowledge the unreasonable nature of the obsessions, and moreover, psychotic disorders have many symptoms which are not characteristic of OCD (e.g., hallucinations and formal thought disorder).

Obsessive–compulsive personality disorder (OCPD) In OCPD, insight is absent and symptoms are ego-syntonic, whereas in OCD symptoms are ego-dystonic. In some patients, OCD and OCPD coexist, and both should be diagnosed.

Other compulsive-like behaviors OCD must be differentiated from other compulsive behaviors such as paraphilias, gambling, and substance abuse. These activities usually give pleasure to the patient, whereas OCD symptoms are not pleasurable.

Medical disorders Idiopathic OCD should be differentiated from OCD-like symptoms associated with basal ganglia diseases like Sydenham's chorea and Huntington's disease.

Course and Prognosis

The course of OCD is usually chronic and symptoms persist for years if not treated. Some individuals have an episodic illness. About one-third of the patients with OCD have depressive disorder.

Treatment

Treatment includes a combination of pharmacotherapy and psychotherapy (usually behavior therapy), and results of combined pharmacotherapy and psychotherapy produce better results as compared to either of these used alone.

Pharmacotherapy

Selective serotonin reuptake inhibitors (SSRIs) or clomipramine is the first line of treatment. Among SSRIs, fluoxetine, sertraline, citalopram, paroxetine, and fluvoxamine are approved by US Food and Drug Administration (USFDA) for the treatment of OCD in adults. Among tricyclic antidepressants (TCAs), clomipramine is approved for the treatment of OCD, and it is the most selective for serotonin reuptake among TCAs. Clomipramine was the first drug to be FDA approved for the treatment of OCD.

Sertraline (age at least 6 years), fluoxetine (age at least 7 years), fluvoxamine (age at least 8 years), and clomipramine (age at least 10 years) are FDA approved for the treatment of OCD in children.

The standard approach is to start treatment with SSRI or clomipramine. Meta-analyses comparing the different SSRIs and direct head-to-head comparisons have not shown superiority of any one SSRI over the other. Higher doses of drugs are usually required for the treatment of OCD in comparison to those used in depression. The usual therapeutic doses of the SSRIs and clomipramine to treat OCD in adults are given in Table 13.1. Atypical antipsychotic drugs can be used to augment the SSRIs in patients not responding completely to SSRIs. Aripiprazole (5–10 mg/day) or risperidone (1–3 mg/day) are consistently found to be effective as augmenting agents, whereas quetiapine and olanzapine have not been consistently found to be effective. Glutamatergic agents like N-methyl-D-aspartate receptor (NMDA) blocker drugs like memantine have shown benefit in patients with OCD in small uncontrolled studies. Other glutamate-modulating agents like riluzole have shown benefit in profoundly refractory patients in a pair of open-label studies. Topiramate, another glutamate modulator, has shown benefit in two controlled trials. None of the drugs acting on glutamate are FDA approved yet.

Table 13.1 Usual therapeutic doses of the SSRIs and clomipramine to treat OCD in adults

Drug	Starting dose mg/day	Usual therapeutic doses in mg/day
Citalopram	20	40–60
Escitalopram	10	20–30
Sertraline	50	150–200
Fluoxetine	20	60–80
Fluvoxamine	50	200–300
Paroxetine	20	40–60
Clomipramine	25	150–225

OCD, obsessive–compulsive disorder; *SSRIs*, selective serotonin reuptake inhibitors.

Behavior Therapy

Exposure and response prevention is the main behavioral approach. Desensitization, thought stopping, and flooding are also used in OCD.

Exposure and response prevention, commonly referred to as **ERP**, is exposing patient to the thoughts, images, objects, and situations that makes a patient anxious without "neutralizing" them with compulsions. Exposure therapy starts with confronting items and situations that cause anxiety, which a patient is able to tolerate. After the first few times, anxiety does not climb as high and does not last as long. Then the patient is encouraged to move on to more difficult exposure exercises.

During exposure, the patient is advised not to engage in subtle avoidance (e.g., thinking about other things, touching the doorknob only with one finger instead of the whole hand, etc.). Patient is advised to try to stay in the situation until his/her fear drops by at least one-half. Also, focus on overcoming one fear at a time. It is a good idea to do the exposure repeatedly until the first item on the hierarchy no longer causes much of a problem for the patient.

Thought stopping In thought stopping, the patient and the therapist make a list of up to four obsessional thoughts and a longer list of triggering situations. The therapist describes a triggering thought, and when the obsessive or racing thoughts begin (patient expresses start of obsession by hand raise) the therapist shouts "Stop!" Many therapists encourage the client to yell out the "Stop!" This helps focus the attention on the word and away from the obsessive thought. Later, the patient thinks the word "Stop" to himself/herself without needing to say it aloud and the word stop is associated with the cessation of the thought.

Desensitization and flooding are described in Chapter 29, *Psychotherapy.*

Neuromodulation Techniques

Electroconvulsive therapy (ECT) is the oldest neuromodulation technique, and for severe treatment-resistant cases, ECT can be considered.

Repetitive transcranial magnetic stimulation (rTMS) is effective in controlling the symptoms of OCD. Stimulation of supplementary motor cortex or orbitofrontal cortex is effective, and stimulation of dorsolateral prefrontal cortex (DLPFC) is ineffective. Deep brain stimulation (DBS) is FDA approved for disabling OCD not responding with other less invasive treatments.

Psychosurgery

For extreme debilitating cases which are not responding to any treatment, psychosurgery (cingulotomy or subcaudate tractotomy, also known as capsulotomy) has been tried with varying results.

BODY DYSMORPHIC DISORDER

In BDD, the patient has a preoccupation with one or more perceived defects or flaws in his physical appearance that are not observable or appear only slight to others. The patient perceives himself ugly, but actually he looks normal. The patient may try to camouflage his perceived flaws. The patient performs repetitive behaviors (e.g., checking body parts in the mirror, excessive grooming, skin picking, reassurance seeking) or mental acts (e.g., comparing body parts with the same area of others). The appearance preoccupation causes clinically significant socio-occupational impairment. BDD is diagnosed if appearance preoccupation is not better explained by concerns with body weight or fat in an individual whose symptoms meet diagnostic criteria of eating disorder.

Muscle dysmorphia is a form of BDD characterized by the belief that one's body build is too small or insufficiently muscular. It occurs exclusively in males.

HOARDING DISORDER

In HD, the patient has a persistent difficulty in discarding his possessions irrespective of their actual value. This difficulty is due to perceived need to save the items. A person with HD experiences distress at the thought of getting rid of the items. An excessive accumulation of items congests and clutters the living areas, and this cluttering compromises their intended use significantly. The hoarding causes clinically significant socio-occupational impairment and is not attributable to another medical condition (brain injury, Prader Willi syndrome). The HD is diagnosed if it is not better explained by the symptoms of another mental disorder (obsessions in OCD, delusions in schizophrenia, cognitive deficits in major cognitive disorders).

EXCORIATION (SKIN PICKING) DISORDER

Excoriation or skin picking disorder (SPD) is characterized by recurrent picking of one's skin resulting in skin lesions; face, arms, and hands are the most common areas that are picked. The patient makes repeated attempts to stop skin picking. Skin picking causes significant impairment in the socio-occupational functioning of the patient. Excoriation is diagnosed if skin picking is not attributable to physiological effects of a substance (cocaine) or another medical condition (scabies) or another mental disorder (attempts to improve perceived defect in appearance in BDD, delusions or tactile hallucinations in a psychotic disorder, or intention to harm oneself in non-suicidal self-injury).

TRICHOTILLOMANIA

TTM is recurrent pulling of one's hair, which results in hair loss. The patient can pull hairs from any hairy area of the body, but scalp, eyebrows, and eyelids are the most common sites. The patient makes repeated attempts to stop hair pulling. TTM causes significant impairment in the socio-occupational functioning of the patient. TTM is diagnosed if hair pulling is not attributable to another medical condition (dermatological disorder) or another mental disorder (attempts to improve perceived defect in appearance in BDD).

TREATMENT OF OBSESSIVE–COMPULSIVE RELATED DISORDERS

Psychoeducation is a key component of the treatment of BDD, TTM, and SPD. Exploring the patient's explanatory model is a useful first step in understanding the patient's suffering, building a collaborative approach to care.

Cognitive behavioral therapy (CBT) for OCD has been modified for BDD and HD. CBT for OCD includes exposure, response prevention, and cognitive restructuring. Modifications of OCD manual are required to address the social avoidance present in BDD. CBT for HD includes organization skill training, practice with resisting acquisition, and cognitive restructuring.

Habit reversal therapy (HRT) is effective in the treatment of childhood and adult TTM. HRT includes awareness training, competing response training, and social support. **Awareness training** includes self-monitoring and collecting pulled hair. In **competing response training**, hair pulling is substituted with an incompatible action (e.g., fist clenching). **Social support** includes other person reinforcing the competing response and changing the patient's environment so that hair pulling is more effortful and less reinforcing. HRT is efficacious in the treatment of childhood and adult SPD.

Pharmacotherpay

Clomipramine is more effective than desipramine in BDD and TTM. SSRIs are also effective in the treatment of BDD and SPD. SSRIs are first-line treatment in HD and venlafaxine may also be effective in HD. SSRIs and venlafaxine have not shown consistent efficacy in TTM.

OBSESSIVE–COMPULSIVE AND RELATED DISORDERS DUE TO ANOTHER MEDICAL DISORDER

Pediatric neuropsychiatric disorders associated with *Streptococcus* (PANDAS) are hypothesized to be an immune reaction to streptococcal infection which leads to sudden onset of obsessive—compulsive symptoms.

KEY POINTS

- Obsessive–compulsive and related disorders (OCRDs) include obsessive–compulsive disorder (OCD), body dysmorphic disorder (BDD), hoarding disorder (HD), trichotillomania (TTM), and excoriation disorder.
- The OCD is characterized by the presence of obsessions and compulsions.
- Twelve-month prevalence internationally is 1.1–1.8%. In childhood males are affected more, whereas in adults females are affected slightly more than males.
- Abnormality of the serotonergic system, particularly hypersensitivity of the postsynaptic 5HT receptor, is the main hypothesis. However, the potential role of dopamine is also emerging.
- The neurobiological explanation of OCD focuses on aberrant functioning of cortico-striatal-thalamic-cortical (CSTC) circuits.
- Contamination is the most common type of obsession followed by increased hand washing or other rituals like more time spent in taking a bath.
- Second most common type of obsession is doubts followed by repeated checking behavior.
- Blasphemous thoughts are sexual thoughts about God and religious figures or evil thoughts or images during prayer or meditation.
- Yale–Brown obsessive compulsive scale (Y-BOCS) is considered the gold standard for assessing the severity of obsessive–compulsive symptoms.
- Other obsessive spectrum disorders, major depressive disorder, anxiety disorders, Tourette syndrome, obsessive–compulsive personality disorder, and medical disorders like Sydenham's chorea and Huntington disease are common differential diagnoses. Sometimes it is difficult to distinguish OCD with poor insight from psychotic disorders.
- The course of OCD is usually chronic and symptoms persist for years if not treated.
- Treatment includes a combination of pharmacotherapy and psychotherapy, usually behavior therapy.
- Selective serotonin reuptake inhibitors (SSRIs) or clomipramine is the first line of treatment. Among SSRIs, fluoxetine, sertraline, citalopram, and fluvoxamine are US Food and Drug Administration (USFDA) approved for treatment of OCD.
- Glutamatergic agents like N-Methyl-D-aspartate receptor (NMDA) blocker drugs like memantine have shown benefit in patients with OCD in small uncontrolled studies. Other glutamate modulating agents like Riluzole and topiramate have shown benefit in OCD, but none of the drugs acting on glutamate are FDA approved yet.
- Exposure and response prevention are the main behavioral approach. Desensitization, thought stopping, flooding, and implosion therapy are also used in OCD.
- For severe treatment-resistant cases, ECT can be considered.
- Deep brain stimulation (DBS) is FDA approved for disabling OCD not responding with other less invasive treatments.

- For extreme debilitating cases which are not responding to any treatment, psychosurgery (cingulotomy or subcaudate tractotomy, also known as capsulotomy) has been tried with varying results.

SELF-ASSESSMENT

1. Case-based Questions

   A 20-year-old female presented with a history of repeated hand washing, taking more time in bathing. She also had a history of washing the bedsheet and chair if an outsider sat on bed or chair. The patient had these symptoms for the last 1 year and she would spend 3-4 hours in washing rituals. The patient admitted that she had repetitive thoughts that her hands are dirty and she will fall ill, and so she is compelled to perform washing rituals. She also admitted that if she does not indulge in washing rituals, she becomes anxious and these rituals decrease her anxiety. She admitted that these thoughts are excessive and unwanted, and she is not able to stop these thoughts. The patient had no comorbid psychiatric or medical disorder and had no history of any substance abuse or addiction.

   a. What is your provisional diagnosis and discuss how you reached at the diagnosis?
   b. Discuss the differential diagnosis.
   c. Discuss various treatment options for this patient.
   d. Patient does not want to take medication. Choose and describe the treatment modality for her.
2. Discuss the mechanism of action of drugs used to treat OCD.

Chapter 14

Trauma and Stressor-Related Disorders

Abdul Majid · Sandeep Kumar Goyal · AW Khan · Nizam Ud Din

The disorders in which exposure to a traumatic or stressful event is listed as a diagnostic criterion are labeled as trauma and stressor-related disorders. These include post-traumatic stress disorder (PTSD), acute stress disorder (ASD), and adjustment disorder (AD).

Comparative Nosology

ICD-10 classifies the reaction to severe stress and AD in the neurotic, stress related and somatoform disorders, whereas in DSM-5 trauma and stressor-related disorders are a separate entity.

POST-TRAUMATIC STRESS DISORDER

PTSD is characterized by the development of symptoms which start after exposure to one or more traumatic events.

Epidemiology

The 12-month prevalence in US adults is 3.5%, and prevalence in Europe, Asian, African, and Latin American counties is 0.5%–1%. The probability of developing PTSD after a similar level of exposure to traumatic event varies across cultural groups. Highest rates (33% to more than 50%) are found in survivors of rape, military combat, and captivity.

Prevalence is more in females as compared to males. Greater exposure to traumatic events such as rape or interpersonal violence may be the cause of increased prevalence in females.

Impact of trauma seems to be more if it is caused by a human cause (e.g., rape is more disturbing than an earthquake).

Etiology

The biopsychosocial model may explain why some people develop PTSD and others do not.

Risk Factors

Factors such as female gender, age at trauma, race, level of education, childhood abuse, severity of trauma, lack of social support, and additional life stress increase the risk of PTSD. Prior trauma, prior psychological adjustment, family history of psychiatric illness, greater perceived life threat during trauma, lower post-trauma social support, greater emotional distress, and greater dissociation during exposure are various predictors of PTSD.

Genetics

Some people are biologically more vulnerable to negative affect and anxiety. There was greater occurrence of PTSD in children born to mothers who were pregnant and escaped the attack on World Trade Center on September 11, suggesting biological sensitivities. It is estimated that genes determine 30% of the variance in the risk for PTSD.

Clinical Features and Diagnosis

PTSD is characterized by exposure to a traumatic event and presence of symptoms belonging to the four diagnostic categories: intrusion symptoms, avoidance symptoms, negative alterations in cognition and mood, and alteration in arousal and reactivity associated with traumatic events.

A traumatic event may be directly experienced by the person or he/she may have witnessed the event in person occurring to others. Traumatic events in PTSD/ASD include but are not limited to threatened or actual physical assault, threatened or actual sexual violence, being kidnapped, being taken a hostage, terrorist attack, natural or man-made disasters, severe motor vehicle accidents, war, and more.

Flashback is the classical **intrusion symptom** in which the patient feels and acts as if trauma is reoccurring. Other intrusion symptoms are recurrent intrusive distressing memories of the traumatic event, distressing dreams related to the traumatic event, and intense psychological distress or marked physiological reactions at exposure to internal or external cue that symbolize traumatic event.

Avoidance symptoms include avoidance of memories, thoughts, or feelings about the traumatic event and avoidance of external reminders (people, places, objects, or situations) that arouse these distressing memories, thoughts, or feelings about the traumatic event.

Symptoms related to **negative alterations in cognition and mood** beginning or worsening after the traumatic event include inability to remember an important aspect of the traumatic event, persistent and exaggerated negative beliefs about oneself, others or the world, and blaming himself/herself or others as the cause of the traumatic event. The patient feels detached from others and his interest in previously enjoyed activities gets decreased. He experiences inability to experience positive emotions (happiness or satisfaction) and remains in persistent negative emotional state, for example, fear, guilt, and shame.

Symptoms related to **alteration in arousal and reactivity** include anger outbursts, self-destructive behavior, hypervigilance, exaggerated startle response, and problems with concentration and sleep.

PTSD is diagnosed if the duration of disturbance is more than 1 month and the disturbance causes clinically significant impairment in socio-occupational functioning.

Apart from symptoms mentioned above, shame, survivor guilt, self-blame, alexithymia (inability to identify or articulate emotions), mistrust of others, avoidance of close relationships, and psychic numbing are additional symptoms. PTSD can occur at any age. Symptoms usually start within 3 months of trauma, although PTSD can occur after a delay of years called **delayed expression**. The delayed expression means that some symptoms appear immediately after the traumatic event and the delay is in meeting full criteria.

Children often cannot remember the source of symptoms or trauma. In children, repetitive themes during play and persistent nightmares reflect trauma. Children can present with a delay in academic achievement and disruption in the relationship with family and friends. Adolescents present with reckless actions, high-risk sexual behavior, substance abuse, and aggressiveness.

Differential Diagnosis

Other trauma and stressor-related disorders AD stressor can be of any severity, but in PTSD, stressor type and severity are mentioned.

AD can be diagnosed immediately while ASD can be diagnosed only between 3 days and 1 month after exposure to the stressor, and PTSD cannot be diagnosed before 1 month after the traumatic event.

Anxiety disorders and obsessive-compulsive disorder (OCD) In OCD, recurrent intrusive thoughts are not related to the experienced traumatic event. OCD also differs by the usual presence of compulsions and absence of other symptoms of PTSD or ASD. In separation anxiety disorder, symptoms are not related to a traumatic event but are related to separation from home and family. Likewise, arousal symptoms of panic disorder are not related to a traumatic event.

Major depressive disorder (MDD) In MDD, history of a traumatic event may or may not be present and in depression, the patient does not have intrusion and avoidance symptoms.

Dissociative disorders Dissociative disorders may or may not be preceded by a traumatic event. If criteria for PTSD are also met along with dissociative disorder, then a diagnosis of PTSD with dissociative symptoms should be made.

Psychotic disorders Flashbacks of PTSD and ASD must be distinguished from hallucinations and other perceptual disturbances which occur in schizophrenia and other psychotic disorders. Flashbacks can be distinguished from perceptual disturbances by being directly related to the traumatic events and absence of other psychotic symptoms.

Course and Prognosis

Prognosis is good for patients who have acute onset of PTSD symptoms, symptom duration less than 6 months, having strong social support, and receiving early treatment as compared to the prognosis of delayed-onset PTSD and PTSD with comorbid psychiatric illness.

Management of PTSD

The first step in management is to ensure the safety and to prevent the current abuse of the client. The assessment process is often painful for people with PTSD. Hypervigilance, rageful outbursts, and self-harming behavior can occur during the assessment, and the psychiatrist should be sensitive to these issues. Clients should not be forced to share the details of trauma until they feel safe and secure.

Assessment

The goal of assessment is to assess the current level of functioning, support system, coping skills, client's strengths, and resilience, apart from diagnosis and measurement of PTSD symptoms.

Clinician-administered PTSD Scale (CAPS) and PTSD Checklist are assessment tools for adults. Assessment scales for children include PTSD section of Kiddie Schedule for Affective Disorders and Schizophrenia (K-SADS) and child behavior checklist.

Treatment of PTSD is a combination of pharmacological and nonpharmacological therapies. Treatment should begin as early as possible after trauma.

Nonpharmacological Therapies

Prolonged exposure therapy is a behavioral therapy in which patients are exposed to feared stimuli until their anxiety is extinguished. **Cognitive processing therapy** combines exposure therapy, anxiety management training, and cognitive restructuring and is as effective as exposure therapy. **Anxiety management training** combines prolonged activation of traumatic memories with relaxation, cognitive restructuring, and biofeedback. **Stress inoculation training** includes education and training in six coping skills (muscle relaxation, thought stopping, breath control, guided self-dialogue, covert modeling, and role-playing) and is used successfully in treating PTSD. **Eye movement desensitization and reprocessing (EMDR)** and group and family therapy are other treatment options.

Pharmacotherapy

Paroxetine and sertraline are FDA approved for the treatment of PTSD. Venlafaxine and risperidone also show promising results. Evidence for the effectiveness of the benzodiazepines is lacking. For insomnia, low-dose trazodone is preferred over benzodiazepines. Newly developed orexin antagonist suvorexant is promising for trauma-related insomnia. Prazosin shows some efficacy in treatment-resistant PTSD, PTSD comorbid with substance use disorder, and nightmares. There is moderate evidence for the effectiveness of hydrocortisone in the prevention of PTSD if hydrocortisone is administered shortly after trauma.

ACUTE STRESS DISORDER

In both the US and non-US populations, ASD is diagnosed in less than 20% of the cases following traumatic events that do not involve interpersonal assault; higher rates of 20%–50% are found following interpersonal traumatic events (e.g., assault, rape).

Etiology

Risk factors include female gender, prior mental illness, high level of neuroticism, greater perceived severity of the trauma, and avoidant coping style.

Clinical Features and Diagnosis

ASD is associated with symptoms from the five categories of intrusion, negative mood, dissociation, avoidance, and arousal, beginning or worsening after the traumatic event occurred.

Intrusion symptoms include recurrent intrusive distressing memories of the traumatic event, flashbacks, distressing dreams related to the traumatic event, and intense psychological distress or marked physiological reactions at exposure to internal or external cue that symbolize traumatic event.

Negative mood symptom includes persistent inability to experience positive emotions (e.g., happiness, satisfaction).

Dissociative symptoms include an altered sense of the reality of one's surroundings or oneself or inability to remember an important aspect of the traumatic events.

Avoidance symptoms include avoidance of memories, thoughts or feelings about the traumatic event and avoidance of external reminders (people, places, objects, or situations) that arouse these distressing memories, thoughts or feelings about the traumatic event.

Anger outbursts, hypervigilance, exaggerated startle response, problems with concentration and sleep are **arousal symptoms**.

ASD is diagnosed if the duration of disturbance is 3 days to 1 month after trauma exposure and the disturbance causes clinically significant impairment in socio-occupational functioning. ASD is diagnosed after ruling out physiological effects of a substance (medication or alcohol) or medical condition (mild traumatic brain injury).

The patient can also have guilt, panic attacks, or impulsive behavior in addition to the symptoms mentioned above.

Course and Prognosis

ASD may progress to PTSD after 1 month or it may resolve within 1 month. Approximately 50% of individuals who present with PTSD initially had ASD.

Differential Diagnosis

ASD needs to be differentiated from **other trauma and stressor-related disorders (PTSD and AD), OCD, and psychotic disorders**. Differentiating points are the same as discussed in the differential diagnosis of PTSD.

Management

Psychological support, crisis intervention, and emotional first aid are different treatment components. Psychological support strengthens coping mechanisms and crisis intervention is used after disasters. Emotional first aid helps the patient to accept feelings, symptoms, reality, and the need for help. Cognitive behavioral therapy (CBT) is also helpful in acute symptoms after trauma. Treatment should be brief, provided immediately, and as proximately as possible to the scene of trauma.

ADJUSTMENT DISORDER

Individuals from disadvantaged life circumstances experience a high rate of stressors and may be at increased risk for ADs.

Clinical Features and Diagnosis

ADs are characterized by the development of emotional or behavioral symptoms in response to an identifiable stressor occurring within 3 months of the onset of the stressor.

AD is diagnosed if distress is out of proportion to the severity of the stressor and/or causes significant impairment in socio-occupational functioning. AD is not diagnosed if stress-related disturbance meet the criteria for another mental disorder or is an exaggeration of the preexisting mental disorder. Normal bereavement symptoms are not included in AD. Symptoms must not persist for more than the additional 6 months after the end of the stressor.

Subtypes

With depressed mood The prominent symptoms are depressed mood, tearfulness, and hopelessness.

With anxiety Palpitations and agitation are prominent symptoms.

With mixed anxiety and depressed mood Patient has symptoms of both anxiety and depression that do not meet the criteria of anxiety and depressive disorder.

With mixed disturbance of emotions and conduct Both emotional symptoms (depression, anxiety) and disturbance of conduct are predominant symptoms. Disturbance of conduct involves situations in which the rights of others are violated, or age-appropriate societal norms and rules are disregarded (e.g., truancy, vandalism, reckless driving, and fighting).

Differential Diagnosis

Major depressive disorder If criteria of MDD in response to a stressor are met, the diagnosis of AD is not applicable.

Other trauma and stressor-related disorders (PTSD and ASD) Differentiating points are the same as discussed in the differential diagnosis of PTSD.

Management

Psychotherapy (group or individual therapy) is the treatment of choice for AD. Psychotherapy can help persons adapt to the stressor which is not reversible. Crisis management helps patients to resolve the situation quickly by supportive techniques, suggestion, reassurance, and environmental modification.

Antianxiety and antidepressant drugs are used depending on the type of the AD. Pharmacological therapy is used to augment psychotherapies and is not a primary modality.

KEY POINTS

- Trauma and stressor-related disorders include post-traumatic stress disorder (PTSD), acute stress disorder (ASD), and adjustment disorder (AD).
- AD can be diagnosed immediately and ASD can be diagnosed only between 3 days and 1 month after exposure to the stressor; PTSD cannot be diagnosed before 1 month after the traumatic event.
- Traumatic events in PTSD/ASD include but are not limited to threatened or actual physical assault, threatened or actual sexual violence, being kidnapped, being taken a hostage, terrorist attack, natural or man-made disasters, severe motor vehicle accidents, war, and more.

Post-Traumatic Stress Disorder

- The highest rates of PTSD (33% to more than 50%) are found in survivors of rape, military combat, and captivity.
- PTSD is associated with intrusion symptoms, avoidance symptoms, negative alterations in cognition and mood, or alteration in arousal and reactivity associated with traumatic events.
- The first step in management is to ensure the safety of the client and to prevent the current abuse of the client.

- Hypervigilance, rageful outbursts, and self-harming behavior can occur during the assessment and psychiatrists should be sensitive to these issues. Clients should not be forced to share the details of trauma until they feel safe and secure.
- Treatment of PTSD is a combination of pharmacological and nonpharmacological therapies.
- Prolonged exposure therapy, cognitive processing therapy, stress inoculation training, and eye movement desensitization and reprocessing (EMDR) are common nonpharmacological therapies.
- Paroxetine and sertraline are FDA approved for the treatment of PTSD.
- There is moderate evidence for the effectiveness of hydrocortisone in the prevention of PTSD if hydrocortisone is administered shortly after trauma.

Acute Stress Disorder

- ASD is associated with intrusion symptoms, negative mood, dissociation symptoms, avoidance, and arousal symptoms, beginning or worsening after the traumatic event occurred.
- ASD may progress to PTSD after 1 month or it may resolve within 1 month. Approximately 50% of individuals who present with PTSD initially had ASD.
- Psychological support, crisis intervention, and emotional first aid are different treatment components in ASD management. Treatment should be brief, provided immediately, and as proximately as possible to the scene of trauma.

Adjustment Disorder

- AD is characterized by the development of emotional or behavioral symptoms in response to an identifiable stressor occurring within 3 months of the onset of the stressor.
- Psychotherapy is the treatment of choice for AD. Antianxiety and antidepressant drugs are used depending on the type of the AD. Pharmacological therapy is used to augment psychotherapies and is not a primary modality.

SELF-ASSESSMENT

1. Case-based Questions

   A 30-year-old male met with a major car accident while coming back from his office 4 months ago. His car was hit by another car and flipped upside down. He had a fracture in the arm, had no head injury, or loss of consciousness. He now presented to the OPD with a 4-month history of flashbacks while driving. He wakes up with nightmares about the car accident and avoids the place of the accident.

   He has hyperarousal symptoms of difficulty in concentrating on work, irritability, and disturbed sleep. He remains disconnected from the family members. He remembers the accident, but he does not remember about the flipping of the car upside down. He denies persistent and pervasive sadness of mood. The patient has no comorbid psychiatric or medical disorder and has no history of any substance abuse or addiction. He has no history of psychiatric illness in the past.

   a. What is your provisional diagnosis and discuss the reasons for it?
   b. Discuss the treatment options in the case.
2. What are the different categories of symptoms of PTSD and discuss symptoms under each category.
3. Describe the clinical features, differential diagnosis, and treatment of ASD.
4. Write short notes on clinical features and treatment of AD.

Chapter 15

Dissociative Disorders

Sandeep Kumar Goyal · Arvind Sharma · Rupesh Chaudhary

The dissociative disorders are a disturbance in the organization of identity, memory, perception, or consciousness. When memories are separated from access to consciousness, the disorder is dissociative amnesia. Fragmentation of identity and perception results in dissociative identity disorder (DID) and depersonalization disorder, respectively.

Dissociative disorders are frequently associated with trauma (e.g., accident, disaster, or crime victimization). During a traumatic experience, dissociation helps a person to tolerate what might otherwise be too difficult to bear. In traumatic situations, a person may dissociate the memory of the place, circumstances, or feelings about the devastating event, mentally escaping from fear, pain, and horror.

Fragmentation of identity, depersonalization, and derealization are positive dissociative symptoms, whereas amnesia is a negative dissociative symptom.

COMPARATIVE NOSOLOGY

DSM-5 dissociative disorders include DID, dissociative amnesia, and depersonalization/derealization disorder.

ICD-10 classifies the dissociative disorders in the neurotic, stress-related, and somatoform disorders, whereas in DSM-5 dissociative disorders are a separate entity. Dissociative fugue is a distinct diagnosis in ICD-10, whereas in DSM-5 it is classified as a specifier (subtype) of dissociative amnesia.

DISSOCIATIVE IDENTITY DISORDER

DID is characterized by two or more distinct personality states or experience of possession. **Disruption of identity** involves **discontinuity** in the **sense of self** and **sense of control**, accompanied by alterations in affect, behavior, consciousness, memory, perception, cognition, and sensory-motor functioning. The **sense of control** is the subjective awareness of initiating, executing, and controlling one's volitional actions.

Etiology

Physical and sexual abuse is associated with an increased risk of DID. Prevalence of childhood abuse and neglect among those with the disorder is about 90%.

Clinical Features

Discontinuity experience can affect any aspect of an individual's functioning. The patient can have a sudden onset of depersonalization, dissociative amnesia, dissociative fugue, or possession states.

In **depersonalization**, a patient can report that their bodies feel different (small child, opposite gender, or huge and muscular) or may report the perception of voices (e.g., child's voice, crying, or the voice of a spiritual being).

Dissociative amnesia of DID can present as gaps in remote memory of personal life events (e.g., life events such as death of a grandparent or getting married) or lapses in dependable memory (e.g., what happened today, how to use a computer, or drive). The patient may present with the symptom of the discovery of doing an action or task which he does not remember, for example, finding unexplained objects in shopping bags. Amnesia in DID is not limited to traumatic events and the patients are often unable to recall everyday events as well.

Dissociative fugue in which a person discovers dissociative travel is common. The individual may find himself/herself at the beach, night club, or anywhere with no memory of how he/she reached there.

In **possession** form DID, the patient behaves as if a spirit, ghost, demon, or deity has taken control and the patient starts speaking or behaving in a distinctly different manner. All possession states do not meet the criteria of DID. Possession form identities of DID are recurrent, unwanted, and involuntary, cause significant distress, and are not a part of broadly accepted cultural or religious practice.

These symptoms cause significant distress in the socio-occupational functioning. DID is diagnosed if disturbance is not a normal part of cultural or religious practice and is not caused by the physiological effects of a substance or another medical condition.

Differential Diagnosis

Dissociative amnesia DID is characterized by a pervasive discontinuity in the sense of self and sense of control, along with many other dissociative symptoms which are not present in dissociative amnesia.

Bipolar disorders Due to rapid subjective shifts in mood across dissociative states, individuals with DID may be misdiagnosed as having bipolar II disorder.

Post-traumatic stress disorder An individual can be suffering from post-traumatic stress disorder (PTSD) alone or a combination of PTSD and DID. Individuals with comorbid DID present with amnesia for nontraumatic events, intrusions unrelated to the traumatic material, and dissociative flashbacks with amnesia for the content of the flashback.

Psychotic disorders Personified internally communicative inner voices of DID may be mistaken for hallucinations. DID may be differentiated by the predominance of dissociative symptoms and amnesia for the episode.

Personality disorders The personality style on longitudinal history in DID is variable, whereas in personality disorder symptoms are pervasive and persistent.

Factitious disorders and malingering Individuals with feigned symptoms seem undisturbed or even seem to enjoy the disorder, whereas individuals with DID tend to be ashamed of their symptoms, try to underreport their symptoms, or deny the symptoms.

Treatment

Hypnosis may be used as a psychotherapeutic tool and it is also useful in establishing a diagnosis of DID. The focus of psychotherapy is on working through traumatic memories and controlling dissociation. The ultimate goal of psychotherapy in DID is the integration of patient's multiple ego states.

Medicines are used for symptomatic relief (e.g., insomnia and panic attacks) or management of comorbid psychiatric illness. Antidepressants are used for comorbid dysthymia or major depressive disorder. Benzodiazepines are used to control secondary anxiety associated with retrieval of traumatic memories (drug-facilitated interviews). Long-term use of benzodiazepines is not indicated. Antipsychotics are not recommended as they can increase dissociative symptoms.

DISSOCIATIVE AMNESIA

Dissociative amnesia is the inability to recall important autobiographical information.

Etiology

Single or repeated traumatic experiences, for example, war, childhood maltreatment, natural disaster, genocide, are common antecedents. Chances of dissociative amnesia are more with a higher number of adverse childhood experiences, interpersonal violence, and increased severity, frequency, and violence of the trauma.

Clinical Features and Diagnosis

Dissociative amnesia is **potentially reversible**. Memory loss is usually for the events which are of traumatic or stressful nature. It spares procedural memory, and new memory formation is intact, that is, dissociative amnesia is **retrograde**.

Localized amnesia is the most common type in which an individual cannot recall events of a circumscribed period.

In **selective amnesia**, an individual can recall some, but not all, of the events during a discrete period.

Continuous amnesia is the failure to recall successive events as they occur.

An individual with dissociative amnesia may be unaware of his/her memory loss. Some episodes resolve rapidly when an individual is removed from a stressful environment, whereas others persist for an extended period. As the amnesia remits, there may be distress, suicidal thoughts, or PTSD.

Dissociative amnesia is diagnosed if inability to recall cannot be explained by ordinary forgetting. Dissociative amnesia is diagnosed after ruling out other disorders which can produce memory loss (e.g., alcohol or substance abuse, complex partial seizures, transient global amnesia, sequelae of head injury, DID, PTSD, major or mild neurocognitive disorder).

Differential Diagnosis

Dissociative identity disorder DID is characterized by many other dissociative symptoms which are not present in dissociative amnesia.

PTSD and ASD Amnesia is a diagnostic criterion in PTSD and ASD. Some individuals with PTSD cannot recall a traumatic event. When amnesia extends beyond the immediate time of trauma, comorbid dissociative amnesia is diagnosed.

Substance-related disorders There may be episodes of blackouts associated with substance intoxication (e.g., alcohol). Amnestic episodes occurring only in the context of substance intoxication help to identify the substance-induced amnesia from dissociative amnesia.

Post-traumatic amnesia due to brain injury History of trauma, unconsciousness, disorientation, confusion, and abnormalities on neuroimaging, visual field defects, anosmia, and new onset of seizures point toward post-traumatic amnesia.

Seizure disorder Patients with complex partial seizures may present with purposeless wandering, whereas behavior during dissociative fugue is usually purposeful, goal-directed, and lasts for many days.

Factitious disorder and malingering Individuals with malingering or factitious disorder continue their symptoms even during hypnotic and barbiturate-facilitated interviews.

Normal ageing Dissociative amnesia is associated with stressful events and is more specific and extensive.

Treatment

In dissociative amnesia, recovery may occur when the patient is removed from a stressful or threatening situation. As mentioned earlier in DID, drug-facilitated interviews may be helpful in controlling anxiety associated with retrieval of traumatic memories. Hypnotic techniques such as age regression, self-hypnosis, and screen technique can help in getting access to dissociated unavailable memories. Screen technique allows recollection of memories without flashbacks.

DEPERSONALIZATION/ DEREALIZATION DISORDER

Depersonalization/derealization disorder is characterized by the presence of persistent or recurrent episodes of depersonalization, derealization, or both.

Etiology

Temperamental Individuals with the depersonalization/derealization disorder are characterized by harm avoidant temperament and immature defenses (idealization, projection, and acting out).

Environmental There is an association between depersonalization/derealization disorder and childhood interpersonal traumas. Physical abuse, witnessing domestic violence, growing up with a seriously impaired mentally ill parent, and unexpected death or suicide of a family member are some other stressors associated with depersonalization/derealization disorder.

Clinical Features and Diagnosis

Depersonalization is characterized by a feeling of unreality or unfamiliarity with oneself ("I am no one") or aspects of self like thoughts ("my thoughts do not feel like my own"), feelings, sensations (touch, hunger, thirst, and libido), body, or actions. In derealization, there is unfamiliarity with the surroundings (individuals or objects appear unreal, foggy).

In depersonalization/derealization disorder, reality testing remains intact. These symptoms cause clinically significant distress in social or occupational functioning. Depersonalization/derealization symptoms can be present in anxiety disorder or schizophrenia. Depersonalization/derealization disorder is diagnosed after ruling out medical or mental disorders which can produce similar symptoms, for example, seizures, schizophrenia, panic disorder, major depressive disorder, acute stress disorder, PTSD, or another dissociative disorder or physiological effects of a substance.

Individuals with depersonalization/ derealization disorder may think that they are going crazy and there is fear of irreversible brain damage. They have a subjectively altered sense of time (too fast or too low). They can have ruminations or obsessional preoccupation (whether they really exist).

Differential Diagnosis

Other dissociative disorders Depersonalization/derealization is not diagnosed if symptoms occur only during DID. Symptoms of dissociative amnesia do not overlap with depersonalization/derealization.

Anxiety disorders Depersonalization/derealization is not diagnosed if symptoms occur only as part of panic disorder, social anxiety disorder, and specific phobia. Depersonalization/derealization can be diagnosed if it persists after the panic disorder has been treated.

Psychotic disorders Presence of intact reality testing differentiates depersonalization/derealization from psychotic disorders.

Substance-induced disorders Depersonalization/derealization is not diagnosed if it occurs during substance intoxication or withdrawal. Marijuana, cocaine, and psychostimulants can cause persistent depersonalization/derealization.

Mental disorders due to another medical condition Onset after 40 years of age or presence of atypical symptoms suggests the possibility of an underlying medical cause. Seizure disorders, brain tumor, migraine, vertigo, metabolic abnormalities, and Meniere's disease are common causes. Temporal lobe epilepsy is most commonly implicated.

Treatment

Depersonalization/derealization disorder is usually transient and may remit without treatment. It may respond to self-hypnosis. By inducing transient depersonalization symptoms, the patient can understand the symptoms and learn to control them. Screen technique can also be helpful. Antidepressants can be used for comorbid depression. Antianxiety and antipsychotic drugs can be used for comorbid anxiety disorders (generalized anxiety or phobia) and psychotic disorders, respectively.

OTHER DISSOCIATIVE DISORDERS

Dissociative Trance Disorder

Dissociative trance disorder is recognized by temporary loss of the customary sense of personal identity without replacement by an alternate sense of identity, whereas possession trance includes alternation in the state of consciousness with the exchange of identity with a new one. The new identity is usually attributed to spirit, deity, or another person (usually a dead relative).

Ganser Syndrome

It is characterized by the approximate answers or passing over (*vorbeigehen*) the correct answer for a related but incorrect one. Answer misses the mark but indicates that question is understood (e.g., naming red color as blue or answering 3 + 3 = 8). Associated symptoms are clouding of consciousness, disorientation, and visual and auditory hallucinations. It must be accompanied by other dissociative symptoms such as amnesia, conversion symptoms, or trance-like behavior.

KEY POINTS

- Fragmentation of identity, depersonalization, and derealization are positive dissociative symptoms, whereas amnesia is a negative dissociative symptom.

Dissociative Identity Disorder (DID)

- DID is characterized by two or more distinct personality states or experience of possession.
- Disruption of identity in DID can affect any aspect of an individual's functioning. The patient can have a sudden onset of depersonalization, dissociative amnesia, dissociative fugue, or possession states.
- Hypnosis may be used as a psychotherapeutic tool and it is also useful in establishing a diagnosis of DID.
- Medicines are used for symptomatic relief (e.g., insomnia and panic attacks) or management of comorbid psychiatric illness only.

Dissociative Amnesia

- Dissociative amnesia is the inability to recall important autobiographical information. It is diagnosed if inability to recall cannot be explained by ordinary forgetting.
- It is potentially reversible. Memory loss is usually for the events which are of traumatic or stressful nature. It spares procedural memory and new memory formation is intact, that is, dissociative amnesia is retrograde.
- In dissociative amnesia, recovery may occur when the patient is removed from the stressful or threatening situation.

Depersonalization/Derealization Disorder

- Depersonalization/derealization disorder is characterized by the presence of persistent or recurrent episodes of depersonalization, derealization, or both.
- In depersonalization/derealization disorder, reality testing remains intact.
- Depersonalization/derealization disorder is usually transient and may remit without treatment. It may respond to self-hypnosis.

Ganser syndrome

- Ganser syndrome characterized by the approximate answers or passing over (*vorbeigehen*) the correct answer for a related but incorrect one. Answer misses the mark but indicates that question is understood (e.g., naming red color as blue).

SELF-ASSESSMENT

1. Define dissociative disorders and enumerate various dissociative disorders and discuss etiology, clinical features, and treatment of dissociative identity disorder.
2. Discuss etiology, clinical features, and treatment of dissociative amnesia.
3. Write short notes on:
   a. Ganser syndrome
   b. Dissociative trance disorder
   c. Depersonalization/derealization disorder

Chapter 16

Somatic Symptom and Related Disorders

Mitali Soni Loya · Vaibhav Dubey

Somatic symptom and related disorders include "somatic symptom disorder," "illness anxiety disorder," "psychological factors affecting another medical condition," "factitious disorder," and "conversion disorder" (functional neurological symptom disorder).

The diagnosis of somatic symptom and related disorders is made based on positive symptoms (distressing somatic symptoms plus abnormal thoughts, feelings, and behaviors related to somatic symptoms). All the disorders share prominence of somatic symptoms associated with significant distress and impairment in patients. The requirement of the medically unexplained symptoms has been removed in DSM-5. However, medically unexplained symptoms remain a key feature in conversion disorder and pseudocyesis (false pregnancy).

Comparative Nosology

This category of disorders was known as somatoform disorders in DSM-IV-TR and included somatization disorder, hypochondriasis, conversion disorder, pain disorder, and body dysmorphic disorder. DSM-5 brought about significant changes in this category by removing hypochondriasis (now diagnosed as illness anxiety disorder), pain disorder (subsumed under somatic symptom disorder), and body dysmorphic disorder (included under *Obsessive–Compulsive and Related Disorders*). DSM-5 added "psychological factors affecting another medical condition" and "factitious disorder" to somatic symptom and related disorders which were grouped elsewhere in DSM-IV-TR.

Etiology

Various factors that predispose for the somatic complaints include the genetic/biological factors, the environmental influences, psychological, and behavioral elements. The aforementioned contributing factors converge into the final common pathway of "somatic presentations."

Genetic and biological vulnerability (increased pain sensitivity and proprioceptive acuity), early traumatic experiences (violence, abuse), and learning factors (having received more attention during physical illness and lack of attention on the description of nonsomatic emotional distress) cause physical expression of emotional conflicts. These traits are more common in certain cultures that stigmatize psychological suffering and show more concern toward medical disorders.

Biological factors There is little information on the biology of somatoform disorders. Studies done by using brain imaging techniques like fMRI (functional magnetic resonance imaging) have shown differences in patients with conversion disorder and functional somatic syndromes such as irritable bowel syndrome to the controls or patients with organic pathology. Preliminary brain imaging studies have found hypometabolism of the dominant hemisphere and hypermetabolism of the nondominant hemisphere and have implicated impaired hemispheric communication as the cause of the conversion disorder.

Personality factors People with histrionic personality or who tend to dramatize are found to be predisposed for conversion disorder.

Psychoanalytic theory As per psychoanalytic theory, **primary gain** forms the basis of conversion disorder. The conversion of a patient's conflict to somatic symptoms occurs without conscious awareness.

Behavior theory The behavioral theory focuses on the **secondary gain** (in the form of extra attention, sympathy, leave from school/workplace). According to this theory, people with poor coping skills learn to deal with adverse situations in a faulty manner. They learn the maladaptive behavioral patterns which grant them secondary gain.

Environmental factors There may be a history of childhood abuse and neglect.

SOMATIC SYMPTOM DISORDER

The core symptom of somatic symptom disorder is the presence of one or more somatic symptoms that are distressing or cause significant disruption of daily life. Individuals with somatic symptom disorder have disproportionate and persistent thoughts about the seriousness of one's symptoms.

Somatic symptom disorder is diagnosed if the symptoms are present for more than 6 months.

If the somatic symptom is predominantly pain, it is diagnosed as somatic symptom disorder with predominant pain (previously pain disorder).

It should be noted that the presence of a medical diagnosis does not exclude the possibility of having a comorbid somatic symptom disorder. The focus has thus been shifted to the symptoms present (and the preoccupation with somatic symptoms) rather than the absence of any disease.

The symptoms may be associated with medical illness, like becoming severely disabled following an uncomplicated myocardial infarction, even if it did not result in any disability. Individuals with somatic symptom disorder have high levels of worry about their illness. These patients imagine the worst outcome of their illness even when there is evidence to the contrary. This worry leads to excessive utilization of medical care and consulting multiple doctors.

Treatment

The patients usually resist psychiatric treatment although they may accept treatment in a medical setting. Symptoms should be seen as real and should not be dismissed. The physician should carry out a detailed examination which reassures the patient that the physician is not abandoning him. Unnecessary "symptom-driven" visits should be discouraged and patient should be encouraged for a timely scheduled regular follow-up. Treating the underlying mood or anxiety disorders can reduce the somatic symptoms caused by them. Specific treatment, including cognitive behavioral therapy (CBT), other psychotherapies like group therapy, and teaching coping skills can be useful.

ILLNESS ANXIETY DISORDER

Patients with illness anxiety disorder have a preoccupation with having or acquiring a serious illness. The preoccupation persists despite appropriate medical evaluation and reassurance.

The somatic symptoms are usually not present in illness anxiety disorder or are mild in intensity. The preoccupation with having or acquiring a serious illness is disproportionate to the medical illness present (if any) or the risk of developing a medical condition. They spend a great deal of time searching for suspected disease on the internet. Their preoccupation is not decreased by medical reassurance or negative diagnostic tests. The individuals have a high level of anxiety about health and repeatedly examine themselves for signs of illness or avoid appointments with the doctor.

Illness anxiety disorder is diagnosed if illness preoccupation is present for at least 6 months and is not better explained by other mental disorders, for example, somatic symptom disorder, body dysmorphic disorder or delusional disorder, somatic type, etc. although specific illness that is feared may change over the 6 months of time.

DSM-5 defines two types of illness anxiety disorder: care-seeking type and care-avoidant type.

Treatment

Like in somatic symptom disorder, the patients usually resist psychiatric treatment although they may accept treatment in a medical setting. The role of regular scheduled physical examinations in illness anxiety disorder is controversial. Group therapy can be beneficial if the group is homogenous with patients of same disorder. Insight–oriented psychotherapy, CBT, and hypnosis can be useful. Selective serotonin reuptake inhibitors (SSRIs) have been reported to be clinically useful to decrease the anxiety caused by the fear of having or acquiring a serious illness. Antipsychotic agents such as risperidone have been recommended for delusional syndromes.

PSYCHOLOGICAL FACTORS AFFECTING OTHER MEDICAL CONDITIONS (PFAOMC)

In this disorder, there is a presence of some medical symptom or condition which gets worsened due to one or more psychological or behavioral factors. These factors influence the course of the medical condition, or interfere with its treatment, or constitute an additional well-established risk factor for the individual, or tend to influence the pathophysiology, or precipitate/exacerbate the symptoms of the medical condition. These psychological factors are not better explained by another psychiatric diagnosis like depression, panic disorder, or post-traumatic stress disorder. Common clinical examples include denying the need for the treatment of acute chest pain, anxiety exacerbating the symptoms of asthma or chronic occupational stress increasing the chances of developing hypertension. Psychological factors can affect diabetes, cancer, coronary disease, migraine, irritable bowel syndrome, fibromyalgia, etc.

Treatment

Treatment includes psychoeducation about the role of emotional and behavioral factors in aggravating the underlying medical condition. CBT can help the patients in stress management.

FACTITIOUS DISORDER

The primary feature of factitious disorder is voluntary production of physical or psychological signs and symptoms. There is falsification of signs and symptoms of a disease or induction of injury on self or in another without any obvious external rewards.

The disorder is of two types:

1. Factitious disorder imposed on self
2. Factitious disorder imposed on others

Factitious disorder imposed on self (also known as *Munchausen syndrome*) This disorder has also been named as hospital addiction, polysurgical addiction, and professional patient syndrome. Munchausen syndrome was named by *Richard Asher* after a German soldier, famous for the tales of his impossible achievements. In factitious disorder, the patients deliberately produce or exaggerate the signs or symptoms of the illness in the absence of obvious external rewards. The patient may induce skin lacerations, add blood to urine, induce GI bleeding; also includes laxative-induced diarrhea and induced fever.

Patients with factitious disorder are familiar with signs and symptoms of most disorders that require admission to a hospital. They present history so well that they can get admission to a hospital. Physical examination may reveal several self-inflicted scars or injuries, or multiple surgical scars most commonly on abdomen giving rise to "**gridiron**" or "**washboard**" abdomen. They may insist on undergoing surgery and claim adhesions from previous surgeries. They may ask for discharge from the hospital when they feel that their factitious behavior is caught. They visit other hospital and this cycle continues.

Factitious disorder imposed on others (also known as *Munchausen syndrome by proxy*) In this disorder, the caretaker tries to simulate or induce the symptoms of an illness voluntarily and consciously in a child or a person under care. The victim is usually a child and the most common inducer being the biological mother. The victim undergoes unnecessary medical and surgical treatments. The purpose of deception is the desire for the attention given by the medical practitioner. This diagnosis is applied to the inducer and not the victim. The victim may be given a diagnosis of medical abuse.

Factitious disorder should be differentiated from malingering, in which the patient intentionally feigns signs and symptoms of a disease for some personal gain such as compensation or leave from work. The factitious disorder is diagnosed after ruling out a delusional disorder or other psychotic disorders.

Treatment

No specific psychiatric therapy has been effective in treating factitious disorders.

The major goal in the management of factitious disorder is early recognition of the disorder. Role of confrontation is controversial. Majority of the patients leave the hospital when disease is diagnosed. Pharmacotherapy of factitious disorders is of limited use. In factitious disorder by proxy, child welfare services can be notified.

CONVERSION DISORDER (FUNCTIONAL NEUROLOGICAL SYMPTOM DISORDER)

Conversion disorder is characterized by voluntary motor or sensory symptoms which cannot be explained by another mental or medical disorder and cause clinically significant impairment in socio-occupational functioning. The clinical examination shows incompatibility between symptoms and recognized neurological and medical conditions.

The term "conversion" stands for the conversion of anxiety arising from the psychic conflict into a loss of function of a body part. The term conversion was first used by Freud who hypothesized that symptoms of conversion disorder reflect unconscious conflicts. It is important to note that though the disorder has a psychological basis, the physical symptoms are not produced deliberately.

DSM-5 has made two important modifications in this category. First, it has added a new name for the disorder in parenthesis, that is, "functional neurological symptom disorder." Second, it lays the criteria that the diagnosis can be made only when the symptom is incompatible with or cannot be explained by a known neurological disorder.

Symptom Types

- Weakness or paralysis
- Abnormal movements (tremor, dystonic movement, myoclonus, gait disturbance)
- Astasia-abasia: It is frequently encountered in conversion disorder. The patient presents with gait abnormality despite normal motor functions
- Swallowing symptoms (dysphagia, globus hystericus)
- Pseudoseizures
- Anesthesia or sensory loss
- Sensory symptoms (visual, olfactory, or hearing disturbance)

The patient may present with non-neurological syndromes such as pseudo cyesis (false pregnancy) or psychogenic vomiting.

Associated Features

Primary gain By converting internal conflicts into physical symptoms, the patient keeps internal conflicts out of awareness and this is known as primary gain.

Secondary gain The patient receives benefits as a result of assuming sick role (e.g., being excused from daily responsibilities and receiving support and care that might not otherwise be expected).

The patient appears inappropriately unconcerned about their physical symptoms. This phenomenon is known as ***La belle indifference*** and is characteristic (but not pathognomonic) of conversion disorder.

Treatment

Approach to the patient Special attention should be given to the history of trauma, abuse (sexual or physical), and family history of conversion symptoms. Physical examination should be done paying particular attention to rule out neurological diseases. Routine laboratory studies and procedures like electroencephalograms (to distinguish between epilepsy and pseudoseizures), MRI, X-rays, lumbar puncture, and so on can be done to rule out possible organic etiologies.

Reassurance Many conversion syndromes may remit spontaneously with understanding and support as they have an acute benign course. Early intervention can prevent the potential chronicity of the disorder.

Hypnotherapy The information stored in the unconscious is thought to be responsible for the conflict and is presented in the form of bodily symptoms in conversion disorder. Resolving the conflicts of such patients by methods like hypnosis is thought to be an effective treatment. Sodium amytal has also been used for bringing conflict-causing traumatic events from unconscious to conscious mind.

Pharmacological treatment Comorbid depression and anxiety may respond to pharmacological interventions.

KEY POINTS

Somatic Symptom Disorder

- The core symptom of somatic symptom disorder is the presence of one or more somatic symptoms that are distressing or cause significant disruption of daily life.
- It should be noted that the presence of a medical diagnosis does not exclude the possibility of having a comorbid somatic symptom disorder. The focus has thus been shifted to the symptoms present (and the preoccupation with somatic symptoms) rather than the absence of any disease.

Illness Anxiety Disorder

- Patients with illness anxiety disorder have a preoccupation with having or acquiring a serious illness.
- The somatic symptoms are usually not present or are of mild intensity. The preoccupation with having or acquiring a serious illness is disproportionate to the medical illness present (if any) or the risk of developing a medical condition.

Factitious Disorder

- The primary feature of factitious disorder is voluntary production of physical or psychological signs and symptoms. There is falsification of signs and symptoms of a disease or induction of injury on self or in another without any obvious external rewards.
- Factitious disorder imposed on self is also known as Munchausen syndrome. This disorder has also been named as hospital addiction, polysurgical addiction, and professional patient syndrome.

Conversion Disorder

- Conversion disorder is characterized by voluntary motor or sensory symptoms which cannot be explained by another mental or medical disorder and the clinical examination shows incompatibility between symptoms and recognized neurological and medical conditions.
- The term "conversion" stands for the conversion of anxiety arising from the psychic conflict into a loss of function of a body part.
- Conversion disorder is characterized by primary gain and secondary gain.
- By converting internal conflicts into physical symptoms, the patient keeps internal conflicts out of awareness and this is known as **primary gain**.
- The patient receives benefits as a result of assuming sick role (e.g., being excused from daily responsibilities and receiving support and care that might not otherwise be expected) and this is known as **secondary gain**.
- The patients appear inappropriately unconcerned about their physical symptoms in conversion disorder. This phenomenon is known as ***La belle indifference*** and is characteristic (but not pathognomonic) of conversion disorder.

SELF-ASSESSMENT

1. Case-based Questions

   A 50-year-old male was referred by the cardiologist. The patient visited the cardiac outpatient department with a complaint of chest pain for the last 1 year. The patient had preoccupation that he has a severe cardiac illness and he was worried that he will die soon. He was evaluated by many general physicians and was reassured that he has no cardiac illness. The cardiologist performed a comprehensive health check-up of the patient with detailed history, physical, and system examination as well as relevant investigations, that is, electrocardiogram (ECG), Treadmill test (TMT), and coronary angiography, and all the findings were normal. The patient continued to have a preoccupation with having a serious cardiac illness. He was referred to psychiatry OPD and psychiatric history and examination found no abnormality other than a preoccupation of having a severe cardiac illness. The patient has no comorbid medical disorder and has no history of any substance abuse or addiction. He has no past history of psychiatric illness.

   a. What is your provisional diagnosis?
   b. Discuss the clinical features of the disorder.
   c. How will you manage this patient?
2. Describe the clinical features and treatment of conversion disorder.
3. Write short notes on:
   a. Factitious disorder
   b. Somatic symptom disorder
   c. Psychological factors affecting other medical conditions

Chapter 17

Feeding and Eating Disorders

Arshad Hussain · Yuman Kawoos

Eating disorders represent a wide range of conditions where a person is excessively preoccupied with body weight, shape, eating behaviors, or the type of food that is taken. People who suffer from eating disorders spend a lot of time thinking about their food intake and the consequences associated with it.

Various eating disorders are anorexia nervosa (AN), bulimia nervosa, pica, binge-eating disorder, rumination disorder, and avoidant/restrictive food intake disorder (AFRID).

ANOREXIA NERVOSA

The term AN is derived from the Greek term for loss of appetite, but the term is a misnomer since appetite loss is not found classically in the disorder.

Epidemiology

A 12-month prevalence of AN is 0.4% in young females. The lifetime prevalence of AN is 0.5%–2% with a peak age of onset of 13–18 years. It is more common in females as compared to males, with female to male ratio 10 : 1.

Etiology

The exact etiology of eating disorders is not known, although interplay between biological, social, and psychological factors has been implicated.

Biological Relatives of patients with eating disorders have an increased risk of inheriting the disorder. Twin studies have estimated heritability of AN between 33% and 84%. Abnormalities of the hypothalamic-pituitary axis, gonadotropin hormones, and other neuroendocrine dysfunctions have been seen.

Social factors Factors like society's emphasis on thinness and exercise have been found to play a role in the causation of AN.

Psychological Psychologically, it is thought that many patients experience their bodies under the control of their parents and starvation may be an effort to gain validation of their individuality and uniqueness.

Clinical Features and Diagnosis

Patients with AN have an intense fear of gaining weight and becoming obese even though having significantly low weight. The patient has a disturbance in the way in which one's body weight or shape is experienced. They lose weight by decreasing the total food intake relative to requirements, leading to significantly low body weight for age and gender. Some patients are not able to restrict their food intake and typically engage in binge eating followed by purging behaviors. Patients abuse laxatives or diuretics and engage in self-induced vomiting secretly.

A patient is brought to a physician with complaints of weight loss or amenorrhea. Patients develop physical signs as the disease progresses such as hypotension, hypothermia, bradycardia, delayed capillary filling, and lanugo hair. Salivary gland enlargement, dental enamel erosion, and scarring on the dorsum of hand (**Russell's sign**) may be present in individuals who self-induce vomiting. In severe cases, electrolyte abnormalities, ECG changes like QTc prolongation, fatigue, mild cognitive dulling, and seizures can occur.

Subtypes

Restricting type No recurrent episodes of binge eating and purging in the last 3 months.

Binge-eating/purging type Recurrent episodes of binge eating and purging in the last 3 months.

Severity

The level of severity is based on BMI in adults.

- **Mild:** BMI ≥ 17 kg/m^2
- **Moderate:** BMI > 16–16.99 kg/m^2
- **Severe:** BMI > 15–15.99 kg/m^2
- **Extreme:** BMI < 15 kg/m^2

Diagnostic Markers

The following laboratory abnormalities may be observed in AN and presence of the diagnostic factors given in Box 17.1 may serve to increase diagnostic confidence.

Treatment

A holistic approach is needed to treat such patients. The family needs to be actively involved in the management plan.

Hospitalization In some instances, hospitalization of the patient is required for restoring electrolyte imbalances, dehydration, and maintaining hemodynamics. As a general rule, patients of AN who are 20% below expected weight for their height are recommended hospitalization. Rapid weight gain is not recommended in such cases.

Box 17.1 Diagnostic markers in anorexia nervosa

Hematology
- Leukopenia with lymphocytosis
- Mild anemia
- Thrombocytopenia

Serum chemistry
- Increased blood urea nitrogen (dehydration)
- Hypomagnesemia
- Hypozincemia
- Hypophosphatemia
- Hyperamylasemia
- Hypercholesterolemia
- *Metabolic alkalosis (elevated serum bicarbonates)
- *Hypochloremia
- *Hypokalemia

Endocrine
- Decreased T_3 and elevated reverse T_3
- Low serum estrogen

ECG
- Bradycardia
- QTc prolongation

Bone mass
- Osteopenia
- Osteoporosis

EEG
- Diffuse abnormalities reflecting metabolic encephalopathy

*Due to self-induced vomiting.

A diet of 1,500–1,800 kcal/day consumed in three to four supervised meals is considered a safe starting point for AN. The patient should be monitored for signs of refeeding syndrome (Box 17.2), which is a rare but fatal complication.

Psychotherapy Cognitive behavioral therapy (CBT) is the most extensively studied and utilized psychotherapeutic technique for treatment of AN. CBT helps the patient to challenge distorted thoughts and alter distorted behaviors (e.g., eating, exercise, and compensatory behaviors).

Medications Antidepressants like selective serotonin reuptake inhibitors (SSRIs) have been used to treat AN. Antidepressants do not have a significant impact on the core symptoms of the illness and do not help in weight gain or reduce anxiety and depression. Weight restoration itself reduces symptoms of anxiety and depression. SSRIs, even after weight restoration, do not offer significant effect on relapse prevention. Olanzapine has shown promising results in promoting weight gain and reducing obsessionality which often marks the illness, but olanzapine use for treatment of AN remains under study.

BULIMIA NERVOSA

People with bulimia nervosa have recurrent episodes of eating large quantities of food followed by compensatory behaviors (e.g., forced vomiting, excess use of laxatives, doing excess exercise, fasting for long periods, or a combination of these behaviors).

Epidemiology

The 12-month prevalence of bulimia nervosa is 1%–1.5% in young females. Its onset is in late adolescence as compared to AN. Nearly half of bulimia patients have a comorbid mood disorder (bipolar and depressive disorders) and more than half have comorbid anxiety disorders.

Etiology

Biological It has been seen that first-degree relatives of bulimia patients have increased risk for inheriting the disorder. Also, raised endorphin levels are seen in some bulimia patients who vomit and raised endorphin levels may mediate the feeling of well-being after vomiting in these patients. Patients with bulimia nervosa may have delayed gastric emptying, increased stomach capacity, and reduced

Box 17.2 Signs and symptoms of refeeding syndrome

- **Lab abnormalities:** Hypophosphatemia, hypokalemia, hypomagnesemia, thiamine deficiency, glucose intolerance
- **ECG abnormalities:** Dysrhythmias, torsades de pointes
- **Physical symptoms:** Edema, respiratory difficulty, muscular weakness, gastrointestinal disturbances (constipation, diarrhea)

secretion of cholecystokinin (a hormone that helps to signal satiety after eating food).

Psychological Some patients with bulimia nervosa are psychologically not able to separate from their parents and the regurgitation may represent wish to separate. Bulimia nervosa patients tend to exhibit high levels of novelty seeking, impulsivity, and harm avoidance.

Clinical Features and Diagnosis

Bulimia nervosa is characterized by recurrent episodes of binge eating occurring at least once a week for 3 months. Binge eating is eating an amount of food that is definitely larger than most people would eat in a similar period of time under similar circumstances. Binge eating is followed by recurrent inappropriate compensatory behaviors in order to prevent weight gain. Compensatory behaviors include self-induced vomiting, misuse of laxatives, diuretics, fasting, or excessive exercise.

People suffering from bulimia nervosa have low to normal body weight. They present with chronically inflamed sore throat, swollen salivary glands in the neck, worn tooth enamel, and decaying teeth as a result of exposure to stomach acid. These patients usually have intestinal distress from laxative abuse, and rectal prolapse has been seen in some individuals with this disorder.

Treatment

Psychotherapy

Psychotherapy has been found to show significant impact on the outcome of illness. CBT helps to identify and restructure distorted thoughts and beliefs that may be maintaining the unhealthy behaviors. It has been used in combination with SSRIs to improve the symptomatology in such patients. CBT is beneficial in the individual as well as group setting. Interpersonal psychotherapy (IPT) reduces binge eating and purging.

Pharmacotherapy

Fluoxetine in doses of 20–60 mg is FDA approved for treatment of bulimia nervosa. Apart from decreasing binge eating and purging, it also helps in improving comorbid depression and anxiety. Bupropion is contraindicated for bulimia nervosa due to increased risk of seizures in patients who are actively purging.

PICA

It involves consumption of non-nutritive substances over a considerable time period of at least 1 month to a level which warrants clinical attention. The substances ingested vary as per age and availability, and include chalk, clay, paper, soap, paint, coal, pebbles, or ice. The eating of non-nutritive substances must be inappropriate to age and should not be culturally acceptable practice. A cut-off age of 2 years is suggested for diagnosis of pica to exclude the normal mouthing behavior of children seen in that age group. The eating of nonnutritive substances has also been seen in other mental disorders like schizophrenia and intellectual disability, but a separate diagnosis of pica should be made only if the eating behavior is sufficiently severe to warrant additional clinical attention. Pica has been associated with mineral deficiencies like zinc or iron.

Clinical Significance

Pica is associated with complications like lead poisoning due to ingestion of lead paints, intestinal obstruction, or perforation because of ingesting clay or pebbles and trichobezoar due to ingestion of hair.

Treatment

Treatment of the complications is the first priority. Lead poisoning is treated by chelating agents like ethylenediaminetetraacetic acid (EDTA) and intestinal obstruction may need surgery. After treating them, we treat the underlying disorder causing pica. In some patients, correcting an iron or zinc deficiency cures pica. Behavioral treatment approaches like mild aversion therapy (mild electric shock or an emetic drug) show improvement in some.

RUMINATION DISORDER

Rumination disorder is characterized by repeated regurgitation of food over a period of at least 1 month. The patient rechews, re-swallows, or spits out the regurgitated food. Rumination disorder is diagnosed if regurgitation is not explained by gastrointestinal or medical condition (gastroesophageal reflux, pyloric stenosis). Rumination disorder cannot be diagnosed in the presence of another eating disorder.

BINGE EATING DISORDER

The patients with binge eating disorder have episodes of binge eating, but unlike bulimia nervosa these binge eating episodes are not followed by compensatory mechanisms.

AVOIDANT/RESTRICTIVE FOOD INTAKE DISORDER

AFRID is characterized by persistent disturbance in eating behavior (e.g., apparent lack of interest in eating; avoidance based on sensory characteristics of food; concerns about aversive consequences of eating), leading to clinically significant consequences (e.g., weight loss, nutritional deficiency, psychosocial impairment). In DSM IV, AFRID was referred as feeding disorder of infancy or early childhood.

KEY POINTS

- Anorexia nervosa (AN), bulimia nervosa, and binge-eating disorder, rumination disorder, avoidant/restrictive food intake disorder (ARFID), and pica are various eating disorders.

Anorexia Nervosa

- AN is restriction of energy intake relative to requirements, leading to significantly low body weight.
- In AN, the patient has either an intense fear of gaining weight or of becoming fat or persistent behavior that interferes with weight gain, even though at significantly low weight.
- In AN, the patient has disturbance in the way in which one's body weight or shape is experienced.
- AN is of two types: restricting type and binge-eating/purging type.
- The level of severity is based on BMI in adults.

- The patients of AN who are 20% below expected weight for their height are recommended hospitalization.
- Patient should be monitored for signs of refeeding syndrome, which is rare but with fatal complication.
- Cognitive behavioral therapy (CBT) helps AN patients to challenge the distorted thoughts and alter distorted behaviors (e.g., eating, exercise, and compensatory behaviors).

Bulimia Nervosa

- People with bulimia nervosa have recurrent episodes of eating large quantities of food followed by compensatory behaviors (e.g., forced vomiting, excess use of laxatives).

Pica

- Pica is consumption of non-nutritive substances for at least 1 month to a level which warrants clinical attention. The substances ingested include chalk, clay, paper, soap, paint, coal, pebbles, or ice.
- A cut-off age of 2 years is suggested for diagnosis of pica to exclude the normal mouthing behavior of children seen in that age group.
- Pica is associated with complications like lead poisoning due to ingestion of lead paints, intestinal obstruction, or perforation because of ingesting clay or pebbles and trichobezoars due to ingestion of hair.
- Treating complications is the priority. Lead poisoning is treated by chelating agents like ethylenediaminetetraacetic acid (EDTA) and intestinal obstruction may need surgery. After treating them, we treat the underlying disorder causing pica.
- In some patients, correcting an iron or zinc deficiency cures pica.
- Behavioral treatment approaches like mild aversion therapy (mild electric shock or an emetic drug) show improvement in some patients of pica.

SELF-ASSESSMENT

1. Case-based Questions
   A 25-year-old female is brought to psychiatry OPD with a history of refusing to eat leading to severe weight loss. As per parents, these symptoms started 6 months back. She avoids eating high-calorie food and also does extensive exercise. Her food intake gradually decreased and now she consumes boiled vegetables and skimmed milk yogurt only. Her BMI is 15.5 kg/m^2. In spite of such a low BMI, she is not willing to increase her food intake fearing weight gain. She keeps on measuring her waist daily. Her menstrual periods are scanty and infrequent.
   a. What is your provisional diagnosis?
   b. Discuss the clinical features of the disorder.
   c. How will you manage this patient?
2. Describe the etiology, clinical features, and treatment of bulimia nervosa. How will you differentiate bulimia nervosa from binge-eating disorder?
3. Write short notes on:
   a. Pica
   b. Rumination disorder
   c. Avoidant/restrictive food intake disorder
   d. Etiology of anorexia nervosa

Chapter 18

Elimination Disorders

Sandeep Kumar Goyal · Jitendra Jeenger · Ankit Mangla

Elimination disorders include enuresis and encopresis. The first reference of nocturnal enuresis (NE) can be found in Ebers Papyrus of 1550 BC. The term enuresis is derived from the Greek word *enourein*, meaning "to void urine."

ENURESIS

Enuresis is repeated voiding of urine during the day or at night into bed or clothes in children aged ≥ 5 years. It can be involuntary or intentional. According to new terminology of the International Children's Continence Society (ICCS), the terms nocturnal incontinence and enuresis are now synonymous.

Epidemiology

Enuresis is a very common but often an underestimated disorder. Prevalence of enuresis is around 10% in children aged 5–7 years and decreases to 5% in children aged 10 years. Most of the individuals become continent by adolescence, but approximately 1% of the patients remains incontinent in adulthood. The prevalence of enuresis is more in males as compared to females. The relative risk of having a child with enuresis is more for previously enuretic fathers than for previously enuretic mothers. Attention deficit/hyperactivity disorder (ADHD) is the most commonly reported comorbidity which is present in nearly 20% of children with enuresis.

Etiology

Environmental Delayed toilet training and psychosocial stress are common environmental factors associated with enuresis. The birth of a sibling, the start of school, the breakup of the family, and moving to a new home are common psychosocial stressors in young children.

Genetic Enuresis has a strong genetic component. The concordance rate is more in monozygotic twins than in dizygotic twins. Enuretic children have a delay in the development of normal circadian rhythm of urine production, leading to nocturnal polyuria, and reduced functional bladder capacities with bladder hyperactivity. Overactive bladder and small bladder are common causes of secondary nocturnal enuresis (SNE).

Voluntary, intentional enuresis is present in oppositional defiant disorder (ODD) or a psychotic disorder.

Diagnosis and Clinical Features

As per DSM-5, this behavior should be present at least twice a week for at least three consecutive months. Enuresis is diagnosed if this behavior is not a result of direct effects of a drug, like a diuretic, an antipsychotic, or another medical condition like seizure, diabetes, or spina bifida.

Severity is measured by frequency of urination and quantity is not a diagnostic criterion.

Subtypes

Nocturnal only Enuresis during night-time sleep

Diurnal only During waking hours

Nocturnal and diurnal A combination of nocturnal and diurnal

However, recently NE has also been further classified into monosymptomatic NE (MNE) and non-monosymptomatic NE (NMNE) by the absence or presence of daytime voiding symptoms.

Monosymptomatic nocturnal enuresis Enuresis with no daytime or other lower urinary tract symptoms and without the history of bladder dysfunction.

Non-monosymptomatic nocturnal enuresis Enuresis with daytime or any other lower urinary tract symptoms.

Lower urinary tract symptoms relevant to this definition are increased/decreased voiding frequency, daytime incontinence, urgency, hesitancy, straining, a weak stream, intermittency, holding maneuvers, a feeling of incomplete emptying, post-micturition dribble, and genital or lower urinary tract pain.

Diagnostic Evaluation in Urinary Incontinence in Children

A detailed history of enuresis (onset, frequency, the presence of daytime symptoms, predominant period of night when bed-wetting occurs, and family history of enuresis) is necessary, which can be taken by careful history taking.

Physical examination is essential in identifying any anatomical disorders of spine or external genitalia.

Age adjusted bladder capacity or expected bladder capacity can be calculated by the following formula:

For children >1 year:

$$\text{Capacity (mL)} = [\text{Age (in years)} + 2] \times 30$$

Bladder diary A bladder diary (Fig. 18.1) is a tool used for better understanding of symptoms of overactive bladder (OAB); it is essential for the assessment of presence of lower urinary tract symptoms. It is a daily record of the patient's fluid input and urinary output which helps to identify issues with urinary urgency, urinary frequency, and incontinence episodes.

Date	Time	Voided volume	Fluid intake	Urinary leakage
01.01.2020	06:00	450 mL	–	No
	07:00	–	Water 150 mL	No
	08:00	–	–	Yes
	09:00	150 mL	–	No
	09:30	–	Coffee 50 mL	–
	...			
	...			
	...			

Figure 18.1 Example of a bladder diary.

Urinalysis is required to rule out urinary tract infections and glycosuria.

Ultrasound KUB This is required if history and examination are suggestive of non-monosymptomatic enuresis (daytime symptoms). USG of the bladder, when the child feels that bladder is full, can be used to estimate functional bladder capacity which can be compared with expected bladder capacity as per age of the child. If the actual bladder capacity is less than 50% of the expected capacity, it is indicative of small bladder.

Uroflowmetry If neurogenic bladder is suspected.

Differential Diagnosis

Neurogenic bladder or another medical conditions producing polyuria Diagnosis of enuresis is not made in the presence of neurogenic bladder or any medical condition producing polyuria or urgency (diabetes mellitus, diabetes insipidus, or urinary tract infection). However, diagnosis of enuresis can be made if urinary incontinence was present before the onset of the medical condition and/or urinary incontinence persists after the treatment of the medical condition.

Course and Prognosis

Enuresis can be primary or secondary. Primary enuresis is the type in which an individual has never been continent since birth (never dry), whereas in secondary enuresis an individual develops incontinence after a period of being urinary continent (previously dry) for at least 6–12 months. The rate of spontaneous remission is 5%–10% per year, and in approximately 1% of the cases, enuresis continues into adulthood.

Treatment

The organic causes of enuresis should be ruled out. The first step is to review the appropriate toilet training. If toilet training was not done correctly, parents and patient should be given adequate toilet training.

Behavior Therapy

The Bell and Pad method of conditioning is the primary intervention. A pad attached to a bell is placed on the bed, and when enuresis happens, moisture completes a circuit in the pad and the ringing of the bell wakes the child. On continuous use, the child learns to awaken before wetting.

Use of alarm clock set after 2–3 hours of sleep, when maximum bladder capacity is expected, is shown to produce results equal to bell and pad method.

Evening fluid restriction, micturition before sleep, and rewards for dry nights are also useful in the treatment of enuresis.

Pharmacotherapy

When the bell and pad method is not successful or feasible, pharmacotherapy is indicated.

Imipramine in the dosage of 75–125 mg shows positive response in the majority of the children. Imipramine can be started at 25 mg and can be gradually increased as per the response. A pretreatment baseline ECG is also recommended. The maximum dose is 5 mg/kg body weight per day and ECG monitoring is recommended at doses greater than 3.5 mg/kg/day.

Desmopressin acetate (DDAVP) is now considered the first-line drug for enuresis, as it is remarkably free of risks and adverse effects, but potentially dangerous hyponatremia may result if the drug is combined with excessive fluid intake. Treatment with DDAVP produces results comparable to the bell and pad method. It is present as a nasal spray and oral tablets. Recently, a sublingual preparation DDAVP Melt is also available, which has better efficacy and lower side effect profile.

Hyponatremic seizures are reported with long-term use of DDAVP. FDA concluded that intranasal formulation is no longer indicated in the treatment of primary nocturnal enuresis (PNE). Treatment with DDAVP tablet should be halted during illnesses, which can produce a disturbance in the fluid or electrolyte balance. The patient should be advised not to use more than 250 mL of fluid at night when DDAVP is used. Periodic monitoring of serum sodium would be prudent.

Anticholinergic drugs are the first-line treatment for overactive bladder; they act by suppressing premature detrusor contractions and increasing the bladder capacity by antagonizing cholinergic muscarinic receptors in bladder, thus relieving the symptoms of urgency, frequency, and also NE. **Oxybutynin** has a well-documented efficacy in the treatment of detrusor overactivity and is a drug of the first choice in patients with this disorder.

Reboxetine, a noradrenaline reuptake inhibitor, is found to be effective in cases resistant to other therapies. In one study, reboxetine monotherapy at a dose of 4–8 mg at bedtime resulted in dryness in 32% of the children who had enuresis that was resistant to enuresis alarm, desmopressin, or anticholinergics.

ENCOPRESIS

Encopresis is repeated passage of feces into inappropriate places.

Epidemiology

Approximately 1% of the 5 years old have encopresis, and it is more common in males than in females.

Etiology

Factors associated with encopresis include early and harsh bowel training, neurological delay, ADHD, conduct disorder, psychosocial stressors, and childhood sexual abuse.

Painful defecation can lead to constipation and a cycle of withholding behavior, which makes encopresis more likely.

Diagnosis and Clinical Features

As per DSM-5, this behavior should be present at least once every month for at least three consecutive months. The chronological age of the child must be at least 4 years or equivalent developmental level. It can be involuntary or intentional.

Subtypes

1. **With constipation and overflow incontinence (retentive encopresis):** This is the most common type of encopresis (approximately 75%). Feces in this subtype are characteristically poorly formed and leakage occurs mostly during the day. The incontinence resolves after treatment of constipation.
2. **Without constipation and overflow incontinence (nonretentive encopresis):** Feces are likely to be of normal form and consistency. Non-retentive encopresis is usually associated with ODD, conduct disorder. The child may

use this type of behavior as a control mechanism.

DSM-5 recognizes the two above mentioned subtypes, although there is a third subtype also, in which children are encopretic because they cannot adequately control the anal sphincter or do not recognize the need to defecate in time.

Diagnostic Evaluation

Physical examination and abdominal X-ray are useful to assess the degree of constipation present. Barium enema or anorectal manography may be used to exclude other medical conditions such as Hirschsprung's disease.

Differential Diagnosis

Encopresis with constipation and overflow incontinence can be caused by faulty nutrition, stenosis of the anus or rectum, adverse effects of medicines, non-gastrointestinal medical disorders (endocrine or neurological, e.g., abnormal innervation of the anorectal region, neuronal intestinal dysplasia, or spinal cord damage), and Hirschsprung's disease. In Hirschsprung's disease, signs appear shortly after birth.

Course and Prognosis

Encopresis can be primary or secondary. Primary encopresis is the type in which an individual has never been fecal continent. Secondary encopresis is the type in which the individual develops incontinence after a period of fecal continence.

Treatment

Treatment is primarily behavioral approach consisting of educational and physiological components. Educational interventions of the child and family are aimed at correcting misconceptions and reducing the anxiety of soiling. Physiological intervention is initial bowel catharsis followed by a daily dose of laxatives. Laxatives are not necessary if the patient is not constipated. Behavioral component involves daily timed interval on the toilet and rewards (star charts) on success. Lifestyle modifications include adequate fluid and dietary fiber.

Pharmacological treatment for encopresis is not extensively studied. Few case reports describe the role of imipramine at doses of 25–75 mg. Imipramine can be helpful in non-retentive encopresis.

KEY POINTS

Enuresis

- Enuresis is repeated voiding of urine during the day or at night into bed or clothes in children aged ≥ 5 years. It can be involuntary or intentional.
- Delayed toilet training and psychosocial stress (the birth of a sibling, the start of school, and the breakup of the family) are common environmental factors associated with enuresis.
- Enuresis has a strong genetic component.
- Enuresis can be primary or secondary. Primary enuresis is the type in which an individual has never been continent since birth (never dry), whereas in secondary enuresis an individual develops incontinence after a period of being urinary continent (previously dry) for at least 6-12 months.

- The organic causes of enuresis should be ruled out before starting treatment.
- The parents and patient should be given adequate toilet training, if toilet training was not done correctly.
- The Bell and Pad method of conditioning is the primary intervention.
- Use of alarm clock set after 2–3 hours of sleep, when maximum bladder capacity is expected, is shown to produce results equal to bell and pad method.
- Evening fluid restriction, micturition before sleep, and rewards for dry nights are also useful in the treatment of enuresis.
- Imipramine in the dosage of 75–125 mg shows positive response in the majority of the children.
- Desmopressin acetate (DDAVP) is now considered the first-line drug for enuresis. Treatment with DDAVP produces results comparable to the bell and pad method.
- Oxybutynin has a well-documented efficacy in the treatment of detrusor overactivity and is a drug of the first choice in patients with this disorder.
- Reboxetine, a noradrenaline reuptake inhibitor, is found to be effective in cases resistant to other therapies.

Encopresis

- Encopresis is repeated passage of feces into inappropriate places.
- DSM-5 recognizes two subtypes: With constipation and overflow incontinence (retentive encopresis) and without constipation and overflow incontinence (non-retentive encopresis).
- Treatment of encopresis is primarily behavioral approach consisting of educational and physiological components.
- Educational interventions of the child and family are aimed at correcting misconceptions and reducing the anxiety of soiling.
- Behavioral component involves daily timed interval on the toilet and rewards (star charts) on success. Lifestyle modifications include adequate fluid and dietary fiber.

SELF-ASSESSMENT

1. Case-based Questions
   A 7-year-old child presents to OPD with complaints of bed-wetting at night. Bed-wetting occurs daily at nighttime only. His mother reports that he has never been continent since birth. The patient feels embarrassed by his symptom of bed-wetting and avoids night stay at relative's place.
   a. What is your provisional diagnosis?
   b. How will you evaluate the child?
   c. Describe the various treatment options.
2. Define encopresis and discuss the etiology, types, and treatment of encopresis.

Chapter 19

Sleep and Sleep Disorders

Ravi Gupta

Sleep is a state of altered consciousness, which is characterized by the absence of communication to and from the environment. This means that events occurring in the surroundings are not perceived by the brain. It is different from coma by the fact that arousal is possible during sleep by any extraneous or internal stimulus.

Humans spend nearly one-third of their lives in sleep, and sleep plays a vital role in health. Sleep deprivation and sleep disorders have been linked to many adverse consequences that include cognitive, emotional, cardiovascular, and metabolic adverse effects (Table 19.1). Despite this, sleep disorders are often missed or ignored in clinical practice. In this chapter, the clinical presentation of common sleep disorders shall be discussed along with management strategies.

Table 19.1 Consequences of sleep deprivation and untreated sleep disorders

Domain	Symptoms
Cognitive	• Poor attention and concentration • Memory lapses • Compromised information processing
Emotional	• Anxiety • Depressed mood • Perceptual disturbances • Impaired quality of life • Fibromyalgia • Somatic symptom disorder • Enhanced pain perception
Cardiovascular	• Systemic hypertension • Pulmonary hypertension • Atherosclerosis • Cardiac arrhythmias
Cerebrovascular	• Stroke
Metabolic	• Metabolic syndrome • Impaired glycemic control • Diabetes mellitus
Economic	• Work absenteeism • Increased health resource utilization • Accidents

PHYSIOLOGY OF SLEEP

Physiological Processes Governing Sleep

The onset of sleep is dependent on the interaction of two different processes: **circadian process** and **homeostatic process**. The circadian process is governed by the suprachiasmatic nucleus, which is the master clock in the body. Environmental signals like light, food, and social cues influence the functioning of the suprachiasmatic nucleus. These influencing factors are known as zeitgebers. In the absence of light, suprachiasmatic nucleus sends signals to the pineal body to release melatonin, a sleep-inducing hormone. That is the reason we fall asleep at night.

On the other hand, sleep debt or time elapsed since last restful sleep regulates the homeostatic process. Longer the person is awake, higher the sleep debt and higher the sleep pressure. That is why people fall asleep when they are sleep deprived.

To induce sleep, these two mechanisms require being in synchrony.

Sleep Architecture

Physiologically, sleep is characterized by two distinct stages known as rapid eye movement (REM) and non-rapid eye movement (NREM) sleep. NREM sleep is further divided into three distinct stages—N1, N2, and N3 sleep (Table 19.2). Normally, sleep starts with N1 stage, progressively goes to the N3 stage, and then to REM sleep. NREM and REM stages alternate at the interval of 90–120 minutes (Fig. 19.1).

Table 19.2 Stages of sleep: Sleep architecture

S. No.	Sleep Stage	Remarks	Electrophysiological characters	Physiological changes
1.	N1	Normally, sleep initiates through the N1 stage and makes 5%–10% of total sleep time	Slowing of EEG to theta range, increasing synchrony, the appearance of vertex waves, and reduction of muscle tone	Regularization of breathing, heart rate, and lowering of blood pressure
2.	N2	The highest proportion of all sleep stages varying between 50%–60%	Further slowing and increasing synchronization of EEG, K complexes and sleep spindles, and reduction of muscle tone	Further lowering of respiratory and heart rate and lowered blood pressure
3.	N3	Occupies 20%–30% of total sleep time; maximum in the first half of sleep period, known as deep sleep	Characterized by the appearance of delta waves and a reduction of muscle tone	Regularization of the above physiological activities; secretion of growth hormone

(*Continued*)

Table 19.2 *(Continued)*

S. No.	Sleep Stage	Remarks	Electrophysiological characters	Physiological changes
4.	Rapid eye movement (REM) sleep	Also known as dreaming sleep; occupies 20%–25% proportion of total sleep time; more toward morning time	Low-voltage mixed frequency activity in EEG; the appearance of REMs and profound muscle atonia	All physiological activities variable; brain metabolism higher than non-REM sleep

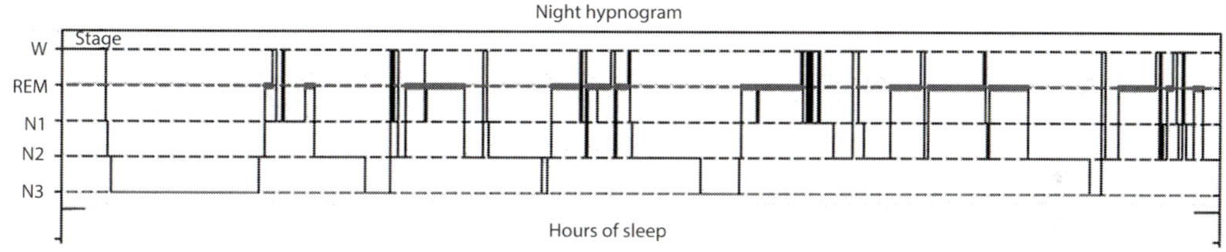

Figure 19.1 Hypnogram showing cyclical sleep stages.

Time from the sleep onset to the first epoch of REM sleep is called **REM latency**. A short REM latency can result from withdrawal from tricyclic antidepressants (TCAs) or monoamine oxidase inhibitor (MAOI), amphetamines, barbiturates, and alcohol. Patients with narcolepsy also have short REM latency. Long REM latency results from use of REM-suppressing medications, including TCAs, MAOIs, amphetamine, barbiturates, and alcohol.

SLEEP DISORDERS

Sleep disorders are characterized by any of the following symptoms:

- Reduction in total sleep time: Insomnia
- Increment in total sleep time: Hypersomnia
- Mismatch between sleep schedule and environmental timing: Circadian rhythm sleep disorders
- Sleep-related breathing disorder: Sleep apnea
- Abnormal simple movements during sleep: Sleep-related movement disorders
- Abnormal complex movements/behaviors during sleep: Parasomnias

Insomnia

Insomnia is characterized by a delay in initiating sleep (>30 min spent to fall asleep at usual bedtime), difficulty maintaining sleep (>30 min spent awake after sleep initiation), or waking up earlier than the usual wake-time (>30 min earlier than usual wake time) when the person has adequate opportunity to sleep. Nighttime symptoms must be present at least three nights a week and negatively influence the cognition, mood, and health the subsequent day. In the absence of daytime symptoms, insomnia cannot be diagnosed. When symptoms are present for more than 3 months, it is termed as *chronic insomnia*.

Insomnia of shorter duration is termed as *short-term* or *acute insomnia*.

Types

Earlier, insomnia was differentiated into *primary* and *secondary insomnias. Primary insomnia* was considered to arise de novo without any apparent pathology. *Secondary insomnia* was considered to represent sleep disturbance due to some other pathology, (e.g., secondary to psychiatric disorders, poor sleep hygiene, medical disorders, and substance abuse). Advancement in the pathophysiological understanding of insomnia has shown that this classification was arbitrary, as pathophysiological overlapping exists across different types of insomnias. Thus, *International Classification of Sleep Disorders, 3rd edition (ICSD-3)* classifies insomnia in two subtypes—*short-term* and *chronic*. Whenever a person reports that insomnia is clinically significant, it is diagnosed as an independent disorder even in the presence of other psychiatric and medical disorders.

Pathophysiology

Pathophysiologically, insomnia is a state of hyperarousal, characterized by the absence or reduction of metabolism in the cortical areas during sleep where it is otherwise expected. It is precipitated in a genetically predisposed person due to some acute incidents (e.g., stress, pain, and substance use, to name a few). Some of the persons with insomnia may develop pathological behaviors that perpetuate insomnia (e.g., abusing stimulants or hypnotics, become worried of not able to get sleep, and spending excessive time in bed in an attempt to fall asleep). Perpetuating factors help in the transformation of acute insomnia into chronic.

Differential Diagnosis

Insomnia must be differentiated from other sleep disorders (e.g., sleep deprivation, short sleepers, circadian rhythm sleep disorders, and restless legs syndrome [RLS], to name a few).

Treatment

Treatment of insomnia varies according to the type of insomnia. However, regardless of the type, an attempt is made to identify the precipitating and perpetuating factors, and they should be addressed. For short-term insomnia, hypnotics are the drug of choice. Two different types of hypnotic agents are available—benzodiazepines and "Z" drugs.

For chronic insomnia, cognitive behavior therapy for insomnia (CBT-I) is preferred.

Hypersomnia

Hypersomnia is characterized by an increase in total sleep time and excessive daytime sleepiness in the absence of any disturbance in nighttime sleep or circadian rhythm sleep disorders. The three main causes for hypersomnia are narcolepsy, idiopathic hypersomnia, and Kleine–Levin syndrome (KLS).

Narcolepsy

Narcolepsy is characterized by an irresistible urge to fall asleep during the daytime, lasting for at least 3 months. There may be multiple such episodes in a day and naps are usually refreshing. In addition, the patient has short REM latency or sleep onset REM periods (SOREMPs) on objective testing by multiple sleep latency test (MSLT). During MSLT, where five opportunities for napping are provided spread across a day, at least two naps must show SOREMPs. Patients with narcolepsy also report sleep paralysis, which is defined as the inability to move any part of the body on waking up. It is a short-lasting frightening condition where people feel as if somebody is sitting on his or her chest or feeling of breathlessness. It occurs due to the maintenance of generalized atonia of REM sleep during wakefulness. After awakening, this condition is terminated by any external or internal stimulus. Because of short REM latency, patients also report dream-like feeling at sleep onset (hypnogogic hallucinations). Based on the presence of cataplexy, narcolepsy is divided into two subtypes—narcolepsy with or without cataplexy. Cataplexy is a sudden loss of muscle tone resulting in dropping of jaw or buckling of knees or fall precipitated by an emotional stimulus.

Pathophysiology Pathophysiologically, narcolepsy is an autoimmune disorder characterized by the loss of hypocretin neurons in the posterior hypothalamus. At times, other medical conditions such as Prader–Willi syndrome, multiple sclerosis, myotonic dystrophy, or hypothalamic injury may precipitate symptoms of narcolepsy.

Treatment Treatment of narcolepsy consists of improving daytime sleepiness, improving nighttime sleep, reducing sleep deprivation, and addressing cataplexy if present.

Gamma-hydroxybutyric acid (GHBA) is the drug of choice for narcolepsy that improves nocturnal sleep maintenance and daytime alertness. In addition, stimulants like modafinil may be used to improve daytime alertness. Cataplexy may be addressed by selective serotonin reuptake inhibitors. In addition, planned naps may help in reducing irresistible urges of sleep.

Idiopathic Hypersomnia

It is characterized by prolonged periods of sleep (>11 hours/day) or excessive daytime sleepiness. These patients have short sleep latency (<8 min) during the MSLT, but unlike narcolepsy have less than two episodes of SOREMPs. These patients report prolonged **sleep inertia** (take longer than 1 hour to be alert after waking up) and have sleep efficiency >90%. Sleep efficiency is the proportion of time spent in sleep divided by the time spent in bed with the intention to stay asleep. This condition often starts in late adolescence and remains fairly stable over the years. Pathophysiology is poorly understood. It must be differentiated from other disorders of hypersomnolence, obstructive sleep apnea (OSA), and insufficient sleep syndrome. Stimulants are used for the management of symptoms.

Kleine–Levin Syndrome

It is characterized by episodic hypersomnia (>11 hours/day) lasting for at least 2 days to 5 weeks. These episodes usually occur at least once in every 18 months. During the episode, patients show other symptoms such as perceptual disturbances, cognitive abnormalities, hyperphagia, and hypersexuality. One of these symptoms along with at least two episodes of hypersomnia is essential for the diagnosis of KLS. In between the episodes, patients are asymptomatic. This disorder must be differentiated from tumors of the third ventricle, encephalitis, Lyme disease, bipolar disorder, major depressive disorder, substance use disorders, and other causes of hypersomnolence. Carbamazepine and lithium have been found effective in the management of KLS.

Circadian Rhythm Sleep Disorders

As already discussed, all living animals have circadian biological rhythm. This rhythm appears due to the activity of biological clock inside the suprachiasmatic nucleus. The biological clock consists of a cascade of proteins and second messenger systems. Various genes determine the structure and functioning of components of the biological clock. Usually, environmental light and other stimuli entrain (reset) the biological clock every day so that a synchrony is maintained between the subjective timing (night or day determined by the biological clock) and environmental timing. Consequent to entrainment, humans feel sleepy at night.

However, at times people may develop a mismatch between subjective timing and environmental timing. This is dependent on the functionality of the constituents of biological clock that is in turn controlled by genes, learned behavior, and availability of environmental lighting.

Advanced sleep-wake phase disorder (ASWPD) is characterized by early bedtime and early wake time compared to socially acceptable sleep-wake times. For example, these persons go to bed early in the evening and wake up early in the morning. They feel fresh, as long as they are allowed to follow their schedule. However, this schedule imparts significant problems in social, personal, and occupational functioning. Another source of trouble is when they are supposed to remain awake late in the evening because of some obligation. At that time, they feel sleepy. These people are often called "larks." To be a clinically significant condition, this schedule must be present for at least 3 months.

Delayed sleep-wake phase disorder (DSWPD) is characterized by delayed bedtime and delayed wake time. These patients go to bed late at night and wake up late in the morning. They are often termed as "owls." Like ASWPD, these patients have normal total sleep time and refreshing sleep, as long as they are allowed to follow their natural cycle. However, when they have to wake up early in the morning, they feel sleepy and irritable. Symptoms must be present for at least 3 months; and when the person is forced to follow environmental timing the symptoms must interfere with personal, social, and occupational functioning.

ASWPD and DSWPD disorders may be mistaken for either insomnia or hypersomnia. Objective measures using actigraphy are required to make the diagnosis of both the disorders. A combination of hypnotics, stimulants, timed light therapy, and chronotherapy is used for the treatment of these conditions.

Shift work-sleep disorder appears when a person has to work at least partly during usual sleep timing. It appears as a combination of insomnia and hypersomnia. When work-shift overlaps with usual sleep episode, symptoms of sleepiness appear, and when they intend to fall asleep outside usual sleep schedule, symptoms of insomnia are reported. The final output is a reduction in total sleep time. Both symptoms and shift working must be present for at least 3 months to be clinically significant. It should be differentiated from other causes of hypersomnolence and insomnia. Management involves proper spacing of work shifts, the optimal interval between the change of shifts, planned naps, and use of stimulants and hypnotics.

The **jet lag disorder** is characterized by a reduction in the total duration of sleep consequent to travel for at least two time zones, leading to a mismatch between internal biological and environmental clock. Daytime symptoms like fatigue or gastrointestinal disturbances appear within 1–2 days after such travel. Traveling toward east advances the environmental clock while travel to west delays the environmental clock. Thus, depending on the time zone crossed, patients may develop mismatch with the environmental timing. Melatonin may help in the management of the condition.

Sleep-Related Breathing Disorders

Sleep-related breathing disorders include **sleep apnea** (complete cessation of breathing during sleep), **sleep-related hypoventilation** (which is characterized by hypercapnia), and **sleep-related hypoxemia**. Among these, sleep apnea is most important and is discussed here.

Sleep Apnea

Sleep apnea is characterized by periodic cessation of breathing during sleep. Polysomnographically, it may take one of the two forms—OSA and central sleep apnea (CSA). Clinically, OSA presents with complaints of snoring, snorting, nocturnal polyuria, sleep-talking, daytime somnolence or fatigue, morning headache, memory lapses, and reduced libido. However, snoring is frequently absent in patients with CSA, and they often complain of chronically nonrefreshing sleep and frequent awakenings at night along with daytime somnolence. In both conditions, a vigilant bed partner may provide a history of witnessed pauses in breathing during sleep.

OSA is more common as compared to CSA. Obesity, male gender, use of hypnotics, alcohol, smoking, advancing age, micrognathia, and maxillary retrusion are risk factors for the development of OSA. It usually appears due to a combination of a reduction in pharyngeal muscle tone during sleep along with an anatomical reduction in the caliber of the upper airway.

Obesity by an increasing amount of adipose tissue in parapharyngeal pads of fat and tongue (macroglossia) reduces the caliber; micrognathia and maxillary retrusion may reduce the caliber by bringing the tongue and soft palate closer to the posterior pharyngeal wall, respectively.

However, CSA is associated with altered sensitivity of central chemoreceptors to CO_2 and hypocapnia (reduced CO_2 in the blood) during wakefulness. These conditions are often mistaken for insomnia, hypersomnia, depression, somatic symptom disorders, and fibromyalgia.

Whole night level 1 polysomnography is the gold standard for the diagnosis of both conditions (Figs 19.2 and 19.3).

Treatment

Treatment of OSA involves increasing the upper airway caliber by providing air splint during sleep (use of continuous positive airway pressure [CPAP] or

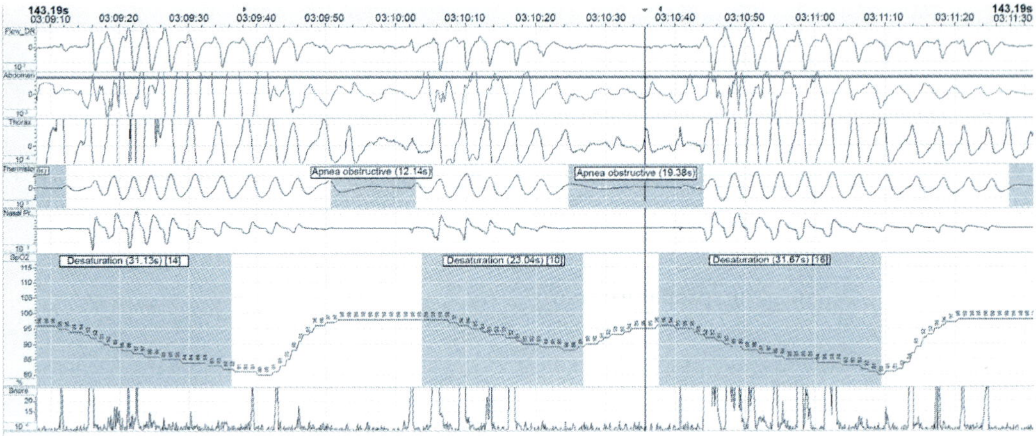

Figure 19.2 2-min epoch showing obstructive sleep apnea. See flattening in thermistor and flow channels with reduction of amplitude in thorax and abdominal channels along with paradoxical respiration. Associated hypoxemia is also evident.

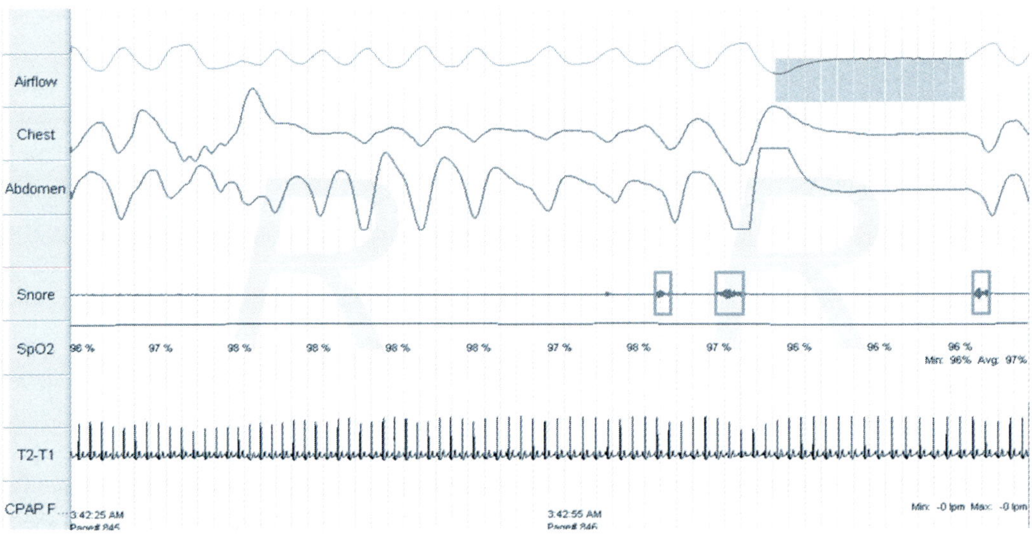

Figure 19.3 2 minutes epoch showing central sleep apnea. Flow channel as well as thorax and abdominal movement depict the absence of signals.

bi-level positive airway pressure), weight reduction, and adopting a healthy lifestyle. Surgery is offered in the presence of a correctable anatomical defect (e.g., adenotonsillar hypertrophy, micrognathia, and maxillary retrusion). In other cases, surgery is usually reserved in cases which do not tolerate PAP therapy. Isolated soft tissue surgeries like palatoplasty, pharyngoplasty, and wedge glossectomy do not offer lasting benefit and recurrence is common. Hence, multistage surgery is preferred.

CSA is managed with the help of CPAP therapy. In addition, medications like carbonic anhydrase inhibitors (e.g., acetazolamide that induce bicarbonaturia and metabolic acidosis) may provide relief in some cases.

Sleep-Related Movement Disorders

These disorders are simple movements that are seen during the preparation for intended sleep, during the transition of sleep and wakefulness, or during sleep. This group includes a number of disorders, (e.g., RLS, sleep starts, sleep-related bruxism, periodic limb movement during sleep, and sleep-related leg cramps).

RLS is characterized by an urge to move legs that are often accompanied by dysesthesia in leg muscles. Symptoms are seen during late evening or night and interfere with sleep onset. Movement of legs or massage brings relief in symptoms as long as these activities are continued and they worsen by periods of rest. These symptoms must be differentiated from leg edema, arthralgia of leg joints, leg myalgia, and varicose veins. Functional deficiency in dopamine in the central nervous system is considered the pathophysiological mechanism of this disorder. Iron deficiency anemia, chronic kidney disease, and rheumatoid arthritis are some of the risk factors for the disorder.

Dopaminergic drugs like levodopa and non-ergot derivatives (e.g., ropinirole, pramipexole) are used for the management of symptoms.

Periodic limb movement disorder (PLMD) is characterized by recurring leg movement during sleep, which interferes with the quality of sleep and consequent daytime symptoms—fatigue, lethargy, sleepiness, and mood changes. In the absence of daytime symptoms, PLMD cannot be diagnosed. PLMD is common among patients having RLS.

Sleep starts are characterized by a sudden jerky movement in the body at the transition between wakefulness to sleep that usually awakens the person from sleep. These are normal variants seen during sleep deprivation, fever, alcohol withdrawal, and stress. Patients need to be reassured only.

Parasomnias

These are complex movements or behaviors or experiences that are seen either during NREM or REM sleep. They are seen at the transition of sleep and wakefulness or within the sleep.

NREM sleep parasomnias are also known as disorders of arousal from NREM sleep. They occur due to incomplete awakening from sleep and continued dream activity that is expressed as behavior. The person has difficulty in waking up and has amnesia for the episode after waking up. It may present in one of these forms—confusional arousal, sleepwalking, sleep terrors, and sleep-related eating disorder.

Confusional arousal is characterized by incomplete awakening and confused behavior during partial wakefulness from sleep. However, unlike sleepwalking, the patient does not move outside bed. Unlike sleep terrors, they do not appear frightened. **Sleep terrors** clinically present as an episode where the person partially awakens from sleep, often screaming and difficult to be consoled along with sympathetic overactivity.

NREM parasomnias often arise out of deep sleep (N3 sleep), and hence usually appear in the first half of sleep period.

Symptoms are common among children and thought to arise from an immature brain. However, if they are seen in an adult, further evaluation of sleep is indicated to find out the underlying pathology.

Benzodiazepines help in the maintenance of sleep and provide relief in symptoms.

REM sleep parasomnias may present as any of the following symptoms—an REM sleep behavior disorder (REMBD), recurrent isolated sleep paralysis, and nightmare disorder. They are common toward morning time as they arise out of REM sleep. They occur due to a mismatch between sleep-wakefulness and muscle atonia.

REMBD is characterized by episodes of dream enactment, which the patient is not aware of. When awakened, the patient is usually able to recall the dream. This occurs due to the loss of atonia, which is normally present during REM sleep. Dementia, Parkinson's disease, and drugs that interfere with REM atonia (e.g., selective serotonin reuptake inhibitors) are the risk factors for REMBD. Clonazepam is effective in the management of REMBD.

Clinical presentation of **sleep paralysis** is explained under the head *Narcolepsy*. It occurs due to the persistence of atonia during wakefulness from REM sleep. Isolated recurrent sleep paralysis is common during periods of stress, sleep deprivation, and alcohol withdrawal. Reassurance is often sufficient; however, when clinically significant, clonazepam offers relief.

Nightmare disorder is characterized by waking up from the dreams that are dysphoric and often can be recalled. The patient immediately becomes alert, contrary to sleep terrors. Daytime symptoms, for example, mood changes, fatigue, memory lapses, poor concentration, are often seen. At times, the patient develops a fear of falling asleep or from the dark. Impairment in personal, social, and occupational functioning is often seen.

KEY POINTS

- Insomnia, hypersomnia, circadian rhythm sleep disorders, sleep apnea, sleep-related movement disorders, and parasomnias are various sleep disorders.

Insomnia and Hypersomnia

- International Classification of Sleep Disorders, 3rd edition (ICSD-3) classifies insomnia into two subtypes–short-term and chronic. When symptoms are present for more than 3 months, it is termed as chronic insomnia. Insomnia of shorter duration is termed as short-term or acute insomnia.
- The three main causes for hypersomnia are narcolepsy, idiopathic hypersomnia, and Kleine-Levin syndrome (KLS).
- *Narcolepsy* is characterized by an irresistible urge to fall asleep during the daytime, lasting for at least 3 months. In narcolepsy, the patient has short rapid eye movement (REM) latency or sleep onset REM periods (SOREMPs) on objective testing by multiple sleep latency test (MSLT). During MSLT, at least two naps must show SOREMPs.

- Other symptoms of narcolepsy are sleep paralysis, hypnogogic or hypnopompic hallucinations, and cataplexy.
- Narcolepsy is an autoimmune disorder characterized by the loss of hypocretin neurons in the posterior hypothalamus.
- Gabahydroxybutyric acid (GHBA) is the drug of choice for narcolepsy that improves nocturnal sleep maintenance and daytime alertness. Stimulants like modafinil may be used to improve daytime alertness.
- Idiopathic hypersomnia is characterized by prolonged periods of sleep (>11 hours/day) or excessive daytime sleepiness. These patients have short sleep latency (<8 min) during the MSLT, but unlike narcolepsy have less than two episodes of SOREMPs.
- *KLS* is characterized by episodic hypersomnia (>11 hours/day) lasting for at least 2 days to 5 weeks. During the episode, patients show other symptoms such as perceptual disturbances, cognitive abnormalities, hyperphagia, and hypersexuality.

Circadian Rhythm Sleep Disorders

- Advanced sleep-wake phase disorder (ASWPD), and delayed sleep-wake phase disorder (DSWPD), shift work-sleep disorder, and jet lag disorder are various circadian rhythm sleep disorders.

Sleep-Related Breathing Disorders

- Sleep apnea is an important sleep-related breathing disorder. Sleep apnea can be obstructive sleep apnea (OSA) or central sleep apnea (CSA). Whole night level 1 polysomnography is the gold standard for the diagnosis of both conditions.
- Clinically, OSA presents with complaints of snoring, snorting, nocturnal polyuria, sleep-talking, daytime somnolence or fatigue, morning headache, memory lapses, and reduced libido.
- Obesity, male gender, use of hypnotics, alcohol, smoking, advancing age, micrognathia, and maxillary retrusion are risk factors for the development of OSA.
- Treatment of OSA includes continuous positive airway pressure (CPAP) or bi-level positive airway pressure and weight reduction.
- Surgery is offered in the presence of a correctable anatomical defect (e.g., adenotonsillar hypertrophy, micrognathia, and maxillary retrusion).

Sleep-Related Movement Disorders

- Restless legs syndrome (RLS) is characterized by an urge to move legs that are often accompanied by dysesthesia in leg muscles. Dopaminergic drugs such as levodopa and non-ergot derivatives (e.g., ropinirole, pramipexole) are used for the management of symptoms.

Parasomnias

- Parasomnias are complex movement or behaviors or experiences that are seen either during non-rapid eye movement (NREM) or REM sleep.
- NREM sleep parasomnias may present in one of these forms–confusional arousal, sleepwalking, sleep terrors, and sleep-related eating disorder. Benzodiazepines help in the maintenance of sleep and provide relief in symptoms.
- REM sleep parasomnias may present as any of the following symptoms–an REM sleep behavior disorder (REMBD), recurrent isolated sleep paralysis, and nightmare disorder. They are common toward morning time as they arise out of REM sleep.

SELF-ASSESSMENT

1. Case-based Questions

   A 48-year-old obese male presents to psychiatry OPD with persistent daytime sleepiness for the past 2 years. He complains of a feeling of tiredness the whole day. He has comorbid hypertension and diabetes mellitus. His wife reports that he snores loudly and wakes up gasping from sleep.

   The patient smokes approximately 10–12 cigarettes daily for the last 20 years. He has no comorbid psychiatric or medical disorder and has no history of any other substance abuse. On physical exam, he has a BMI of 36, macroglossia, and maxillary retrusion.

   a. What is your provisional diagnosis?
   b. How will you evaluate the patient?
   c. Describe the various treatment options.
2. Discuss clinical features, diagnosis, and treatment of narcolepsy. How narcolepsy is different from idiopathic hypersomnia?
3. Discuss restless leg syndrome.
4. Describe rapid eye movement sleep behavior disorder (REMBD).
5. Write short notes on:
   a. Circadian rhythm sleep disorders
   b. Sleep stages
6. How will you differentiate central and obstructive sleep apnea?

Chapter 20

Sexual Dysfunctions and Gender Dysphoria

SK Kar · Adarsh Tripathi

Sexual disorders are common clinical entities. The clinically reported sexual disorders in medical settings are only the tip of the iceberg. Myths, stigma, as well as discussion on sex/sexuality/sexual disorders being a taboo subject in Indian culture mostly attribute to underreporting of sexual disorders.

Sexual dysfunctions commonly seen in males are erectile dysfunction and premature ejaculation (PME), whereas in females are decreased desire and arousal.

NORMAL SEXUALITY

Normal sexual development depends on the integrity of biological, psychological, as well as social factors (Fig. 20.1). Sex chromosomes (X and Y) determine the sex of the individual. Gender-specific sex hormones (gonadal hormones) help in the development and maturation of sexual organs. The integrity of the hypothalamic-pituitary-gonadal axis as well as the hypothalamic-pituitary-adrenal axis is highly essential in normal sexual development. However, the psychological and social factors also play a pivotal role in sexual development. Any breach in the harmony of these factors, which determine healthy sexual development, may cause sexual disorders.

Many psychiatric disorders may cause or exacerbate the underlying sexual

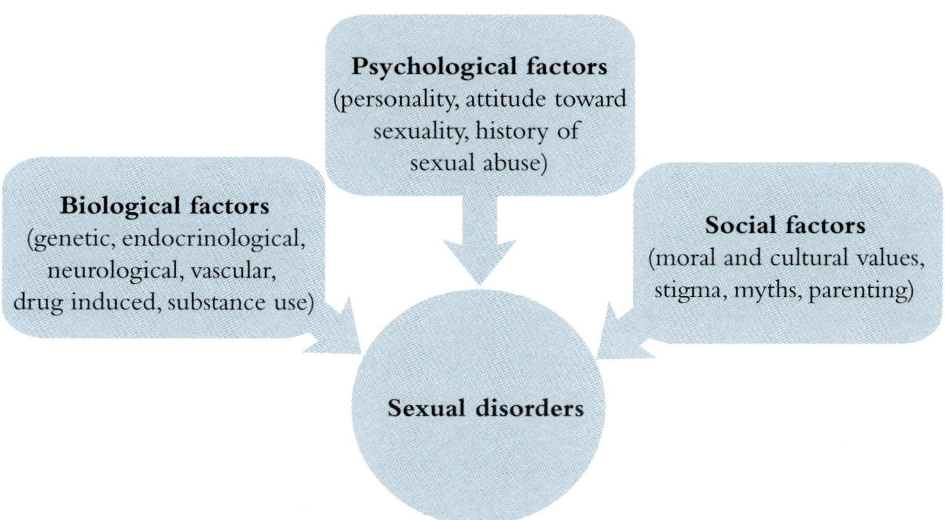

Figure 20.1 Factors attributing to sexual disorders.

dysfunction. Patients with depression, anxiety disorders, and schizophrenia may report about decreased libido. Psychotropic medications (selective serotonin reuptake inhibitors [SSRIs] and antipsychotic drugs) may cause sexual dysfunctions.

Masturbation is a self-stimulating sexual behavior to obtain gratification. It is a healthy sexual behavior. Masturbation becomes the major mode of sexual gratification when the partner is not available or ill or the sexual relation is not satisfactory. It is considered abnormal when it becomes a compulsive behavior and uncontrolled.

Homosexuality refers to sexual behavior characterized by sexual attraction and orientation toward the same gender. Homosexual females and males are known as *lesbians* and *gays*, respectively. Initially, it was considered as a form of sexual perversion; however, over the past four decades the notion toward homosexuality has changed and it is considered as a normative sexual behavior and not a disease entity.

CLASSIFICATION OF SEXUAL DISORDERS

Sexual disorders can be classified as male sexual disorders and female sexual disorders. According to the nature of sexual dysfunction, they can be broadly classified as disorders of sexual interest (increased or decreased libido, arousal disorder), disorders of sexual excitement (erectile dysfunction), disorders of orgasm (anorgasmia, PME), and sexual pain disorder (vaginismus).

Sexual disorders can also be classified as **lifelong disorders** (refers to conditions of sexual dysfunction since the first encounter) or **acquired disorders** (refers to previous normal sexual functioning). Sexual disorders can be **generalized** (associated with all situations and partners) or **situational** (associated with the specific situation or partner).

COMMON SEXUAL DYSFUNCTIONS

Common sexual dysfunctions include PME, delayed ejaculation, erectile dysfunction, female orgasmic disorder, female sexual interest/arousal disorder, genito-pelvic pain/penetration disorder, and medication-induced/substance-induced sexual dysfunction.

Premature Ejaculation

It is characterized by ejaculation occurring in a persistent or recurrent pattern within approximately 1 minute following vaginal penetration and before the individual wishes it. It can be a lifelong condition or may be acquired. It can be situational or generalized. The severity of PME can be mild (ejaculation occurring within 30 seconds to 1 minute of vaginal penetration), or moderate (ejaculation occurring within 15–30 seconds of vaginal penetration), or severe (ejaculation occurring within 15 seconds of vaginal penetration). As per DSM-5, for definitive diagnosis, the symptoms must persist for more than 6 months and must be experienced on almost all or all (approximately 75%–100%) occasions of sexual activity. Premature ejaculation is diagnosed if sexual dysfunction is unexplainable with any other nonsexual psychiatric condition, or medical condition. Various factors (partner related, relationship related, individual specific, sociocultural, and stress) play a role in the development of PME. The presence of psychiatric comorbidities like anxiety disorders increases the risk of PME. Opioid withdrawal can cause PME. Many medical conditions like thyroid disorders and prostatitis can also attribute to PME. PME is found to be associated with polymorphism of dopamine and serotonin transporter gene. PME results in decreased self-confidence in sexual performance, which subsequently may affect the sexual performance resulting in further worsening of premature ejaculation.

Delayed Ejaculation

It is characterized by a marked delay in ejaculation or absence of ejaculation on almost all or all (approximately 75%–100%) occasions of partnered sexual activity and without the individual desiring delay. Delayed ejaculation is diagnosed if the symptoms are unexplainable by any other nonsexual psychiatric condition, or medical condition. For the definitive diagnosis, a minimum period of 6 months is required. Delayed ejaculation produces significant psychological distress. The causes of delayed ejaculation are surgical injury involving lumbar sympathetic and parasympathetic nerves, multiple sclerosis, neuropathy (diabetic, alcoholic), opioid use, SSRIs, and antipsychotic drugs. Relationship difficulties, negative attitudes toward sex, depression, anxiety, and stress as well as childhood sexual abuse may also increase the risk of delayed ejaculation. It can be a lifelong condition or may be acquired. It can be situational as well as generalized.

Erectile Dysfunction

It is characterized by marked difficulty in obtaining an erection during sexual activity, or/and marked difficulty in maintaining an erection until the completion of sexual activity, or marked decrease in erectile rigidity. Erectile dysfunction is diagnosed if the symptoms are present on almost all or all occasions (75%–100%) of sexual activity for at least 6 months and are not explained by any other nonsexual psychiatric condition or medical condition. It can be a lifelong condition or may be acquired. It can be situational as well as generalized. Erectile dysfunction produces significant psychological distress in both partners. The causes of erectile dysfunction can be biological (e.g., hypogonadism, drug induced, injury to the nerve responsible for the erection of the penis), psychological (anxiety related to performance, depression, poor self-image) as well as sociocultural (e.g., negative attitude toward sexuality). The prevalence of erectile dysfunction increases with increasing age, with half of the men reporting the problem after the age of 60 years. Various risk factors that may attribute to erectile dysfunction are increasing age, diabetes, sedentary lifestyle, smoking, and dyslipidemia. Patients with erectile dysfunction should undergo certain investigations to rule out medical disorders. The investigations needed for a complete evaluation of erectile dysfunction are as follows:

- Fasting and postprandial glucose
- Lipid profile
- Liver and renal function test
- Serum level vitamin B_{12} and folate
- Serum testosterone level
- Thyroid function test
- Penile Doppler ultrasonography and dynamic infusion cavernosography
- Nerve conduction study of the pudendal nerve

Patients, who report erection with a different partner, or during masturbation, or sleep (nocturnal erection), or in the early morning, are most likely to have a psychogenic cause of erectile dysfunction rather than any medical or surgical cause.

Treatment of underlying medical abnormality (if any) is likely to improve erectile dysfunction. Erectile dysfunction can be treated with phosphodiesterase inhibitors (sildenafil, tadalafil).

Female Orgasmic Disorder

It is characterized by a significant delay to the lack of orgasm in a female during sexual activity. Many patients also complain about the reduction in the intensity of orgasmic sensations. For the definite diagnosis, the symptoms should persist for more than 6 months and should not be explained with any other nonsexual psychiatric illness or medical cause. It can be a lifelong condition or may be acquired and can be situational as well as generalized.

Female Sexual Interest/ Arousal Disorder

Female sexual interest/arousal disorder (FSIAD) is defined in the DSM-5 as lack of, or significantly reduced, sexual interest/arousal. DSM-IV-TR (Diagnostic and Statistical Manual of Mental Disorders, Fourth Edition, Text Revision) had separate diagnoses of hypoactive sexual desire disorder (HSDD) and female sexual arousal disorder (FSAD). FSIAD is characterized by absent to reduced interest in sexual activity and sexual thoughts (fantasies), poor initiation of sexual activity, and reduced to absent sexual excitement or pleasure during sexual encounters. The counter-responses to sexual stimuli in these individuals are often absent or diminished.

As per DSM-5, FSIAD is diagnosed if the symptoms persist for more than 6 months, and are unexplainable with any nonsexual psychiatric disorder or medical condition. Commonly, females with this disorder present with lack of sexual pleasure with sexual activities. It can be a lifelong condition or may be acquired and can be situational as well as generalized.

Genito-Pelvic Pain/Penetration Disorder

It is characterized by persistent or recurrent difficulties associated with vaginal penetration, marked vulvovaginal pain during penetration attempts, anxiety or fear about vulvovaginal pain in anticipation of or as a result of vaginal penetration, and tightening of pelvic floor muscles during attempted vaginal penetration. It is also referred to as vaginismus. It can be a lifelong condition or may be acquired. As per DSM-5, for definitive diagnosis, the symptoms must persist for more than 6 months, and the sexual dysfunction is not better explained by any other nonsexual psychiatric or medical conditions. Dyspareunia refers to recurrent and persistent pain during sexual intercourse. Often patients with this disorder complain of dyspareunia.

Medication-Induced/Substance-Induced Sexual Dysfunction

It is characterized by the development of any form of sexual dysfunction (evident from the history, physical examination, or laboratory investigations) during, soon after substance intoxication, or withdrawal, or use of medication. Sexual dysfunction causes significant impairment and distress in the individual. The symptoms of sexual dysfunction should not develop during the phase of delirium associated with substance use, or withdrawal, or medication use. Substances that can commonly cause sexual dysfunction are opioids, sedatives and hypnotics (e.g., benzodiazepines, barbiturates), stimulants, and alcohol. Withdrawal of the above substances also causes sexual dysfunction. Medications like hormonal contraceptives, antipsychotics (e.g., haloperidol, olanzapine, risperidone), antidepressants (e.g., tricyclic antidepressants, SSRIs), cabergoline, sympathomimetic agents, and sympatholytic agents can also cause sexual dysfunction.

ASSESSMENT OF SEXUAL DISORDERS

Assessment of sexual disorders is the basic prerequisite of their management. The assessment of sexual disorders follows the steps shown in Figure 20.2.

A careful, detailed history taking is important in patients with sexual disorders. History should include the sociodemographic details of the patients, onset and progression of the symptoms, distress and impairment due to the symptoms, substance abuse, comorbid medical and

Approach

History taking: Developmental history, sexual orientation, nature of dysfunction, current sexual functioning, co-morbid medical or psychiatric illness, history of sexual abuse, attitude towards sexuality, sexual myths, history of sexually transmitted disease, use of contraception, nature and quality of relationship with partner

General physical examination: Body habitus (feminine and masculine), development of breast, axillary and pubic hair, thyroid enlargement, clinical signs of medical illnesses (respiratory, cardiac, neurological)

Examination of the genitalia: Genital anatomy, deformity of the genitalia, primary and secondary sexual characteristics, any lesion or discharge from the genitalia

Laboratory investigations (depending upon the nature of sexual dysfunction): Hematological—Complete hemogram, organ function tests (thyroid, liver, kidney), serum cortisol, gonadal hormone level estimation, serum level of vitamin B_{12} and folate

- Penile Doppler
- Nerve conduction studies (pudendal nerve)
- Radiological—X-ray of spine, CT scan/MRI of spinal cord (for spinal cord and nerve root lesions)

Figure 20.2 Focus points for evaluation in sexual disorders.

psychiatric disorders, premorbid sexual functioning, and context of sexual dysfunction (situational or generalized). Physical examination and examination of the external genitalia is an important but often neglected part of the clinical evaluation in sexual disorders. Laboratory investigations are intended to rule out various medical causes of sexual dysfunction. Many of these investigations are done when there is clinical suspicion of a particular or group of medical conditions. The investigations that are recommended for ruling out common medical conditions are complete hemogram, blood sugar, lipid profile, and hormone assays (thyroid function test, serum testosterone, serum prolactin).

MANAGEMENT OF SEXUAL DISORDERS

Broadly, the management of sexual disorders is classified into two categories:

1. Pharmacological treatment
2. Psychological treatment

Pharmacological Treatment

Pharmacological management has a limited role in the treatment of sexual disorders other than PME or erectile dysfunction.

In erectile dysfunction, most commonly phosphodiesterase 5 (PDE-5) inhibitors (sildenafil, tadalafil, vardenafil) are used. They are short-acting and facilitate the erection of the penis by enhancing blood flow to the penis. The vasodilatation is mediated by nitric oxide. The most common side effect of PDE-5 inhibitors is headache. They can cause priapism (painful, prolonged erection of the penis), which may require urgent surgical intervention. PDE-5 inhibitors should be avoided in patients already using nitrates for coronary artery disease. Other agents that may be useful in erectile dysfunction are phentolamine (oral and injectable), papaverine (injectable), and prostaglandin analogs-alprostadil (oral, injectable as well as intraurethral). For patients complaining of decreased libido, dopaminergic agents like L-dopa, bromocriptine, cabergoline, selegiline, and bupropion may be useful.

Androgens (testosterone) may also improve the sexual drive and may be useful in patients with erectile dysfunction. Similarly, antiandrogens (estrogens, progesterone) are used in patients with compulsive sexual behavior (hypersexuality).

Delayed or retrograde ejaculation often occurs in patients taking SSRIs. Stoppage of SSRIs and switching to antidepressants like bupropion or mirtazapine reduces the sexual side effects of SSRIs, including delayed ejaculation.

Flibanserin is the first FDA-approved medication for low sexual desire in premenopausal women. An injectable medication, bremelanotide, has been approved by the FDA recently (June 21, 2019) as a treatment for low sexual desire in premenopausal women. The medication should be injected in the abdomen or thigh at least 45 minutes before anticipated sexual activity. It should not be used more than once a day or more than eight times a month.

Psychological Treatment

Among the psychological treatments, cognitive behavior therapy (CBT) is an evidence-based treatment modality. It helps in modifying the maladaptive patterns of thinking and behavior in patients with sexual disorders. Sex education by promoting positive sexual health and resolving sexual myths reduces distress.

It is helpful in patients with PME and erectile dysfunction.

Dual-sex therapy is a unique technique developed by **Masters and Johnson** for erectile dysfunction. In this technique, both the partners participate. This technique facilitates communication and sexual expression between the partners. During the sessions, the couple learns to arouse each other in a graded manner without indulging in intercourse in the initial period and subsequently learning various methods of genital stimulation. The anxiety related to sexual performance is reduced significantly, thereby enhancing performance.

Patients with genito-pelvic pain (vaginismus) are advised to serially dilate the vaginal introitus by lubricated dilators.

Patients with PME benefit from *squeeze technique* (partner applies pressure at the coronal ridge of glans at the height of excitement with an impending sense of ejaculation). The regular practice of this technique raises the threshold of ejaculation. The *stop-start technique* is also useful for delaying ejaculation. In this method, the female partner stimulates the male partner till there is an impending sense of ejaculation and then suddenly stops the stimulation. The male partner loses arousal before ejaculation. This process is repeated several times to increase the threshold of ejaculation.

Controlled masturbation by the use of a vibrator is recommended for females with lifelong orgasmic disorder. Relaxation exercises, aerobic exercises, hypnotherapy, mindfulness training, and various other behavioral techniques have been successfully used in sexual dysfunctions.

Other treatment modalities that may be useful in sexual dysfunction are surgery (vascular surgery in atherosclerotic changes of blood vessels supplying to the penis) and the use of prosthesis (implants). These may be useful in patients with erectile dysfunction. Vacuum pump devices with band techniques (applying elastic band at the root of the penis after erection from vacuum device) are also used for erectile dysfunction.

PARAPHILIC DISORDERS

These disorders are also known as sexual perversions. The individuals with paraphilic disorder get sexual excitement from nonconventional and rather objectionable ways that may affect another individual or group of individuals adversely. They are often considered as criminal acts (offenses). These behaviors are often intense and follow a persistent pattern. The common types of paraphilic disorders are as follows:

1. **Voyeurism:** It refers to watching the sexual activities or private parts of others secretly to derive sexual excitement.
2. **Exhibitionism:** It refers to showing/displaying one's genitalia publicly to derive sexual excitement.
3. **Frotteurism:** It refers to man's rubbing his penis against the body parts of a fully clothed woman to achieve orgasm.
4. **Sexual sadism:** It refers to inflicting pain, suffering, or humiliation to the partner or an individual to derive sexual excitement.
5. **Sexual masochism:** It refers to seeking pain, suffering, and humiliation from the partner to get sexual excitement.
6. **Fetishism:** It refers to acts of deriving sexual gratification from nonliving objects (fetish objects) associated with the opposite gender (e.g., undergarments, stockings, shoes, and other belongings).

7. **Pedophilia:** It refers to the acts of deriving pleasure by indulging in sexual activities with small children.
8. **Transvestism:** It refers to the acts of deriving sexual gratification by cross-dressing.

GENDER DYSPHORIA (GENDER IDENTITY DISORDER)

Earlier it was known as gender identity disorder. Gender dysphoria refers to a condition which results from disparity or mismatch between the anatomically and physiological gender with that of psychological gender (emotionally and cognitively perceived gender). The individual experiences significant distress as the individual is identifying the self with the opposite gender.

Children suffering from gender dysphoria have an intense desire to be of the opposite gender. They prefer to wear clothes of the opposite gender. They play cross-gender roles in fantasy play (e.g., a boy playing as a mother in fantasy play). They like playmates of the opposite gender. They prefer toys and games meant for the other gender and reject the toys meant for the same gender. They dislike their sexual anatomy and desire to have sexual characteristics of the opposite gender.

Boys with gender dysphoria often have Barbie dolls as their favorite toy and girls as preferred playmates. They may insist on sitting to urinate and wish for the removal of testis or penis. Girls with gender dysphoria dislike feminine toys such as dolls and like rough and tumble play with boys. They may refuse to urinate in the sitting position. They do not want to develop breasts or menstruate.

Adults suffering from gender dysphoria have a marked incongruence between one's experienced gender and assigned gender and have a strong desire to be of opposite gender. They want to get rid of their primary and/or secondary sex characteristics and have a strong desire for the primary and/or secondary sex characteristics of the other gender. They report that they have typical feelings and reactions of the other gender.

For the definite diagnosis, the symptoms must persist for more than 6 months and must produce significant psychosocial distress.

Treatment

In adolescents, gonadotropin-releasing hormone (GnRH) can be used to temporarily block puberty by blocking the hormones responsible for secondary sex characteristics. This gives adolescents and their family time to choose the best option available.

Treatment of adults who identify as transgender includes psychotherapy, hormone therapy, and surgery.

Hormonal supplementations are recommended, too, for bringing the gender-specific changes. Hormone treatment of transgender men is by testosterone which leads to increased muscle mass and libido, cessation of menses, increased body hair, and enlargement of the clitoris. Transgender women are given estrogen, testosterone blockers, or progesterone. This leads to breast growth. Sex drive, erection, and ejaculation decrease and body hair also decrease.

The most common type of surgery for both trans-men and trans-women is chest surgery or top surgery. Bottom surgery is less common. Bottom surgery for women is vaginoplasty, also known as sex reassignment surgery.

Family intervention may be required in case of gender dysphoria. Nonacceptance by family and society is another major cause of distress in individuals with gender dysphoria. Family education facilitates the acceptance of gender dysphoria and helps in the social integration of the patient in a graceful manner.

KEY POINTS

Premature Ejaculation

- **Premature ejaculation (PME)** is characterized by ejaculation occurring in a persistent or recurrent pattern within approximately 1 minute following vaginal penetration and before the individual wishes it.
- The severity of PME can be mild (ejaculation occurring within 30 seconds to 1 minute of vaginal penetration), or moderate (ejaculation occurring within 15–30 seconds of vaginal penetration), or severe (ejaculation occurring within 15 seconds of vaginal penetration).
- The presence of psychiatric comorbidities like anxiety disorders increases the risk of PME. Opioid withdrawal can cause PME. Many medical conditions like thyroid disorders and prostatitis can also attribute to PME.
- Patients with PME benefit from *the squeeze technique* or *stop-start technique*.

Delayed Ejaculation

- **Delayed ejaculation** is characterized by a marked delay in ejaculation to the absence of ejaculation on almost all or all (approximately 75%–100%) occasions of partnered sexual activity and without the individual desiring delay.
- The causes of delayed ejaculation are surgical injury involving lumbar sympathetic and parasympathetic nerves, multiple sclerosis, neuropathy (diabetic, alcoholic), opioid use, SSRIs, and antipsychotic drugs.

Erectile Dysfunction

- **Erectile dysfunction** is characterized by marked difficulty in obtaining an erection during sexual activity, or/and marked difficulty in maintaining an erection until the completion of sexual activity, or marked decrease in erectile rigidity.
- In erectile dysfunction, most commonly phosphodiesterase 5 (PDE-5) inhibitors (sildenafil, tadalafil, vardenafil) are used.
- *Dual-sex therapy* is a unique technique developed by **Masters and Johnson** for erectile dysfunction.

Female Sexual Disorders

- **Female orgasmic disorder** is characterized by a significant delay to the lack of orgasm in a female during sexual activity.
- **Female sexual interest/arousal disorder (FSIAD)** is defined in the DSM-5 as lack of, or significantly reduced, sexual interest/arousal. DSM-IV-TR had separate diagnoses of hypoactive sexual desire disorder (HSDD) and female sexual arousal disorder (FSAD).
- FSIAD is characterized by absent to reduced interest in sexual activity and sexual thoughts (fantasies), poor initiation of sexual activity, and reduced to absent sexual excitement or pleasure during sexual encounters.

- **Genito-pelvic pain/penetration disorder** is characterized by persistent or recurrent difficulties associated with vaginal penetration, marked vulvovaginal pain during penetration attempts, anxiety or fear about vulvovaginal pain in anticipation of or as a result of vaginal penetration, and tightening of pelvic floor muscles during attempted vaginal penetration.
- Flibanserin is the first FDA-approved medication for low sexual desire in premenopausal women.
- An injectable medication, bremelanotide, has been approved by the FDA recently (June 21, 2019) as a treatment for low sexual desire in premenopausal women. The medication should be injected in the abdomen or thigh at least 45 minutes before anticipated sexual activity. It should not be used more than once a day or more than eight times a month.

Paraphilic Disorders

- In **paraphilic disorders**, the individuals get sexual excitement from nonconventional and rather objectionable ways that may affect another individual or group of individuals adversely.
- Voyeurism, exhibitionism, frotteurism, sexual sadism, sexual masochism, fetishism, pedophilia, and transvestism are the common types of paraphilic disorders.

Gender Dysphoria

- **Gender dysphoria** refers to a condition which results from disparity or mismatch between the anatomically and physiological gender with that of psychological gender (emotionally and cognitively perceived gender). The individual experiences significant distress as the individual is identifying the self with the opposite gender.
- Treatment of adults who identify as transgender includes psychotherapy, hormone therapy, and surgery.

SELF-ASSESSMENT

1. Case-based Questions
   Mr "A" was born as a male and registered as a male on the birth certificate. In his childhood and adolescence, he used to dress like a male, would play outdoor team sports with his friends. At the age of 21, he disclosed to his family members that he feels as if he is female and does not like his beard and moustache. Gradually he started dressing up as a female and would request others to call "Her" as Miss "B" (female name). He told his family members that he wants to become a female by sex reassignment surgery.
   a. What is your provisional diagnosis?
   b. How will you manage this patient?
2. Define and enumerate various paraphilic disorders.
3. Define premature ejaculation and discuss its treatment.
4. Define erectile dysfunction and discuss its assessment and management.
5. Enumerate the various female sexual disorders and discuss clinical features and management of genito-pelvic pain/penetration disorder.
6. Write pharmacotherapy of low sexual desire in premenopausal females.

Chapter 21

Psychiatric Disorders in Childhood and Adolescence

Nidhi Chauhan

Children and adolescents constitute an important chunk of the total population of the world and are no exception to the development of mental health problems. The most common psychiatric disorders in children and adolescents are neurodevelopmental disorders (intellectual disability, autism spectrum disorders, attention-deficit/hyperactivity disorder (ADHD), specific learning disorder, tic disorder, etc.). Autism spectrum disorders, ADHD, and intellectual disability have been discussed in Chapters 6, 7, and 8, respectively. This chapter pertains to adult-like psychiatric disorders in children and adolescents. Like adults, children and adolescents too are vulnerable and may have adult-like psychiatric disorders. The important point here is to remember that psychiatric disorders in children and adolescents may differ from psychiatric disorders in adults in their manifestations, symptomatology, course, prognosis, choice of medications, and response to treatment. A brief overview of major psychiatric disorders in children and adolescents is presented in this chapter.

SCHIZOPHRENIA AND OTHER PSYCHOTIC DISORDERS

Schizophrenia is among the most devastating psychiatric disorders affecting children and adolescents. Although it is rare before the age of 10, the incidence of schizophrenia rises steadily through childhood into adolescence and young adulthood. The diagnostic criteria are the same for children and adolescents as well as adults.

Childhood-onset schizophrenia (COS) is typically different from adult-onset schizophrenia, in being more insidious in onset, predominant negative symptoms, greater disorganization, less systematized delusions (owing to cognitive immaturity), and hallucinations in different modalities. Overall, the prevalence is 0.9 per 10,000 at the age of 13 with a steady increase in prevalence thereafter.

Assessment of a child or adolescent with COS entails a detailed history, mental status examination, and a thorough physical examination. The developmental age of the child should always be taken into account as it will determine their ability to understand as well as express psychotic symptoms. A wide array of organic brain disorders (epilepsy, Wilson disease, metachromatic leukodystrophy) and drugs/medicines (steroids, cocaine, cannabis, etc.) can present with psychotic symptoms and a child with COS requires careful examination and evaluation.

Treatment

Management includes treatment with antipsychotics along with family counseling, individual psychotherapy, psychoeducation, provisions of educational and social benefits, and rehabilitation. Pharmacotherapy involves use of typical and atypical antipsychotics. Table 21.1 shows first-generation and second-generation antipsychotics approved by FDA for treatment of schizophrenia in children.

In children, the propensity of extrapyramidal side effects (tremors, rigidity) with typical antipsychotics is higher compared to the adult population. The propensity of weight gain and metabolic adverse effects with atypical antipsychotics is also more in children. However, the dictum is to start with an atypical antipsychotic as a first-line agent. Because of the increased risk of serious side effects with first-generation antipsychotics, they often are not recommended for use in children until other options have been tried without success.

Table 21.1 First- and second-generation antipsychotics approved by FDA for treatment of schizophrenia in children

Generic name	Approved age group in schizophrenia
First-generation antipsychotics	
Chlorpromazine	1–12 years
Loxapine	≥12 years
Perphenazine	12 years
Thiothixene	12 years
Thioridazine	2 years
Trifluoperazine	6 years
Second-generation antipsychotics	
Aripiprazole	13–17 years
Olanzapine	
Quetiapine	
Risperidone	
Lurasidone	
Paliperidone	≥12 years

BIPOLAR AFFECTIVE DISORDER

Bipolar affective disorder presents quite differently from adults. The most common presentation of a manic episode in children is irritability, anger outbursts, and violent behavior. It is rare for the prepubertal child to show grandiosity or euphoria. In DSM-5, diagnostic criteria for bipolar disorder in children and adolescents are same as used for adults.

Treatment

Lithium is the only US FDA-approved mood stabilizer for the treatment of mania in children as young as 12 years. Chlorpromazine is indicated in children 1–12 years for the treatment of manic episode. Table 21.2 shows second-generation antipsychotics approved by FDA for treatment of bipolar disorder in children.

Lurasidone is indicated as monotherapy for the acute management of depressive episodes associated with bipolar I disorder in adolescent (10–17 years) patients.

Table 21.2 Second-generation antipsychotics approved by FDA for treatment of bipolar disorder in children

Generic name	Approved age group in bipolar disorder (manic/mixed episode)
Aripiprazole	10–17 years
Olanzapine	13–17 years
Quetiapine	10–17 years
Risperidone	10–17 years

UNIPOLAR DEPRESSION

It tends to manifest in slightly different ways according to the developmental level of the child. Prepubertal children present with somatic complaints, psychomotor agitation, and mood congruent hallucinations. Anhedonia, hopelessness, psychomotor retardation, and delusions are more in adolescents and adults with depression as compared to depression in young children. Sadness of mood, irritability, suicidal thoughts, and insomnia are present with same frequency regardless of age. Older children and adolescents may present with conduct issues, substance abuse, academic decline, or impaired concentration.

Treatment

Fluoxetine is the only antidepressant approved by the US FDA for the treatment of preadolescent and adolescent depression, whereas escitalopram is approved for the treatment of adolescent depression only.

DISRUPTIVE MOOD DYSREGULATION DISORDER

To address concerns about the potential of overdiagnosis of bipolar disorder in children, a new diagnosis, disruptive mood dysregulation disorder (DMDD), is added to the depressive disorders for children up to 12 years. DMDD is for children with persistent irritability and frequent episodes of extreme behavioral dyscontrol.

DMDD is characterized by severe recurrent temper outbursts manifested verbally or behaviorally that are grossly out of proportion in intensity or duration to the situation, and are inconsistent with the development level. These temper outbursts must occur on an average 3 or more times per week. The mood between the temper outbursts remains irritable or angry most of the day and is observable by others. These symptoms must be present for 12 or more months and during these 12 months, the patient should not be symptom-free for 3 or more than 3 consecutive months. These symptoms must be present at least in two out of three settings (i.e., at home, at school, with peers). The age of onset should be before 10 years and diagnosis should not be made for the first time before the age of 6 years or after the age of 18 years. There should not be a period lasting more than 1 day when the criteria for mania or hypomania (except duration) are fulfilled. These symptoms should not be occurring as a part of a depressive disorder or any other psychiatric illness (autism spectrum disorder, separation anxiety disorder, posttraumatic stress disorder) or due to the physiological effects of a substance or to another medical or neurological condition.

A diagnosis of DMDD cannot coexist with a diagnosis of a manic episode, bipolar affective disorder, intermittent explosive disorder, and oppositional defiant disorder. However, it can be reliably made coexistent with major depressive disorder, ADHD, substance use disorder, and conduct disorder.

About 2%–5% of children and adolescents may have DMDD, with males at higher risk. Conversion to bipolar affective disorder later in life is rare, but may develop into depressive disorder or anxiety disorder. However, an important consideration should be given to differentiating it from bipolar disorder, oppositional defiant disorder, ADHD, depressive disorder, and anxiety disorder.

Treatment

There are no FDA-approved drugs for management of DMDD since it is a newer diagnosis. Treatment may include antidepressants for depressive symptoms, stimulants for aggression, and antipsychotics and/or valproate for mood dysregulation. Other modalities that can be used are anger management techniques and problem-solving skills.

KEY POINTS

- The most common psychiatric disorders in children and adolescents are neurodevelopmental disorders.
- Like adults, children and adolescents may have adult-like psychiatric disorders.
- The psychiatric disorders in children and adolescents may differ from psychiatric disorders in adults in their manifestations, symptomatology, course, prognosis, choice of medications, to treatment.

Childhood-Onset Schizophrenia

- Childhood-onset schizophrenia (COS) is typically different from adult-onset schizophrenia, in being more insidious in onset, predominant negative symptoms, greater disorganization, less systematized delusions (owing to cognitive immaturity), and hallucinations in different modalities.
- The diagnostic criteria of schizophrenia are the same for children and adolescents as well as adults.

Bipolar Affective Disorder

- Lithium is the only US FDA-approved mood stabilizer for the treatment of mania in children as young as 12 years.
- Chlorpromazine is indicated in children 1–12 years for the treatment of manic episode, whereas aripiprazole, quetiapine, and risperidone are FDA approved for children and adolescents 10–17 years and olanzapine in children and adolescents 13–17 years.
- Lurasidone is indicated as monotherapy for the acute management of depressive episodes associated with bipolar I disorder in adolescent (10–17 years) patients.

Unipolar Depression

- Fluoxetine is the only antidepressant approved by the US FDA for the treatment of preadolescent and adolescent depression, whereas escitalopram is approved for the treatment of adolescent depression only.

Disruptive Mood Dysregulation Disorder

- Disruptive mood dysregulation disorder (DMDD) is characterized by severe recurrent temper outbursts manifested verbally or behaviorally that are grossly out of proportion in intensity or duration to the situation and are inconsistent with the development level.
- The mood between the temper outbursts remains irritable or angry most of the day and is observable by others.

SELF-ASSESSMENT

1. Discuss the treatment of childhood-onset schizophrenia.
2. Describe disruptive mood dysregulation disorder.

Chapter 22

Disruptive, Impulse Control, and Conduct Disorders

Darpan Kaur · Sandeep Kumar Goyal

Disruptive, impulse control, and conduct disorders include conditions involving problems in the self-control of emotions and behavior. Problems of emotional or behavioral regulation may be present in other disorders also, but these disorders result in behaviors that violate the right of others. These disorders include oppositional defiant disorder (ODD), intermittent explosive disorder (IED), conduct disorder (CD), antisocial personality disorder, pyromania, and kleptomania.

Antisocial personality disorder is discussed in Chapter 27, *Personality Disorders*.

Comparative Nosology

In ICD-10, ODD is a subtype of CD, whereas DSM-5 diagnoses ODD and CD separately. In ICD-10, pathological gambling, trichotillomania, kleptomania, pyromania, and IED are classified as habit and impulse control disorders. In DSM-5, IED, kleptomania, and pyromania are classified along with ODD and CD as disruptive, impulse control and conduct disorders, whereas trichotillomania is classified as OCD spectrum disorder and gambling disorder under nonsubstance related disorders in substance related and addictive disorders.

CONDUCT DISORDER

CD consists of an enduring repeated pattern of behavior in which the basic rights of others or age-appropriate societal rules are violated. Symptoms begin in childhood or adolescence.

Epidemiology

CD is seen more commonly in boys than girls, with ratios varying across different studies from 4:1 to 12:1 and lifetime prevalence rates range from 2% to 10%. CD can develop into antisocial personality disorder in as high as 40% of children. Hence, early identification and appropriate management are very important.

Etiology

CD occurs by complex interaction of biological, psychological, and sociological factors.

Biological Factors

Genetic Factors Clustering of CD in families can be due to genetic factors, shared environmental factors, or interaction between the genetic predisposition and adverse environmental factors. Twin and adoption studies show significant genetic influence.

Genetic research of CD patients indicates 50% genetic influence. Eleven percent variance is due to shared environment and rest due to the environment unique to the individual.

Shared environment includes antisocial parents, maternal depression, paternal alcoholism, urban environment, and low socioeconomic status.

Example of interaction of genetic predisposition and adverse environment is polymorphism of the MAO-A gene. Boys with sexual or physical abuse in the developmental period and gene variant with low MAO-A activity have two times more risk of developing CD as compared to those with gene variant coding for high MAO-A activity. In boys without a history of abuse, variations in MAO-A were not related to the development of CD.

Physiological Factors Individuals with CD, aggression, and antisocial behavior have physiological under arousal and decreased sensitivity to stress.

Neurotransmitters CD is associated with the lower dopamine and norepinephrine levels in the CNS.

Psychological Factors

Cognitive Factors Poor academic performance, especially delays in reading, is also associated with CD. Individuals with CD fail to encode social cues accurately.

Parent factors Poor monitoring of a child's whereabouts and peers, coercive family process, and harsh discipline practices are associated with disruptive behavior in the child.

Opiate dependence, depression, and antisocial personality of the parents are associated with increased risk of CD in children.

Traumatic factors Childhood physical and sexual abuses are associated with depression, anxiety, and conduct problems in children and adolescents.

Sociological Factors

Peer factors CD is associated with the rejection of the aggressive child by peers followed by association with a deviant peer group.

Social factors Aggression, crime, and antisocial behavior are associated with general social deprivation such as poverty, low socioeconomic status, unemployment, residing in violent neighborhoods, and so on.

Protective Factors

Protective factors (Box 22.1) exert a buffering effect in youth at high risk for CD. Protective factors are more than absence of risk factors.

Clinical Features and Diagnosis

CD commonly presents with behaviors that violate the rights of others or societal norms. These behaviors fall into four main types—aggression to people or animals,

Box 22.1 Protective factors in conduct disorder

Child factors

- Female gender
- Easy temperament
- High IQ
- Internal locus of control
- High self-esteem
- Academic competence
- Social competence

Familial and extrafamilial factors

- Good parent–child relations
- High functioning parents
- Intact family structure
- Highly educated parents
- External supports
- Good friendship
- Availability of opportunities
- Safe neighborhoods
- Safe schools

destruction of property, theft, and serious rule violations.

Children with CD show aggression in the form of bullying others, using a weapon like brick, gun, or knife, cruelty to people and animals, and stealing items of nontrivial value with confronting a victim (purse snatching) or without confronting a victim (shoplifting, forgery). Children with CD may be involved in the destruction of property by means of setting fire or by any other means. Lying, forcing someone into sexual activity, staying out at night in spite of the parental prohibition, and showing truancy from school before the age of 13 are common symptoms. Sometimes children with CD may run away from home overnight.

Some of the problems associated with CD can also lead to legal issues.

CD causes impairment in social, academic, or occupational functioning. In an individual of more than 18 years, CD is diagnosed after ruling out antisocial personality disorder.

CD is divided into childhood-onset and adolescent-onset, depending upon the onset before or after 10 years of age. Early-onset CD has a poor prognosis.

Treatment

The treatment of CD consists of comprehensive assessment followed by multidisciplinary management approaches.

Some severe cases of CD may need inpatient treatment depending on the severity of the situation, risk of harm to self or others, history of severe violence, and aggression.

Psychotherapy

Primary prevention is the gold standard in CD. Psychotherapy plays an important role in the treatment of CD. Multimodal interventions targeting child, family, parents, teachers, peers, and education of the child are more effective than intervention with a single focus.

The multifocused therapy combines parent management training (PMT), and child skill building therapies. PMT teaches positive and less harsh discipline practices, monitoring of the child, and positive feedback for the child. Skill building of the child includes training in social skills, anger management strategies, and problem-solving techniques.

Rehabilitation is very important in the management of CD.

Pharmacotherapy

Pharmacotherapy is primarily recommended for comorbid disorders and target symptoms such as impulsivity, mood lability, irritability, and aggression. Atypical antipsychotics, mood stabilizers, and Lithium are moderately effective in aggression associated with CD.

Psychostimulants such as methylphenidate, atypical antipsychotics, and α_2 agonists (guanfacine) may be used for antisocial symptoms in the context of attention-deficit/hyperactivity disorder (ADHD). Antidepressants such as SSRIs can be used for depression and anxiety disorders.

OPPOSITIONAL DEFIANT DISORDER

The ODD is characterized by persistent and frequent negativistic, hostile, and defiant behavior without violation of social norms or rights of others and is more frequent, more intense, and more persistent across the child's development than in an individual of similar age and development.

Comparative Nosology

As described earlier, as per ICD-10 ODD is a subtype of CD, whereas ODD is a separate diagnostic entity in DSM-5.

Etiology

Etiology is best explained by the complex interaction between biological and environmental risk and protective factors. Difficult temperament (overactivity, inattention, low adaptability to new situations) is associated with increased risk of generalized psychopathology, including ODD. Difficult temperament is a weak predictor of the development of ODD, but when it is combined with adverse environmental conditions like family dysfunction, marital conflict, and parental psychopathology, the prediction for ODD and CD is stronger.

Clinical Features and Diagnosis

Symptoms of the ODD include losing temper, getting annoyed, becoming angry, vindictiveness, and argumentative with authority figures. Children with ODD often refuse to comply with requests from authority figures, deliberately annoy others, and blame others for their own mistakes.

The symptoms are often present at home but may not be present at school. Symptoms are prominent while interacting with adults or peers whom the child knows well. ODD is diagnosed if the symptoms are present during the interaction with at least one person who is not a sibling for at least 6 months. The symptoms of the ODD cause distress in the individual or others in his or her immediate social context.

ODD is diagnosed after ruling out psychotic illness, depressive or bipolar disorder, or substance use, and disruptive mood dysregulation disorder.

Treatment

Primary treatment of ODD is family therapy in which parents are trained in child management techniques. The PMT program focuses on teaching parents to alter their behavior to discourage the child's oppositional behavior and encourage appropriate behavior. Behavior therapy (BT) teaches parents to reinforce or praise appropriate behavior and ignore (not reinforce) undesired behavior. Individual psychotherapy may also be effective and the child learns less provocative behavior. Self-esteem of the child should be restored first. Eliminating harsh, punitive parenting and increasing positive parent-child interactions may be beneficial in reducing oppositional defiant behaviors.

IMPULSE CONTROL DISORDERS

Impulse control disorders are characterized by the inability to resist an intense impulse, drive, or temptation to perform a particular act that is harmful to self or others or both.

Pyromania

Pyromania is the recurrent, deliberate, and purposeful fire setting on more than one occasion. Pyromania is associated with tension or affective arousal before the act and pleasure, gratification, or relief after setting the fire. The individual has a fascination with fire. Fire setting is not done for a monetary reason, as an expression of sociopolitical ideology, to conceal criminal activity, to express anger, in response to delusion or hallucinations, or as a result of the impaired judgment. Pyromania is diagnosed after excluding CD, manic episode, and antisocial personality disorder. Pyromania occurs more frequently in boys. Fire setting often begins in childhood, but typical age of onset of pyromania is unknown. Individuals suffering from pyromania show no remorse to their act. Alcohol intoxication, below average IQ, sexual dysfunction, and resentment toward authority figures are associated features. Some fire setters become sexually aroused by the fire.

No single treatment is effective, so a number of modalities should be tried. The treatment program should include supervision of the patients to prevent an episode of fire setting. Incarceration may be the only method to prevent a recurrence. BT can be administered in the institution.

Kleptomania

Kleptomania is a condition characterized by a repeated failure to resist impulses to steal objects that are not needed for personal use or their monetary value. It is associated with tension before stealing and pleasure, gratification, or relief at the time of committing the theft. The stealing is not done to express anger and is not in response to a delusion or a hallucination. Kleptomania is diagnosed after ruling out CD, a manic episode, and antisocial personality disorder. The articles and items that are stolen are generally described to be of trivial value. It occurs more in women than men (F:M = 3:1); kleptomania usually begins in adolescence.

Insight-oriented psychotherapy and psychoanalysis are effective. Insight-oriented psychotherapy may help individuals who feel guilt and shame. SSRIs such as fluoxetine and fluvoxamine appear to be effective.

INTERMITTENT EXPLOSIVE DISORDER

IED is characterized by episodes of failure to control aggressive impulses. Symptoms include verbal aggression (temper tantrums, verbal arguments, or fights) or physical aggression toward property, animals, or other individuals, occurring on an average twice weekly for a period of 3 months.

Expressed aggression during outbursts is out of proportion to the provocation and is not premeditated. The recurrent aggressive outbursts cause marked distress in the individual or impairment in occupational or interpersonal functioning or are associated with financial or legal consequences.

Minimum age of the patient should be at least 6 years. IED is diagnosed after ruling out other causes of recurrent aggressive outbursts (e.g., schizophrenia, antisocial or borderline personality disorder, ADHD, CD, head trauma, Alzheimer disease, or substance intoxication).

Combined pharmacological and psychotherapeutic approach gives best results. Group therapy and family therapy may be beneficial. The goal of psychotherapy is to help the patient to recognize and verbalize feelings that precede the explosive outbursts instead of acting them out. Lithium is useful in decreasing aggression in general. Carbamazepine and valproate are reported to be helpful.

KEY POINTS

- Disruptive, impulse control, and conduct disorders include oppositional defiant disorder (ODD), intermittent explosive disorder (IED), conduct disorder (CD), antisocial personality disorder, pyromania, and kleptomania.

Conduct Disorder

- Conduct disorder commonly presents with behaviors that violate the rights of others or societal norms.
- These behaviors fall into four main types–aggression to people or animals, destruction of property, deceitfulness or theft, and serious rule violations.
- Pharmacotherapy is primarily recommended for comorbid disorders and target symptoms such as impulsivity, mood lability, irritability, and aggression.
- Primary prevention is the gold standard in conduct disorder intervention.
- Multimodal interventions targeting child, family, parents, teachers, peers, and education of the child are more effective than intervention with a single focus.
- The multifocused therapy combines parent management training (PMT), and child skill building therapies.

Oppositional Defiant Disorder

- The oppositional defiant disorder is characterized by persistent and frequent negativistic, hostile, and defiant behavior without violation of social norms or rights of others.
- Primary treatment of oppositional defiant disorder is family therapy in which parents are trained in child management techniques.
- Parent management training program focuses on teaching parents to alter their behavior to discourage the child's oppositional behavior and encourage appropriate behavior.
- Behavior therapy teaches parents to reinforce or praise appropriate behavior and ignore (not reinforce) undesired behavior.

Impulse Control Disorders

- Impulse control disorders are characterized by the inability to resist an intense impulse, drive, or temptation to perform a particular act that is harmful to self or others or both. They include pyromania and kleptomania.

Intermittent Explosive Disorder

- It is characterized by episodes of failure to control aggressive impulses. Symptoms include verbal aggression (temper tantrums, verbal arguments, or fights) or physical aggression toward property, animals, or other individuals occurring on an average twice weekly for a period of 3 months.

SELF-ASSESSMENT

1. Case-based Questions

   Master ABC, a 14-year-old adolescent, was brought by his parents with a history of behavioral problems, lying, beating animals, getting aggressive toward others, stealing money from home, stealing items from friends, missing his classes frequently, and not listening to his parents and elders. Mother reports that in the last 6 months he fled from home thrice and came back the next day. There was no history of comorbid seizures, substance abuse, psychosis, mania, depression, anxiety, and attention deficit/hyperactivity disorder. Birth and development history revealed full-term normal delivery and normal developmental milestones. Mental status examination (MSE) revealed no abnormalities of thought, perception, or mood.

   a. What is your provisional diagnosis?
   b. How will you treat this patient?

2. Define impulse control disorders. Enumerate various impulse control disorders. Write a short note on any one impulse control disorder.
3. Write short notes on:
   a. Etiology of conduct disorder
   b. Clinical features and treatment of oppositional defiant disorder
   c. Intermittent explosive disorder

Chapter 23

Substance-Related Disorders

Naresh Nebhinani · Navratan Suthar · Pooja Patnaik Kuppili

Psychoactive substances are compounds that can alter one's state of mind, consciousness, or mood. Alcohol; opioids; tobacco; cannabis; sedative, hypnotic, or anxiolytic; inhalants; hallucinogens; and stimulants are different classes of substances that are commonly abused.

Trends in substance use vary globally. Cannabis is the most commonly used illicit drug while alcohol is the most commonly used licit substance.

Comparative Nosology

The DSM-IV-TR had the concept of abuse and dependence. A significant change in the DSM-5 is that substance abuse and substance dependence are no longer separate criteria. DSM-5 merged the criteria for substance abuse and substance dependence to make a diagnosis of substance use disorder (SUD).

ICD-10 uses the categories of harmful use and dependence syndrome.

Diagnostic Classification

In DSM-5, substance-related disorders are broadly divided into the following four diagnostic categories:

Substance Use Disorder

SUD is characterized by a maladaptive pattern of substance use which leads to clinically significant impairment or distress.

It is characterized by tolerance, withdrawal symptoms, craving, substance use in situations in which it is physically hazardous (driving, operating machinery), use for longer duration or in larger amount, failure to fulfill major role obligations, and continued use despite knowledge of having a persistent or recurrent physical or psychological problem caused or exacerbated by the substance.

Substance Intoxication

It is a syndrome characterized by clinically significant maladaptive psychological or behavioral changes that are substance-specific, occurs as a result of recent ingestion or exposure to the substance, and is not explained by another medical condition or mental disorder.

Substance Withdrawal

Substance withdrawal is also a substance-specific syndrome that results from the abrupt cessation of heavy and prolonged use of a substance, which leads to clinically significant distress or impairment.

Substance-Induced Mental Disorder

Substance-induced mental disorder is classified as intoxication, withdrawal, and other substance/medication-induced mental disorders (psychotic disorders, bipolar and related disorders, depressive disorders, anxiety disorders, obsessive–compulsive and related disorders, sleep disorders, sexual dysfunctions, delirium, and neurocognitive disorders).

Etiology

The biopsychosocial model, which is the integration of biological, psychological, and social theories, can to an extent explain the heterogeneity of SUDs.

The various etiological factors in SUDs are briefly summarized in Box 23.1.

Psychodynamic Factors

The psychodynamic theories compare substance abuse to "masturbatory equivalent" or conceptualize as a form of regression to the oral phase. Recent psychodynamic theories view drug use as a reflection of disturbed ego functioning, that is, inability to deal with reality. Some patients use the substance as a form of self-medication to deal with underlying psychiatric illness (e.g., alcohol for panic disorder or amphetamines for depression).

Learning and Conditioning

As per theories of learning, substance use is conceptualized as a form of learned behavior. Positive reinforcement is caused by drug-induced euphoria or alleviation of

Box 23.1 Etiological factors of substance use disorders

Etiological factors

Biological factors
- Genetic vulnerability (family history of substance dependence)
- Biochemical factors (e.g., the role of neurotransmitters)
- Individual differences in susceptibility to the effects of different drugs
- Comorbid psychiatric or physical disorders

Psychological factors
- Curiosity
- Impulsivity
- Early initiation of drug use
- High novelty seeking
- High sensation seeking
- Poor self-esteem

Social factors
- Peer pressure
- Modeling (imitating behavior of significant others)
- Easy availability of substance
- Poor social/family support
- Childhood trauma or loss
- Parental substance use
- Permissive social attitude/sociocultural milieu
- Rapid urbanization

withdrawal symptoms caused by use of the drug. The paraphernalia (needles, bottles, or cigarette packs) can become secondary reinforcers and also acts as a cue that signals the availability of the substance. This paraphernalia is associated with craving for the substance.

Neural Pathways and Neurotransmitters

The reward circuit which chiefly includes the **mesocorticolimbic pathway** is the most important pathway implicated in the feeling of reward. The ventral tegmental area (VTA) of the midbrain, which contains dopaminergic neurons, has a projection to the prefrontal cortex (PFC) as well as to the part of the limbic system that is nucleus accumbens (NA). The PFC is implicated in stress-induced relapse and amygdala for cue-induced relapse. The main neurotransmitters involved are opioid, dopamine, and gamma-aminobutyric acid (GABA).

Under normal conditions, the circuit controls an individual's responses to natural rewards such as food, sex, and social interactions. In simplistic terms, activation of the pathway tells the individual to repeat what it just did to get that reward.

Approach to Management of SUD

Complete abstinence and harm reduction approach are the main approaches in the management of SUD.

Complete Abstinence

In complete abstinence, the patient is advised against using any psychoactive substance. This has been the conventional and widely preferred approach. However, in the context of frequent relapses and difficulty maintaining abstinence, a harm reduction approach is being increasingly recognized.

Harm Reduction

Harm reduction refers to interventions alleviating the harmful/problematic behaviors due to substance use. Controlled drinking, nicotine replacement therapy, opioid substitution therapy (OST), provision of "shooting alleys" (i.e., safe injection sites, disposable needles, and syringes), and needle exchange programs are some of the harm reduction techniques.

ALCOHOL-RELATED DISORDERS

Some of the commonly used alcoholic beverages are beer, wine, spirits (whiskey, rum, gin, vodka, brandy).

Screening Tests

MAST (Michigan Alcoholism Screening Test) and CAGE questionnaire can be used in the community setting to detect problem drinkers.

C = Have you ever felt you should **cut down** on your drinking?

A = Have people **annoyed** you by criticizing your drinking?

G = Have you ever felt bad or **guilty** about your drinking?

E = Have you ever had a drink first thing in the morning to steady your nerves or to get rid of a hangover (**eye-opener**)?

Alcohol Intoxication

The alcohol intoxication or "drunkenness" is characterized by slurring of speech, dizziness, incoordination, unsteady gait, ocular abnormalities such as nystagmus, diplopia, impairment of attention or memory, and stupor or coma.

In India, the legal limit for driving is 30 mg/100 mL (Section 185 of the Motor Vehicle Act. 1988), where as in the United Kingdom, it is 80 mg/100 mL. Impairment markedly increases with the increase of blood alcohol concentrations (BAC) (Table 23.1).

Alcohol Withdrawal

The onset of uncomplicated withdrawal occurs within 8 hours after the last drink, peaks on the second day, and remains for 2–5 days (Table 23.2). The alcohol withdrawal state is a hyper-glutamatergic and hypo-GABAergic state. It is characterized by autonomic hyperactivity marked by tremors, anxiety, sweating, tachycardia, increased pulse or blood pressure, and gastrointestinal upset. Psychotic symptoms such as hallucinations and delusions can also occur. Alcohol withdrawal can be complicated by seizures (rum fits) or delirium called delirium tremens (DT). Malnutrition, medical comorbidity, and dehydration are some of the predisposing factors for developing DT.

Table 23.2 Timeframe of onset of symptoms of alcohol withdrawal

Withdrawal symptoms	Time of development (after the last alcohol drink)
Tremor	6–8 hours
Psychotic and perceptual symptoms	8–12 hours
Seizures (rum fits)	12–24 hours
Alcohol delirium (DTs)	48–72 hours

Delirium Tremens

Alcohol withdrawal delirium is a medical emergency with around 20% mortality rate (especially if untreated). Delirium tremens (DT) is heralded by a triad of clouding of consciousness, perceptual abnormalities such as hallucinations, and coarse tremors.

The best treatment for DT is prevention. DT should be managed as an emergency, with an oral or parenteral benzodiazepine such as IV lorazepam, along with multivitamins (especially thiamine) and IV fluids. A high calorie-carbohydrate diet is also important.

Table 23.1 Impairment at various blood alcohol concentrations

BAC (mg/dL)	Likely impairment
20–30	Slowness in motor performance and thought process
30–80	Increase in motor and cognitive problems
80–200	Incoordination and judgment errors Lability of mood Cognitive deterioration
200–300	Nystagmus, marked slurring of speech, and alcoholic blackouts
>300	Impaired vital signs and possible death

Withdrawal Seizures

Alcohol withdrawal seizures/rum fits are generalized tonic–clonic seizures (GTCS). Status epilepticus is a rare occurrence. Antiepileptic medication is not recommended. Hypoglycemia, electrolyte abnormalities such as hyponatremia, and hypomagnesemia caused by alcohol use could also lower the seizure threshold. Benzodiazepines (e.g., lorazepam) are preferred to manage withdrawal seizures.

Complications of Alcohol Use

Wernicke–Korsakoff Syndrome

Alcohol-induced persisting amnestic disorders are of two types: **Wernicke's encephalopathy** and **Korsakoff's syndrome**. The acute and completely reversible condition is known as Wernicke's encephalopathy. The chronic state Korsakoff syndrome has a poor prognosis with only 20% improvement. It results from thiamine (Vitamin B1) deficiency, which is an essential coenzyme.

Wernicke's encephalopathy is characterized by the presence of the triad of symptoms, namely change in mental state (confusion), ocular disturbances (ophthalmoplegia, nystagmus), and ataxia. Once it is diagnosed, thiamine should be initiated immediately to prevent its progression into the Korsakoff syndrome. A high carbohydrate diet or intravenous glucose should be started after thiamine supplementation. Thiamine is usually started orally in a dose of 100 mg two to three times daily and then continued for 1–2 weeks. If timely treated, it resolves within a few days/weeks or otherwise it might evolve into Korsakoff syndrome.

Korsakoff syndrome is characterized by confabulation, recent memory impairment, and amnesia of anterograde type. Treatment of Korsakoff syndrome is also oral thiamine in a dose of 100 mg, twice or thrice a day for 12 weeks to 1 year.

Laboratories Tests

The laboratory tests that provide objective evidence of alcohol consumption as well as help in assessing the degree of impairment are known as state markers of heavy drinking (Table 23.3).

A combination of γ-glutamyl transferase (GGT) and carbohydrate deficient transferrin (CDT) is better than either test alone for the identification of heavy drinking and monitoring abstinence.

Table 23.3 State markers of heavy drinking

Test	Relevant result
γ-Glutamyl transferase (GGT)	>35 U/L
Carbohydrate deficient transferrin (CDT)	>3%
Mean corpuscular volume (MCV)	>91.0 μm^3
Aspartate aminotransferase (AST)	>45 IU/L
Alanine aminotransferase (ALT)	>45 IU/L
Uric acid	• >6.4 mg/dL for men • >5 mg/dL for women

Treatment

It involves detoxification, that is, management of acute withdrawal state and maintenance treatment (Table 23.4).

1. *Acute (Detoxification)*

The benzodiazepines are the drug of choice in the detoxification phase to control alcohol withdrawal symptoms. Benzodiazepines help to control the seizure activity, delirium, anxiety, tachycardia, and tremors associated with alcohol withdrawal. Chlordiazepoxide or lorazepam are preferred drugs. Short-acting drugs like lorazepam, oxazepam, and temazepam are preferred in the case of hepatic impairment and geriatric age group.

In DT, antipsychotics are used along with benzodiazepines to control agitation and hallucinations.

2. *Maintenance therapy*

Anticraving Agents

Naltrexone and acamprosate are two USFDA-approved anticraving agents, while topiramate and baclofen are not approved by USFDA but used to reduce the craving for alcohol.

Naltrexone It is an opioid antagonist, reduces the craving, and acts by antagonizing the effects of endogenous endorphins released by alcohol intake.

Acamprosate It acts as an NMDA receptor antagonist and causes enhancement of GABA signaling via positive allosteric modulation of $GABA_A$ receptors. In severe renal insufficiency (creatinine clearance less than 30 mL per hour), acamprosate is contraindicated.

Table 23.4 Pharmacological management of alcohol use disorder

<table>
<tr><th>Phase of treatment</th><th colspan="3">Treatment/drugs</th></tr>
<tr><td>Acute (detoxification)</td><td colspan="3">• Benzodiazepine (diazepam, chlordiazepoxide, lorazepam)
• Vitamin supplements (especially thiamine)
• Intravenous fluids
• Motivational enhancement therapy (MET)</td></tr>
<tr><td rowspan="3">Maintenance therapy</td><td rowspan="2">Pharmacological</td><td>Aversive/deterrent agents</td><td>• Disulfiram</td></tr>
<tr><td>Anticraving agents</td><td>• Naltrexone
• Acamprosate
• Baclofen
• Topiramate</td></tr>
<tr><td>Psychosocial</td><td colspan="2">• Motivational enhancement therapy
• Cognitive behavioral therapy (CBT)
• Relapse prevention counseling (RPC)
• Behavioral therapies
• Group therapy
• Family therapy
• Self-help groups such as alcohol anonymous (AA)</td></tr>
</table>

The combination of acamprosate plus naltrexone may be more effective than either drug alone.

Deterrent Drug

Disulfiram This FDA-approved drug acts via inhibiting aldehyde dehydrogenase, resulting in the build-up of acetaldehyde in the blood causing unpleasant symptoms of nausea, vomiting, flushing, throbbing headache, tachycardia, hypertension, sweating, thirst, dyspnea, chest pain, vertigo, and blurred vision. These unpleasant symptoms are known as a **disulfiram alcohol reaction**. The treatment of severe disulfiram alcohol reaction is mainly supportive to prevent shock.

The dose range is 250–500 mg per day. Disulfiram should be started at least 12 hours after the last drink. Patients must not consume alcohol or use any products containing alcohol such as vinegar, aftershave, and cough syrup while taking disulfiram.

Psychosocial Interventions

Motivational enhancement therapy (MET) It is a counseling approach that helps patients to resolve their ambivalence of stopping substance use behaviors and engaging in treatment.

Cognitive behavioral therapy (CBT) CBT to promote self-control, development of coping ability, and social skills.

Relapse prevention counseling (RPC) It uses CBT techniques for identification and prevention of high-risk situation to maintain abstinence.

Behavioral therapies These therapies help in modifying the attitude and behavior of patients, engaging them in drug abuse treatment, and providing incentives for them to remain abstinent.

OPIOID USE DISORDERS

The opiates are a group of compounds derived from milky exudates of unripe seed capsules of the poppy plant *Papaver somniferum*. Commonly abused substances include natural opiates like opium (afeem), poppy husk (bhukki/dode), poppy seeds (khuskhus), codeine, morphine, and synthetic compounds such as heroin, pethidine, dextropropoxyphene, and diphenoxylate. The most dependence-producing derivatives are morphine and heroin. Various routes of consumptions are oral, snorting, chasing, intravenous (**mainlining**), intramuscular (**blind dating**), and subcutaneous injections (**skin-popping**).

Opioid use disorder is of great public health importance because of the higher occurrence of infections such as HIV, hepatitis B and C virus with intravenous opioid use.

Acute Intoxication

It is manifested as respiratory depression, pinpoint pupil, bradycardia, hypotension, and subnormal core body temperature. Later, it can progress to delayed reflexes, coma, and death. It can be treated with naloxone 0.2–0.4 mg to a patient in coma to aid in the maintenance of respiration. A higher initial dose of 1–2 mg is given to patients with apnea or cardiorespiratory arrest. An increase in respiratory rate and pupillary dilatation are signs of improvement. If no response is seen within 2–3 minutes of IV administration of naloxone higher doses (1–2 mg), repeated doses are administered while maintaining ventilation and oxygenation.

The primary goal of naloxone administration is to restore adequate ventilation (above 12 respirations per minute) and oxygenation (above 92%) rather than full alertness.

Withdrawal Syndrome

It usually starts within 12–24 hours. Peaking of symptoms is noted on the first to third day. The symptoms decrease and subside within a week or 10 days of last opioid use. Body aches, abdominal and muscular cramps, restlessness, rhinorrhea, lacrimation, diarrhea, sweating, yawning, gooseflesh, tachycardia, and pupillary dilation are the characteristic withdrawal symptoms noted.

Laboratory Tests

- Urinary opioids testing: It detects the presence of opiates in urine. The testing can be done to check abstinence from opioids and before the start of naltrexone therapy. Drugs are first detected in urine 2–6 hours after the use. Morphine, heroin, codeine, and hydrocodone can be detected in urine for 1–3 days after the last use.
- Patients with a history of IV drug abuse should be tested for hepatitis B, hepatitis C, and HIV.

Treatment

It involves detoxification, that is, management of acute withdrawal state and maintenance treatment (Table 23.5). Immediate management goals include detoxification and management of comorbid medical illness. Short-term goals include promoting abstinence, treatment of comorbid medical or psychiatric conditions, and reintegration into the family. Long-term goals mainly focus on promoting abstinence, relapse prevention, rehabilitation, reintegration into the community, and enhancing functioning.

Three main detoxification strategies are as follows:

1. Symptomatic treatment (with nonopioid medication)
2. Agonist-assisted detoxification
3. Antagonist-assisted detoxification with symptomatic treatment

Table 23.5 Pharmacological management of opioid use disorder

Phase of treatment	Treatment	Drugs/therapy
Acute (detoxification)	a. Symptomatic treatment	• Clonidine for autonomic hyperactivity symptoms (e.g., sweating, restlessness, tremor, and rhinorrhea) • Clonazepam for anxiety • Zolpidem or zopiclone for insomnia • Loperamide for diarrhea • Metoclopramide for nausea and vomiting • Ibuprofen for aches and pain

(*Continued*)

Table 23.5 *(Continued)*

Phase of treatment	Treatment	Drugs/therapy
	b. Agonist-assisted detoxification	• Buprenorphine: Partial opioid agonist • Methadone: Full opioid agonist
	c. Antagonist-assisted detoxification	• Naltrexone is used 2–3 days after the last dose of full agonist opioid. It is started at low doses of 3–6 mg and titrated to a full dose of 50 mg per day • Withdrawal symptoms are treated symptomatically with clonazepam and clonidine
Maintenance	Opioid substitution therapy	• Buprenorphine • Methadone
	Opioid antagonist	• Naltrexone
	Psychosocial therapy	• Motivational enhancement therapy • Cognitive behavior therapy • Relapse prevention counseling • Behavioral therapies • Others: Family therapy, group therapy, and self-help groups such as Narcotic Anonymous

1. *Detoxification*

a. Methadone: It is a full agonist at μ receptor. It is a long-acting synthetic opiate with a half-life of 24 hours. Usual dose is 20–80 mg/day (maximum dose = 120 mg).

b. Buprenorphine: It is a partial opiate agonist available as sublingual preparation. It produces less euphoria than methadone. Supervised administration is the norm to prevent diversion. Because of its slow dissociation from opioid receptors, it can also be given thrice weekly.

c. Clonidine: It is an α_2 agonist, acts by inhibiting the noradrenergic release. It is given orally 0.1–0.3 mg, 3–4 times a day, and tapered off in 10–14 days. Sedation and postural hypotension are common side effects.

2. *Maintenance Treatment*

Once the detoxification phase is complete, the patient is started on maintenance therapy. Following options are available:

- **Opioid substitution therapy:** OST is a form of harm reduction strategy. Here, the focus is on the patient receiving licit, medically safe compounds orally instead of illicit unsafe psychoactive substances taken through high-risk

behaviors. The patient can be put on either of the following two regimens:
- Methadone maintenance
- Buprenorphine maintenance

- **Opioid antagonists (naltrexone):** Naltrexone is a long-acting μ-opioid antagonist. If the patient restarts opioid use while on naltrexone, the reinforcing effects of opioids will gradually extinguish as naltrexone prevents the euphoric effects of opioids. The major limitation of the antagonist treatment model is the need for supervision for taking medication. The dose of the naltrexone is 50 mg daily. Naltrexone can be used thrice in a week (100 mg on Monday and Wednesday and 150 mg on Friday). Naltrexone is also available as a monthly intramuscular injection which is FDA approved. Implantable naltrexone with 3–6 months duration is available in some countries (Russia).

  Naltrexone can precipitate withdrawal symptoms in patients actively consuming opioids; so to prevent precipitation of withdrawals symptoms, naltrexone should be prescribed after making sure a washout period of 5 days after short-acting opioids such as heroin and at least 10 days for longer-acting opioids such as methadone after the last dose of the opioids. Opioid Free State can be determined by urine toxicology, and even after a negative urine screen test if any doubt persists, naloxone challenge test should be done.
- **Naloxone challenge test**: This test is performed to assess physical dependence. Subcutaneous or intravenous injection of naloxone is administered. A positive test is indicative of physical dependence and consists of symptoms and signs typical of opioid withdrawal.

Education and Needle Exchange

Other than the opioids abstinence, proper education about the transmission of HIV is also important. Emphasis must be laid on promoting safe-sex practices and free needle-exchange programs.

TOBACCO-RELATED DISORDERS

Cigarettes, cigars, snuff, chewing tobacco, and pipes are the various modes of consumption of tobacco in descending order.

Tobacco Withdrawal

Withdrawal symptoms result after cessation or reduction in the use of tobacco after use for many weeks. The common withdrawal symptoms include anxiety, depressed mood, irritability, frustration, insomnia, difficulty concentrating, restlessness, and increased appetite. Insomnia, increased cough, constipation, and mouth ulcers can also occur. Craving is common.

Treatment

Psychiatrists must give clear advice to stop tobacco use and a quit date must be discussed. The decision of abrupt or gradual cessation should be decided according to the patient's preference, severity, and risk factors. The first follow-up visit should be within 48–72 hours after quitting due to the high risk of relapse.

The Fagerstrom test of nicotine dependence (FTND) is commonly used as a screening test for the intensity of physical addiction to nicotine.

Psychosocial Therapies

5A's model of tobacco cessation intervention is the most widely accepted and well-proved psychological therapy for smoking (Box 23.2).

Box 23.2 5A's model of tobacco cessation intervention

- **Ask** about tobacco use: Screen current and past tobacco use
- **Advice** to quit or reinforce people who have quit
- **Assess** for the desire to quit
- **Assist** patients with different strategies
- **Arrange** follow up

Identifying and addressing high-risk situations is a key component of *relapse prevention. Stimulus control* involves the removal of environmental cues for smoking. *Aversive therapy* is based on the concept of learning theory, where smokers smoke rapidly in succession until they develop nausea. Thereby, smoking gets associated with an unpleasant sensation (nausea) rather than a pleasant sensation.

Pharmacological Therapies

Nicotine replacement therapies (NRTs)

Out of the five FDA-approved NRTs, chewing gums, lozenges, and patches are available as over-the-counter medicines, whereas NRT inhaler and NRT nasal spray are available on prescription only. NRT is advised for a short period of maintenance (6–12 weeks) followed by tapering gradually for another 6–24 weeks.

Non-nicotine prescription medications

Non-nicotine therapy may help smokers who failed NRT. The FDA-approved agents are sustained-release preparation (SR) of bupropion, and varenicline.

- **Bupropion:** Doses of 300 mg per day double the quit rates in smokers with or without a history of depression.
- **Varenicline:** It relieves both craving and withdrawal and also reduces the reinforcing effects of nicotine by blocking dopaminergic stimulation responsible for smoking reinforcement.

Preclinical and clinical trials are going on for the development of a vaccine against nicotine.

CANNABIS-RELATED DISORDERS

Cannabis is the most commonly used illicit substance globally.

Cannabis Preparations

It is obtained from the hemp plant, which is scientifically called *Cannabis sativa.* Delta-9-tetrahydrocannabinol (Δ9-THC) is the principal psychoactive constituent. The rolled marijuana cigarettes are commonly called "joints." The various preparations of cannabis are bhang, ganja, charas (hashish), and hash oil.

Cannabis Use Disorder

Cannabis consumption leads to the dilation of the conjunctival blood vessels (red eye) and a mild increase in heart rate. Orthostatic hypotension may be present at high doses. Increased appetite and dry mouth are common symptoms of cannabis intoxication.

Long-term cannabis use leads to cerebral atrophy, increased seizure vulnerability, chromosomal damage, birth defects, menstrual irregularities, impaired immune response, and alteration in testosterone concentration.

Very mild or no physical dependence is noted with cannabis. Psychological dependence could be mild to severe. Early age of onset, greater duration, and frequency of use are associated with increased risk of dependence.

Cannabis Intoxication

Cannabis intoxication increases the user's sensitivity to the external stimuli, makes colors seem brighter, and subjectively slows the appreciation of time. Often, cannabis users experience the phenomenon of depersonalization and derealization. Motor skills are also impaired by cannabis use.

Cannabis Withdrawal

Withdrawal symptoms start appearing within 1–2 weeks after cessation and include craving, irritability, depressed mood, nervousness, anxiety, tremors, decreased sleep and appetite, weight loss, vivid dreaming, sweating, restlessness, headache, and abdominal pain.

Cannabis-Induced Psychotic Disorder or Hemp Insanity

Cannabis-induced psychotic disorder is uncommon compared to transient paranoid ideation. It is usually found in patients who take highly potent preparations of cannabis for a long time. Psychotic episodes in cannabis users are referred to as hemp insanity. Rarely, "bad trip" experience can be caused by cannabis, which is often reported with the intoxication of hallucinogens.

Flashbacks

Persons using cannabis can experience sensations related to cannabis intoxication (flashback) days or weeks after they last used cannabis.

Amotivational Syndrome

It is controversial whether this syndrome is related to cannabis use or characterological trait in a subgroup of persons regardless of cannabis use. It is characterized by a person's unwillingness to initiate or persist in any task which requires constant attention. It is associated with heavy and long-term cannabis use.

Treatment

Treatment of cannabis use rests on the principles of abstinence and support. Abstinence can be achieved by either hospitalization or on an outpatient basis. Monitoring is done with the help of urine drug screens, which can detect cannabis for up to 4 weeks after the last use. For support, various therapies can be utilized such as individual, family, and group psychotherapies.

An antianxiety drug can be used for the short term to treat withdrawal symptoms. Antidepressants may be used to treat cannabis dependence in a person whose cannabis dependence is related to underlying depressive disorder.

SEDATIVE, HYPNOTIC, OR ANXIOLYTIC-RELATED DISORDERS

The three major groups of drugs are benzodiazepines, barbiturates, and barbiturate-like substances.

Benzodiazepines

Alprazolam, nitrazepam, diazepam, and clonazepam are some of the commonly abused benzodiazepines.

Flunitrazepam (Rohypnol) is a "club drug" (as used in clubs for rave parties) and also known as "date rape drug," as it causes rapid sedation on adding it with alcohol and facilitates promiscuous sexual behavior and rape.

Nonbenzodiazepine sedatives such as zolpidem, zaleplon, and eszopiclone, commonly known as "Z drugs," can also lead to drug abuse and dependence.

Barbiturates

Before the introduction of benzodiazepines, barbiturates were frequently prescribed; however, these are not commonly prescribed these days due to high abuse potential. Secobarbital (also known as "reds," "red devils," "seggies," and "downers"), pentobarbital (known as "yellow jackets," "yellows," and "nembies"), and a secobarbital–amobarbital combination (known as "reds and blues," "rainbows," "double trouble," and "tooies") are some of the commonly abused barbiturate drugs.

Barbiturate-Like Substances

The most commonly abused barbiturate-like substance is methaqualone, often used by young people to heighten the pleasure of sexual activity. The street names for methaqualone include "**mandrakes**" and "soapers." Other barbiturate-like substances include meprobamate (Equanil) and chloral hydrate.

Treatment of Benzodiazepines Overdose

Benzodiazepines in contrast to barbiturates have a large margin of safety when taken in overdose. Most persons with benzodiazepine overdose respond to a cumulative dose of 1–3 mg of benzodiazepine receptor antagonist flumazenil.

Benzodiazepines Withdrawal and Treatment

Anxiety, dysphoria, obsessive ruminations, and paranoia are mood disturbances in benzodiazepine withdrawal. Sleep disturbances include insomnia, altered sleep-wake cycle, and daytime drowsiness. Physical signs and symptoms include tachycardia, increased blood pressure, agitation, hyper-reflexia, tremor, myoclonus, muscle and joint pain, nausea, ataxia, tinnitus, diaphoresis, grand mal seizures, hyperpyrexia, and death. Perceptual disturbances include hyperacusis, depersonalization, illusion, and hallucinations.

Some clinicians prefer switching to a longer acting benzodiazepine (e.g., diazepam, clonazepam) and others recommend stabilizing on the drug the patient was taking or phenobarbital. The basic principle for safe withdrawal is a gradual tapering of the drug (10%–25% every few days, if tolerated). Antiepileptic drugs such as Carbamazepine may also be useful in the treatment of benzodiazepine withdrawal to prevent seizures. Equal emphasis is placed on nonpharmacological interventions of relapse prevention.

Treatment of Barbiturates Intoxication

Treatment includes gastric lavage, activated charcoal, and monitoring of vital signs. If the patient is comatose, IV fluid line should be established, the airway should be secured with an endotracheal tube, and the patient should be mechanically ventilated if needed.

Barbiturates Withdrawal and Treatment

Withdrawal symptoms can be mild (e.g., anxiety, weakness, sweating, and insomnia) or can be severe (e.g., seizures, delirium, cardiovascular collapse, and death). Most symptoms appear in the first 3 days of abstinence and seizures usually occur on the second or third day.

Withdrawal symptoms are treated by using a loading dose of phenobarbital. An adequate dose is 30 mg of phenobarbital for every 100 mg of the short-acting substance.

INHALANT-RELATED DISORDERS

Inhalant drugs (also called volatile substances or solvents) are volatile hydrocarbons with various routes of administration through the nose or mouth to enter the bloodstream via the transpulmonary route. Inhalants are readily available in the community in the form of paint products, correction fluid, fuels, and more. Inhalant use is associated with several psychiatric problems such as conduct disorder, mood disorders, suicidality, and physical and sexual abuse or neglect.

Clinical Features

At small dose, disinhibition, euphoria, and excitement occur. High doses of inhalants can cause psychological symptoms of fearfulness, perceptual disturbances such as illusions, auditory, and visual hallucinations, and distortions of body size. The neurological manifestations are slurring of speech, decreased rate of speech, and ataxia. Long-term use can lead to irritability, memory impairment, and emotional lability. Tolerance can occur in some users.

Withdrawal symptoms include insomnia, irritability, tremors, jitteriness, sweating, nausea, vomiting, tachycardia, and occasional delusions and hallucinations.

Treatment

The cornerstone of treatment of inhalant use disorder is largely nonpharmacological, consisting of motivation enhancement therapy and RPC. Withdrawal usually resolves spontaneously, and hence may not require any specific management. It primarily incorporates reassurance, support, and physical monitoring.

However, the serious effects of intoxication such as coma, bronchospasm, cardiac arrhythmias, trauma, and burns should receive medical attention. Sedative drugs such as benzodiazepines are contraindicated as they worsen inhalant intoxication.

Severe agitation and psychosis should be managed with antipsychotic, haloperidol. Sedative drugs should be avoided as they may aggravate the psychosis.

HALLUCINOGEN-RELATED DISORDERS

Hallucinogens are diverse substances that produce alterations in perception, cognition, affect, sense of meaning, or sense of self. They are referred by various terms such as psychedelics and psychotomimetics.

Phencyclidine (PCP) and related arylcyclohexamines (ketamine) are termed as dissociative anesthetics. Their actions are mediated by noncompetitive N-methyl-D-aspartate (NMDA) receptor antagonist. **PCP** is also known as **angel dust**.

The effect of **classic hallucinogens** is mediated by agonism or partial agonism of the $5HT_{2A}$ receptor, and the prototype drug of this type is lysergic acid diethylamide (LSD). Other drugs in this group are psilocybin derived from mushroom, mescaline (the active component of hallucinogenic cacti), and dimethyltryptamine (DMT).

MDMA (3, 4-methylenedioxymethamphetamine), commonly known as **ecstasy** (is structurally similar to classic hallucinogens, e.g., mescaline), produces feelings of love and closeness toward other people with little or no alteration in the perception or thought process that are prominent in classic hallucinogens.

PCP is smoked or snorted, whereas ketamine is frequently injected, snorted, or ingested.

Hallucinogen Use Disorder

Long-term use of hallucinogen is uncommon; therefore, psychological dependence rarely occurs.

Hallucinogen Intoxication

Hallucinogen intoxication presents as altered mental status. Patients are agitated, fearful, or experience panic or paranoia. All types of hallucinogens can produce anxiety, agitation, inappropriate labile affect, visual illusions or hallucinations, paranoia, or other delusions.

Hallucinogen Persisting Perception Disorder

Hallucinogen users sometimes report of a *flashback* of hallucinogenic symptoms long after ingesting a hallucinogen. This is diagnosed as hallucinogen persisting perception disorder.

Hallucinogen-Induced Psychotic Disorders

PCP-induced psychosis is often indistinguishable from schizophrenia. Thought disorder and negative symptoms may be prominent.

The most common adverse effect of LSD and related substances is known as "*bad trip*." It is described as similar to an acute panic reaction to cannabis. A bad trip can occasionally produce true psychotic symptoms.

Hallucinogen-Induced Mood Disorder

Hallucinogen abusers may experience short-lasting manic symptoms with grandiose delusions, or depression-like feelings, or mixed symptoms and hallucinogen-induced mood symptoms generally remit after elimination of the substance from the body.

Hallucinogen-Induced Anxiety Disorder

Anxiety is the most common symptom for which a person seeks help in an emergency room. Panic disorders with agoraphobia are the most common anxiety disorders in these patients.

Treatment

Hallucinogen Intoxication

A basic principle in treatment is providing supportive care. Benzodiazepines are the preferred drug to treat anxiety symptoms. Sometimes, restraint is also required.

Hallucinogen Persisting perception Disorder and Hallucinogen-Induced Psychosis

In hallucinogen persisting perception disorder, pharmacological therapy includes long-acting benzodiazepines such as clonazepam and anticonvulsants such as valproic acid and carbamazepine.

Antipsychotics should be used only in the case of hallucinogen-induced psychoses. Treatment of hallucinogen-induced psychoses does not differ from other psychoses. The second dimension of treatment is behavioral. The patients are advised to avoid other stimulants such as over-the-counter drugs, caffeine, and alcohol.

STIMULANT-RELATED DISORDERS

As per DSM-5, stimulants are classified as amphetamine-like substances, structurally dissimilar agents with similar effects (methylphenidate), and cocaine. Amphetamines are commonly used illicit substances and are known by street names like ice, crystal, crystal meth, and speed.

In ICD-10 and DSM-IV-TR, stimulants and cocaine are described separately, but in DSM-5, cocaine and amphetamine are combined into stimulant use disorders.

Cocaine is extracted from *Erythroxylum coca*. **Crack cocaine** or "rocks" is a freebase form of cocaine. This form is highly potent, and hence extremely addictive.

Snorting (inhaling fine powder) is the most common method of using cocaine. Other methods of consumption are subcutaneous or intravenous injection and smoking (freebasing).

Psychological symptoms of stimulant intoxication include mood changes, hallucinations, and delusions. Typical paranoia consists of worry that the police or a drug dealer is planning to attack the cocaine user. Physical symptoms include changes in heart rate, blood pressure, thermoregulation, pupillary dilatation, GI disturbances, and cardiopulmonary symptoms. In severe intoxication, the patient can have seizures, arrhythmia, hyperpyrexia, and death.

Stimulant withdrawal is characterized by dysphoria, fatigue, disturbances in sleep, appetite, and psychomotor activity.

Treatment

Treatment of patients with stimulant-related disorders is often begun in outpatient settings, as withdrawal syndrome rarely requires specific medical intervention. Indications of inpatient treatment include psychiatric or medical conditions independently requiring admission (e.g., depression with suicidal ideation or complications of stimulant use such as a cerebrovascular accident or myocardial infarction), a lack of response to outpatient treatment, and need to remove the patient from the environment that may sustain drug use.

There are no specific pharmacological treatments for amphetamine or cocaine intoxication or withdrawal. Supportive care is the mainstay of the treatment. Stimulant withdrawal is generally mild, self-limited, and is not associated with delirium.

Agitation or paranoia may need monitoring and short-term treatment with benzodiazepines or antipsychotics. Unscheduled urine testing must be done frequently during the follow-up period.

Disulfiram has shown potential benefits in cocaine dependence.

"Cocaine bugs" is a form of delusional parasitosis found in cocaine users. Patients describe them as insects or bugs crawling beneath the skin. Treatment includes abstinence from the psychoactive substance, and using antipsychotics.

A vaccine to treat cocaine use disorders has been developed and a trial has shown a significant increase in cocaine-free urine when adequate antibody titers were achieved. A vaccine against methamphetamine is in preclinical stages.

CLUB DRUGS

LSD, γ-hydroxybutyrate (GHB), ketamine, methamphetamine, MDMA (ecstasy), and Rohypnol or "roofies" (flunitrazepam) are known to be consumed at dance clubs, bars, and rave parties. Hence, they are called "club drugs". GHB, ketamine, and Rohypnol are called "date rape drugs."

POLYSUBSTANCE DEPENDENCE

A diagnosis of polysubstance dependence can be considered if there has been repeated use of substances of at least three of the above described categories (excluding nicotine and caffeine), meeting criteria for dependence as a group but not for any single substance for the past 1 year. However, the concept of polysubstance dependence has been dropped from DSM-5.

KEY POINTS

- Psychoactive substances are compounds that can alter one's state of mind, consciousness, or mood.

Alcohol-Related Disorder

- The alcohol intoxication or "drunkenness" is characterized by slurring of speech, dizziness, incoordination, unsteady gait, ocular abnormalities such as nystagmus, diplopia, impairment of attention or memory, and stupor or coma.
- The alcohol withdrawal state is characterized by autonomic hyperactivity marked by tremors, anxiety, sweating, tachycardia, increased pulse or blood pressure, and gastrointestinal upset. Psychotic symptoms such as hallucinations and delusions can also occur.
- Alcohol withdrawal can be complicated by seizures (rum fits) or delirium called delirium tremens (DT).
- Delirium tremens is heralded by a triad of clouding of consciousness, perceptual abnormalities such as hallucinations, and coarse tremors.
- Alcohol withdrawal seizures/rum fits are generalized tonic–clonic seizures (GTCS). Status epilepticus is a rare occurrence.
- A combination of γ-glutamyl transferase (GGT) and carbohydrate deficient transferrin (CDT) is better than either test alone for the identification of heavy drinking and monitoring abstinence.
- The benzodiazepines are the drug of choice in the detoxification phase to control alcohol withdrawal symptoms.
- Naltrexone and acamprosate are two USFDA-approved anticraving agents and disulfiram is USFDA-approved deterrent drug.

Opioid-Related Disorder

- Commonly abused substances include natural opiates like opium (afeem), poppy husk (bhukki/dode), poppy seeds (khuskhus), codeine, morphine, and synthetic compounds such as heroin, pethidine, dextropropoxyphene, and diphenoxylate.
- Acute intoxication of opioids is manifested by respiratory depression, pinpoint pupil, bradycardia, hypotension, and subnormal core body temperature. It can be treated with Naloxone 0.2–0.4 mg to a patient in coma to aid in the maintenance of respiration.
- Body aches, abdominal and muscular cramps, restlessness, rhinorrhea, lacrimation, diarrhea, sweating, yawning, gooseflesh, tachycardia, and pupillary dilation are the characteristic opioid withdrawal symptoms.
- Three main detoxification strategies are:
  - Symptomatic treatment
  - Agonist-assisted detoxification
  - Antagonist-assisted detoxification with symptomatic treatment

Tobacco-Related Disorder

- Tobacco withdrawal symptoms include anxiety, depressed mood, irritability, frustration, insomnia, difficulty concentrating, restlessness, and increased appetite. Insomnia, increased cough, constipation, and mouth ulcers can also occur.
- Out of the five FDA-approved nicotine replacement therapies (NRTs), chewing gums, lozenges, and patches are available as over-the-counter medicines, whereas NRT inhaler and NRT nasal spray are available on prescription only.
- Bupropion and varenicline are FDA-approved non-nicotine replacement therapy.

Cannabis-Related Disorder

- Cannabis is the most commonly used illicit substance globally.
- Delta-9-tetrahydrocannabinol (Δ9-THC) is the principal psychoactive constituent.
- Cannabis intoxication increases the user's sensitivity to the external stimuli, makes colors seem brighter, and subjectively slows the appreciation of time.
- Very mild or no physical dependence is noted with cannabis.
- Cannabis abuse is associated with flashbacks and amotivational syndrome.

Sedative, Hypnotic, or Anxiolytic-Related Disorders

- Benzodiazepine overdose is treated with benzodiazepine receptor antagonist flumazenil.
- Benzodiazepines withdrawal is characterized by anxiety, dysphoria, obsessive ruminations, paranoia, hallucinations, insomnia, daytime drowsiness, tachycardia, increased blood pressure, agitation, hyper-reflexia, tremor, myoclonus, nausea, ataxia, tinnitus, diaphoresis, grand mal seizures, hyperpyrexia, and death.
- Benzodiazepine withdrawal can be managed by switching to a longer acting benzodiazepine (e.g., diazepam, clonazepam).
- Antiepileptic drugs such as carbamazepine may also be useful in the treatment of benzodiazepine withdrawal to prevent seizures.
- Treatment of barbiturate intoxication includes gastric lavage, activated charcoal, and monitoring of vital signs. If the patient is comatose, IV fluid line should be established, the airway

should be secured with an endotracheal tube, and the patient should be mechanically ventilated if needed.

- **Barbiturates** withdrawal symptoms can be mild (e.g., anxiety, weakness, sweating, and insomnia) or can be severe (e.g., seizures, delirium, cardiovascular collapse, and death).
- Barbiturate withdrawal symptoms are treated by using a loading dose of phenobarbital. An adequate dose is 30 mg of phenobarbital for every 100 mg of the short-acting substance.

Inhalant-Related Disorders

- Inhalants use is associated with several psychiatric problems such as conduct disorder, mood disorders, suicidality, and physical and sexual abuse or neglect.

Hallucinogen-Related Disorders

- Hallucinogens are of two types: PCP (phencyclidine) and related arylcyclohexamines (ketamine) and classic hallucinogens that include lysergic acid diethylamide (LSD), psilocybin, mescaline, and dimethyltryptamine (DMT).
- All types of hallucinogens can produce anxiety, agitation, inappropriate labile affect, visual illusions or hallucinations, paranoia, or other delusions.
- Hallucinogen use is associated with flashbacks and a bad trip.
- PCP-induced psychosis is often indistinguishable from schizophrenia.

Stimulant-Related Disorders

- DSM-5 classifies stimulants as amphetamine-like substances, structurally dissimilar agents with similar effects (methylphenidate), and cocaine.
- **Crack cocaine** or "rocks" is a freebase form of cocaine.
- Psychological symptoms of stimulant intoxication include mood changes, hallucinations, and delusions.
- There are no specific pharmacological treatments for amphetamine or cocaine intoxication or withdrawal.

Club Drugs

- LSD, γ-hydroxybutyrate (GHB), ketamine, methamphetamine, MDMA (ecstasy), and Rohypnol or "roofies" (flunitrazepam) are known to be consumed at dance clubs, bars, and rave parties. Hence, they are called "club drugs."
- GHB, ketamine, and Rohypnol are called "date rape drugs."

SELF-ASSESSMENT

1. Case-based Questions

   A 40-year-old male is brought to the casualty of the hospital in a comatose condition. On examination, the patient has a respiratory rate of 8 per minute, a heart rate of 50 per minute, a blood pressure of 80/40, and a temperature of 36° centigrade. The patient has pinpoint pupils reacting to light. On ECG, patient has a sinus rhythm. Family members report that the patient has no comorbid psychiatric or medical disorder. Family members are not aware of any substance abuse by the patient.

  a. What is your provisional diagnosis and discuss the reasons for it?
  b. How will you manage the patient?

2. Write short notes on:
   a. What are the two main approaches in the substance use disorders?
   b. CAGE questionnaire.
   c. Discuss the various state markers of heavy drinking.
   d. Disulfiram.
   e. Delirium tremens.
   f. Discuss the various FDA-approved drugs for nicotine dependence.
   g. Treatment of benzodiazepine withdrawals.
   h. Cannabis-related disorder.
   i. Inhalant-related disorder.
   j. Classify hallucinogens and discuss various hallucinogen-induced psychiatric illnesses.
   k. Clinical features and treatment of stimulant intoxication and withdrawal.
   l. Naltrexone.

Chapter 24

Geriatric Psychiatry

Sandeep Kumar Goyal

Geriatric psychiatry deals with preventing, diagnosing, and treating psychological disorders in older adults. Advances in medical technology have led to an increase in the number of people 65 years of age and older. The characteristics of this age group include chronic medical illnesses, concomitant use of medications, and drug–drug and drug–disease interactions. Apart from medical disorders, reduced financial resources due to retirement, death of spouse or friends leading to loneliness, and dependence on others for activities of daily living are stressors that are often present in the elderly.

Psychiatric history taking and mental status examination follow the same format as in young adults. Medical history includes all major diseases, trauma, hospitalizations, and treatment interventions. The medical illness may present with psychiatric symptoms, for example, sadness of mood, delusions, and hallucinations may precede other symptoms of Parkinson disease by months and psychiatric disorder may present with somatic symptoms such as weight loss and malnutrition. A review of the medications (currently using or used in the recent past) is important. Drugs may induce depression (antihypertensive), delirium (anticholinergic), or cognitive impairment (sedatives).

Memory disturbances, depression, and anxiety are considered part of a normal aging process, which they are not. It may be difficult for healthcare professionals not trained in psychiatry or geriatrics to distinguish signs of psychiatric illness from the normal aging process. The elderly suffer from the same disorders as young adults, in addition to some disorders specific to old age, for example, **dementia**. The presentation of psychiatric illnesses may be different in the elderly as compared to younger people. In this chapter, symptoms in the elderly that are different from the young adults are discussed.

Depression Depression in the elderly may present with more somatic complaints. The elderly with depression have melancholic features characterized by hypochondriasis, low self-esteem, worthlessness, and self-accusatory trends about sex, paranoid, and suicidal ideation. Cognitive impairment in depressed elderly patients can be confused with true dementia.

Schizophrenia Schizophrenia usually begins in late adolescence, and first episode onset after 65 is rare. As age increases, psychopathology usually decreases.

Somatoform disorders Somatic complaints are common among the elderly. Hypochondriasis is also common in the elderly. These patients should be reassured by repeated general physical examination, and invasive procedures should be avoided if medically not indicated.

Sleep disorders Primary insomnia, nocturnal myoclonus, restless leg syndrome, and sleep apnea are common in the elderly.

Dementia Dementia is discussed in Chapter 26, *Neurocognitive Disorders II: Major and Mild Neurocognitive Disorder.*

PSYCHOPHARMACOLOGICAL TREATMENT OF ELDERLY

A pretreatment medical evaluation and review of the currently used medications should be done. The physician should know the pharmacodynamics and pharmacokinetics of the prescribed drugs as well as the interaction of the prescribed drugs with the drugs patient is already taking and the effect on preexisting medical illness. Elderly patients may have comorbid medical illnesses which may change the pharmacokinetic properties of the drug (Table 24.1).

Table 24.1 Effect of existing diseases on pharmacokinetics of the drugs in the elderly

Disease	Effect on pharmacokinetics
Renal disease	Decreased renal clearance of drugs
Liver disease	Decreased metabolism of drugs

With aging, body fat increases which leads to the wide distribution of lipid-soluble drugs, resulting in prolonged action of these drugs. The **golden rule** is to use the lowest possible dose to achieve the desired therapeutic effect. The dictum is "**start low and go slow**."

KEY POINTS

- Geriatric psychiatry deals with preventing, diagnosing, and treating psychological disorders in older adults.
- The characteristics of this age group include chronic medical illnesses, concomitant use of medications, and drug-drug and drug-disease interactions.
- The elderly suffer from the same disorders as young adults, in addition to some disorders specific to old age, for example, dementia.
- The presentation of psychiatric and physical illnesses may be different in the elderly as compared to younger people.
- The physician should know the pharmacodynamics and pharmacokinetics of the prescribed drugs as well as the interaction of the prescribed drugs with the drugs patient is already taking and the effect on preexisting medical illness.
- The **golden rule** is to use the lowest possible dose to achieve the desired therapeutic effect. The dictum is "**start low and go slow**."

SELF-ASSESSMENT

1. Describe the various psychiatric disorders in the elderly and factors affecting pharmacological treatment of psychiatric disorders in the elderly.

Chapter 25

Neurocognitive Disorders I: Delirium

Sandeep Grover · Devakshi Dua

DSM-5 defines neurocognitive disorders as those in which the primary clinical deficit is in cognitive function, which is acquired rather than developmental and reflects a decline from the previous level of functioning. The neurocognitive disorders are categorized as delirium and major and mild neurocognitive disorders.

Delirium is possibly the only psychiatric disorder, which definitely has an underlying organic etiology. It is often under-recognized and undertreated. If not treated adequately, it is associated with increased risk of mortality, a significant increase in the length of hospital stay, healthcare expenditures, functional decline, and distress to the patient and the caregivers.

Delirium is known by various alternative terms, that is, intensive care unit (ICU) psychosis, encephalopathy, acute confusional state, acute organic syndrome, acute brain failure, postoperative psychosis, toxic psychosis, and cerebral insufficiency.

EPIDEMIOLOGY

The prevalence of delirium in different inpatient settings varies considerably, with rates as high as 80% reported for those admitted in various ICUs. Prevalence is much higher among patients requiring mechanical ventilation. It is reported that about 30%–50% of patients admitted in medical inpatient setting suffer from delirium. Although delirium is reported across all age groups, in general prevalence is higher among the elderly and those with more severe medical illnesses.

RISK FACTORS AND ETIOLOGICAL FACTORS FOR DELIRIUM

Various risk factors that are associated with the development of delirium are broadly categorized as predisposing and precipitating factors. Box 25.1 shows risk factors and etiological factors with some overlap between precipitating factors and etiological factors. Most of the patients have more than one etiological/precipitating factors associated with the emergence of delirium.

PATHOGENESIS OF DELIRIUM

The major neurotransmitter involved in delirium is acetylcholine. The major neuroanatomical area is the reticular formation and the major pathway implicated is the dorsal tegmental pathway.

CLINICAL FEATURES

Delirium characteristically manifests as an acute onset confusional state, often having a fluctuating course and is often

Box 25.1 Predisposing/precipitating factors and etiological factors for delirium

Predisposing factors

- Alcohol abuse
- Cognitive impairment
- Comorbid illnesses (e.g., chronic renal or hepatic disease, stroke)
- Dehydration or malnutrition
- Dementia
- Elderly (65 years and older)
- Male gender
- Metabolic derangements
- Poor functional ability (e.g., immobility, low level of activity)
- Sensory impairment—visual and hearing
- Severe medical disease
- Treatment with drugs with anticholinergic properties

Precipitating factors

- Admission to ICU
- Iatrogenic events (surgery, any intervention)
- Indwelling catheter
- Malnutrition
- More than three medications
- Pain
- Prolonged sleep deprivation
- Use of physical restraints

Etiological factors

- Acute vascular lesions (stroke, trauma)
- Endocrinopathies (hypoglycemia, diabetic ketoacidosis, hypothyroidism, hyperthyroidism, Cushing syndrome)
- Hypoxia
- Infection (sepsis, urinary tract infection, pneumonia)
- Intracranial pathology (meningitis, encephalitis)
- Malignancies
- Metabolic disturbances (electrolyte imbalance)
- Nutritional deficiencies
- Substance withdrawal (alcohol)
- Toxins
- Trauma
- Use of heavy metals
- Use of medications (anticholinergic)

short-lasting. Symptoms may show a diurnal pattern, with worsening at night; in between, the patient may have lucid intervals of normal functioning. Impairment in attention and awareness is considered as the core symptom of delirium. Other common clinical features of delirium are listed in Box 25.2.

Box 25.2 Clinical features of delirium

- **Impaired attention:** Reduced ability to focus, sustain, and shift attention. While examining the patient, this is noted in the form of forgetting instructions, distraction toward irrelevant stimuli, asking the same question again and again.
- **Reduced awareness:** Reduced orientation to the environment.
- **Decreased level of consciousness**
- **Disruption of sleep and wakefulness:** Fragmented sleep at night with or without day time drowsiness, experiencing vivid dreams and nightmares—difficulty distinguishing dreams from real perceptions.
- **Emotional disturbance:** Irritability, dysphoria, anxiety, or euphoria.
- **Psychomotor disturbance:** Based on the level of psychomotor activity, delirium is subtyped as a hyperactive, hypoactive, and mixed subtype. A **hyperactive subtype** is characterized by increased motor activity, manifested in the form of agitation (pulling out the tubes/drains/catheters, repeated attempts of getting out of bed, wander around in the ward/house), increased speech output, a faster rate of speech and increased movements.

  A **hypoactive subtype** is characterized by lower activity levels, that is, both motor movements and speech output (reduction in activity level, delay in responding to queries or not responding at all, a marked reduction in verbal output, apathetic, withdrawn).

  A **mixed subtype** is characterized by symptoms of both subtypes. Among the various subtypes of delirium, hypoactive subtype is often missed.
- **Disorders of thought:** Delusions (usually persecutory), poor organization of speech, bizarre or illogical thinking.
- **Disorders of memory:** Improper recollection about meals, intake of medicines, people visiting them, inability to recollect things recently discussed.
- **Disorientation:** Not oriented to the time, place, person.
- **Perceptual disturbances:** Hallucinations (visual more common than auditory), illusions (may misinterpret wrinkles on the bedsheets as animate objects with attempts to clean the bedsheet to remove the animate objects, the noise of ICU machines misinterpreted as a gunshot, different alarms of a machine considered as police siren).

DIAGNOSIS

Diagnosis of delirium can be made as per the DSM-5 or ICD-10 criteria. DSM-5 criteria emphasize disturbance in attention, awareness and cognition whereas ICD-10 requires symptoms should be present *in each one* of the following areas: impairment of consciousness and attention; global disturbance of cognition; psychomotor disturbances; disturbance of the sleep-wake cycle; and emotional disturbances.

Scales

Apart from DSM-5 or ICD-10 criteria, various instruments like the Confusion Assessment Method (CAM) and Confusion Assessment Method for the Intensive Care Unit (CAM-ICU) can be used to screen patients for delirium. These instruments have been shown to have high sensitivity and specificity for diagnosing delirium.

DIFFERENTIAL DIAGNOSIS

As delirium is characterized by a broad spectrum of symptoms that overlap with many other psychiatric conditions, it is important to consider dementia, depression, and psychosis as differential diagnoses (Table 25.1).

ASSESSMENT OF DELIRIUM

Assessment of delirium involves making a correct diagnosis and looking for the underlying causes. A thorough physical examination must be carried out. Relevant investigations should be carried out to confirm possible metabolic derangements, for example, serum electrolytes, renal function test, liver function test,

Table 25.1 Differential diagnosis of delirium

Features	Delirium	Dementia	Depression	Schizophrenia
Onset	Acute	Insidious	Variable	Variable
Consciousness	Marked fluctuations	Clear till late stages	Generally no impairment	Generally no impairment
Attention	Impaired	Impairment-late stages	Poor attention	Poor attention
Orientation	Disoriented	Disorientation is seen in later stages	Usually oriented	Usually oriented
Memory	Poor short-term memory	Poor short- and long-term memory	Usually intact	Usually intact
Diurnal fluctuation	Fluctuations common	Maybe present	Morning worsening	Usually not seen
Psychotic symptoms	Fleeting, simple	Less common	Less common	Persistent, complex
Hallucinations	Visual > auditory; tactile	Usually absent	If present, are auditory	Mostly auditory
Mood	Fluctuating	Flat, apathetic	Sadness	Apathetic/flat

hemogram, and arterial blood gas analysis. Neuroimaging can be ordered for patients with focal neurological signs, history of head injury or when no cause for delirium is found. Electroencephalogram (EEG) can differentiate delirium from depression or psychosis by showing diffuse bilateral slowing of the background rhythm.

Besides physical examination and investigations, a careful history of substance use, especially alcohol use, is required. Toxicology screening can be done if substance abuse is suspected and history provided is contradictory. Additionally, a review of the medication chart is required to rule out any contributory factor, and in such a scenario, management may involve the removal of the offending agent.

MANAGEMENT

Management of delirium involves the stoppage of unnecessary medications, management of underlying cause, use of nonpharmacological measures, and the use of pharmacological treatments.

If any correctable specific etiological factor(s) are found, these must be corrected at the earliest. Nonpharmacological measures are considered as first-line management of delirium (Box 25.3). Certain measures like reorientation cues can be carried out by the family members multiple times a day by telling the patient about the day, time, and place. Additionally, having a calendar and clocks can help in improving the orientation.

Antipsychotics are usually considered in a patient who is agitated, restless, has hallucinations and delusions. Among the various antipsychotics, low dose haloperidol is the most commonly used agent. However, in recent times, many antipsychotics like quetiapine, risperidone, and olanzapine have also been used successfully in the management of delirium. Antipsychotics are used for a short duration and in the lowest effective dose (Table 25.2). While using antipsychotics, it is important to monitor the electrocardiogram (ECG) for any

Box 25.3 Nonpharmacological management of delirium

- Frequent reorientation
- Talking slowly but clearly, and using clear verbal instructions while talking to patients
- Establishing proper eye contact
- Bring familiar belongings from home, e.g., favorite blanket or night clothes
- Minimal physical restraints
- Regulation of bowel/bladder
- Adequate nutrition
- Early mobilization
- Minimize change of staff
- Minimize room changes
- Correction of sensory deprivation by providing spectacles or hearing aid, if the patient was using them earlier

Table 25.2 Antipsychotic dose used for management of delirium

Antipsychotics	Usual starting dose in patients with delirium
Haloperidol	0.25–0.5 mg Bid
Olanzapine	1.25–2.5 mg OD/Bid
Risperidone	0.25–0.5 mg OD/Bid
Quetiapine	6.25–12.5 mg OD/Bid

QTc prolongation. Benzodiazepines are particularly indicated for the management of delirium precipitated by alcohol and benzodiazepine withdrawal. Insomnia can be treated with benzodiazepines with short half-life.

KEY POINTS

- Delirium is possibly the only psychiatric disorder, which definitely has an underlying organic etiology.
- Visual and hearing impairment, treatment with drugs with anticholinergic properties, severe medical disease, metabolic derangements, dehydration or malnutrition, poorer functional ability (e.g., immobility, low level of activity), elderly (65 years and older), cognitive impairment, dementia, comorbid illnesses (e.g., chronic renal or hepatic disease, stroke), alcohol abuse, and male gender are predisposing factors.
- More than three medications, malnutrition, iatrogenic events (surgery, any intervention), indwelling catheter, use of physical restraints, pain, admission to ICU, and prolonged sleep deprivation are common precipitating factors.
- Infection, alcohol withdrawal, electrolyte imbalance, trauma, hypoxia, meningitis, encephalitis, endocrinopathies, stroke, malignancies, toxins, use of heavy metals, and use of medications (anticholinergic) are common etiological factors.
- The major neurotransmitter involved in delirium is acetylcholine. The major neuroanatomical area is the reticular formation and the major pathway implicated is the dorsal tegmental pathway.
- Delirium characteristically manifests as an acute onset confusional state, often having a fluctuating course and is often short-lasting. Symptoms may show a diurnal pattern, with worsening at night; in between, the patient may have lucid intervals of normal functioning. Impairment in attention and awareness is considered as the core symptom of delirium.
- Confusion Assessment Method (CAM) and Confusion Assessment Method for the Intensive Care Unit (CAM-ICU) can be used to screen patients for delirium.
- Dementia, depression, and psychosis are important differential diagnoses.
- Management of delirium involves the stoppage of unnecessary medications, management of underlying cause, use of nonpharmacological measures, and the use of pharmacological treatments.
- Nonpharmacological measures are considered as first-line management of delirium.
- Antipsychotics are usually considered in a delirious patient who is agitated, restless, has hallucinations and delusions.
- Benzodiazepines are particularly indicated for the management of delirium precipitated by alcohol and benzodiazepine withdrawal.

SELF-ASSESSMENT

1. Case-based Questions

   A 65-year-old male, who is suffering from hypertension since 10 years (is on a combination of amlodipine 5 mg/day and atenolol 50 mg/day), diabetes mellitus since 5 years (is on metformin 500 mg twice per day), has hearing impairment (using hearing aid in the right ear), developed fever and loose motions a week prior to presentation to the emergency department. For the last 3 days, the patient is very restless, seeing things which others cannot see, picking up at clothes, fearful, disoriented to time, place, and person, forgetful, and has disturbed sleep. All these symptoms worsen during the evening and the night time, and the patient becomes very agitated. There is no associated history of head injury, past psychiatric history, history of long-standing cognitive deficits, substance dependence, and similar episodes in the past. On physical examination, he has signs of dehydration (i.e., dry skin, dry mouth) and on mental status examination, he is found to uncooperative, agitated, is trying to get up from the bed again and again, has poor attention and concentration, is not aware of where he is, misrecognizes his wife as his sister, is able to tell his own name but is not able to tell his address, and has poor short- and long-term memory.

   a. What is your provisional diagnosis?
   b. What are the predisposing and precipitating factors?
2. Discuss the etiology, clinical features, and management (nonpharmacological and pharmacological) of delirium.
3. Write short note on:
   a. Differential diagnosis of delirium

Chapter 26

Neurocognitive Disorders II: Major and Mild Neurocognitive Disorder

Nimmy Chandran · KS Shaji

Dementia is an acquired neuropsychiatric disorder characterized by a progressive decline from the previous level of intellectual capacity in clear consciousness. **Celsus** used the term dementia for the first time. DSM-5 now uses the term of major and mild neurocognitive disorder (NCD) for dementia, whereas ICD-10 retains the term dementia.

EPIDEMIOLOGY

Around 50 million people have dementia worldwide, and 60% of them live in low- to middle-income countries. Dementia is a disorder of elderly, even though the onset before the age of 65 years can occur in around 2% of patients.

The prevalence of dementia (largely congruent with major NCD) is 1%–2% at age 65 and as high as 30% by age 85. The strongest risk factor for major NCD is age. Female gender is associated with a higher prevalence of dementia in general and Alzheimer disease in specific, whereas education and employment are protective factors for cognitive impairment among the elderly people.

ETIOLOGY

Major NCDs can be due to many causes (Box 26.1). The most common type of dementia is Alzheimer followed by vascular dementia. Other causes include dementia with Lewy bodies and frontotemporal dementia (FTD). Reversible causes of dementia include drugs with anticholinergic activity, endocrine causes such as hypothyroidism, normal pressure hydrocephalus, intracranial tumors, infections, and vitamin B_{12} or folate deficiency. It is important to identify treatable causes of dementia early so that identified treatable cause can be managed promptly and cognitive symptoms can be reversed.

CLINICAL FEATURES AND DIAGNOSIS

The following symptoms are usually seen in patients with dementia.

Memory impairment (initial recent memory impairment followed by remote memory impairment), aphasia (word-finding difficulties, word substitution, mispronouncing words, and difficulty in remembering names), praxis (earlier symptoms of difficulty in using familiar tools, machines, losing previously acquired skills, and later difficulty in dressing and feeding), agnosia (difficulty in recognizing familiar objects), impairment in executive functioning (difficulty in planning, organizing, sequencing, and abstracting), changes in social functioning,

Box 26.1 Etiologies of major neurocognitive disorder

Neurodegenerative causes

- Alzheimer disease
- Dementia with Lewy bodies
- Frontotemporal dementia
- Parkinson disease

Vascular causes

- Infarction
- Binswanger disease
- Hemodynamic insufficiency (e.g., hypoperfusion or hypoxia)

Structural and neoplastic causes

- Normal pressure hydrocephalus
- Brain tumor

Endocrine causes

- Hypothyroidism
- Hypercalcemia
- Hypoglycemia

Nutritional causes

- Vitamin B_{12} deficiency
- Thiamine deficiency
- Niacin deficiency

Infectious disease

- HIV disease
- Prion disease
- Neurosyphilis
- Cryptococci

Metabolic causes

- Hepatic insufficiency
- Renal insufficiency
- Wilson disease
- Metachromatic leukodystrophy

Traumatic causes

- Subdural hematoma
- Dementia pugilistica

Intoxication

- Alcohol
- Heavy metals
- Anticholinergic medications
- Irradiation

and visuospatial functioning (difficulty in navigation) are common symptoms of dementia.

Major NCD is characterized by **significant cognitive decline** from a previous level of performance in one or more of the cognitive domains (memory and learning, language, executive functioning) and the cognitive decline **interferes** with independence in everyday activities.

In mild NCD, **cognitive decline** from the previous level of performance is **modest** in comparison to a **significant decline** in major NCD. In mild NCD, cognitive deficits **do not interfere** with the person's independence in everyday activities.

The diagnosis is made by clinical examination, mental status examination (MSE), and on information from the patient's family. The cognitive decline should be documented by standardized neuropsychological testing or by quantified clinical assessment. Major and mild NCD are diagnosed if cognitive deficits do not occur exclusively in the context of a delirium and is unexplainable by other psychiatric illness like major depressive disorder (MDD) or schizophrenia.

Neuropsychiatric Manifestations

Behavioral changes include mood changes, anxiety, personality changes, psychosis, sleep disturbance, and agitation. Non-cognitive symptoms and behaviors occurring in subjects with dementia are known as behavioral and psychological symptoms of dementia (BPSD).

Depressive symptoms are present in half of the patients and major depression has a prevalence of 10% in these patients. Anxiety is present in 60% of the patients and presents as a fear of being alone. FTD presents as disinhibition and impulsivity. Psychosis presents as paranoia and belief that belongings have been stolen. The patient may have hallucinations; visual hallucinations are the most common. They may see dead relatives. Dementia patients have altered sleep-wake cycles and fragmented sleep. Agitation increases with an increasing level of dementia. These patients are at risk of wandering as cognitive impairment increases.

Depending on the initial involvement in the brain, there is a significant difference in the clinical presentation of cortical dementias (e.g., FTD, Binswanger disease, Creutzfeldt–Jakob disease) and subcortical dementias (e.g., Huntington, Parkinson, AIDS dementia complex). Differences between cortical and subcortical dementia are given in Table 26.1.

MAJOR OR MILD NEUROCOGNITIVE DISORDER DUE TO ALZHEIMER DISEASE

Alzheimer disease was named after **Alois Alzheimer** who described this condition in 1907. It is the most common cause of dementia. Onset is insidious with gradual progression of impairment in memory and learning. Alzheimer disease is diagnosed if there is no mixed etiology, that is, the absence of neurodegenerative, cerebrovascular, neurological, mental, or systemic diseases. NCD due to Alzheimer disease

Table 26.1 Differences between cortical and subcortical dementia

	Subcortical dementia	Cortical dementia
Language	No aphasia	Early aphasia
Memory	Recall impairment > recognition	Recall and recognition impaired
Calculation	Preserved until late	Involved early
Frontal system abilities (executive function)	Disproportionately affected	The degree of involvement consistent with other impairments
Attention and recall	Impaired	Impaired
Visuospatial skills	Impaired	Impaired
Personality	Apathetic	Unconcerned
Abstraction	Impaired	Impaired
Mood	Depressed	Euthymic
Speech	Dysarthric	Articulate until late
Coordination	Impaired	Normal until late
Motor speed	Slowed	Normal
Adventitious movements	Chorea, tremors, tics	Absent

is diagnosed after the general criteria for major or mild NCD are met.

DSM-5 added criteria, for diagnostic certainty, dividing the Alzheimer disease as probable or possible. **Probable Alzheimer disease** is diagnosed (both major and mild NCD) if there is evidence of a causative Alzheimer disease genetic mutation from the genetic testing or autosomal dominant family history coupled with autopsy confirmation or genetic test in an affected family member.

Neuropathology

Amyloid deposits are the hallmark of Alzheimer disease. Alzheimer dementia shows linkage to chromosomes 1, 14 and 21. The amyloid precursor protein (APP) gene is on the long arm of chromosome 21. APP breakdown leads to the production of 42 amino acid peptide β/A4 protein, which is the major constituent of senile plaques. Amyloid plaques can be seen in Down syndrome also. Classic neuropathological findings are senile plaques, neurofibrillary tangles, neuronal loss, synaptic loss, and degeneration of neurons. Neurofibrillary tangles are made up of phosphorylated tau protein, which can be seen in Down syndrome, Parkinson's dementia complex, dementia pugilistica, and normal elderly people.

VASCULAR NEUROCOGNITIVE DISORDER

In vascular NCD (vascular dementia), the cognitive deficit is temporally correlated to the cerebrovascular event. The decline is prominent in complex attention and frontal executive function. There is evidence for cerebrovascular disease from history, physical examination, or neuroimaging. Clinical features can vary according to the type of vascular lesion.

FRONTOTEMPORAL DEMENTIA

FTD is also known as Pick's disease. It has a behavioral variant and language variant. FTD of language variant usually begins with speech and language impairment. Progressive difficulties with word finding, object naming, grammar, or word comprehension can be present. The behavioral variant of FTD starts with behavioral symptoms like disinhibition, apathy, loss of empathy, stereotyped or compulsive/ritualistic behavior, hyperorality, dietary changes, and a prominent decline in social cognition and/or executive abilities.

NEUROCOGNITIVE DISORDER WITH LEWY BODIES

NCD with Lewy bodies (Lewy body dementia) has core diagnostic features of fluctuating cognition with pronounced variation in attention and alertness. It also has recurrent well-formed and detailed visual hallucinations, and features of Parkinsonism with onset following the development of cognitive decline. Other features that are suggestive of Lewy body dementia are rapid eye movement, sleep behavior disorder, and severe neuroleptic sensitivity.

MAJOR NEUROCOGNITIVE DISORDER DUE TO HIV

This occurs during the late stage of AIDS. It usually follows a subcortical dementia pattern with impaired executive function, slowing of processing speed, problems with attentional tasks, and difficulty in learning new information. There can be acquired abnormality in motor functioning and a decline in motivation.

Prognosis is considered to be poor and there is no role for acetylcholinesterase inhibitors and the mainstay of treatment is highly active antiretroviral therapy (HAART).

Scales

There are multiple screening tools available to screen for cognitive deficits. Mini-Mental Status Examination (MMSE) is a widely used short screening tool. Montreal Cognitive Assessment (MoCA) is most commonly used for screening of dementia. Clinical Dementia Rating (CDR) Scale is used to assess the severity of dementia. Functional Assessment Staging (FAST) is useful in tracking the course of Alzheimer disease.

Differential Diagnosis

1. **Age-related cognitive decline:** Also known as benign senescent forgetfulness, it differs from dementia in being mild in intensity and not interfering significantly in a person's socio-occupational functioning.
2. **Delirium:** It can be differentiated with the help of a careful history, considering the onset and course. Delirium is characterized by rapid onset, diurnal variation of cognitive impairment, nocturnal exacerbation of symptoms, disturbance of sleep-wake cycle, and disturbance in attention and perception. It can be superimposed on patients with dementia.
3. **Major depressive disorder:** Cognitive impairment in a patient with depression is known as pseudodementia. The differences between dementia and pseudodementia are given in Table 26.2.
4. **Factitious disorder:** Person simulating memory loss behaves inconsistently.

COURSE AND PROGNOSIS

The course and prognosis of major or minor NCD depend on the cause. In most of the cases, the onset is insidious. Sudden onset can be seen in NCD due to vascular events. Progressive cognitive decline leads

Table 26.2 Differences between dementia and pseudodementia

Pseudodementia	Dementia
The family is always aware of the dysfunction	The family may not be aware of the dysfunction
Acute onset	Onset insidious
Short duration	Long duration
Rapid progression	Slow progression
Previous history of psychiatric complaints	Unusual
The patient complains about the memory impairment	The patient usually will not complain
Emphasize their failures	Appear glad in their accomplishments
Little effort to perform the task	Struggle to perform
Communicate their distress	Appear unconcerned

to functional impairment and severe disability in most of the cases.

EXAMINATION

A detailed physical and neurological examination should be done. Screening tests like MMSE and severity rating scale like CDR and FAST can be done.

Laboratory investigations include complete hemogram, serum electrolytes, renal function tests, liver function tests, vitamin B_{12}, folate level, thyroid stimulating hormone, HIV, and syphilis test. These help us to rule out the treatable contributing factors or causes of dementia.

Structural neuroimaging (CT head/MRI brain) is used to rule out the abnormalities in the brain that can cause dementia, including mass lesions like tumors or metastasis, cerebrovascular events, subdural hematoma, and normal pressure hydrocephalus.

Molecular neuroimaging can identify biomarkers of different dementia. The absence of amyloid deposits on positron emission tomography (PET) indicates that dementia is unlikely to be of Alzheimer disease. Single-photon emission computed tomography (SPECT) or fluorodeoxyglucose (FDG)-PET can be used to find the etiology of dementia by measuring blood flow or metabolic rate in various regions of the brain (e.g., diminished uptake in frontal and temporal lobe regions in FTD).

Electroencephalogram (EEG) is not indicated in the routine evaluation of dementia. In Creutzfeldt–Jakob disease, EEG can show periodic sharp wave complexes.

TREATMENT

Various pharmacological and nonpharmacological treatment modalities are available for dementia.

Pharmacotherapy

For cognitive impairment, acetylcholinesterase inhibitors and N-Methyl-D-aspartate (NMDA) receptor antagonists are used. Donepezil, rivastigmine, galantamine, and tacrine are various cholinesterase inhibitors used to treat mild to moderate cognitive impairment in Alzheimer disease. They increase the concentration of acetylcholine by preventing the inactivation of acetylcholine by enzyme cholinesterase. Tacrine can cause hepatotoxicity therefore not used commonly. Rivastigmine and galantamine cause gastrointestinal adverse effects. Rivastigmine patches are now available. Memantine is an NMDA receptor antagonist and it protects neurons from an excessive amount of glutamate, which may be neurotoxic. Memantine is FDA approved for moderate to severe Alzheimer disease.

Preventive measures like diet, exercise, control of hypertension, and diabetes are important for vascular dementia. Surgical removal of carotid plaques in selective patients might be helpful.

The behavioral and psychological symptoms of dementia are very troublesome for the patient and the caregivers. Risperidone, olanzapine, and aripiprazole have shown significant improvement in agitation, psychosis, and behavioral disturbance. For insomnia, first nonpharmacological measures like improved sleep hygiene and increasing daytime wakefulness via social and physical activity should be advised. Benzodiazepines can be used for insomnia, but they should be avoided as they can cause cognitive and gait disturbances. Antidepressants can be used for depression.

Psychotherapy

Reminiscence therapy helps the patient to recall and relive past life events and results in short-term improvement in mood and cognition. Stimulation-oriented therapies focus on enhancing the involvement of patients in pleasurable activities like games, music, and art to improve their cognitive abilities. Examples of stimulation-oriented therapies include recreational therapy (craft, games), art therapy, pet therapy, multisensory stimulation, and exercise.

Caregiver interventions in dementia are of utmost importance as they help the caregivers to understand the nature of symptoms of dementia and the course of the illness. Caregivers should be educated about the importance of legal and financial planning, and the need to take precautions for ensuring the safety of patients. WHO **iSupport** is an e-health solution developed by WHO that provides information and skills training for caregivers of people living with dementia.

KEY POINTS

- Dementia is an acquired neuropsychiatric disorder characterized by a progressive decline from the previous level of intellectual capacity in clear consciousness.
- **Celsus** used the term dementia for the first time.
- DSM-5 now uses the term of major and mild neurocognitive disorder (NCD) for dementia, whereas ICD-10 retains the term dementia.
- The strongest risk factor for major NCD is age. Female gender is associated with a higher prevalence of dementia in general and Alzheimer disease in specific, whereas education and employment are protective factors for cognitive impairment among older people.
- The most common type of dementia is Alzheimer followed by vascular dementia.
- Reversible causes of dementia include drugs with anticholinergic activity, endocrine causes like hypothyroidism, normal pressure hydrocephalus, intracranial tumors, infections, and Vitamin B_{12} or folate deficiency.
- Memory impairment, aphasia, praxis, agnosia, impairment in executive functioning, changes in social functioning, and visuospatial functioning are common symptoms of dementia.
- Behavioral changes include mood changes, anxiety, personality changes, psychosis, sleep disturbance, and agitation.
- Depressive symptoms are present in half of the patients and major depression has a prevalence of 10% in these patients.
- Anxiety is present in 60% of the patients, and presents as a fear of being alone.
- Frontotemporal dementia (FTD) presents as disinhibition and impulsivity.
- Psychosis presents as paranoia and belief that belongings have been stolen.
- The patient may have hallucinations; visual hallucinations are the most common.
- These patients are at risk of wandering as cognitive impairment increases.
- Cortical dementias include FTD, Binswanger disease, and Creutzfeldt-Jakob disease, and subcortical dementias include Huntington, Parkinson, and AIDS dementia complex.
- In subcortical dementias, speech is dysarthric and coordination is impaired early as compared to cortical dementias. Subcortical dementias are associated with slowed motor speech and abnormal movements such as chorea, tremors, or tics.
- In vascular neurocognitive disorder (vascular dementia), the temporal correlation with the cerebrovascular event and onset of cognitive deficit can be established.
- FTD has a behavioral variant and a language variant.

- NCD with Lewy bodies (Lewy body dementia) has core diagnostic features of fluctuating cognition with pronounced variation in attention and alertness. It also has recurrent well-formed and detailed visual hallucinations, and features of Parkinsonism with onset following the development of cognitive decline.
- Major neurocognitive disorder due to HIV usually follows a subcortical dementia pattern with impaired executive function, slowing of processing speed, problems with attentional tasks, and difficulty in learning new information. There is no role for acetylcholinesterase inhibitors medicines, and the mainstay of treatment is highly active antiretroviral therapy (HAART).
- Montreal Cognitive Assessment (MoCA) is most commonly used for screening of dementia.
- Structural neuroimaging (CT head/MRI brain) is used to rule out the abnormalities in the brain that can cause dementia, including mass lesions like tumors or metastasis, cerebrovascular events, subdural hematoma, and normal pressure hydrocephalus.
- For cognitive impairment, acetylcholinesterase inhibitors and N-Methyl-D-aspartate (NMDA) receptor antagonists are used.
- Donepezil, rivastigmine, galantamine, and tacrine are various cholinesterase inhibitors used to treat mild to moderate cognitive impairment in Alzheimer disease. Memantine protects neurons from an excessive amount of glutamate.
- Risperidone, olanzapine, and aripiprazole have shown significant improvement in agitation, psychosis, and behavioral disturbance.

SELF-ASSESSMENT

1. Case-based Questions

   A 70-year-old lady was brought to our hospital by the family members. According to family members, she had progressive forgetfulness for 3 years. She would forget the names of familiar persons and would also forget where she kept her belongings. Family members would often find her searching for her belongings in the household.

   Moreover, sometimes she would accuse neighbors or other family members of stealing things. She was not interacting well with others, which was unlike her previous self, and her speech output was reduced. She was not as fluent as she used to be.

   She also had difficulty in self-care. She was unable to take a bath or brush her teeth properly. She would even go out of her house and family members would have difficulty in finding her. She would find it difficult to return home and had to be brought back.

   On examination, she was poorly groomed and ill-kempt. Her general physical examination was within normal limits. On mental status examination (MSE), she had impaired memory and language functions. Her thinking was concrete. Neurological examination was normal.

   a. What is your provisional diagnosis?
   b. How will you evaluate the patient?
   c. How will you manage the patient?
2. Write short notes on:
   a. Alzheimer disease
   b. Vascular dementia
   c. Frontotemporal dementia
   d. Lewy body dementia
   e. Major neurocognitive disorder due to HIV

Chapter 27

Personality Disorders

Sathya Prakash · Pratap Sharan

Gordon Allport defined personality as the "*dynamic organization within the individual of those psychophysical systems that determine his/her unique adjustment to his/her environment.*" The definition involves three important terms—**dynamic, psychophysical**, and **adjustment**. Each organism has to deal with its environment continually, to survive. A successful adjustment would enhance the organism's survival and poor adjustment puts its survival at risk. Personality is something that enables an organism to adjust. This system that enables the organism to adjust is organized dynamically. In other words, the machinery used to deal with the environment at one point may be redundant at another point in time. And what is the nature of this machinery? It is psychophysical. It has a physical, physiological, or biological aspect and a psychological aspect. The physical aspects refer to the neural structure, neurotransmitters, hormones, and genetics. Psychological aspects may hinge upon patterns learned from others, or figured out during times of need.

PERSONALITY DISORDER

The DSM-5 defines a personality disorder as "an enduring pattern of inner experience and behavior that deviates markedly from the expectations of the individual's culture, is inflexible and pervasive across a broad range of personal and social situations, has an onset in adolescence or early adulthood, is stable over time, and leads to distress or impairment in social, occupational, or other areas of functioning."

The DSM-5 has clarified further that the deviant experience and behavior must manifest in two or more areas amongst cognition, affectivity, interpersonal functioning, and impulse control. A personality disorder is diagnosed if this enduring pattern is not better explained by another mental disorder or a medical condition (e.g., head trauma) or physiological effects of a substance (e.g., a drug of abuse or a medication).

Relationship Between Personality, Temperament, and Character

Personality comprises of several components. The **temperament** provides a broad framework or a repertoire of potential behaviors and experiences to which the individual is biased or predisposed. However, what eventually manifests may be a modified version of the above, as a result of voluntary, willful alterations made by the individual—the realm of **character**.

Temperament

Temperament refers to the body's *biases in the modulation of conditioned behavioral responses to prescriptive physical stimuli*.

Although each organism can respond to external stimuli in a multitude of ways, the range of such responses is broadly restricted by the organism's internal, biological machinery. Because the restriction is not absolute, it has been termed as a bias. In other words, a person with a particular temperament is more likely to respond in one particular way than the other, when faced with a certain challenge or scenario. A large part of the temperament is considered to be **biological** and **heritable**, and therefore resistant to change.

Four types of temperaments have been identified. They are as follows:

Harm Avoidance

The harm avoidance trait refers to a tendency or bias toward not engaging in behaviors that have a likelihood of resulting in punishment or frustrative nonreward. Even if the likelihood of such an outcome is low, there is a bias toward not engaging in such behaviors. The advantage of such a temperament is that it is likely to result in meticulous planning to avoid negative outcomes. The downside is that a lot of time, energy, and resources are spent in avoiding a potential danger, which has a very low likelihood of happening. Gamma aminobutyric acid (GABA) and serotonin are considered to be the principal neuromodulators of this temperament. They are primarily operative in the ascending neurons of the dorsal raphe nuclei.

Novelty Seeking

Positive and heritable bias in initiating activities in response to novelty, signals of reward, and active avoidance of conditioned signals of punishment characterize this temperament. The most distinctive feature of this trait is exploratory approach behavior and therefore it is named novelty seeking. Advantages include explorative abilities leading to newer ideas and discoveries, whereas downside includes impulsiveness, easy boredom, and potentially higher exposure to danger. Dopamine is considered the principal neuromodulator for this temperament. The mesolimbic and mesocortical dopaminergic projections are believed to be the primary physical basis for this temperament.

Reward Dependence

Reward dependence is a heritable bias in the maintenance of behavior in response to rewarding social cues. This may result in affectionate relationships, concern for others, and a generally tender-hearted nature. Downsides are poor objectivity, suggestibility, sensitivity to others' responses, and dependence on others. Noradrenergic projections from the locus ceruleus and serotonergic projections from the median raphe are believed to be the primary neurobiological basis for this temperament.

Persistence

Persistence refers to a heritable bias to behaviors persisting despite frustration, unreliable reward, and fatigue with only intermittent reinforcement. In other words, rewards that are available unpredictably or in the distant future can maintain behaviors even when there is no immediate reward. This temperament can be highly adaptive to achieve difficult, complicated, and long-term goals. It may come, though, at the cost of temporary strain and anxiety. The ventral striatum, including the nucleus accumbens, is believed to be the seat of regulation of persistence. Glutamate as well as serotonin are the principal neuromodulators of this temperament.

Character

The character is what one **voluntarily** and **intentionally** makes out of oneself. It has been described as "**rational** and **volitional**." For example, depending upon one's character, a novelty-seeking temperament may lead one to explore and unravel the mysteries of nature, become a scientist, or experiment with different substances of abuse.

Three dimensions of character have been identified, as described next.

Self-directedness It measures the individual's "executive competence." In other words, individuals high on self-directedness are responsible, goal-oriented, and self-accepting. They are very effective in serving the real-world needs and goals.

Cooperativeness It measures the "legislative functions" of the individual. Individuals scoring high on this character trait gel well within groups, are considerate of other people's feelings, and do not do so well in solitary pursuits. They view themselves as part of society as a whole and therefore are empathetic and tolerant.

Self-transcendence This can be seen as a measure of the "judicial functions" of the individual. Persons with significant self-transcendence attributes see themselves as an integral part of the universe as a whole. They may not fit so well within a materialistic society, but have unique adaptive advantages from an existential perspective.

CLASSIFICATION OF PERSONALITY DISORDERS

The DSM-5 classifies personality disorders into three clusters: A, B, and C. ICD-10 has a broadly similar approach regarding individual personality disorders, though it does not follow the cluster concept.

Cluster A consists of:
- Paranoid personality disorder
- Schizoid personality disorder
- Schizotypal personality disorder

Cluster B consists of:
- Antisocial personality disorder
- Borderline personality disorder
- Histrionic personality disorder
- Narcissistic personality disorder

Cluster C consists of:
- Avoidant personality disorder
- Dependent personality disorder
- Obsessive–compulsive personality disorder

Etiology

Biological Theories

Genetics

The cluster 'A' personality disorders seem to have a link with schizophrenia and related psychotic conditions. Schizotypal personality disorder has the most evidence, with lesser evidence for the other two personality disorders, belonging to the cluster. A paranoid personality disorder may be closer to delusional disorder.

In the case of cluster B personality disorders, a strong element of heritability indicative of transmitted genetic material exists for antisocial personality disorder. However, additional environmental factors like poor parental upbringing may add to the risk. However, the genetic vulnerabilities do not seem to be as specific as with cluster A personality disorders. For instance, the same genetic material when combined with a different set of environmental influences can result in one of the cluster C personality disorders as well.

Persons with any of the three cluster C personality disorders frequently demonstrate other members in the family with traits from one or more of the three personalities that make up this cluster, suggesting some role of genetics. However, part of this transmission could be environmentally mediated as well. The relative contribution from genetic vis-à-vis environmental factors is somewhat unclear for these personality disorders.

Neurochemistry

Persons with schizotypal personality disorder have been shown to have lower levels of dopamine in the striatum. Also, the level of the dopamine metabolite homovanillic acid is lower in the cerebrospinal fluid (CSF) of these persons. This is correlated with their decreased motivation and desire to venture out and socialize.

In persons with cluster B personality disorders, 5-hydroxy-indole-acetic acid (5-HIAA; a serotonin metabolite) levels in the CSF are lower. Studies have also demonstrated that more the psychopathology (like low mood and impulsivity), more the deficit, that is, lower the levels of serotonin. This is attributable to a lower synthesis of serotonin and higher levels of serotonin transporters.

Psychophysiology

Abnormalities with eye movement (e.g., abnormal saccades during smooth pursuit eye movements) have been observed in cluster A personality disorders, particularly schizotypal personality disorder. Increased frequency of slow waves over the temporal region has been observed in the EEG recordings of persons with antisocial personality disorder.

Psychological Theories

Cognitive theory

The cognitive theory assumes that thoughts influence emotions, which in turn results in certain behaviors. Abnormalities in thoughts lead to abnormal emotions and abnormal behaviors. These abnormal thoughts may be set off by internal or external triggers. Cognitive distortions actively aid the continued preservation of abnormal thoughts. In personality disorders, the abnormalities are primarily seen in the interpersonal areas and produce maladaptive responses to life situations.

Psychoanalytic theory

From a psychoanalytic perspective, personality is codetermined by temperament, character, and superego.

CLINICAL FEATURES

It is important here to point out though that more often than not, persons present with a mixture of multiple traits from different personalities rather than a pure form where traits belonging to a single personality are present.

Paranoid Personality Disorder

The prevalence of paranoid personality is estimated to be at around 2%–4%. The central feature of this personality disorder is a pervasive distrust of others leading to needless and unwarranted suspiciousness. All the diagnostic criteria are the fallout of this central theme. Persons with a paranoid personality are therefore preoccupied with doubts about the loyalty of partners and friends. They tend to hold grudges and are unforgiving of perceived insults or slights. They may respond with a vengeance in scenarios where others may not be able to recognize that an insult or demeaning event even took place. Fear of sharing information with others due to the fear of the same being used against them makes them poor confiders. They may have suspiciousness regarding fidelity of their spouse without justification and they may gather evidence to support their beliefs. Because of their somewhat unusual behavior, they may elicit an unpleasant response from others, which in turn serves to confirm their beliefs about others being nasty and untrustworthy. They read hidden meanings (that are demeaning) of other's benign remarks. They may misinterpret remarks by colleagues or friends, for example, humorous remarks may be viewed as a serious attack on character. As with any personality disorder, these observations must not occur exclusively during or must not be a direct result of schizophrenia, bipolar disorder, other psychiatric disorders, general medical conditions, or effects of a substance of abuse or medication. However, when faced with stress, individuals with a paranoid personality may briefly develop delusions or intense ideas of suspiciousness bordering on delusions, which alone must not preclude the diagnosis of a paranoid personality. Such states typically last no more than a few minutes to a few hours.

How then is the suspiciousness seen here different from that of a persecutory delusion seen in a psychotic condition? Unlike in a delusion, persons with a paranoid personality can see the unwarrantedness of their beliefs and actions briefly when faced with countering information, evidence, or reassurance. Also, broadly, they can see reality and therefore can function to a significant extent.

Sometimes, a psychotic disorder, schizophrenia, or delusional disorder may develop over and above a preexisting paranoid personality disorder, but not necessarily so.

Schizoid Personality Disorder

Studies estimate the prevalence of this personality disorder between 3% and 5%. It is characterized by a general sense of detachment from social connections and a limited range of emotional expressions in a social or interpersonal setting. The person usually lacks friends and other social connections, except for first-degree relatives. Solitary activities are generally preferred. Emotional coldness, indifference to praise or criticism, and little interest in sexual activities with another person are seen. They are typically seen as loners in their younger years. They may do well in activities or professions that do not involve social interaction such as mathematics and computers, but where human interaction is needed, dysfunction may become apparent.

As with other categories, to make a confident diagnosis of this disorder, general medical condition, substance use, medication effect, or alternative psychiatric diagnoses must not explain the clinical picture.

Schizotypal Personality Disorder

Epidemiological studies from the West suggest a prevalence of 0.6%–4.6% for this disorder. They are believed to be less frequent in clinical populations or possibly the diagnosis is missed in a number of cases.

Similar to persons with a schizoid personality, persons with schizotypal personality have limited ability and interest in social interactions. The result may be that the person has hardly any social relationships, besides his/her first-degree relatives. However, the deficits seen here are somewhat qualitatively different from schizoid personality and there are additional deficits as well. The anxiety in social scenarios does not seem to reduce with familiarity and repeat meetings. Additionally, the anxiety is centered on a sense of paranoia rather than low confidence or negative perceptions of self. People around might perceive the individual as odd and eccentric. Individuals with schizotypal disorder may have constricted and inappropriate affect. They may have idea that they are the ones being referred to in conversations around them or the media or that other people's actions are in some way relevant to them. Also, it might seem to them that people are looking at them in crowds even when this is not the case. Unlike in a psychotic disorder, these are not rigidly held like a delusion, but are nevertheless, significant and may influence behavior. Odd beliefs or magical thinking, not in keeping with the person's culture may be present. The person may believe he or she has magical powers and can sense events before they happen or can read other's thoughts. The person may speak in a vague, overelaborate, and metaphorical way without actual derailment or incoherence.

Although for a diagnosis of this disorder, alternative psychiatric diagnoses, substance use, general medical condition, or medication-related effects need to be ruled out, schizophrenia may develop in individuals having a preexisting schizotypal personality disorder.

Notably, the ICD-10 does not regard schizotypal personality as a personality disorder, but instead classifies it as a separate condition under the psychotic disorders section.

Antisocial Personality Disorder

The ICD-10 terms this disorder as **dissocial personality disorder**. Western literature suggests prevalence rates ranging from 0.2% to 3.3%. Specific populations like those with substance use disorders, prisons, and forensic settings may have a much higher prevalence.

This personality disorder is characterized by a general disregard for the feelings of others and violation of their rights. The pattern is seen since childhood where the diagnostic term conduct disorder is used. The DSM-5 states that to make a diagnosis of antisocial personality disorder, the person must be at least 18 years old with a diagnosis of conduct disorder before the age of 15. Typical behaviors involve a lack of respect for law and social norms, putting the individual at risk for arrest. Deceit, lying, conning, and similar behaviors merely for pleasure or for material gains are frequently seen. Disregard for others may manifest as irresponsible behavior and lack of concern for others' safety. Such lack of concern may be coupled with a lack of remorse, which may or may not be accompanied by a superficial demeanor of remorse. Impulsiveness, aggression, and inability to or failure to plan systematically are additional features. Aggression may be seen against animals, humans, or property depending on the age and situation. The victims may be blamed for their stupidity and the individual may rationalize his/her behavior. Lack of support to the family, both emotional and financial, and erratic presence at work may be seen. These behaviors must be distinguished from that due to the direct effect of another psychiatric disorder like schizophrenia or bipolar disorder. Individuals with antisocial personality disorder have a high prevalence of substance use disorders. A diagnosis of antisocial personality must be based on the above descriptions, which are consistently and inflexibly present and not merely based on an isolated criminal behavior not accompanied by these personality traits.

Borderline Personality Disorder

Epidemiological studies suggest a prevalence rate ranging from 1% to 6% for this personality disorder.

Borderline personality disorder (BPD) is characterized by a pervasive, generalized instability involving one's identity, self-image, interpersonal relationships, emotions, and a tendency to marked impulsivity. BPD is characterized by unstable and intense interpersonal relationships. Relationship difficulties arise as a result of impulsive decision-making and a tendency to overvalue a person initially and then markedly undervalue or devalue him/her later. The emotions and mood are markedly variable, often in relation to interpersonal stresses. Self-mutilating behaviors and suicidal gestures or attempts are seen. Impulsivity may be apparent in multiple areas, as manifested by erratic patterns of spending, sexual relationships, eating, substance use, driving, and so on. Difficulty regulating anger, stress-related paranoia, and dissociative symptoms may also occur. Chronic feelings of emptiness, referring to a scary feeling of not existing, or isolation from others are often present, which the person might struggle to articulate. Frantic efforts (to prevent abandonment), associated with dramatic behaviors, might be apparent when confronted with situations that reflect real or imagined abandonment.

The ICD-10 replaces this section with a disorder termed as "**emotionally unstable personality disorder**," which is further divided into an impulsive type and a borderline type.

Histrionic Personality Disorder

Epidemiological studies suggest a prevalence rate of 1%–2% for this personality disorder.

The hallmark of this personality disorder is an excessive display of emotions and tendency to draw attention across a wide range of scenarios or settings. If the person is not the center of attention, he or she may feel uncomfortable. Persons with this disorder tend to be seductively or provocatively dressed. They tend to overestimate the intimacy of a relationship. They may show self-dramatization, theatricality, and exaggerated public display of emotions, for example, temper tantrums or sobbing on minor occasions. The person is easily suggestible, displays a wide range of emotions, and speaks in a very impressionistic manner, which, however, lacks significant content.

Narcissistic Personality Disorder

Epidemiological studies from the West suggest a prevalence of up to 6% in the general population. The ICD-10 does not classify this as a separate disorder.

The central feature here is a preoccupation or fantasy of being grandiose that might be apparent in imagination, or behavior, or both. Need for praise and admiration by others and lack of empathy for others are associated central features of this personality disorder. The person with this kind of personality has an exaggerated sense of self-importance and expects others to automatically comply with and behave in accordance with his/her mental image of himself/herself; this may not always happen, leading to disappointment with its associated emotional and behavioral repercussions. The person needs excessive admiration, attention, and special treatment from others. The person fantasizes about unlimited power, money, beauty, youth, intelligence, ideal love, and the like. Lack of empathy is reflected in an inability to care for others' feelings or understand the other person's situation. The person thinks that he or she is special and should associate with other special people only. The person may show exploitative behavior toward others in friendships and relationships. Excessive discussion about oneself, one's problems as well as achievements, in front of others to the disregard of discussion about others may be seen. The person seems to be unable to let go of a sense of one being special and unique. When faced with real-life situations to the contrary, underlying poor self-esteem may become exposed. Many people with a narcissistic personality may be legitimately very skilled or intelligent, but this is not necessarily the case. Even when one is legitimately skilled or intelligent or in some way superior to others around, narcissistic personalities tend to overestimate their superiority over others. These symptoms must not be part of a bipolar disorder, schizophrenia, delusional disorder, effect of a substance of abuse, medication, or a general medical condition to make a diagnosis of narcissistic personality disorder.

Avoidant Personality Disorder

The prevalence of this personality disorder is estimated to be around 2%–3% based on epidemiological studies from the West. It is referred to as the **anxious [avoidant] personality disorder** in ICD-10.

An avoidant personality disorder is characterized by a pervasive pattern of social inhibition and hypersensitivity to negative evaluation. The person avoids occupational activities that involve interpersonal contact fearing criticism or rejection. Social situations are avoided unless one is sure of being liked or accepted. Even in intimate relationships, steps are taken cautiously to avoid rejection or embarrassment, either real or imagined. The person feels he or she is inferior to others and is afraid to engage with people, take risks, and do new things unless there is an overwhelming evidence that success is likely. These features may lead them to take up jobs involving little interpersonal interaction and allow them to stay largely by themselves. Anxiety disorders like social phobia are closely related. However, in an anxiety disorder, a clear onset may be apparent, although not necessarily so, whereas in the case of the personality disorder, these tendencies are seen from childhood and continue through adulthood.

Dependent Personality Disorder

Epidemiological studies suggest a prevalence rate of less than 1% for this personality disorder.

In this disorder, there is a pervasive pattern of being submissive, excessive clinging, and need to be taken care of by others. Constant reassurance and guidance from others are needed even for simple decisions to allay severe anxiety. The person may do uncomfortable things to please or stay away from the imagined displeasure of the person from whom he or she receives reassurance and support. He or she may also be extremely hesitant to disagree because of fear of loss of approval. Ending of one relationship may trigger frantic efforts to find another source of emotional support and shelter. They allow other people to take initiative and assume responsibility for major areas of their life. They have difficulty initiating projects on their own and feel helpless when alone. However, the anxiety and lack of confidence in one's abilities preclude such independent initiation of new projects.

Obsessive–Compulsive Personality Disorder

Prevalence estimates for this disorder range from 2% to 8% in the general population, making it one of the most prevalent personality disorders. It is termed **anankastic personality disorder** in ICD-10.

Marked preoccupation with rules, lists, and details is apparent, such that the main point about the activity is lost. This results in an odd sense of clinging to perfection about rules, such that the task may be delayed significantly. Regardless of economic necessity and cultural values, there is involvement in work to the exclusion of leisure activities. They have rigid ideas about morality and ethics. There is a tendency to avoid discarding things that may not be important and retaining them for some potential imagined use in the future. This may also extend into miserly spending patterns, with the idea of hoarding money for the future. There is a poor ability to tolerate uncertainty, and the associated rigidity is complementary to this trait.

Personality Change due to Another Medical Condition

When a personality change happens due to the direct pathophysiological effects of a medical or neurological condition, the presentation is categorized under this section. Depending on the predominant symptoms, they may be categorized as the labile type (marked mood fluctuations), disinhibited type (sexual indiscretions), aggressive type, apathetic type (demonstrating indifference), paranoid type, and combined type (some combination of the above).

MANAGEMENT

Psychotherapy

Supportive psychotherapy is a very useful form of therapy that is used during periods of crisis in personality disorders. Although not seen as a standalone therapy to create personality transformation, it is a low resource-consuming method that manages "acute exacerbations," and thereby enables a significant reduction of morbidity in settings where other, more comprehensive forms of intervention are either not available, accessible, and not affordable or are associated with poor compliance.

Classical psychoanalysis, psychoanalytic psychotherapy, and psychodynamic psychotherapy were for long considered the treatment of choice for personality disorders, but have been criticized for lack of scientific evidence in well-planned studies.

Cognitive behavioral therapy (CBT) is adapted with modifications for the treatment of personality disorders.

Dialectical behavior therapy (DBT) is based on cognitive-behavioral principles and is currently the only empirically supported treatment for BPD.

DBT includes four modes of treatment:

a. **Group skills training:** In group format, the patients learn behavioral, emotional, cognitive, and interpersonal skills.
b. **Individual therapy:** In individual therapy, skills learned during group training are reviewed. Pathological behavioral patterns in the last week that could have been corrected by using learned skills are also reviewed.
c. **Telephonic consultation:** The therapist is available for phone consultation 24 hours a day. Patient is encouraged to call when he is in a crisis, which may lead to self-injurious behavior.
d. **Consultation team:** Therapists meet weekly to review their work with patients.

These components work together to teach behavioral skills that target common symptoms of BPD, including an unstable sense of self, chaotic relationships, fear of abandonment, emotional lability, and impulsivity such as self-injurious behaviors.

Pharmacotherapy

Medications are not considered the mainstay of treatment of personality disorders. They may be considered in certain individuals for specific purposes.

A BPD is associated with mood fluctuations and mood stabilizers, such as sodium valproate and lamotrigine have demonstrated benefit in such scenarios. Additionally, aripiprazole and olanzapine have also demonstrated utility in this disorder, presumably by a combination of beneficial effects on aggression, quasi-psychotic and micropsychotic symptoms, and mood stabilization. These medications may also benefit aggression in other personality disorders like antisocial personality disorder. Impulsivity may benefit from serotonergic antidepressants; however, this runs the risk of worsening mood cycling. Very often, superadded depressive episodes develop in persons with these cluster B personality disorders. In such instances, antidepressants may accord a lot more benefit.

Anti-anxiety medicines such as benzodiazepines may accord dramatic short-term relief, but may become counterproductive in the intermediate to long term. There is a high risk of dependence. Also, medications are frequently overdosed as a part of impulsive self-harm attempts. Benzodiazepines can occasionally also trigger paradoxical aggression and disinhibition.

Antipsychotics may also accord some benefit in paranoid and schizotypal personality disorders, but the responses are variable and far from satisfactory. If a superimposed delusional disorder or psychotic disorder has become manifest, the benefits may be much more apparent.

Anxiety, low self-esteem, and low mood seen in cluster C personality disorders may respond partially to antidepressants. Many a time, it is the comorbid anxiety or depressive disorder that responds to the medicines. This should not divert the clinician's attention away from the need for psychotherapy for the underlying personality disorder.

KEY POINTS

- **Personality** is defined as "dynamic organization within the individual of those psychophysical systems that determine his/her unique adjustment to his/her environment."
- The DSM-5 defines a **personality disorder** as "an enduring pattern of inner experience and behavior that deviates markedly from the expectations of the individual's culture, is inflexible and pervasive across a broad range of personal and social situations, has an onset in adolescence or early adulthood, is stable over time, and leads to distress or impairment in social, occupational, or other areas of functioning."
- **Temperament** refers to the body's *biases in the modulation of conditioned behavioral responses to prescriptive physical stimuli.*
- Temperament is of four types: Harm avoidance, novelty seeking, reward dependence, and persistence.
- The **harm avoidance** trait refers to a tendency or bias toward not engaging in behaviors that have a likelihood of resulting in punishment or frustrative nonreward.
- **Novelty seeking** is a positive and heritable bias in initiating activities in response to novelty, signals of reward, and active avoidance of conditioned signals of punishment characterizes this temperament.
- **Reward dependence** is a heritable bias in the maintenance of behavior in response to rewarding social cues.
- **Persistence** refers to a heritable bias to behaviors persisting despite frustration, unreliable reward, and fatigue with only intermittent reinforcement.
- The **character** is what one **voluntarily** and **intentionally** makes out of oneself. It has been described as "**rational** and **volitional**."
- The character has three dimensions: Self-directedness, cooperativeness, and self-transcendence.
- The DSM-5 classifies personality disorders into three clusters: A, B, and C.
- Cluster A consists of paranoid personality disorder, schizoid personality disorder, and schizotypal personality disorder.
- Cluster B consists of antisocial personality disorder, borderline personality disorder, histrionic personality disorder, and narcissistic personality disorder.
- Cluster C consists of avoidant personality disorder, dependent personality disorder, and obsessive-compulsive personality disorder.
- As per biological theories, genetics plays an important role in the etiology of personality disorders.
- Persons with schizotypal personality disorder have been shown to have lower levels of dopamine in the striatum.
- In persons with cluster B personality disorders, 5-hydroxyindoleacetic acid (5-HIAA; a serotonin metabolite) levels in the cerebrospinal fluid are lower.
- As per cognitive theory, abnormalities in thoughts lead to abnormal emotions and abnormal behaviors.
- From a psychoanalytic perspective, personality is co-determined by temperament, character, and superego.
- The central feature of **paranoid personality disorder** is a pervasive distrust of others leading to needless and unwarranted suspiciousness.
- A **schizoid personality disorder** is characterized by a general sense of detachment from social connections and a limited range of emotional expressions in a social or interpersonal setting.

- Persons with **schizotypal personality disorder** have limited ability and interest in social interactions. However, the deficits seen here are somewhat qualitatively different from schizoid personality. The anxiety in social scenarios does not seem to reduce with familiarity and repeat meetings. Additionally, the anxiety is centered on a sense of paranoia rather than low confidence or negative perceptions of self.
- An **antisocial personality disorder** is characterized by a general disregard for the feelings of others and violation of their rights.
- A **borderline personality disorder** is characterized by a pervasive, generalized instability involving one's identity, self-image, interpersonal relationships, emotions, and a tendency to marked impulsivity. It is characterized by unstable and intense interpersonal relationships.
- The hallmark of **histrionic personality disorder** is an excessive display of emotions and a tendency to draw attention across a wide range of scenarios or settings. If the person is not the center of attention, he or she feels uncomfortable.
- The central feature of **narcissistic personality disorder** is a preoccupation or fantasy of being grandiose that might be apparent in imagination, or behavior, or both. Need for praise and admiration by others and lack of empathy for others are associated central features of this personality disorder.
- An **avoidant personality disorder** is characterized by a pervasive pattern of social inhibition and hypersensitivity to negative evaluation.
- In **dependent personality disorder**, there is a pervasive pattern of being submissive, excessive clinging, and need to be taken care of by others. Constant reassurance and guidance from others are needed even for simple decisions to allay severe anxiety.
- In **obsessive–compulsive personality disorder**, marked preoccupation with rules, lists, and details is apparent, such that the main point about the activity is lost.
- **Supportive psychotherapy** is a very useful form of therapy that is used during periods of crisis in personality disorders. It is a low resource-consuming method that manages "acute exacerbations."
- **Dialectical behavior therapy** is considered the treatment of choice for borderline personality disorder.
- Medications are not considered the mainstay of treatment of personality disorders. They may be considered in certain individuals for specific purposes.
- A borderline personality disorder is associated with mood fluctuations and mood stabilizers such as sodium valproate and lamotrigine, and antipsychotics like aripiprazole and olanzapine have demonstrated benefit in such scenarios. These medications may also benefit aggression in other personality disorders like antisocial personality disorder.
- Very often, superadded depressive episodes develop in persons with these cluster B personality disorders. In such instances, antidepressants may accord a lot more benefit.
- Antipsychotics may also accord some benefit in paranoid and schizotypal personality disorders, but the responses are variable and far from satisfactory.
- Anxiety, low self-esteem, and low mood seen in cluster C personality disorders may respond partially to antidepressants.

SELF-ASSESSMENT

1. Define personality and personality disorders.
2. Define temperament. Enumerate types of temperament and describe various temperaments in brief.
3. Define character and its various dimensions.
4. Classify personality disorders and discuss their etiology.
5. Describe the clinical features of any one personality disorder.
6. Discuss the management of personality disorders.

Chapter 28

Additional Conditions Requiring Clinical Attention

Sandeep Kumar Goyal

This chapter deals with conditions that do not fall under the categories dealt in other chapters of this book.

POSTPARTUM PSYCHIATRIC DISORDERS

Postpartum psychiatric disorders have been classified into five major categories:

i. Postpartum blues (PBs)
ii. Postpartum depression (PPD)
iii. Postpartum psychosis (PP)
iv. Postpartum post-traumatic stress disorder (PTSD)
v. Postpartum anxiety disorder

The current psychiatric nosology has not classified postpartum psychiatric disorders as a distinct entity. DSM-5 has replaced the specifier "with postpartum onset" for depressive and bipolar disorders with the specifier "**with peripartum onset**." "With peripartum onset" specifier is used if the onset of mood symptoms occurs during pregnancy or within the 4 weeks following delivery.

Postpartum Blues

PBs or baby blues are the most common constellation of mood symptoms experienced by a female in the immediate postpartum period. PBs are transient. Symptoms start after 3rd postpartum day, peak by day 5, and spontaneously resolve by 10th day. At least 20%–25% of the females suffering from PBs may experience PPD. Fast mood shifts, weeping, anxiety, insomnia, irritability, anorexia, lack of energy, and feeling overwhelmed with newborn caregiving tasks are common symptoms.

Postpartum Depression

PPD is the most common postpartum psychiatric disorder. It affects 10%–15% of postpartum women. In addition to the postpartum time specifier, the symptoms are similar to that of a major depressive episode. In PPD, the negative thoughts are mainly related to the newborn. Additionally, feelings of guilt or inability to care for the infant and a preoccupation with the infant's well-being or safety are present. Risk factors for PPD include past or family history of depression and history of PPD in a previous childbirth.

Postpartum Psychosis

PP has an acute and abrupt onset and is the most severe of perinatal mood disorders. It affects 0.1%–0.2% (1 in 1,000 to 1 in 500) of postpartum females. PP is a psychiatric and obstetrical emergency. History of psychosis in previous pregnancies, history of bipolar disorder, and family history of psychotic illness are risk factors for the development of PP. Elation, lability of mood, rambling speech, disorganized behavior, and hallucinations or delusions (delusions of guilt, paranoid or grandiose delusions, and auditory hallucinations) are the most common symptoms. Disorientation, deficits in judgment, and high level of impulsivity are also common. Sometimes, delusions are related to the infant, especially that the infant is possessed, has special powers, is divine, or is dead.

Postpartum Post-traumatic Stress Disorder

It is generally characterized by tension, nightmares, flashbacks, and autonomic hyperarousal symptoms. These symptoms can persist for some weeks or months and may recur toward the end of the next pregnancy. This can also result in secondary tocophobia.

Postpartum Anxiety Disorder

Postpartum anxiety disorders are underdiagnosed. The prevalence of generalized anxiety disorder and obsessive compulsive disorder is more in postpartum women as compared to the general population. The most common feature of postpartum anxiety disorder is nocturnal vigilance (the mother remains awake and repetitively checks the infant's breathing, which results in sleep deprivation). The mother may present with excessive worries and preoccupation with the health and safety of their children, which is known as "maternity neurosis."

Diagnosis and Screening Tools

Tools such as the "Edinburgh Postnatal Depression Scale" de-emphasize symptoms common to the perinatal period (sleep and eating disturbances, weight gain, fatigue, and decreased sexual interest) and is widely used. This is validated in pregnant and postpartum females.

Organic etiology should be excluded using appropriate laboratory investigations and physical examination. Sometimes, Sheehan syndrome which is a rare medical condition can mimic postpartum psychiatric disorders. A careful neurological evaluation should be done.

Treatment

Untreated mental illness can lead to clinical deterioration and is an independent risk for pregnancy outcome. Nonpharmacological treatments such as outpatient psychotherapy or mindfulness-based stress reduction can be beneficial in mild to moderate anxiety or depression. The treatment plan should be formulated with the involvement of the patient and family members. Interpersonal therapy (IPT) might be beneficial in some cases. In cases of PP, separation from the infant might be necessary. Reassurance, emotional support, and skill development to facilitate coping are important tools.

In moderate to severe depression and PP, pharmacotherapy is indicated. The safety and hazards of the use of psychotropic medications during lactation should be addressed. The aim of treatment in the perinatal period is to minimize exposure to both untreated illness and psychotropic drugs. Most of the drugs cross the placenta and medication transfer to the baby via lactation is lesser than placental transfer. If fetal exposure to a particular psychotropic has already occurred, it is reasonable to continue that drug during lactation rather than switching to one with lower risk.

MALINGERING

Malingering is a willful production of false or grossly exaggerated physical or psychological symptoms motivated by external incentives such as avoiding work, obtaining financial compensation, evading criminal prosecution, or obtaining drugs. Under some circumstances, malingering can be an adaptive behavior such as a case of prisoner of war.

Malingering is suspected if any combination of the following is noted:

1. Medico-legal context of presentation.
2. The marked discrepancy between an individual's claimed stress or disability and the objective findings and observations.
3. Lack of cooperation during the diagnostic evaluation and in complying with the prescribed treatment regime.

Malingering can be differentiated from the factitious disorder by the fact that symptom production in factitious disorder is not motivated by external incentives. In factitious disorder, the apparent aim is to assume the sick role.

DISASTER-RELATED PSYCHIATRIC DISORDERS

WHO defines disaster as "a severe disruption, ecological and psychosocial, which greatly exceeds the coping capacity of the affected community."

There is no single accepted definition of disaster. However, there are some common characteristics across all definitions. They are as follows:

a. Sudden onset
b. Unpredictability
c. Uncontrollability
d. Huge magnitude of destruction
e. Human loss and suffering
f. Greatly exceed the coping capacity of the affected community

Disasters can be natural (earthquake) or human-made. Human-made disasters can be intentional (terrorist activity) or unintentional (nuclear accident at Chernobyl). In terms of evoking mental health morbidity, natural disasters are mild, human errors and technological accidents are moderate, and willful acts like terrorism are most severe.

Common Psychiatric Disorders in Disaster-Exposed Persons

Exposure to disasters can lead to different mental health illnesses. Up to two-thirds of the survivors may have complicated grief.

The prevalence of mental morbidity in the disaster-affected population varies from 8.6% to 57.3%. Affected people also have subsyndromal symptoms, in addition to diagnosable psychiatric disorders. The majority of them report medically unexplained somatic symptoms.

Most common disaster-related disorders are adjustment disorders, depression, PTSD, nonspecific somatic symptoms, and substance abuse. Relapse of preexisting psychiatric disorders is also common.

PTSD is one of the most common post-disaster psychopathologies. The prevalence of PTSD is approximately 30%–40% among direct victims and 10%–20% among rescue workers.

The severity of the disaster, a threat to life, loss of family members, and duration of exposure are the common risk factors for the development of post-disaster mental illness. The key pre-disaster risk factors for post-disaster mental illness include female gender, young age, and prior mental health problems.

Role of Mental Health Professionals

Disaster mental health services had a paradigm shift from curative to holistic, integrated, and preventive approach of disaster management, and include **six "Rs"** such as Readiness (preparedness), Response (immediate action), Relief (sustained rescue work), Rehabilitation (long-term remedial measures using community resources), Recovery (returning to normalcy), and Resilience (fostering).

The role of mental health professionals is psychosocial rehabilitation, in addition to diagnosing and treating psychiatric disorders. Rehabilitation should start as early as possible in high-risk groups in the affected area. Training of community workers is an important step in disaster management to deprofessionalize the service delivery. Involving the local community helps in capacity building. Disaster relief workers are at risk of compassion fatigue, burnout, and vicarious trauma. It is essential to monitor the disaster relief worker's mental and physical health status. Rehabilitation should be culturally appropriate and empower the affected community to enhance their competence to cope with future disasters.

BEREAVEMENT, GRIEF, AND MOURNING

Bereavement is the state of having suffered the loss of a loved one. It is the time after a loss during which grief is experienced and mourning occurs.

Mourning is the external expression of grief. It includes rituals that mark someone's death such as funerals, wakes, or memorial services. Mourning is the process by which grief is resolved.

Grief is a subjective feeling in response to the death of a loved one and also from other losses such as health, home, and country.

Normal Grief Reactions

The period of acute grief includes elements of both the "separation response" (i.e., a specific response to separation from a loved one) and the response to stress. Numbness, disbelief, yearning, angry protest, searching behaviors, and sadness are common symptom patterns. Other transient symptoms include symptoms identical to the deceased, a sense of a deceased's on-going presence (seeing the face, hearing the voice, or feeling the touch). Yearning is the most pathognomonic phenomenon. The bereaved person may become confused about his or her identity or social role and may tend to disengage from usual activities.

Circumstances of death influence the outcome of grief. Sudden unexpected death leads to emotional shock, especially if it involves untimely death of children. When dying is prolonged, family members have **anticipatory grief**. The prior loss adds to vulnerability (e.g., multiple premature deaths and separations). Social support is protective and helps the bereaved.

The early bereavement period is associated with increased risks of myocardial infarction, Takotsubo (stress) cardiomyopathy, or both. It is also associated with increased risk of mood, anxiety, and substance use disorders.

Phases of Grief

Grief is not a linear process with concrete boundaries, but rather, a combination of overlapping, fluid phases that vary from person to person.

Shock and denial In this phase, the bereaved person feels that the loss is not real. The patient can have somatic symptoms like numbness.

Yearning and searching In this phase, the bereaved is acutely aware of the void left in his life from the loss. The bereaved continues identifying with the person who has died, looking for constant reminders of the deceased.

Despair and detachment In this stage, the bereaved has hopelessness and despair as well as anger and questioning. The bereaved person feels that life will never make sense again without the person who died. Bowlby and Parkes suggest that if we do not progress through this phase, we will continue to be consumed by anger and depression and that our attitude toward life will remain negative and hopeless.

Reorganization and recovery In this phase, faith in life starts to be restored and recovery begins. In this phase, our grief is not fully resolved, but for Bowlby, the loss recedes to a hidden section of the brain, where it continues to influence us but is not at the forefront of the mind.

Duration

Grief usually subsides by 4–6 months. Grief persisting beyond this suggests the possibility of pathological grief.

Complicated Bereavement

Complicated bereavement is known by a variety of other names (e.g., abnormal, atypical, distorted, morbid, traumatic, unresolved, etc.). This condition is characterized by intense grief, lasting longer than expected according to social norms, which causes impairment in daily functioning. Complicated grief has a prevalence of approximately 10%–20% after the death of a romantic partner, and prevalence in parents who have lost children is even more. The prevalence of complicated grief is highest among females older than 60 years. History of mood or anxiety disorders, alcohol or drug abuse, and multiple losses are common risk factors.

The rates of suicidal ideation among patients with complicated grief are high, so clinicians should be sensitized to evaluate suicidal intent and plans in these patients.

The Brief Grief Questionnaire and the Inventory of Complicated Grief are self-report questionnaires commonly used to screen patients for complicated grief.

Traumatic Bereavement

When violent death occurs such as homicide or as a result of war or terrorism, the bereaved may experience a complex mixture of traumatic stress and grief reactions called traumatic grief.

Bereavement and Depression

Grief may precipitate depression in preexisting vulnerabilities. It is important to differentiate normal and pathological grief from depression. Marked psychomotor retardation is not observed in normal grief. The bereaved person may have the guilt of omission (guilt about not doing certain things which could have saved the deceased), but they do not have the guilt of commission. Worthlessness and psychotic symptoms and active suicidal ideation point toward mood disorder. **Mummification** (keeping the belongings of the deceased person as they were before his or her death) and severe anniversary reactions indicate psychopathology.

Bereavement and PTSD

Unnatural and violent deaths such as homicide and suicide are more likely to precipitate PTSD in surviving loved ones than natural death. Individuals who experience bereavement as a result of traumatic death may experience both PTSD and persistent complex bereavement disorder (PCBD).

Treatment

Psychotherapy is the first-line treatment. Complicated grief treatment is based on identifying and resolving complications of grief and facilitating adaptation to loss. Antidepressant medication is commonly used.

STRESS

Stress is defined as a situation that disturbs or can disturb the normal physiological or psychological functioning of the individual.

Hans Selye defined stress as a nonspecific bodily response to any demand caused by either pleasant or unpleasant conditions. He also described **general adaptation syndrome** characterized by three phases, that is, alarm reaction, the *stage of resistance* in which adaptation is achieved, and the *stage of exhaustion* in which adaptation may be lost.

Response to Stress

Stressors activate noradrenergic and serotonergic systems in the brain. Stress also activates corticotropin-releasing factor (CRF) secretion, which triggers the secretion of adrenocorticotropic hormone (ACTH). ACTH stimulates the synthesis and release of glucocorticoids from the adrenal cortex. Glucocorticoids inhibit immune functioning and increase energy use and cardiovascular activity (in the service of the "flight or fight" response).

Life Events, Personality, and Stress

A life event is a significant experience that can lead to an increase in stress. Both positive and negative life events can lead to stress.

Individuals vary widely in their subjective response to a similar stressful event depending on a number of factors, including the individual's personality, social support system, and importance of relation with person or institution. To make an extreme example, death of spouse may be absolutely shattering for one person with a close relationship, while for another, with a serious conflict, death of spouse may be actually a relief from stress.

Childbirth is a positive experience, but it can be stressful for the parents. Chronic stress and resulting anxiety predispose some individuals to psychosomatic disorders. The susceptibility of the organ system to be affected by stress can be genetic or acquired (lungs weakened by smoking).

In addition to life stresses, certain personalities are associated with certain psychosomatic disorders. A person with coronary personality (hard-driving and competitive) is predisposed to coronary disease. *Friedman* and *Rosenman* defined two types of personalities: Type A and B. Type A personality is similar to coronary personality and Type B is calm and relaxed and not predisposed to coronary disease.

TYPE A PERSONALITY

Friedman and Rosenman described Type A personality. They found that Type A personality has a higher risk of heart disease and high blood pressure than Type B.

"Type A personality" has a set of behavioral responses collectively known as Type A behavior pattern (TABP).

Typical responses of TABP include competitiveness, time urgency, and hostility.

Competitiveness Type A individuals tend to be very competitive and they strive toward goals without feeling a sense of joy in their efforts or accomplishments.

Time urgency They become impatient with delays and unproductive time, schedule commitments too tightly, and try to do more than one thing at a time.

Hostility They are easily aroused to anger or hostility. These persons see the worse in others, display anger, envy, and a lack of compassion. Hostility appears to be the main factor linked to heart disease and is a better predictor than the TABP as a whole.

People with Type B personality tend to be more tolerant of others and experience lower levels of anxiety than Type A individuals.

KEY POINTS

Postpartum Disorders

- Postpartum blues or baby blues are the most common constellation of mood symptoms experienced by a female in the immediate postpartum period. Postpartum blues are transient.
- PPD is the most common postpartum psychiatric disorder. It affects 10%–15% of postpartum women. In addition to the postpartum time specifier, the symptoms are similar to that of a major depressive episode.
- PP has an acute and abrupt onset and is the most severe of perinatal mood disorders. It affects 0.1%–0.2% (1 in 1,000 to 1 in 500) of postpartum females. Elation, lability of mood, rambling speech, disorganized behavior, and hallucinations or delusions are the most common symptoms.
- Postpartum post-traumatic stress disorder is generally characterized by tension, nightmares, flashbacks, and autonomic hyperarousal symptoms.
- Postpartum anxiety disorders are underdiagnosed. The most common feature is nocturnal vigilance (the mother remains awake and repetitively checks the infant's breathing, which results in sleep deprivation).
- Nonpharmacological treatments such as outpatient psychotherapy or mindfulness-based stress reduction can be beneficial in mild to moderate anxiety or depression.
- In moderate to severe depression and postpartum psychosis, pharmacotherapy is indicated.

Malingering

- Malingering is a willful production of false or grossly exaggerated physical or psychological symptoms motivated by external incentives.
- Malingering can be differentiated from the factitious disorder by the fact that symptom production in factitious disorder is not motivated by external incentives.

Disaster

- WHO defines disaster as "a severe disruption, ecological and psychosocial, which greatly exceeds the coping capacity of the affected community."
- Up to two-thirds of the survivors may have complicated grief.
- Most common disaster-related disorders are adjustment disorders, depression, post-traumatic stress disorder, nonspecific somatic symptoms, and substance abuse. Relapse of preexisting psychiatric disorders is also common.
- Disaster mental health services had a paradigm shift from curative to the holistic, integrated, and preventive approach of disaster management.
- The role of mental health professionals is psychosocial rehabilitation, in addition to diagnosing and treating psychiatric disorders.

Bereavement, Grief, and Mourning

- Bereavement is the state of having suffered the loss of a loved one. It is the time after a loss during which grief is experienced and mourning occurs.
- Mourning is the external expression of grief. It is the process by which grief is resolved.
- Grief is a subjective feeling in response to the death of a loved one and also from other losses such as health, home, and country.
- Numbness, disbelief, yearning, angry protest, searching behaviors, and sadness are common symptom patterns.
- The early bereavement period is associated with increased risks of myocardial infarction, Takotsubo (stress) cardiomyopathy, or both. It is also associated with increased risk of mood, anxiety, and substance use disorders.
- Grief usually subsides by 4–6 months. Grief persisting beyond this suggests the possibility of pathological grief.
- Complicated bereavement is characterized by intense grief, lasting longer than expected according to social norms, which causes impairment in daily functioning.
- Complicated grief treatment is based on identifying and resolving complications of grief and facilitating adaptation to loss. Antidepressant medication is commonly used.

Stress

- *Hans Selye* defined stress as a nonspecific bodily response to any demand caused by either pleasant or unpleasant conditions.
- General adaptation syndrome is characterized by three phases, that is, alarm reaction, the *stage of resistance* in which adaptation is achieved, and the *stage of exhaustion* in which adaptation may be lost.

Type A Personality

- Friedman and Rosenman described Type A personality. They found that Type A personality has a higher risk of heart disease and high blood pressure than Type B.
- "Type A personality" has a set of behavioral responses collectively known as Type A Behavior Pattern (TABP).
- Typical responses of TABP include competitiveness, time urgency, and hostility.

SELF-ASSESSMENT

1. Write short notes on:
   a. Postpartum disorders
   b. Malingering
   c. Disaster
   d. Type A personality
   e. Stress
2. Define grief. Describe phases of grief, complicated bereavement, and its treatment.

Chapter 29

Psychotherapy

Nitin Gupta · Sushmita Bhattacharya

"Psychotherapy" can be simply defined as a mode of nonpharmacological treatment to address problems of psychological nature. A more conventional definition remains given by **Lewis R Wolberg** in 1967, in which psychotherapy was defined as

"The treatment, by psychological means, of problems of an emotional nature in which a trained person deliberately establishes a professional relationship with the patient with the objective of

1. removing, modifying or retarding existing symptoms,
2. mediating disturbed patterns of behavior, and
3. promoting positive personality growth and development."

Psychotherapy utilizes a verbal or nonverbal mode of communication to decrease the emotional distress (or emotional pain) of the patient and facilitate changes in emotions, attitudes, and behavior. There are various types of therapies with different indications and different degrees of effectiveness. They also vary in the duration as well as the setting (i.e., individual, family, or group setting).

This chapter will briefly cover various types of psychotherapeutic approaches, major principles behind these approaches, the Indian context of psychotherapy, and the problems in this field.

TYPES OF PSYCHOTHERAPIES

Psychotherapies can be broadly divided into three main groups:

1. **Reconstructive psychotherapy:** It aims at developing insight into unconscious conflicts, based on the premise that past experiences have retarded the normal psychological growth. It includes classical psychoanalysis and psychoanalytically-oriented (psychodynamic) psychotherapy.
2. **Re-educative psychotherapy:** It aims at changing/modifying the person's attitude, thinking, or behavior.
3. **Supportive psychotherapy:** It aims at achieving an emotional equilibrium by solving current problems.

PSYCHOANALYSIS AND PSYCHOANALYTICAL PSYCHOTHERAPY

The essential principle of **Freudian psychoanalysis** is the recognition and resolution of unconscious conflicts and gaining insight into the intrapsychic (internal psychological) events, with the resolution of symptoms being an indirect result. The main technique used was "**free association**," with a focus on utilizing the concepts of "**resistance**" and "**transference**" of the patient during therapy.

"**Free association**" is a technique in which the patient is allowed to communicate or speak freely, whatever comes to mind, in an unguided manner.

"**Resistance**" refers to the unwillingness by the patient to discuss a particular topic or opposing the treatment in any form.

"**Transference**" is the reflection of a patient's relationship with a significant other onto the therapist. The defense mechanisms (unconscious psychological strategies brought into play to cope with reality) are also identified during psychoanalysis.

Apart from Sigmund Freud, many other techniques of psychoanalysis were developed by other workers (Carl Jung – **Jungian psychoanalysis**; Alfred Adler – **individual psychology**; Harry Stack Sullivan – **interpersonal psychoanalysis**; Melanie Klein – **object relations theory**). The work done by Freud is referred to as "**classical or orthodox psychoanalysis**," to distinguish it from the more recent variations known as "**psychoanalytic psychotherapy**." Classical psychoanalysis is a long and enduring process, which can take up to 2–5 years and hence is often considered to be less cost and resource-effective.

Psychoanalytically oriented brief psychotherapy is usually not very long (done over a few weeks/months) and more direct. Emphasis on the interpretation of transference, resistance, and defense mechanism is less in comparison to traditional (classical) psychoanalysis. The focus is more on the current interpersonal events. This form of therapy is suitable for all neurotic disorders like depression, anxiety, conversion disorder, and obsessive–compulsive disorder (OCD) as well as personality disorders.

BEHAVIOR THERAPY

Behaviorism or **behavior therapy** uses techniques based on theories of operant conditioning, classical conditioning, and social learning. A behavioral approach involves thinking about problems as being "learned behaviors" and teaching patients to learn new ways of behaving (and sometimes thinking) to reduce symptoms and improve functioning and quality of life. It is a time-limited approach and considered to be cost-effective. Some important behavioral techniques are given in Box 29.1.

COGNITIVE THERAPY OR COGNITIVE BEHAVIOR THERAPY

Cognitivism evolved in the 1950s in response to behavioral and psychoanalytic schools of therapy. **Albert Ellis** developed **rational emotive behavior therapy** (REBT) and soon after **Aaron T. Beck** developed **cognitive therapy**. Both these therapies are based on the premise that

Box 29.1 Behavioral techniques

Systematic desensitization

Systematic desensitization was developed by **Dr Joseph Wolpe** and is based on the principle of **counterconditioning**. It includes three primary steps:

1. **Relaxation training:** First, the patient is taught to be in a state of complete relaxation via relaxation exercises.

(*Continued*)

Box 29.1 *(Continued)*

2. **Hierarchy construction:** Next step is the construction of hierarchy (ranking) of anxiety-provoking events or situations in descending order.
3. **Desensitization of the stimulus:** Then, the patient is exposed to the object/situation which evokes anxiety (starting with least anxiety provoking and then moving up in the hierarchy list), while in a relaxed state. Exposure can be done either with the help of imagery or in reality (called "in vivo exposure"). Gradually, the patient is able to remain relaxed on exposure to the anxiety-provoking stimulus. It is the treatment of choice in phobias, obsessive-compulsive disorders, and other anxiety disorders.

Flooding

Flooding is based on the premise that escaping from feared stimuli reinforces the anxiety through conditioning, and anxiety (along with associated avoidance behavior) can be extinguished by not allowing the patient to escape the situation. In flooding, the patient is exposed to the feared stimuli, and it is ensured that escape is not possible. The therapist encourages the patient to confront the feared situation directly and response (avoidance behavior) is prevented.

Operant strategies for the modification of behavior

These strategies are based on the "**operant model**," which means that a behavior operates on the environment; the chance of recurrence of behavior is determined by the behavior's consequences.

1. **Positive reinforcement:** Rewarding the acceptable or desired behavior, which is likely to increase the behavior.
2. **Negative reinforcement:** Strengthening a desirable behavior by removing the negative outcome if the behavior is performed.
3. **Modeling:** Learning new behavior by copying it from another person such as a therapist or parent.
4. **Time-out:** Temporarily withdrawing the person from the environment where undesirable behavior has occurred.
5. **Punishment:** Reducing the undesirable behavior by providing aversive stimulus (punishment) on its occurrence.

Aversion therapy

- Undesirable behavior is followed by a noxious or unpleasant stimulus (punishment), which is likely to decrease the occurrence of undesirable behavior.
- Aversion therapy is generally indicated for substance dependence, sexual deviations (exhibitionism), and certain other behaviors with impulsive or compulsive qualities (e.g., nail-biting, trichotillomania).
- Noxious (painful and undesirable) stimuli that can be used are low voltage electrical stimuli, drugs that produce unpleasant effects like vomiting (disulfiram), social disapproval, or even corporal (physical) punishment.
  However, it is not used much nowadays.

the way we think or perceive an event or situation further influences our emotions and behaviors (**cognitive model**). These therapies attempt to make a change in the patient's thinking and belief system to bring about a sustained change in the patient's mood and behavior.

In contrast with the psychodynamic therapies, these are oriented to the present and aimed at solving current problems. Cognitive and behavioral approaches were combined during the 1970s, resulting in cognitive behavioral therapy (CBT), and since then, CBT has gained widespread acceptance as the treatment of choice for numerous disorders like depression, anxiety, and OCD.

SUPPORTIVE PSYCHOTHERAPY

Supportive psychotherapy attempts at alleviating or removing the distress of the person and restoring functioning to the normal level, by addressing the current problem at hand. It is usually of shorter duration and does not attempt to change the personality structure of the patient. Some of the principles of supportive therapy include **guidance, ventilation**, and **catharsis** (emotional expression of feelings), **prestige suggestion** (giving a message in a persuasive manner in order to have maximum credibility and make the person feel good), **tension control** and **release**, and **environmental manipulation** (bringing about changes in the environment for ensuring results at a psychological level).

GROUP THERAPY

Group therapy is both a time- and cost-effective form of therapy, which involves working together with a group of people under the guidance of a skilled therapist with a pre-established common goal. It is most commonly used in the treatment of substance dependence, but can be used in other psychiatric disorders like schizophrenia, affective (mood) disorders, and eating disorders. It provides a platform for mutual support and understanding and counters isolation experienced by the patients and relatives.

FAMILY THERAPY

Family therapy focuses on the family as the unit of intervention, to modify how different family members interact and relate with each other. It can be used to address relationship problems in family (which are present either primarily or occurring secondary to psychiatric illness), to improve the family's coping (how the family manages the various stressors they encounter) in case of presence of psychosocial stressors, and to manage the expressed emotions (emotional and behavioral ways of psychological expression of the family members toward their patient who is suffering from a mental illness) of family.

MARITAL AND SEXUAL THERAPIES

Marital (or couples) therapy aims at resolving the conflicts between a couple (married or unmarried but in a steady relationship) over a range of parameters like social, emotional, financial, and sexual. It also involves different psychotherapeutic approaches with a focus on restructuring the couple's interaction, teaching to cope with problems effectively, and reducing the distress present in the relationship.

Sexual therapy is also primarily intended for couples, but can also be used for individuals. Masters and Johnson therapy is a widely used and effective therapy for sexual problems.

HISTORY OF PSYCHOTHERAPY IN INDIA

Ancient Indian scriptures and spiritual materials are filled with references to psychotherapeutic techniques, with one of the most astounding discourses in psychotherapy coming from the Bhagavad Gita. There has been evidence of the existence and use of psychotherapy in India since time immemorial.

The beginning of the psychoanalytic movement in India can be pinpointed in the early 20th century when the **Indian Psychoanalytic Society** was founded by Girindra Shekhar Bose in 1922 in Kolkata. He was a pioneer of modern psychotherapy and practiced his concept of psychoanalysis around the same time when Freud was practicing psychoanalysis. His work was followed by the work of several philosophers, who emphasized the relevance of Indian culture, religion, and philosophy in practicing psychotherapy. Surya, Jayaram, Dhairyam, Neki, Varma, and Sethi were among the many who emphasized that psychotherapy in the Indian context differed much from its Western counterpart. There is less focus on autonomy, privacy, and confidentiality and the structure of psychotherapy provided is less formal and circumscribed. Also, there is less emphasis on intrapsychic explanations. The concepts of interdependence (Varma) and the **Guru-Chela relationship** (Neki) were also given.

Many authors have attempted to apply the knowledge of traditional concepts in psychotherapy. "Shivite" symbols in psychoanalysis (Nand), legends of Savitri (Surya and Jayaram), and the Hanuman complex (Wig) are some examples. Several authors have also opined that Indian patients are likely to be more open to the traditional concepts of karma, reincarnation, and faith healing and often have magical expectations of cure.

PROBLEMS IN THE FIELD OF PSYCHOTHERAPY AND FUTURE DIRECTIONS

The field of psychotherapy has seen a relatively slow pace of progress; there seems to be a general decline in interest in psychotherapy, especially with the increased interest in the development and use of medications for the treatment of psychiatric illnesses. Interest and pace have also been retarded due to the increasing influence and evidence of the "**biological basis of etiology**" for various psychiatric disorders.

Additionally, there has been a **lack of empirical research in psychotherapies** from the developing countries, including India. Much of the research has been descriptive with small samples. There is an urgent requirement for research in this area to assess the effectiveness of psychotherapeutic interventions.

Advancements in the method of delivery of psychotherapeutic techniques worldwide also need to be acknowledged and inculcated. Unique and newer approaches like computer-based CBT and telepsychiatry can also have a place in the

Indian mental health scenario, although there is still a long way to go before they can be fully utilized in India.

To conclude, it can be said that there is much scope for further progress in this field. Psychotherapy should be viewed as a day-to-day nurturing activity and serve the purpose of self-actualization. The preventive and promotive role of psychotherapy needs to be tapped in the future.

KEY POINTS

- As per **Lewis R Wolberg**, psychotherapy is the treatment, by psychological means, of problems of an emotional nature, in which a trained person deliberately establishes a professional relationship with the patient with the objective of removing, modifying, or retarding existing symptoms, mediating disturbed patterns of behavior, and promoting positive personality growth and development.
- The essential principle of **Freudian psychoanalysis** is the recognition and resolution of unconscious conflicts and gaining insight into the intrapsychic events, with the resolution of symptoms being an indirect result.
- The main technique used was "**free association**," with a focus on utilizing the concepts of "**resistance**" and "**transference**" of the patient during therapy.
- In **psychoanalytically oriented brief psychotherapy**, emphasis on the interpretation of transference, resistance, and defense mechanism is less in comparison to traditional (classical) psychoanalysis. The focus is more on the current interpersonal events.
- **Behavior therapy** involves thinking about problems as being "learned behaviors" and teaching patients to learn new ways of behaving (and sometimes thinking) to reduce symptoms and improve functioning and quality of life.
- Systematic desensitization, flooding, aversion therapy, and operant strategies for modification of behavior are common techniques used in behavior therapy.
- **Albert Ellis** developed **rational emotive behavior therapy (REBT)** and **Aaron T. Beck** developed **cognitive therapy**. Both these therapies are based on the premise that the way we think or perceive an event or situation further influences our emotions and behaviors (**Cognitive Model**).
- **Supportive therapy** attempts at alleviating or removing the distress of the person and restoring functioning to the normal level, by addressing the current problem at hand. Some of the principles of supportive therapy include guidance, ventilation, and catharsis, prestige suggestion, tension control and release, and environmental manipulation.
- **Group therapy** involves working together with a group of people under the guidance of a skilled therapist with a pre-established common goal. It is most commonly used in the treatment of substance dependence.
- **Family therapy** focuses on the family as the unit of intervention, to modify how different family members interact and relate with each other. It can be used to address relationship problems in the family, to improve the family's coping in case of the presence of psychosocial stressors, and to manage the expressed emotions of the family.
- **Marital (or couples) therapy** aims at resolving the conflicts between a couple over a range of parameters like social, emotional, financial, and sexual.
- Many authors have attempted to apply the knowledge of traditional concepts in psychotherapy. "Shivite" symbols in psychoanalysis (Nand), legends of Savitri (Surya and Jayaram), and the Hanuman complex (Wig) are some examples.

SELF-ASSESSMENT

1. Define psychotherapy and describe various types of psychotherapies.
2. Define behavior therapy and describe various behavior therapy techniques in brief.
3. Write short notes on:
   a. Psychoanalysis
   b. Cognitive therapy
   c. Supportive therapy
   d. Group therapy
   e. Family therapy

Chapter 30

Psychopharmacology I: Antidepressants and Antianxiety Drugs

Dinesh Kumar Badyal · Sandeep Kumar Goyal

ANTIDEPRESSANTS

The various antidepressants include the following:

A. **Selective serotonin reuptake inhibitors (SSRIs):** Fluoxetine, paroxetine, fluvoxamine, sertraline, citalopram, and escitalopram
B. **Selective serotonin–norepinephrine reuptake inhibitors (SNRIs):** Duloxetine, venlafaxine, desvenlafaxine, and milnacipran
C. **Serotonin partial agonist and reuptake inhibitor (SPARI):** Vilazodone
D. **Atypical antidepressants:** Mirtazapine, bupropion, trazodone, and tianeptine
E. **Tricyclic antidepressants (TCAs):** Imipramine, amitriptyline, doxepin, nortriptyline, amoxapine, clomipramine, and reboxetine
F. **Monoamine oxidase inhibitors (MAOIs):** Phenelzine, isocarboxazid, tranylcypromine, rasagiline, and moclobemide
G. **Multimodal:** Vortioxetine
H. **Melatonin receptor agonist:** Agomelatine

A. Selective Serotonin Reuptake Inhibitors

Fluoxetine was the first SSRI introduced in the United States. SSRIs are preferred antidepressants, as the efficacy is almost similar to the earlier used TCAs without dry mouth, retention of urine, or blurring of vision seen with TCAs.

Mechanism of Action

There is selective inhibition of serotonin transporters (SERTs), and hence they inhibit serotonin reuptake. The SSRIs lack clinically significant receptor activity at muscarinic cholinergic, H_1, M_1 adrenergic, M_2 adrenergic, β adrenergic, $5HT_1$, and $5HT_2$ receptors. Among SSRIs, paroxetine has the highest affinity for muscarinic cholinergic receptors, so it can cause dry mouth, constipation, urinary hesitancy, and blurred vision.

Pharmacokinetics

SSRIs have long plasma half-lives allowing once a day administration. Fluoxetine has the longest half-life which is 4–6 days and its active metabolite has a half-life of 7–9 days.

Therapeutic Uses

SSRIs are FDA approved for major depressive disorder (MDD), obsessive–compulsive disorder (OCD), post-traumatic stress disorder (PTSD), premenstrual dysphoric disorder (PMDD), panic disorder, and social phobia. Not all SSRIs have FDA approval for these indications, but they have a common spectrum of action. FDA-approved indications are as follows:

1. **Depression:** All SSRIs except fluvoxamine are FDA approved for the treatment of depression in adults. Fluoxetine is additionally approved for use in children suffering from a major depressive disorder.
2. **Obsessive–compulsive disorder:** Fluoxetine, fluvoxamine, paroxetine, and sertraline are approved for the treatment of OCD in adult patients. Fluoxetine, fluvoxamine, and sertraline are approved for the treatment of children with OCD (aged 6–17 years).
3. **Anxiety disorders:** SSRIs are used to treat anxiety disorders, for example, panic disorder (fluoxetine, paroxetine, and sertraline), social anxiety disorder (paroxetine and sertraline), and generalized anxiety disorder (escitalopram and paroxetine).
4. **Post-traumatic stress disorder:** Paroxetine and sertraline are FDA approved for PTSD.
5. **Bulimia nervosa:** Fluoxetine is indicated in the treatment of bulimia nervosa.
6. **Premenstrual dysphoric disorders:** Fluoxetine, paroxetine, and sertraline are FDA approved for the treatment of premenstrual dysphoric disorders.

Adverse Effects

Nausea, anorexia, vomiting, flatulence, dyspepsia, and loose stools are common gastrointestinal adverse effects. Initial nausea settles down as tolerance develops. There can be CNS stimulation reported as insomnia and restlessness. Avoid fluoxetine if the patient is agitated. SSRIs, especially fluoxetine, cause headaches; otherwise, SSRIs are effective prophylactic agents for a migraine and tension-type headache. SSRIs can cause functional impairment of platelet aggregation but not a reduction in platelet number. Sexual dysfunction can manifest as a lack of libido or delayed orgasm. Paroxetine has mild anticholinergic activity and can cause dry mouth and constipation. SSRIs can cause hyponatremia and syndrome of the inappropriate antidiuretic hormone. All SSRIs cause QTc prolongation. Citalopram has the most pronounced effect on the QT interval.

Emotional blunting is a side effect that is often overlooked. Patients report that they are not able to cry in emotional situations. Excessive yawning is a side effect that is also often overlooked. SSRIs may rarely cause extrapyramidal symptoms (e.g., akathisia, dystonia, and tremor).

Serotonin Syndrome

Serotonin syndrome occurs when SSRIs are prescribed to a patient taking other drugs that increase serotonin levels (i.e., MAO inhibitors or lithium). This syndrome is characterized by diarrhea, restlessness, hyperthermia, muscle rigidity, extreme agitation, autonomic instability, delirium, coma, status epilepticus, cardiovascular collapse, and death. Treatment of serotonin syndrome consists of removing the offending agent, supportive care with nitroglycerine, cyproheptadine, cooling blankets, mechanical ventilation, and paralyzing agents.

B. Selective Serotonin-Norepinephrine Reuptake Inhibitors

SNRIs are dual reuptake inhibitors, as these drugs inhibit both norepinephrine and serotonin uptake transporters. SNRIs lack affinity for other receptors, especially muscarinic, histaminergic, and alpha- and beta-adrenergic receptors. This selectivity differentiates SNRIs from TCAs.

Therapeutic Uses

Venlafaxine is FDA approved for the treatment of MDD, generalized anxiety disorder, social anxiety disorder, and panic disorder. Venlafaxine can also be used in PTSD and premenstrual dysphoric disorders (off-label use). **Desvenlafaxine** is FDA approved only for major depressive disorder.

Duloxetine is FDA approved for major depressive disorder, generalized anxiety disorder, diabetic peripheral neuropathic pain, fibromyalgia, and chronic musculoskeletal pain. It is also used to treat stress incontinence (off-label use).

Milnacipran is USFDA approved for fibromyalgia only, but it is approved for major depressive disorder in many countries, including France and Japan.

Adverse Effects

Nausea is the most common treatment-emergent adverse effect (TEAE) associated with venlafaxine. Venlafaxine (above 225 mg/day) and duloxetine (above 60 mg/day) can increase blood pressure. Venlafaxine can lead to sexual dysfunction (decreased libido and delayed ejaculation) and anxiety. Other TEAE are nausea, dry mouth, somnolence, fatigue, constipation, decreased appetite, and hyperhidrosis.

Duloxetine is contraindicated in severe renal dysfunction and hepatic insufficiency. It should be used with caution in patients with narrow-angle glaucoma.

C. Serotonin Partial Agonist and Reuptake Inhibitor

Vilazodone

Vilazodone is a dual-acting serotonergic antidepressant. It is a partial agonist of the $5HT_{1A}$ receptor and selective serotonin reuptake inhibition. Due to its dual mechanism of action, it is termed as **SPARI**. It is FDA approved for the treatment of major depressive disorder in adult patients. Bioavailability of vilazodone increases if it is administered with food and it has a bioavailability of 72% with food.

Therapeutic response is usually seen after 1–2 weeks of treatment. No dose adjustment is recommended for elderly and mild, moderate, or severe renal impairment and mild to moderate hepatic impairment. It has not been studied in patients with severe hepatic impairment. Diarrhea, nausea, and decreased libido are common side effects.

D. Atypical Antidepressants

These drugs are different from typical antidepressants in structure and also act on targets different from the target for typical or conventional antidepressants.

Mirtazapine

Mirtazapine acts by antagonism of presynaptic α_2 adrenergic receptors and postsynaptic $5HT_2$ and $5HT_3$ receptors. Consequently, adrenergic and serotonergic transmission improves relieving the symptoms. Mirtazapine does not affect monoamine uptake.

Therapeutic Indications

Mirtazapine is FDA approved for the treatment of depression.

Side Effects

Somnolence is the most common side effect. Dry mouth, increased appetite, constipation, weight gain, dizziness, myalgias, and disturbing dreams are other side effects. Insomnia and sexual dysfunction are not problems with this drug. However, there can be sedation due to action on histamine receptors so that it can be preferred in depression with insomnia.

Bupropion

Bupropion improves adrenergic and dopaminergic transmission by dopamine and norepinephrine reuptake inhibition.

Therapeutic Indications

It is FDA approved for major depressive disorder, seasonal affective disorder, and smoking cessation. Other uses may include neuropathic pain and weight loss. Bupropion can be added to SSRIs to treat the sexual side effects of SSRIs and it may also be helpful in hypoactive sexual desire disorder.

Side Effects

Headache, insomnia, dry mouth, tremor, and nausea are the most common side effects. Bupropion can cause psychotic symptoms (e.g., hallucinations, delusions, and catatonia). It can cause seizures in 0.1%–0.2% of the patients on bupropion at doses of 450 mg per day. Weight gain and sexual side effects are uncommon. Bupropion is least likely to cause a manic switch in a patient of bipolar disorder. Bupropion is contraindicated in patients of seizure disorder, patients undergoing abrupt discontinuation of alcohol and sedatives, including benzodiazepines (BZDs), and patients with a current or past diagnosis of bulimia or anorexia nervosa.

Trazodone

Trazodone is a weak inhibitor of serotonin reuptake and a potent antagonist of $5HT_{2A}$ and $5HT_{2C}$ receptors. It is FDA approved for the treatment of the major depressive disorder. Trazodone is also used for insomnia and erectile dysfunction.

Tianeptine

Unlike other antidepressants, it increases 5HT reuptake, so tianeptine is a serotonin reuptake enhancer. It is preferred in depressive disorder with psychosomatic symptoms. Adverse effects include gastrointestinal symptoms and body aches.

E. Tricyclic Antidepressants

TCAs block the transporter site for norepinephrine and serotonin, thus increasing the synaptic concentrations of these neurotransmitters. Secondary effects of the TCAs include antagonism at the muscarinic acetylcholine, histamine H_1, and α_1 and α_2 adrenergic receptors.

Therapeutic Uses

Treatment and prophylaxis of major depressive disorder is the principal indication of TCAs and clomipramine is FDA approved for the treatment of OCD. Amitriptyline has shown good efficacy in neuropathic pain and prophylaxis of migraine.

Imipramine is effective in enuresis. Amoxapine blocks D_2 receptors also and has an antipsychotic property in addition to antidepressant action, so it can be used in psychotic depression.

Adverse Effects

The typical adverse effects of TCA include dry mouth, retention of urine, and blurring of vision (anticholinergic effects). TCAs can cause changes in heart rate (tachycardia), flattened T waves, QT prolongation, and ST segment depression. As they prolong conduction time, TCAs are contraindicated in patients with preexisting conduction defects. Orthostatic hypotension, sedation, increased blood pressure, palpitations, profuse sweating, and sexual dysfunction are other common side effects. Amoxapine can cause extrapyramidal adverse effects. Tolerance to hypotensive and anticholinergic effects occurs.

F. Monoamine Oxidase Inhibitors

MAOIs were approved as antidepressants in 1950. Their use is limited by potentially lethal hypertension and need to use a restrictive diet. They have dangerous interactions causing a hypertensive crisis, with some food items containing tyramine and DOPA (e.g., cheese, beer, wine, pickled meat and fish, and yeast extract). The reaction is known as the **cheese reaction**. These drugs have several other adverse effects, including orthostatic hypotension, insomnia, sexual dysfunction, and weight gain.

Phenelzine, isocarboxazid, tranylcypromine, and rasagiline are various MAOIs.

Moclobemide is a reversible and selective MAO-A inhibitor known as RIMA (reversible inhibitors of MAO-A). With moclobemide, dietary restrictions are not required. It is an effective antidepressant with efficacy comparable to TCAs in mild to moderate depression.

G. Multimodal

Vortioxetine

Vortioxetine is a multimodal antidepressant drug that acts through 5HT receptor activity and SERT inhibition. It acts as $5HT_3$, $5HT_7$, $5HT_{1D}$ antagonists, $5HT_{1B}$ partial agonist, $5HT_{1A}$ agonist, and SERT inhibitor. Vortioxetine is FDA approved for the treatment of major depressive disorder. Most of the other antidepressants, except vilazodone, are unimodal agents with a single primary mechanism of action that acts through SERT inhibition. It is recently launched in India (September 2018).

Vortioxetine-treated patients also show **improvement in MDD-related cognitive dysfunction**. Cognitive benefits of vortioxetine are partly mediated by improvement in depressive symptoms and partly by the direct effect of vortioxetine on cognitive function.

Side Effects

The most common side effects reported with vortioxetine are nausea, vomiting, constipation, diarrhea, headache, dizziness, itching, decreased appetite, and abnormal dreams. TEAEs, including insomnia, somnolence, and weight gain, occur at rates comparable to placebo with all doses, and sexual dysfunction is comparable to placebo at doses 5–15 mg. A 20 mg dose is associated with an increased incidence of treatment-emergent sexual dysfunction. No dose adjustment is required in patients with mild to moderate hepatic impairment, mild to severe renal impairment, and end-stage renal disease.

H. Melatonin Receptor Agonist

Agomelatine

Agomelatine is an MT_1 and MT_2 melatonin receptor agonist and $5HT_{2C}$ antagonist. Agomelatine is indicated for the treatment of depression in Europe, but it is not USFDA approved yet. Nausea and dizziness are the most common side effects. No dose adjustment is recommended for renal impairment. It should not be administered to patients with even mild hepatic impairment. The manufacturer recommends baseline liver function tests and follow-up tests at 6, 12, and 24 weeks.

Use of Antidepressants Drugs in Pregnancy and Lactation

All SRIs (SRI = SSRI + SNRI), except paroxetine, are in FDA pregnancy category C (drugs for which animal reproduction studies have shown an adverse effect on the fetus; there are no adequate and well-controlled studies in humans, but potential benefits may warrant the use of the drug in pregnant women despite potential risks). Association of paroxetine with cardiac septal defects led to change in its FDA pregnancy category to "D" (drugs for which there is positive evidence of human fetal risk based on adverse reaction data from investigational or marketing experience or studies in humans, but potential benefits may warrant use of the drug in pregnant women despite potential risks) in 2005. Bupropion and mirtazapine also belong to pregnancy category C.

Use of MAOIs is contraindicated in pregnancy, and if pregnancy occurs and the patient is taking MAOIs, the drug should be discontinued.

Sertraline and paroxetine concentration in an infant is less than 2% of adjusted maternal dose, whereas citalopram, fluoxetine, and venlafaxine have more than 10% of the adjusted maternal dose in the infant. Breastfed infants of fluoxetine-treated mothers gain less weight after birth.

The estimated infant dose of duloxetine through breast milk is 0.14% of the maternal dose.

ANTIANXIETY DRUGS

The various antianxiety drugs include the following:

A. Benzodiazepines:
Diazepam, alprazolam, nitrazepam, oxazepam, lorazepam, and chlordiazepoxide

B. Azapirones:
Buspirone and ipsapirone

C. SSRIs/SNRIs:
Selective serotonin reuptake inhibitors (SSRIs)
Fluoxetine, paroxetine, fluvoxamine, sertraline, citalopram, and escitalopram
Selective serotonin-norepinephrine reuptake inhibitors (SNRIs)
Duloxetine and venlafaxine

D. Adrenergic antagonists:
Propranolol

A. Benzodiazepines (BZDs)

BZDs act on the $GABA_A$ receptor–Cl channel complex. BZD bind to a site known as "BZD receptors." These drugs increase the action of GABA on $GABA_A$ receptor–Cl Chanel complex. The increased action leads to increased chloride conductance and hence hyperpolarization. The hyperpolarization inhibits neuronal transmission; this action decreases symptoms of anxiety. The BZDs act preferentially on midbrain ascending reticular formation and on the limbic system.

Most of the BZDs can be given orally. Midazolam is given parenterally. Most of BZD have active metabolites that add to their action and duration (e.g., oxazepam is an active metabolite of diazepam).

Therapeutic Uses

BZDs are used in a variety of disorders due to their action on various targets.

1. **Anxiety:** BZDs are the drug of choice in the generalized anxiety disorder. They can be prescribed on a need basis or daily for a short duration, during which other drugs or psychosocial interventions show a therapeutic response. Alprazolam is a preferred drug here due to its additional mood-elevating action. Oxazepam is a preferred option in the elderly and hepatic disorders due to its short half-life and inactive metabolites.
2. **Catatonia:** Lorazepam is frequently used to treat acute catatonia associated with bipolar disorder or schizophrenia.
3. **Epilepsy:** Diazepam is preferred in status epilepticus in children by rectal route. Clonazepam is used in myoclonic and petit mal epilepsy.
4. **Alcohol withdrawal:** BZDs are used to manage the withdrawal symptoms of alcohol. Chlordiazepoxide, lorazepam, and oxazepam are used.
5. **Insomnia:** BZDs increase quality and duration of sleep and reduce sleep latency, and REM sleep.
6. **Acute agitation:** Midazolam is very useful in controlling the acute agitation in an emergency. Rapid onset of action and minimal residual impairment are the factors that make midazolam a favorite for controlling acute agitation.

Adverse Effects

BZDs have several adverse effects. Drowsiness is the most common side effect. They affect psychomotor and cognitive functions also, and hence driving and operating heavy machinery should be avoided. Amnesia for events can happen. Some patients experience ataxia or dizziness.

Abuse potential is an area of concern. The abrupt withdrawal of BZDs can lead to rebound anxiety.

Pregnancy and Lactation

Previously, BZD exposure during the first trimester was thought to cause cleft lip and cleft palate, but subsequent studies failed to prove the association. Diazepam and chlordiazepoxide are preferred during pregnancy. The use of BZDs in the third trimester can cause a withdrawal syndrome in the newborn. Breastfeeding can cause sedation, hypotonia, and decreased feeding in the infants.

B. Azapirone (Buspirone)

Buspirone acts as an agonist or partial agonist at presynaptic $5HT_{1A}$ receptors and both agonist and antagonist at the D_2 receptor. The onset of action may take up to 2 weeks, so it is not used in acute anxiety conditions. Buspirone is used in generalized anxiety disorder. It is sometimes used to augment SSRIs in OCD. Headache, nausea, dizziness, and rarely insomnia are the most common side effects.

C. SSRI/SNRIs

These are preferred for chronic anxiety states like anxiety disorders and phobias. As already described in SSRIs, various SSRIs are FDA approved in anxiety disorders. **Venlafaxine** is FDA approved for the treatment of generalized anxiety disorder, social anxiety disorder, and panic disorder. **Duloxetine** is FDA approved for generalized anxiety disorder.

D. Adrenergic Antagonists (Propranolol)

This drug is an adjuvant antianxiety drug that is used to control symptoms of anxiety such as palpitations, tremors, and sweating. Propranolol is indicated for the treatment of performance-type social phobia. A 10–40 mg of propranolol is given approximately 30 minutes before the anxiety-provoking situation.

KEY POINTS

Selective Serotonin Reuptake Inhibitors (SSRIs)

- SSRIs act by selective inhibition of serotonin transporters (SERT). This raises serotonin levels in CNS.
- SSRIs are FDA approved for major depressive disorder (MDD), obsessive-compulsive disorder (OCD), post-traumatic stress disorder (PTSD), premenstrual dysphoric disorder (PMDD), panic disorder, social phobia, and generalized anxiety disorder (GAD).
- Fluoxetine is indicated in the treatment of bulimia nervosa.
- Nausea, anorexia, vomiting, flatulence, dyspepsia, and loose stools are common gastrointestinal adverse effects of SSRIs.
- SSRIs can cause hyponatremia and syndrome of the inappropriate antidiuretic hormone. All SSRIs cause QTc prolongation. Citalopram has the most pronounced effect on the QT interval.
- Emotional blunting is a side effect that is often overlooked. Patients report that they are not able to cry in emotional situations.
- A lack of libido and delayed orgasm are sexual side effects.

Selective Serotonin-Norepinephrine Reuptake Inhibitors (SNRIs)

- SNRIs are dual reuptake inhibitors, as these drugs inhibit both norepinephrine and serotonin uptake transporters.
- **Venlafaxine** is FDA approved for the treatment of the major depressive disorder, generalized anxiety disorder, social anxiety disorder, and panic disorder.
- **Duloxetine** is FDA approved for major depressive disorder, generalized anxiety disorder, diabetic peripheral neuropathic pain, fibromyalgia, and chronic musculoskeletal pain. It is also used to treat stress incontinence (off-label use).
- Nausea is the most common treatment-emergent adverse effect (TEAE) associated with venlafaxine.
- Venlafaxine (above 225 mg/day) and duloxetine (above 60 mg/day) can increase blood pressure.
- Venlafaxine can lead to sexual dysfunction (decreased libido and delayed ejaculation) and anxiety.

Serotonin Partial Agonist/Reuptake Inhibitor (SPARI)

- Vilazodone is a partial agonist of the $5HT_{1A}$ receptor and SSRI.
- It is FDA approved for the treatment of major depressive disorder in adult patients.

Atypical Antidepressants

- Mirtazapine acts by antagonism of presynaptic α_2 adrenergic receptors and postsynaptic $5HT_2$ and $5HT_3$ receptors.
- Mirtazapine is FDA approved for the treatment of depression.
- Somnolence is the most common side effect and dry mouth, increased appetite, constipation, weight gain, dizziness, myalgias, and disturbing dreams are other side effects of mirtazapine.
- Bupropion improves adrenergic and dopaminergic transmission by dopamine and norepinephrine reuptake inhibition.
- Bupropion is FDA approved for major depressive disorder, seasonal affective disorder, and smoking cessation.
- Bupropion can cause psychotic symptoms (e.g., hallucinations, delusions, and catatonia).
- Bupropion can cause seizures in 0.1%–0.2% of the patients at doses of 450 mg per day. Bupropion is contraindicated in patients of a seizure disorder.
- Sexual side effects are uncommon with bupropion.
- Bupropion is least likely to cause a manic switch in a patient of bipolar disorder.
- Trazodone is FDA approved for the treatment of the major depressive disorder. Trazodone is also used for insomnia and erectile dysfunction.
- **Tianeptine** increases 5HT reuptake, so tianeptine is a serotonin reuptake enhancer. It is preferred in depressive disorder with psychosomatic symptoms.

Tricyclic Antidepressants (TCAs)

- TCAs block the transporter site for norepinephrine and serotonin, thus increasing the synaptic concentrations of these neurotransmitters. Secondary effects of the TCAs include antagonism at the muscarinic acetylcholine, histamine H_1, and α_1 and α_2 adrenergic receptors.
- Treatment and prophylaxis of major depressive disorder is the principal indication of TCAs and clomipramine is FDA approved for the treatment of OCD. Amitriptyline has shown good efficacy in neuropathic pain and prophylaxis of migraine. Imipramine is effective in enuresis.
- The typical adverse effects of TCA include dry mouth, retention of urine, and blurring of vision (anticholinergic effects).

Monoamine Oxidase Inhibitors (MAOIs)

- MAOIs have dangerous interactions causing a hypertensive crisis with some food items containing tyramine and DOPA (e.g., cheese, beer, wine, pickled meat and fish, and yeast extract). The reaction is known as the **cheese reaction**.
- Phenelzine, isocarboxazid, tranylcypromine, and rasagiline are various MAOIs.
- Moclobemide is a reversible and selective MAO-A inhibitor known as RIMA (reversible inhibitors of MAO-A). With moclobemide, dietary restrictions are not required.

Multimodal

- Vortioxetine is a multimodal antidepressant drug that acts through 5HT receptor activity and SERT inhibition. It acts as $5HT_3$, $5HT_7$, $5HT_{1D}$ antagonists, $5HT_{1B}$ partial agonist, 5 HT_{1A} agonist, and SERT inhibitor. Vortioxetine is FDA approved for the treatment of major depressive disorder.

Melatonin Receptor Agonist

- Agomelatine is an MT_1 and MT_2 melatonin receptor agonist and $5HT_{2C}$ antagonist. Agomelatine is indicated for the treatment of depression in Europe, but it is not USFDA approved yet.

Antidepressants in Pregnancy and Lactation

- All SRI (SRI = SSRI + SNRI), except paroxetine, are in the FDA pregnancy category C. Association of paroxetine with cardiac septal defects led to change in its FDA pregnancy category to "D." Bupropion and mirtazapine also belong to pregnancy category C.
- Sertraline and paroxetine concentration in an infant is less than 2% of adjusted maternal dose, whereas citalopram, fluoxetine, and venlafaxine have more than 10% of the adjusted maternal dose in the infant.

Antianxiety Drugs

- Benzodiazepines (BZDs) are used in a variety of disorders due to their actions on various targets (e.g., anxiety, catatonia, epilepsy, alcohol withdrawal, insomnia, and agitation).
- Buspirone acts as an agonist or partial agonist at presynaptic $5HT_{1A}$ receptors and both agonist and antagonist at the D_2 receptor. The onset of action may take up to 2 weeks, so it is not used in acute anxiety conditions. Buspirone is used in generalized anxiety disorder.
- Propranolol is an adjuvant antianxiety drug that is used to control symptoms of anxiety just as palpitations, tremors, and sweating. Propranolol is indicated for the treatment of performance-type social phobia.

SELF-ASSESSMENT

1. Classify various antidepressants.
2. Describe the mechanism of action, therapeutic indications, and side effects of SSRIs.
3. Write short notes on:
   a. SNRI
   b. SPARI
   c. Mirtazapine
   d. Bupropion
   e. TCAs
   f. MAOIs
   g. Vortioxetine
   h. Agomelatine
4. Classify antianxiety drugs and describe the mechanism of action, therapeutic indications, and side effects of benzodiazepines.

Chapter 31

Psychopharmacology II: Antipsychotics

Sandeep Kumar Goyal

Antipsychotics are the drugs used to treat schizophrenia and other psychotic disorders. The modern era of psychopharmacology began with the discovery of chlorpromazine, the first effective antipsychotic in the early 1950s by **Paul Charpentier**.

FIRST-GENERATION ANTIPSYCHOTICS

First-generation antipsychotics (FGAs) were known by various names such as neuroleptics, major tranquilizers, typical antipsychotics, and dopamine receptor antagonists (DRAs). FGAs are associated with significant extrapyramidal symptoms such as secondary Parkinsonism and tardive dyskinesia (TD).

The various FGAs are:

A. **Phenothiazines:** Chlorpromazine, thioridazine, trifluoperazine, fluphenazine
B. **Diphenylbutylpiperidine:** Pimozide
C. **Thioxanthenes:** Thiothixene
D. **Butyrophenones:** Haloperidol, droperidol, spiperone
E. **Others:** Loxapine, molindone

Low-Potency vs. High-Potency FGAs

Traditionally, antipsychotics are classified as low-potency and high-potency. Fluphenazine and haloperidol are examples of high-potency typical antipsychotics, and chlorpromazine and thioridazine are examples of low-potency antipsychotics.

Pharmacokinetics

Absorption of FGAs administered orally or parentally is good. Steady-state levels of chlorpromazine, haloperidol, and most of the other FGAs are reached in 3–5 days as their half-lives are about 24 hours. Bioavailability is approximately ten times when drugs are administered parentally as compared to oral administration. FGAs are metabolized mainly by the liver.

Pharmacodynamics

FGAs act as dopamine receptor antagonists. The antipsychotic potency of dopamine receptor antagonists is highly correlated with their affinity for D_2 receptors. Dopamine receptor antagonism in the mesolimbocortical system explains the antipsychotic activity, whereas activity in the nigrostriatal system causes extrapyramidal side effects (EPS).

Therapeutic Indications

1. Treatment of schizophrenia and schizoaffective disorders
2. Delusional disorder and other psychotic disorders
3. Mania
    - FGAs have a rapid onset of action as compared to antimanic drugs, so these are combined with antimanic drugs during the first few days of treatment, and antipsychotic drugs

are tapered as the effect of anti-manic drugs starts

4. Depression with psychotic features
5. Delirium and dementia
   - FGAs are useful in treating agitation and psychotic symptoms associated with delirium and dementia
6. Haloperidol and pimozide are the most commonly used drugs to treat motor and vocal tics in Tourette syndrome
7. Huntington disease
8. Ballismus
9. Severe emesis associated with chemotherapy
10. Intractable hiccups

FGAs are **contraindicated** in Parkinson's psychosis and Lewy body disease, as they can worsen Parkinsonism and may precipitate dystonic reactions.

Side Effects

High-potency typical antipsychotics tend to be associated with more EPS and less histaminic (e.g., sedation), alpha-adrenergic (e.g., orthostasis), and anticholinergic (e.g., dry mouth) side effects, while low-potency typical antipsychotics tend to be associated with fewer EPS but more H_1, $alpha_1$, and muscarinic side effects.

Sedation The blockade of the H_1 receptors causes sedation. Chlorpromazine (CPZ) is the most sedating typical antipsychotic.

Neurological FGAs have EPS which can be acute or chronic. Acute EPS occur in the first few days or weeks of treatment and chronic EPS occur after treatment for months or years. Acute EPS include tremors, akinesia (paucity of motion), akathisia, drug-induced Parkinsonism, dystonia, and neuroleptic malignant syndrome (NMS). TD is a chronic EPS.

Tremors These are usually coarse and can interfere with daily activities.

Akathisia It is the most common and most distressing acute EPS. Akathisia is the inability to sit or stand still. It manifests as shifting weight from foot to foot, feeling of inner restlessness, and shifting of body positions in a chair. The patient presents with a complaint of a compelling urge to walk or to initiate movement. Akathisia responds well to beta-blockers, especially propranolol. Anticholinergics and benzodiazepines are also helpful.

Acute dystonia It presents as a spasm of muscles of the head and the neck. Common dystonias are opisthotonos, retrocollis, torticollis, oculogyric crisis (eyes turned upwards), macroglossia, and tongue protrusion. Dystonias respond well to anticholinergic drugs (diphenhydramine or benztropine used IM or IV).

Drug-induced Parkinsonism It presents with rigidity, bradykinesia, shuffling gate, and tremors. Diminished arm swing or decreased facial expressiveness may be the first symptoms. The patient may present with akinesia, that is, difficulty in initiating movements. Drug-induced Parkinsonian symptoms respond well to oral anticholinergic drugs (e.g., trihexyphenidyl). Amantadine is also effective in treating Parkinsonism and akinesia.

Neuroleptic malignant syndrome NMS is a serious side effect of antipsychotic drugs. It is characterized by hyperthermia, rigidity, autonomic instability, including tachycardia, increased blood pressure, tachypnea, diaphoresis, and fluctuating consciousness. It is commonly associated with an increase in creatine phosphokinase (CPK) and aldolase. Elevation in liver transaminases, leukocytosis, myoglobinemia, and myoglobinuria may also be present. It may progress to acute renal failure. NMS is more common with high-potency FGAs. Treatment includes stopping the antipsychotic drug and starting supportive and symptomatic treatment, treating fever, and correcting fluid and electrolyte imbalance. Dantrolene and bromocriptine are useful in treating NMS. Amantadine can be used as an add-on drug if needed.

Tardive dyskinesia TD develops after chronic treatment with antipsychotic drugs and is characterized by abnormal involuntary movements of mouth, tongue, and jaw (lip-smacking, sucking, and puckering), and facial grimacing. Classic TD may present as **fly catcher's tongue** (tongue darting in and out of the mouth) or **bonbon sign** (repeated pushing of the tongue against cheek). Choreoathetoid movements of fingers and toes and slow writhing movements of the trunk can also be present. Antiparkinsonian medicines usually worsen the TD. TD develops in 10%–20% of the patients who are on FGAs for more than 1 year. Second-generation antipsychotics (SGAs) are associated with a lower risk of TD than FGAs. Clozapine does not cause TD and sometimes it can reverse the TD.

Endocrine Dopamine receptor antagonists (DRAs) can increase serum prolactin levels which can produce gynecomastia, galactorrhea, and erectile dysfunction in men. FGAs decrease follicle-stimulating hormone (FSH) and luteinizing hormone (LH) leading to amenorrhea and inhibition of orgasm in women.

Behavioral Decrease in emotional expressiveness, apathy, depression, cognitive impairment, and attention deficits are behavioral side effects of FGAs.

Cardiac Low-potency FGAs such as chlorpromazine and thioridazine cause ECG changes, for example, prolongation of QT and PR intervals, blunting of the T waves, and depression of ST-segment. Thioridazine has the highest risk of prolonging QTc interval, and ECG should be done before and during treatment with thioridazine.

Orthostatic hypotension Low-potency FGAs (chlorpromazine, thioridazine) may cause orthostatic hypotension. Tolerance usually occurs to this side effect, and it is advisable to start FGAs at low doses and gradually increase to the target dose. The patient should be told to stand up slowly or sit with their feet by the side of the bed when arising, to wait for a minute, particularly during the first 2 weeks of the treatment.

Sudden unexplained death Reports of sudden death in patients treated with FGAs can be due to Torsades de pointes secondary to QTc prolongation.

Blood DRAs may be associated with mild leukopenia. Thrombocytopenia and pancytopenia may also occur.

Skin and eye effects Low-potency FGAs, especially chlorpromazine, are associated with blue-grey metallic discoloration of the sun-exposed areas of the skin. This reaction usually occurs after long-term treatment with high doses. Patients receiving CPZ may also develop photosensitivity reactions causing sunburn or rash.

Patients receiving CPZ may also develop granular deposits in the anterior lens and posterior cornea. High doses of thioridazine (more than 1,000 mg per day) may cause retinitis pigmentosa.

Sexual function Thioridazine is associated with retrograde ejaculation. In males, FGAs can cause decreased libido and erectile dysfunction and in females, decreased libido, anorgasmia, and decreased lubrication.

Anticholinergic The anticholinergic side effects of low-potency drugs can lead to dry mouth, constipation, urinary retention, and blurred vision.

Pregnancy and lactation Correlation between using FGAs during pregnancy and congenital malformations is very low. Despite the low risk, FGAs should be avoided during pregnancy, especially in the first trimester, unless the benefit outweighs the risk.

FGAs are secreted in breast milk, so women taking FGAs should be advised against breastfeeding.

Seizure threshold DRAs lower the seizure threshold and are associated with an increased risk of seizures. The risk is clinically important in patients with a prior history of seizures. Low-potency drugs cause more reduction of seizure threshold.

SECOND-GENERATION ANTIPSYCHOTICS

Earlier these were called serotonin-dopamine antagonists (SDAs) considering their high affinity for $5HT_{2A}$ and D_2 receptors. Clozapine, risperidone, olanzapine, quetiapine, ziprasidone, aripiprazole, iloperidone, asenapine, and lurasidone are examples of SGAs. Cariprazine and brexpiprazole are newer drugs (not available in India yet). These were also called atypical antipsychotics as they had antipsychotic effect at doses which caused negligible EPS. Term SGA is preferred as each SGA has unique actions. SGAs have fewer EPS in comparison to FGAS, as they have additional effects on $5HT_{2A}$ receptors which increases dopamine turnover. Among SGAs, clozapine and quetiapine have the lowest EPS.

FDA issued a black box warning for all SGAs for increased mortality in elderly patients with dementia-related psychosis.

Clozapine

Clozapine was the first drug among SGAs.

Pharmacodynamics

Clozapine has a low affinity for D_2 receptors blockade, strong $5HT_2$, $5HT_3$, α_1 and α_2 adrenergic, H_1, and muscarinic receptor blockade. A low affinity for D_2 receptors may be an explanation for the lack of EPS of clozapine.

N-desmethylclozapine metabolite (40%–80% of the concentration of clozapine) is an M_1 receptor agonist, whereas clozapine is a muscarinic antagonist. This metabolite may be a major contributor to the clozapine's superior effects on cognition and negative symptoms compared to other agents.

Indications

1. It is indicated for treatment-resistant schizophrenia (patients who have failed at least two antipsychotic trials, and one of the drugs should be SGA).
2. Clozapine is indicated for reducing the risk of recurrent suicidal behavior in schizophrenia or schizoaffective disorder. So, it may be a preferred agent for patients of schizophrenia with high suicidal risk.
3. Clozapine can suppress abnormal movements in TD.
4. Clozapine is useful in the treatment of psychotic symptoms secondary to dopaminergic drugs used to treat Parkinson disease.

Side Effects

Sedation is a prominent side effect, which can be managed by giving the greater part of the dose at night. **Benign hyperthermia** can be seen during the initial part of the treatment, with a peak incidence on the 10th day. An increase in temperature usually resolves in a few days.

Clozapine causes **tachycardia** and **postural hypotension**. Clozapine-induced tachycardia can be treated with beta-blocker such as atenolol. Propranolol can increase the risk of agranulocytosis, so it should not be prescribed. In postural hypotension support stockings, increased sodium intake and fludrocortisone may be helpful. Tolerance to the hypotensive effects occurs over time and can be managed if the initial dose is low (25 mg per day) and is increased gradually. Paradoxically, hypertension has been reported in less than 4% of the patients on clozapine.

Constipation is the most common gastrointestinal side effect. Interventions may include diet modification, increased fluid intake, use of stool softeners, and exercise.

Hematological side effects of clozapine include neutropenia, decreased WBC count (3%), leukocytosis (0.6%), and eosinophilia (1%). Clozapine causes **agranulocytosis** in less than 1% of the patients. The risk of agranulocytosis is greatest during the first 3 months of the treatment. The risk of agranulocytosis increases with age and is more in females.

Clozapine causes **seizures** in 5%–10% of the patients. The risk of seizure is increased at a dosage of more than 600 mg per day. In patients who receive higher doses or have abnormal EEGs, the addition of an anticonvulsant like valproate or topiramate may be effective. Carbamazepine should not be used, as it can increase granulocytopenia.

Clozapine is associated with an increased risk of **myocarditis** (2.8/100,000 patients). The majority (80%) of the myocarditis occurs during the first 6 months of treatment.

Clozapine and other SGAs carry **black box warning** for increased mortality in elderly patients with dementia-related psychosis.

Sialorrhea during sleep is a troublesome side effect. Clozapine does not increase saliva but decreases swallowing, and the effect is more during sleep. Clonidine patches 0.1 mg once a week or amitriptyline can be used to treat sialorrhea.

Peripheral anticholinergic side effects like dry mouth, blurred vision, constipation, and urinary retention are common.

Clozapine causes weight gain. It can increase the risk of type 2 diabetes mellitus.

The incidence of EPS is much less as compared to other antipsychotics.

Dosage

Clozapine should be started at 12.5–25 mg per day and increased to 25 mg or 50 mg on the second day. It can be increased by 25 mg every 1–2 days until a target dose of 300–450 mg per day is achieved.

Monitoring

In the United States, monitoring of WBC is no longer required; absolute neutrophil count (ANC) needs to be measured. The initial ANC must be ≥1,500/mm^3. Monitoring is weekly for the first 6 months, every 2 weeks for the second 6 months, and monthly after 12 months. Any fever or sign of infection, such as pharyngitis, is an immediate indication for a WBC count. Clozapine treatment should be interrupted for ANC <1,000/mm^3. Clozapine should be stopped if total WBC count falls below 3,000/mm^3 or granulocyte count falls below 1,500 cells per mm^3. A patient who develops agranulocytosis should not get clozapine again. If the total eosinophil count rises above 4,000, clozapine should be stopped.

Risperidone

Risperidone has a potent $5HT_{2A}$ receptor antagonism along with D_2 receptor antagonism. It also antagonizes D_1, D_4, α_1, α_2, and H_1 receptors. Risperidone is metabolized in the liver to paliperidone, which has the same pharmacological profile as the parent compound.

Six mg per day is the optimal dose and dosage above 6 mg is associated with a higher incidence of adverse effects, especially EPS.

Risperidone causes weight gain, nausea, vomiting, rhinitis, erectile dysfunction, and increased pigmentation. It also causes hyperprolactinemia which can lead to galactorrhea and breast enlargement. A depot preparation (Risperdal Consta) is also available, which is administered IM every 2 weeks. Oral risperidone should be coadministered with Risperdal Consta for the initial 3 weeks.

Indications

1. Schizophrenia and schizoaffective disorder.
2. Bipolar I disorder: Risperidone is indicated in adults and children aged 10–17 years as monotherapy or adjunct therapy to lithium or valproate in acute manic or mixed episodes associated with bipolar I disorder.
3. Irritability associated with the autistic disorder in children aged 5–17 years.

Paliperidone

Paliperidone is the major active metabolite of risperidone. The recommended dose is 6 mg per day administered in the morning, and the maximum recommended dose is 12 mg per day. A depot preparation (Invega Sustenna) is also available, which is administered IM every month. The dose of paliperidone should be reduced in renal impairment. It may cause an increase in the QTc interval. It may cause orthostatic hypotension, tachycardia, somnolence, akathisia, dystonia, and Parkinsonism.

Indications

1. Acute and maintenance treatment of schizophrenia.
2. Acute treatment of schizoaffective disorder as monotherapy or adjunctive drug to mood stabilizers or antidepressants.

Olanzapine

Its $5HT_2$ blockade is eight times stronger than the dopamine receptor blockade. It acts as an antagonist at $5HT_{2A/2C}$, $5HT_6$, D_{1-4}, H_1, α_1, M_{1-5}, and $5HT_3$ receptors. Olanzapine has more histaminergic and muscarinic receptor antagonism. A 10–20 mg olanzapine per day is usually sufficient in the treatment and prevention of schizophrenia. Its antihistamine activity may explain weight gain caused by olanzapine. Olanzapine is associated with sedation, constipation, orthostatic hypotension, and tachycardia. Weight gain, hyperlipidemia, and hyperglycemia are potential side effects of olanzapine. It can cause an elevation of alanine aminotransferase (ALT).

Indications

1. It is indicated in the treatment of schizophrenia
2. Acute treatment of manic or mixed episodes associated with bipolar I disorder
3. Maintenance treatment of bipolar I disorder
4. A combination of olanzapine and fluoxetine is indicated for depressive episodes associated with bipolar I disorder
5. Olanzapine–fluoxetine combination is also indicated for treatment-resistant depression
6. It is also effective in schizoaffective disorder, Tourette syndrome, and psychosis in dementia and for producing weight gain in anorexia nervosa

A depot preparation of olanzapine pamoate is also available, which is administered IM every 2 or 4 weeks. This depot is associated with **post-injection delirium/sedation syndrome (PDSS),** which presents with sedation, delirium, EPS, dysarthria, ataxia, dizziness, hypertension, and convulsions. FDA has mandated that this injection should be administered at facilities with access to emergency services and the patient should be observed for at least 3 hours after injection. Before administering a long-acting injection of olanzapine, the patient should be administered oral olanzapine to ensure tolerability.

Quetiapine

Quetiapine's low incidence of EPS may be explained by its high $5HT_{2A}$ binding as compared to D_2 receptors. Another hypothesis proposes that its fast dissociation from the D_2 receptor is sufficient to induce antipsychotic response while minimizing EPS. The usual dose range for both mania and schizophrenia is 400–800 mg per day. Somnolence, postural hypotension, and dizziness are the most common side effects of quetiapine.

Indications

1. Acute treatment of schizophrenia
2. Acute treatment of manic episodes in bipolar I either as monotherapy or adjunct therapy to lithium or valproate
3. Monotherapy for acute treatment for depressive episodes associated with bipolar I or II disorder
4. Maintenance treatment of bipolar I disorder as an adjunct to lithium or divalproex
5. Quetiapine is used to treat insomnia (off-label use)

6. Low EPS potential makes it useful in a dopamine-induced psychosis in Parkinson disease

Ziprasidone

Ziprasidone has a higher affinity for $5HT_2$ receptors and intermediate affinity for D_2 receptors resulting in a high $5HT_2$:D_2 affinity ratio. It is $5HT_{1A}$ agonist and inhibits the reuptake of serotonin and norepinephrine suggesting possible antidepressant action. It prolongs QTc interval by 20 milliseconds at maximum therapeutic blood levels. It should be avoided in combination with other drugs known to produce QTc prolongation. Ziprasidone produces less weight gain as compared to other atypical antipsychotic agents. Somnolence, headache, dizziness, and nausea are common side effects.

Indications

1. Treatment of schizophrenia
2. Acute treatment of manic or mixed episode in bipolar I disorder as monotherapy
3. Maintenance treatment of bipolar I disorder as an adjunct to lithium or valproate

Aripiprazole

Aripiprazole differs from SGAs in having partial agonistic action at D_2 and $5HT_{1A}$ receptors, in addition to antagonistic actions at D_2 and $5HT_{2A}$ receptors. Aripiprazole is an effective antipsychotic with minimal sedation, metabolic effects, and weight gain. Aripiprazole is the only antipsychotic which may reduce levels of prolactin.

Indications

1. Treatment of schizophrenia
2. Acute treatment of manic or mixed episodes in bipolar I disorder as monotherapy, or adjunct therapy with lithium or valproate
3. Adjunct treatment of patients with inadequate response to antidepressants
4. Irritability associated with the autistic disorder
5. Tourette disorder

Lurasidone

It has partial agonistic action at $5HT_{1A}$ receptors, in addition to potent antagonistic action at D_2 and $5HT_{2A}$ receptors. Along with aripiprazole and ziprasidone, it has low liability for metabolic effects. It should be administered with food. Sedation, EPS, and nausea are the most common side effects. For schizophrenia, the recommended starting dose is 40 mg per day and the maximum dose is 160 mg per day and for bipolar depression, the recommended starting dose is 20 mg per day and the maximum dose is 120 mg per day.

Indications

1. Treatment of schizophrenia
2. Treatment of adults with bipolar depression, both as monotherapy and as an adjunct to lithium or valproate

Brexpiprazole

It is a partial agonist at $5HT_{1A}$ and D_2 receptors and antagonist at $5HT_{2A}$ and $\alpha_{1B/2C}$ receptors. It is FDA approved for the treatment of schizophrenia and as an adjunctive treatment of major depressive disorders.

Pregnancy and Lactation

Clozapine and lurasidone are classified as pregnancy category B (animal reproduction studies have failed to demonstrate a risk to the fetus and there are no adequate and well-controlled studies in pregnant women) and all other SGAs are in category C (animal reproduction studies have shown an adverse effect on the fetus and there are no adequate and well-controlled studies in humans, but potential benefits may warrant use of the drug in pregnant women despite potential risks). The risk of gestational diabetes may be increased with all SGAs. Olanzapine has been associated with hip dysplasia, meningocele, ankyloblepharon, and neural tube defects.

Animal studies show that clozapine is excreted in milk and women on clozapine should not breastfeed. Literature suggests that risperidone is excreted in milk and the possibility of EPS/NMS in an exposed infant cannot be ruled out, so the decision to breastfeed while on risperidone should be made after careful risk–benefit analysis. Data regarding the excretion of SGAs in breast milk and effects on an infant is limited to case studies, and the patient should be told about possible adverse effects of breastfeeding.

Metabolic Syndrome

Metabolic syndrome is a risk factor for diabetes mellitus and cardiovascular disease. Metabolic syndrome is diagnosed if three of the following are present:

1. Abdominal obesity (waist circumference >102 cm in men and >88 cm in women)
2. Triglycerides more than or equal to 150 mg/dL
3. HDL cholesterol less than 40 mg/dL in men and less than 50 mg/dL in women
4. Hypertension (blood pressure 130/85 mmHg or more)
5. Fasting plasma glucose 100 mg/dL or more

It is recommended to monitor the patient's blood glucose levels, serum lipids, body weight, waist circumference, and blood pressure when atypical antipsychotics are used for a long time.

Choice of Agent

All SDAs can be used for the initial management of psychotic episodes. In a person not responding to one SDA, other SDAs should be tried. SDAs may take up to 8 weeks to show their full effects. Clozapine is reserved for the patients who have failed at least two antipsychotic trials, including one trial of SGA.

Olanzapine and clozapine should be tapered slowly to prevent cholinergic rebound symptoms (e.g., excessive salivation, nausea, vomiting, diarrhea, diaphoresis, and flushing). Risperidone, quetiapine, and ziprasidone lack anticholinergic effects, and sudden transition from DRA, olanzapine, or clozapine to one of these may cause cholinergic rebound. The risk of cholinergic rebound can be reduced by adding an anticholinergic drug to risperidone, quetiapine, and ziprasidone.

LONG-ACTING ANTIPSYCHOTICS

A patient who has schizophrenia is usually not compliant with drugs due to the lack of insight, and discontinuation of antipsychotic drugs can lead to relapse. Long-acting injections of antipsychotic drugs are an option for patients with poor compliance with drugs. The major drawback of the long-acting antipsychotic injections is that if side effects occur, they persist for several weeks. So, before starting long-acting antipsychotics, it is advisable to start oral preparation and switch to the injectable once tolerance is established or a test dose of long-acting antipsychotic FGAs can be given. For SGAs, test dose is not required as the aqueous base is not allergenic. The lowest therapeutic dose is started and then it can be increased as per the response of the patient. The depot injection is administered at the longest possible licensed interval. There is no evidence that can suggest that administering depot injection at a shorter interval improves efficacy. Long-acting depot injections of flupentixol decanoate, fluphenazine decanoate, haloperidol decanoate, pipotiazine palmitate, zuclopenthixol, risperidone, olanzapine, and paliperidone are available.

If patients on regular depot injections of an FGA are to be switched to depot injection of SDA, the first dose of SDA is given on the day the next injection is due.

KEY POINTS

First-Generation Antipsychotics (FGAs)

- FGAs act as dopamine receptor antagonists. The antipsychotic potency of dopamine receptor antagonists is highly correlated with their affinity for D_2 receptors.
- Dopamine receptor antagonism in the mesolimbocortical system explains the antipsychotic activity, whereas activity in the nigrostriatal system causes extrapyramidal side effects (EPS).
- FGAs are indicated in the treatment of schizophrenia, schizoaffective disorders, delusional disorder, mania, and depression with psychotic features.
- Haloperidol and pimozide are the most commonly used drugs to treat motor and vocal tics in Tourette syndrome.
- The use of FGAs is associated with EPS. Acute EPS include tremors, akinesia, akathisia, drug-induced Parkinsonism, dystonia, and neuroleptic malignant syndrome. Tardive dyskinesia (TD) is a chronic EPS.
- **Neuroleptic malignant syndrome** is characterized by hyperthermia, rigidity, and autonomic instability, including tachycardia, increased blood pressure, tachypnea, diaphoresis, and fluctuating consciousness.
- **Tardive dyskinesia** is characterized by abnormal involuntary movements of mouth, tongue, and jaw (lip-smacking, sucking, and puckering) and facial grimacing.
- Classic TD may present as **fly catcher's tongue** (tongue darting in and out of the mouth) or **bonbon sign** (repeated pushing of the tongue against cheek).
- FGAs increase serum prolactin levels which can produce gynecomastia, galactorrhea, and erectile dysfunction in men and amenorrhea and inhibition of orgasm in women.
- Reports of **sudden death** in patients treated with FGAs can be due to Torsades de pointes secondary to QTc prolongation. Thioridazine has the highest risk of prolonging QTc interval.
- Dopamine receptor antagonists (DRAs) are associated with an increased risk of seizures.

Second-Generation Antipsychotics (SGAs)

- Earlier, these were called serotonin-dopamine antagonists (SDAs) considering their high affinity for $5HT_{2A}$ and D_2 receptors.

Clozapine

- Clozapine has a low affinity for D_2 receptors blockade and a low affinity for D_2 receptors may be an explanation for the lack of EPS of clozapine.
- Clozapine is indicated for treatment-resistant schizophrenia (patients who have failed at least two antipsychotic trials and one of the drugs should be SGA).
- Clozapine can suppress abnormal movements in TD.
- Sedation, tachycardia, and postural hypotension are common side effects. Peripheral anticholinergic side effects like dry mouth, blurred vision, constipation, and urinary retention are also common.
- Clozapine causes **seizures** in 5%–10% of the patients, **myocarditis** (2.8/100,000 patients), and **agranulocytosis** in less than 1% of the patients.
- Clozapine causes sialorrhea during sleep and weight gain and increases the risk of type 2 diabetes mellitus.
- In the United States, monitoring of WBC is no longer required; absolute neutrophil count (ANC) needs to be measured. The initial ANC must be $\geq 1{,}500/mm^3$. Clozapine treatment should be interrupted for ANC $< 1{,}000/mm^3$.

Risperidone

- Risperidone has a potent $5HT_{2A}$ receptor antagonism along with D_2 receptor antagonism.
- Risperidone causes weight gain, nausea, vomiting, rhinitis, erectile dysfunction, and increased pigmentation. It also causes hyperprolactinemia which can lead to galactorrhea and breast enlargement.
- **Indications** include schizophrenia, schizoaffective disorder, bipolar I disorder, and irritability associated with the autistic disorder in children aged 5–17 years.

Paliperidone

- Paliperidone is the major active metabolite of risperidone.
- **Indications** include acute and maintenance treatment of schizophrenia and acute treatment of schizoaffective disorder as monotherapy or adjunctive drug to mood stabilizers or antidepressants.

Olanzapine

- Its $5HT_{1A}$ blockade is eight times stronger than the dopamine receptor blockade.
- Olanzapine is associated with sedation, constipation, orthostatic hypotension, tachycardia, and weight gain.
- **Indications** include schizophrenia, acute treatment of manic or mixed episodes associated with bipolar I disorder, and maintenance treatment of bipolar I disorder.
- A combination of olanzapine and fluoxetine is indicated for depressive episodes associated with bipolar I disorder.

Quetiapine

- Quetiapine's low incidence of EPS may be explained by its high $5HT_{2A}$ binding as compared to D_2 receptors.
- Somnolence, postural hypotension, and dizziness are the most common side effects of quetiapine.
- **Indications** include schizophrenia, acute treatment of manic episodes in bipolar I disorder, acute treatment for depressive episodes associated with bipolar I or II disorder, maintenance treatment of bipolar I disorder as an adjunct to lithium or divalproex, dopamine-induced psychosis in Parkinson disease.

Ziprasidone

- It is a $5HT_{1A}$ agonist and inhibits the reuptake of serotonin and norepinephrine suggesting possible antidepressant action.
- Ziprasidone produces less weight gain as compared to other atypical antipsychotic agents.
- **Indications** include schizophrenia, acute treatment of manic or mixed episode in bipolar I disorder as monotherapy, and maintenance treatment of bipolar I disorder as an adjunct to lithium or valproate.

Aripiprazole

- Aripiprazole differs from SGAs in having partial agonistic action at D_2 and $5HT_{1A}$ receptors in addition to antagonistic actions at D_2 and $5HT_{2A}$ receptors.
- Aripiprazole is an effective antipsychotic with minimal sedation, metabolic effects, and weight gain.
- Aripiprazole is the only antipsychotic which may reduce levels of prolactin.
- **Indications** include schizophrenia, acute treatment of manic or mixed episodes in bipolar I disorder as monotherapy, or adjunct therapy with lithium or valproate.

Lurasidone

- It has partial agonistic action at $5HT_{1A}$ receptors, in addition to potent antagonistic action at D_2 and $5HT_{2A}$ receptors.
- It has low liability for metabolic effects.
- Lurasidone is indicated in schizophrenia and adults with bipolar depression both as monotherapy and as an adjunct to lithium or valproate.

Pregnancy and Lactation

- Clozapine and lurasidone are classified as pregnancy category B and all other SGAs are in category C.

Long-Acting Antipsychotics

- Long-acting injections of antipsychotic drugs are an option for patients with poor compliance with drugs.
- Long-acting depot injections of flupentixol decanoate, fluphenazine decanoate, haloperidol decanoate, pipotiazine palmitate, zuclopenthixol, risperidone (Risperdal Consta), olanzapine pamoate, and paliperidone (Invega Sustenna) are available.

SELF-ASSESSMENT

1. Classify first-generation antipsychotics (FGAs). Discuss the mechanism of action, indications, and side effects of FGAs.
2. Discuss the mechanism of action, indications, and side effects of clozapine.
3. Write short notes on:
   a. Risperidone
   b. Paliperidone
   c. Olanzapine
   d. Quetiapine
   e. Ziprasidone
   f. Aripiprazole
   g. Lurasidone
   h. Metabolic syndrome
   i. Long-acting antipsychotics

Chapter 32

Psychopharmacology III: Mood Stabilizers

Sandeep Kumar Goyal · Prithpal Singh

Mood stabilizers are agents that are useful for the treatment of acute episodes (both mania and depression) and prevention of relapse or recurrence of symptoms without any further worsening of symptoms of either polarity. Lithium and anticonvulsants like valproate, carbamazepine, lamotrigine, and oxcarbazepine are commonly used mood stabilizer drugs. Atypical antipsychotics like olanzapine, quetiapine, and ziprasidone are also indicated in the maintenance treatment of bipolar disorders.

LITHIUM

Lithium is a small monovalent cation which has virtually complete absorption. It is not metabolized at all and excreted in the urine.

Pharmacodynamics

The mechanism of action of lithium is not precisely known, and it shares many common targets with valproic acid and has wide effects on signal transduction pathways within the cell. It suppresses the inositol signaling through the depletion of intracellular inositol. Decreased inositol prevents the formation of inositol phosphate 3 (IP3) and diacylglycerol, and thus blocks transmembrane signaling.

Lithium inhibits glycogen synthase kinase-3 (GSK-3). GSK-3 is involved in gene transcription and synaptic plasticity. It is activated under the conditions of chronic stress such as prolonged exposure to dopamine during mania. This effect on GSK-3 may be key to its therapeutic properties.

Indications

1. Treatment of moderate to severe mania.
2. Prophylaxis of bipolar affective disorder. Lithium reduces the frequency and severity of relapses. It is more effective at preventing manic than depressive relapse. The efficacy of lithium is more in euphoric mania as compared to the dysphoric variant.
3. It provides some protection against antidepressant-induced mania.
4. It is also indicated as an augmentation agent in patients with unipolar depression in case of partial response with antidepressants.
5. Lithium is also used to treat aggression and self-mutilating behavior, to raise the white blood cell count in patients on clozapine and to prevent and treat steroid-induced psychosis.
6. Lithium reduces the risk of suicide in bipolar affective disorder as well as in patients of unipolar depression, and the mechanism of this protective effect is unknown.

Dosage

In a person with normal renal function starting dose is usually 300 mg thrice a day. After 5 days of constant use, serum lithium level is done and the dose is adjusted to get the therapeutic level of 0.6–1 mEq/L or maintenance level of 0.6–0.8 mEq/L. The maximum dose is 1,800 mg per day.

Lithium has a narrow therapeutic index, so patients on lithium should be educated about signs and symptoms of lithium toxicity.

Adverse Effects

Gastrointestinal (GI) Nausea, loss of appetite, and loose stools are common side effects.

Neurological Dysphoria, lack of spontaneity, slow reaction time, and memory impairment are common side effects. Peripheral neuropathy, downbeat nystagmus, pseudotumor cerebri, myasthenia-like syndrome, and lowering of seizure threshold are rare side effects.

Lithium use is associated with a postural tremor in hands and arms. Lithium-induced tremors can be treated by the use of a slow-release preparation, reducing caffeine intake and treatment with propranolol and primidone.

Endocrine Lithium can cause clinical hypothyroidism and goiter, although subclinical hypothyroidism is more common than clinical hypothyroidism. If hypothyroidism occurs, it should be treated with thyroid hormone. Hypothyroidism predisposes to clinical depression.

Lithium can also cause hypercalcemia and hyperparathyroidism.

Cardiac Benign reversible T wave changes are common. Lithium intoxication can lead to varying degrees of heart block, bradyarrhythmias, QTc prolongation, and T wave inversion.

Renal Polyuria is a troublesome renal effect of lithium and nephrogenic diabetes insipidus occurs in about one-third of the patients on lithium. The concentrating defect is not always reversible after discontinuation of lithium. Lithium can cause nonspecific interstitial fibrosis. It also causes a reduction of glomerular filtration rate (GFR) and an increase of creatinine (creatinine creep).

Hematological Lithium use is associated with mild reversible granulocytosis and increased platelet counts.

Dermatological Lithium causes worsening of acne, psoriasis, hair loss, and follicular keratosis.

Miscellaneous Weight gain is a common side effect of lithium. It causes fluid retention.

Lithium Intoxication

GI upset, dysarthria, coarse tremors, and ataxia are initial symptoms. If untreated, it can lead to impaired consciousness, myoclonus, seizure, and coma. Mild cases can be managed by discontinuing the use of lithium. Hemodialysis is the treatment of choice for severe cases.

Lithium Use in Pregnancy and Lactation

Lithium is in FDA pregnancy category D (drugs for which there is evidence of human fetal risk, but potential benefits may warrant the use of the drug in pregnant women despite potential risks). Lithium use in pregnancy is associated with **Ebstein's anomaly**. The risk of atrial and ventricular septal defects may be increased. It can cause goiter, hypotonia, lethargy, and cardiac arrhythmias in the neonate. Polyhydramnios in a pregnant female on lithium can be due to lithium-induced fetal polyuria. To reduce the risk of toxicity in the newborn, the dose of lithium should be reduced shortly before delivery and therapeutic dose should be restarted after delivery to prevent a recurrence. The teratogenic effect of lithium is lower as compared to valproate and carbamazepine.

The use of lithium for breastfeeding mothers has generally been discouraged by the American Academy of Pediatrics (AAP) because of concerns regarding the secretion of the drug through breast milk. Plasma levels in the infant may exceed 10% of the mother's plasma levels, causing toxicity in the infant, especially in cases of dehydration.

Drug Interactions

The risk of extrapyramidal symptoms may be increased if antipsychotic drugs are given along with lithium. Nonsteroidal anti-inflammatory drugs and diuretics decrease renal lithium clearance and increase serum lithium levels. Angiotensin-converting enzyme (ACE) inhibitors and metronidazole also increase lithium concentration. Toxicity can also be increased with methyldopa and calcium channel blockers.

ANTICONVULSANT MOOD STABILIZERS

Anticonvulsants like carbamazepine and valproic acid are shown to be effective as mood stabilizers. Lamotrigine has also shown efficacy in preventing the depressed phase of bipolar disorder and has received FDA indication for bipolar disorder.

Sodium Valproate/Valproic Acid

Valproic acid and its derivatives valproate sodium and divalproex sodium are the first-generation mood-stabilizing anticonvulsants.

Pharmacokinetics

The bioavailability of valproate is almost 100%. The plasma half-life is 10–16 hours. Valproate is highly protein-bound, and an unbound portion is pharmacologically active and can cross the blood–brain barrier.

Pharmacodynamics

The mechanism of action of valproate as anticonvulsant and mood stabilizer is not known exactly. Valproate enhances γ-aminobutyric acid (GABA) neurotransmission by several mechanisms, such as it inhibits the enzyme GABA transaminase (prevents GABA catabolism) and activates glutamate decarboxylase (an increase of GABA synthesis). Whether this GABA enhancement leads to its antimanic effects is controversial as other potent GABAergic drugs are not effective antimanic drugs (e.g., tiagabine, gabapentin, and topiramate).

Lithium, valproate, and carbamazepine inhibit sodium/myo-inositol transport system (SMIT) in astrocytes. Inhibition of inositol and reduced intraneuronal inositol may be related to the mood-stabilizing action. Valproate and lithium cause down-regulation of protein kinase c (PKC). PKC inhibition is a likely contributor to antimanic activity.

Indications

FDA approved for:

1. Monotherapy and adjunctive therapy for patients with complex partial seizures and absence seizures.
2. Treatment of acute manic episodes.
3. Prophylaxis of migraine.

Valproate is also used as a prophylactic treatment of recurrent mania and depression. It is preferred in acute mania with depressive, dysphoric, and mixed symptoms, rapid cycling course (more than four episodes per year), acute dysphoric mania complicated by substance abuse, seizure disorder, EEG abnormalities, head injury, and migraine.

Valproate is also effective on symptoms of irritability, aggressiveness, mood instability, and impulsivity.

Dosage

Divalproex is better tolerated than valproate. It is started at a dosage of 250 mg three times per day, with increase of 250-500 mg every few days to therapeutic threshold (serum level greater than 50 mg/L).

Adverse Effects

Common side effects include GI distress, tremors, sedation, elevation of transaminase levels, leukopenia, thrombocytopenia, hair loss, increased appetite, and weight gain. Most of the common side effects are dose-related and can be decreased by dose reduction. Valproate causes a dose-related increase in homocysteine and cotreatment with folic acid reduces this risk.

Valproate use has been linked with polycystic ovaries and polycystic ovarian syndrome, but this association is controversial as females with epilepsy and obesity appear to be at increased risk for the syndrome.

Rare serious side effects include hepatic failure, pancreatitis, and hyperammonemic encephalopathy.

Valproate Use in Pregnancy and Lactation

Valproate is an FDA pregnancy category D. Its use in pregnancy is associated with neural tube defects such as spina bifida (1%–4%), syndrome of developmental delay, and low IQ. Valproate has been associated with an increased risk of autism. Use of valproate during the first trimester is associated with increased risk of atrial septal defects, cleft palate, hypospadias, polydactyly, and craniosynostosis.

Ideally, valproate should be avoided in females who wish to become pregnant; if valproate needs to be given, it can be supplemented with folic acid, vitamin B_1 and B_6.

Neural tube defects can be detected by fetal USG at weeks 18–20, alpha-fetoprotein, and if needed, amniotic fluid at week 16.

Valproate is compatible with breastfeeding. It is present in breast milk at a concentration of approximately 1%–10% of the mother's serum level.

Drug Interactions

Valproate, when used in combination with lamotrigine and carbamazepine, can increase their concentration by displacing these drugs from protein-binding sites.

The concentration of valproic acid is increased with concurrent administration of drugs that inhibit cytochromes P450 (CYP) enzymes (e.g., fluoxetine, fluvoxamine, cimetidine, and erythromycin).

Carbamazepine

Carbamazepine is a an anticonvulsant mood stabilizer. A long-acting sustained release formulation was approved for the treatment of acute mania in 2002.

Pharmacokinetics

Carbamazepine is absorbed slowly and erratically. The average half-life after a single dose is 26 hours (range 18–54 hours) and it decreases to 12 hours (range 10–25 hours) on long-term use due to autoinduction. Carbamazepine is metabolized by the liver and excreted by the kidneys.

Oxcarbazepine is 96% absorbed and 60% protein-bound. The half-life of oxcarbazepine is 2 hours and its metabolite monohydroxide, which is responsible for anticonvulsant activity, has a half-life of 9 hours.

Pharmacodynamics

The exact mechanism of mood stabilizer action is not known. Carbamazepine binds to voltage-dependent sodium channels in the inactive state and prolongs their inactivation, which leads to decreased voltage-dependent calcium channel activation and therefore synaptic transmission.

It reduces glutamate release and decreases the turnover of dopamine and noradrenaline.

Indications

FDA approved for:

1. Seizure disorder
2. Trigeminal neuralgia
3. Long-acting preparation is FDA approved for acute mania

Carbamazepine is widely used in the treatment of acute mania and prophylaxis. It can be used as a substitute or an adjuvant to lithium in partial responders and is especially helpful in rapid cyclers.

Oxcarbazepine has effects similar to carbamazepine, but is not FDA approved for bipolar disorder.

Dosage

The serum level for antimanic effect has not been established. An 8–12 mg/mL levels are usually associated with good antimanic and anticonvulsant activity. Carbamazepine is started at a dose of 200 mg twice daily (extended-release formulation, 3–4 doses for immediate release) and increased gradually to a maintenance dosage of 800–1,200 mg/day. The maximum dose is 1,200 mg/day.

Adverse Reactions

Mild GI (nausea, vomiting, diarrhea, constipation, and anorexia) and central nervous system (ataxia, drowsiness, diplopia, and dizziness) side effects are most common. Carbamazepine decreases the WBC count by inhibiting the colony-stimulating factor. It is associated with aplastic anemia, pancytopenia, and rarely agranulocytosis (1 in 25,000 to 1 in 100,000 patients). Carbamazepine causes hyponatremia, which can be prevented or reversed by the administration of lithium or demeclocycline. The incidence of hyponatremia is more with oxcarbazepine than carbamazepine. It causes a benign maculopapular rash. It can also cause exfoliative dermatitis, erythema multiforme, Stevens—Johnsons syndrome (SJS), or toxic epidermal necrolysis (TEN). The incidence of rash is less with oxcarbazepine. Carbamazepine is associated with an increase in liver transaminase levels. It can decrease atrial-ventricular conduction and is relatively contraindicated in patients with heart block.

Carbamazepine and Pregnancy

Carbamazepine is in FDA pregnancy category D. Its use in pregnancy is associ ated with neural tube defects such as spina bifida. It is secreted in the milk at a concentration of approximately 50% of that in maternal plasma. The teratogenic effect is less than valproate.

Drug Interactions

Carbamazepine is a potent inducer of cytochrome P4503A4, and it reduces levels of a variety of drugs (e.g., buprenorphine, tramadol, warfarin, phenytoin, topiramate, valproate, lamotrigine, citalopram, bupropion, mirtazapine, doxycycline, aripiprazole, clozapine, olanzapine, risperidone, clonazepam, oral contraceptive pills, prednisolone, methylphenidate, thyroxine etc.). Carbamazepine reduces its own levels by autoinduction.

Drugs that inhibit cytochrome oxidase 3A4 or epoxide hydroxylase increase blood levels of carbamazepine (e.g., fluoxetine, fluvoxamine, valproate, isoniazid, diltiazem, verapamil, erythromycin, clarithromycin etc.).

Lamotrigine

Lamotrigine is approved for the maintenance treatment of bipolar I disorder. It is more effective in the prophylaxis of depressive episodes than manic episodes.

Pharmacokinetics

Lamotrigine has an oral bioavailability of 98%; 55% drug is plasma protein-bound. A large proportion is conjugated to inactivate glucuronide metabolite, and 10% is excreted unchanged in the urine. Half-life in monotherapy is 28 hours and clearance is 40 mL/minute. With carbamazepine or phenytoin (hepatic enzyme inducers) its half-life reduces to approximately half, that is, 14 hours and clearance doubles to approximately 80 mL per minute. With enzyme inhibitor valproate, half-life of lamotrigine doubles and clearance falls approximately to 56 hours and 20 mL/minute, respectively.

Pharmacodynamics

Inhibition of voltage-activated sodium channels may best explain lamotrigine's mechanism of action. It also antagonizes N-type calcium channels. The antiglutaminergic action of lamotrigine may affect mood.

Indications

1. Lamotrigine is indicated for the maintenance treatment of bipolar I disorder. It is more effective in the prophylaxis of depressive episodes than manic episodes. It might also be effective in the acute treatment of bipolar depression but it is not FDA approved for the same.
2. Lamotrigine is indicated in adults and children more than 2 years old as adjunctive therapy for primary generalized tonic--clonic seizures, generalized seizures of Lennox–Gastaut syndrome, and partial-onset seizures.

Side Effects

Lamotrigine is associated with common benign rashes, uncommon serious rash such as Stevens-Johnson syndrome (SJS), and rare hypersensitivity reactions. Risk factors for the rash include age, concurrent administration of valproate, increasing lamotrigine dose too quickly, and starting lamotrigine at a dose more than recommended. Lamotrigine should be stopped at first sign of a rash.

Rash along with eye, mouth, or bladder discomfort, fever, or lymphadenopathy indicates the onset of serious rash. Rare hypersensitivity reactions with multiorgan failure have been reported.

Apart from the risk of rash, lamotrigine is generally well tolerated. Headache, dizziness, diarrhea, nausea, fatigue, rhinitis, dream abnormality, and pruritis are common side effects other than the rash.

Pregnancy and Lactation

Lamotrigine is classified as pregnancy category C (risk cannot be ruled out, human studies are lacking, and animal studies are either positive for fetal risk or lacking as well; however, potential benefit may justify the potential risk). There is possibility of association with cleft lip or palate, but no definite association occurs. Lamotrigine is excreted in breast milk and contraindicated with breastfeeding.

Drug Interactions

Enzyme inducers (carbamazepine, phenytoin, phenobarbital, primidone, and rifampin) decrease lamotrigine concentration by 40%–50% and enzyme inhibitors such as valproate approximately doubles lamotrigine concentration.

Dosage

Lamotrigine blood levels are influenced by concomitant use of valproate or enzyme inducers like carbamazepine. Table 32.1 shows the schedule of dose titration of lamotrigine in adults with bipolar disorder.

Lamotrigine dose needs to be decreased by 25% in patients with moderate to severe hepatic impairment without ascites and 50% in patients with severe hepatic impairment with ascites. The dose needs to be decreased in renal impairment. If a patient stops taking lamotrigine for more than 5 days, it should be restarted according to the initial regime.

Table 32.1 Dose titration of lamotrigine in adults with bipolar disorder

	Lamotrigine without valproate and enzyme inducers mg/day	**Lamotrigine with valproate mg/day**	**Lamotrigine with enzyme inducers (carbamazepine, phenytoin, phenobarbital, primidone, and rifampin) mg/day**
Weeks 1 and 2 dose	25	12.5	50
Weeks 3 and 4 dose	50	25	100
Week 5 dose	100	50	200
Week 6 dose	200	100	300
Week 7 and FDA target dose	200	100	400

KEY POINTS

Lithium

- The mechanism of action of lithium is not precisely known, and it shares many common targets with valproic acid and has wide effects on signal transduction pathways within the cell.
- Indications include mania, prophylaxis of bipolar affective disorder, and augmentation of an antidepressant in patients with unipolar depression in case of partial response with antidepressants.
- Lithium is also effective in aggression, self-mutilating behavior, to raise the WBC count in patients on clozapine, and to prevent and treat steroid-induced psychosis.
- Lithium reduces the risk of suicide in bipolar affective disorder as well as in patients of unipolar depression.
- Lithium has a **narrow therapeutic index**. The therapeutic level of lithium is 0.6–1.0 mEq/L and the maintenance level is 0.6–0.8 mEq/L.
- Nausea, loss of appetite, and loose stools are common gastrointestinal (GI) side effects.
- Dysphoria, lack of spontaneity, slow reaction time, and memory impairment are common neurological side effects.
- Lithium can cause clinical hypothyroidism, hypercalcemia, and hyperparathyroidism.
- Nephrogenic diabetes insipidus occurs in about one-third of the patients on lithium.
- Lithium use is associated with mild reversible granulocytosis and increased platelet counts.
- Lithium causes worsening of acne, psoriasis, hair loss, and follicular keratosis.
- Weight gain is a common side effect of lithium. Lithium causes fluid retention.
- GI upset, dysarthria, coarse tremors, and ataxia are initial symptoms of **lithium intoxication**. If untreated, it can lead to impaired consciousness, myoclonus, seizure, and coma.
- Lithium is in the FDA pregnancy category D. Its use in pregnancy is associated with **Ebstein's anomaly**.

Sodium Valproate/Valproic Acid

- The mechanism of action of valproate as anticonvulsant and mood stabilizer is not known exactly. Valproate enhances γ-aminobutyric acid (GABA) neurotransmission.
- Indications include treatment of acute manic episodes, prophylaxis of migraine, prophylactic treatment of recurrent mania, and depression.
- Common side effects include GI distress, tremors, sedation, elevation of transaminase levels, leukopenia, thrombocytopenia, hair loss, increased appetite, and weight gain.
- Valproate use has been linked with polycystic ovaries and polycystic ovarian syndrome, but this association is controversial as females with epilepsy and obesity appear to be at increased risk for the syndrome.
- Rare serious side effects include hepatic failure, pancreatitis, and hyperammonemic encephalopathy.
- Valproate is an FDA pregnancy category D. Its use in pregnancy is associated with neural tube defects such as spina bifida (1%–4%), syndrome of developmental delay, and low IQ. Valproate has been associated with an increased risk of autism.

Carbamazepine

- The exact mechanism of mood stabilizer action is not known.
- Long-acting carbamazepine preparation is FDA approved for acute mania.
- Oxcarbazepine has effects similar to carbamazepine, but is not FDA approved for bipolar disorder.
- Mild GI (nausea, vomiting, diarrhea, constipation, and anorexia) and central nervous system (ataxia, drowsiness, diplopia, and dizziness) side effects are most common.
- It decreases the WBC count by inhibiting the colony-stimulating factor. It is associated with aplastic anemia, pancytopenia, and agranulocytosis rarely.
- Carbamazepine causes hyponatremia which can be prevented or reversed by the administration of lithium or demeclocycline.
- It can also cause exfoliative dermatitis, erythema multiforme, Stevens–Johnsons syndrome (SJS), or toxic epidermal necrolysis (TEN).
- Carbamazepine is in FDA pregnancy category D. Its use in pregnancy is associated with neural tube defects such as spina bifida. The teratogenic effect is less than valproate.

Lamotrigine

- Inhibition of voltage-activated sodium channels may best explain lamotrigine's mechanism of action. It also antagonizes N-type calcium channels. The antiglutaminergic action of lamotrigine may affect mood.
- Lamotrigine is indicated for the maintenance treatment of bipolar I disorder. It is more effective in the prophylaxis of depressive episodes than manic episodes.
- Lamotrigine is associated with common benign rashes and uncommon serious rash such as Stevens-Johnson syndrome (SJS).
- Risk factors for the rash include age, concurrent administration of valproate, increasing lamotrigine dose too quickly, and starting lamotrigine at a dose more than recommended. Lamotrigine should be stopped at first sign of a rash.
- Lamotrigine is classified as pregnancy category C.

SELF-ASSESSMENT

1. Define mood stabilizers and enumerate various mood stabilizers.
2. Describe the mechanism of action, indications, and side effects of lithium.
3. Describe the mechanism of action, indications, and side effects of valproate.
4. Describe the mechanism of action, indications and side effects of carbamazepine.
5. Describe the mechanism of action, indications, and side effects of lamotrigine.
6. Describe the dosing schedule of lamotrigine. What dose modification of lamotrigine is required if the patient is also taking:
   a. Valproate
   b. Carbamazepine

Chapter 33

Neuromodulation

Nand Kumar · Swarndeep Singh

The human brain is a complex electrochemical organ that comprises around 100 billion (10^{11}) neurons, with each one of them having an average of about 7,000 synaptic interconnections with each other. The activity of the brain can be modulated by the use of electric current, magnetic field, psychopharmacological, and psychological agents either alone or in combination.

The neuromodulation techniques are broadly divided into three categories depending on their degree of invasiveness and seizure-inducing potential as given in Box 33.1.

Box 33.1 Categorization of neuromodulation techniques

A. **Noninvasive and nonseizurogenic** (low risk)
Examples: rTMS, tDCS
B. **Noninvasive and seizurogenic** (medium risk)
Examples: ECT, MST
C. **Invasive and nonseizurogenic** (high risk)
Examples: VNS, DBS

DBS, deep brain stimulation; *ECT*, electroconvulsive therapy; *MST*, magnetic seizure therapy; *rTMS*, repetitive transcranial magnetic stimulation; *tDCS*, transcranial direct current stimulation; *VNS*, vagus nerve stimulation.

ELECTROCONVULSIVE THERAPY

Electroconvulsive therapy (ECT) is the oldest, but still the most effective neuromodulation technique to be used for the treatment of various psychiatric disorders, since its introduction by **Ugo Cerletti** and **Lucio Bini** in 1938 (about eight decades back!). The electric current of sufficient intensity is passed through the brain via electrodes placed over the scalp producing a motor seizure in the subject.

Mechanism of Action

There are several neurobiological changes associated with ECT such as normalization of dexamethasone suppression test, optimization of neurotransmitter levels in different areas of the brain, and neuroplasticity. The exact mechanism of its action is not established. However, there is a consensus that the neurobiological changes associated with the production of seizure rather than the administration of general anesthesia or electrical stimulation are responsible for the therapeutic effects of ECT.

Procedure

ECT is usually given in a dedicated ECT room. In modern times, modified ECT (MECT) is preferred, in which electric current is delivered to the patient under the effect of general anesthesia and muscle relaxant. MECT is associated with a decreased risk of fractures associated with contraction of muscles in seizure episodes as compared to direct ECT.

Pretreatment evaluation includes a complete medical history and standard physical, neurological, and preanesthesia checkup (PAC). Investigations include blood and urine chemistries, ECG and CT or MRI of the brain if the clinician suspects the space-occupying lesion. The presence of space-occupying lesion is no longer considered an absolute contraindication to ECT.

Muscarinic anticholinergic drugs are administered before ECT to minimize oral and respiratory secretions and to prevent bradycardia and asystoles. Atropine is the most commonly used drug. Glycopyrrolate can also be used which causes less cognitive dysfunction and its cardioprotective activity is also less than atropine.

Methohexital, thiopental, ketamine, and propofol are various anesthetic drugs and succinylcholine is used as a muscle relaxant.

The patient should be fasting for at least 6 hours before the treatment. An intravenous line is established and a bite block is inserted just before treatment to protect the patient's teeth and tongue. One hundred percent oxygen is administered at a rate of 5 L/min during the procedure until spontaneous respiration returns.

Electrode Placement

Figure 33.1 depicts the various electrode placements.

Bitemporal placement The electrode is applied about 1 inch above the midpoint of the line connecting the outer canthus of the eye and the external auditory meatus on each side of the individual's head.

Right unilateral placement One electrode is positioned as in bitemporal on the right side (d'Elia placement) and the center of the other electrode is placed 2–3 cm to the right of the vertex of the skull. The use of right unilateral electrode placement instead of bitemporal or bifrontal electrode placement to deliver ECT has been associated with a better cognitive side effect profile.

Bifrontal placement The center of each electrode is placed 5 cm above the outer canthus of the eye along a vertical line perpendicular to a line connecting the pupils.

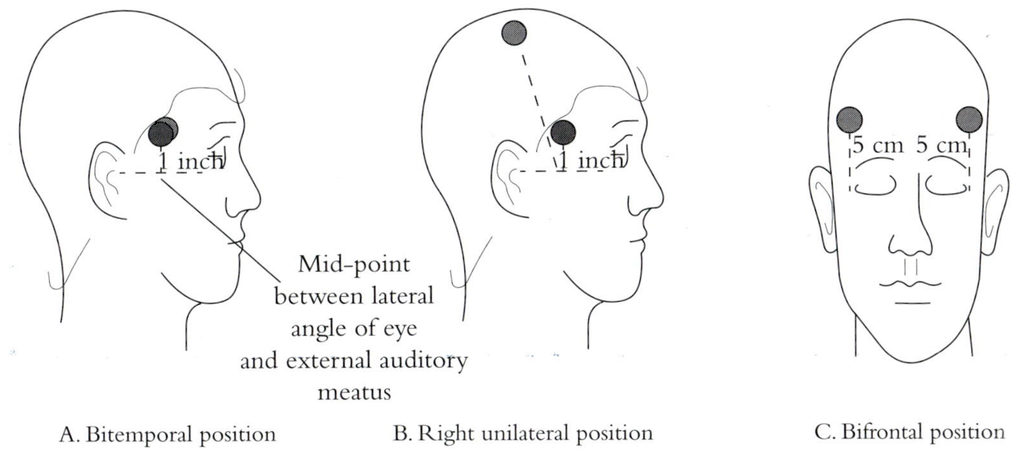

Figure 33.1 Three different electrode placements used for delivering electroconvulsive treatment (ECT).

The electrical stimulus must be strong enough to reach the seizure threshold. The planter extension is the first sign of the seizure and marks the tonic phase that is followed by rhythmic (clonic) contractions.

Electrode placement, the electrical waveform of the stimulus, and the frequency of ECT treatments are three important parameters. The most commonly used technique for ECT in current clinical settings involves placement of electrodes in bitemporal position (Fig. 33.1), with electrical stimulus delivered in brief pulse (0.5–2.0 milliseconds) or ultra-brief pulse (less than 0.5 millisecond) waveform at a dose of 1.5–2.0 times of seizure threshold for an individual patient.

Clinical Applications

ECT is usually used for the management of treatment-resistant cases of depression, mania, and schizophrenia (Table 33.1). It is also used in situations where other treatments are not tolerated or a quicker response is required clinically, such as patients with high suicidality or catatonia.

Table 33.1 Common clinical applications of different neuromodulation techniques in psychiatry

Neuromodulation technique	Use in neuropsychiatric disorders
ECT	• Depression* • Mania • Schizophrenia
rTMS	• Depression* • OCD • Schizophrenia • Substance use disorders • Migraine • Tinnitus
MST	Depression
tDCS	• Depression • OCD • Schizophrenia • Substance use disorders
VNS	Depression*
DBS	• Depression • OCD* • Parkinson disease* • Dystonia* • Tourette syndrome

* FDA approved indication.

DBS, deep brain stimulation; *ECT*, electroconvulsive therapy; *MST*, magnetic seizure therapy; OCD, obsessive–compulsive disorder; *rTMS*, repetitive transcranial magnetic stimulation; *tDCS*, transcranial direct current stimulation; *VNS*, vagus nerve stimulation.

A typical treatment course with ECT will relieve the symptoms of depression within 2–3 weeks of treatments, usually given two to three times per week during the acute course of ECT. The efficacy of ECT varies from about 20% to more than 80%, depending on the technique of ECT and clinical condition for which it is used. ECT is particularly effective in treating patients with psychotic depression, with response rates ranging around 90%. However, the majority of patients relapse within 6 months of treatment with an acute course of ECT in the absence of any maintenance therapy.

Side Effects

The risk of death due to MECT is minimal (about 1 per 10,000 patients), which is comparable with the rate associated with general anesthesia alone. Cognitive impairment is the most common side effect of ECT. It is associated with both anterograde and retrograde amnesia, the latter being at times a persistent side effect in some of the cases. Headache, nausea, muscle aches, and fatigue are a few other commonly reported side effects with ECT. With the advances in technology related to the delivery of electrical current to the human brain, ECT is one of the safest modalities of treatment for psychiatric disorders. The development of ECT machines, capable of delivering brief pulse (0.5–2.0 milliseconds) and ultra-brief pulse of electrical stimulation (less than 0.5 milliseconds), has significantly reduced the cognitive side effects.

REPETITIVE TRANSCRANIAL MAGNETIC STIMULATION

Repetitive transcranial magnetic stimulation (rTMS) is a novel, noninvasive neuromodulation technique in which intense, intermittent magnetic field is applied over different areas of the brain by placing an electromagnetic coil over the scalp of the patient. The magnetic field passes through the skull and other biological tissues between the scalp and brain without any impedance unlike electric current in ECT.

Mechanism of Action

rTMS is administered to awake patients without anesthesia or sedation. When magnetic pulses are applied repeatedly over regular intervals of time, they produce long-lasting effects on the excitability of the cerebral cortex persisting even after the end of the treatment session and it is known as rTMS. The low-frequency rTMS (≤ 1 Hz) inhibits, whereas the high-frequency rTMS (≥ 5 Hz) stimulates the underlying brain area. The rTMS is thought to act at the level of synapses, causing long-term potentiation or depression (LTP/LTD) of synapses, depending on the frequency of stimulation used. Further, recent evidence from animal studies has shown increased expression of genes associated with neural plasticity such as brain-derived neurotrophic factor associated with rTMS.

Procedure

The rTMS is usually delivered on an outpatient basis. All the objects with magnetic properties should be removed before the beginning of the procedure. The rTMS is delivered using an electromagnetic coil placed over the scalp of the patient, which in turn modulates the activity of the underlying target area of the brain depending on the kind of rTMS given and the psychiatric disorder treated. The patient remains conscious throughout the entire procedure. The patient is given earplugs to protect him from the noise produced during the procedure.

Clinical Applications

rTMS has been used in the management of several psychiatric disorders (Table 33.1), with the maximum and strongest evidence for its efficacy in the treatment of depression.

In 2008, the FDA approved the use of rTMS for the treatment of patients with depression, who had failed to respond with at least one adequate antidepressant medication trial during the current episode. A standard rTMS treatment course for depression generally consists of five rTMS sessions per week for 4–8 weeks, depending on the symptom severity and patients' response. The FDA-approved protocol for depression consists of 10-Hz rTMS delivered at a stimulation intensity of 120% motor threshold (magnetic strength necessary to produce activation of the motor cortex in an individual) and a total of 3,000 pulses per session. The recommended target for stimulation is the left dorsolateral prefrontal cortex (DLPFC).

Moreover, newer treatment protocols of delivering rTMS have been developed such as deep TMS (dTMS), which can modulate the activity of even subcortical brain areas such as basal ganglia, and has been shown to be effective in the treatment of depression and obsessive–compulsive disorder (OCD). Recently, in 2018, the FDA approved the use of dTMS for the treatment of OCD.

Side Effects

rTMS is safer than ECT and is tolerated well by most patients; there is a potential risk for occurrence of seizure with rTMS, especially in vulnerable individuals (e.g., concomitant use of drugs with seizure threshold lowering potential). Apart from this, few commonly reported benign side effects associated with rTMS are scalp discomfort at the site of stimulation and mild headache.

VAGUS NERVE STIMULATION

Vagus nerve stimulation (VNS) involves intermittent electrical stimulation of left cervical vagus nerve via two electrodes directly placed over it surgically and connected to a pacemaker-like pulse generator placed subcutaneously in the left upper chest wall. The right vagus nerve is not used as it provides parasympathetic innervation to the heart, and its stimulation is associated with an increased risk of developing bradycardia and cardiac arrest.

Mechanism of Action

Stimulation of the left vagus nerve leads to the stimulation of noradrenergic neurons in the locus ceruleus and serotonergic neurons in the dorsal raphe. The functional neuroimaging studies also suggest that VNS produces distal effects in the orbitofrontal cortex and anterior cingulate cortex, which are hypothesized to be responsible for its antidepressant effect.

Clinical Application

The VNS was approved by the FDA in 2005 for adjunctive treatment of depression, which had failed to respond with at least four antidepressant medication trials or ECT (Table 33.1).

Side Effects

It is generally well tolerated by patients, with hoarseness of voice, dyspnea, neck pain, bradycardia, and surgical site pain being some of the commonly reported side effects.

DEEP BRAIN STIMULATION

Deep brain stimulation (DBS) is a type of functional neurosurgical procedure in which two electrodes are implanted in a specifically targeted region of the brain through stereotactic-guided surgery under general anesthesia.

Mechanism of Action

The hypothesized mechanism of action for DBS includes depolarization blockade, neural jamming, or synaptic inhibition. The DBS produces a reversible lesion with high precision, unlike conventional ablative surgeries.

Clinical Applications

It has been shown to improve symptoms of various psychiatric disorders such as Tourette syndrome, depression, and OCD (Table 33.1). The FDA approved DBS under the humanitarian device exemption category for treatment of disabling OCD not responding with other less invasive treatments. The electrodes are implanted over the anterior limb of the internal capsule in OCD. Although DBS is shown to be beneficial in the treatment of Tourette syndrome and depression, there is lack of controlled studies and consensus regarding the best site for implantation of electrodes for these indications currently.

Side Effects

Further, it is associated with various complications related to any neurosurgical procedure such as intracranial bleeding, infection, or electrode displacement. The DBS also produces neuropsychiatric side effects like mania, depression, or anxiety in a subset of patients.

MAGNETIC SEIZURE THERAPY

Magnetic seizure therapy (MST) is a relatively recent neuromodulation technique, which shares certain aspects with both ECT and rTMS. It involves the use of magnetic pulses similar to rTMS instead of the electric current to stimulate a more focal brain area. However, in contrast to rTMS, the magnetic pulses are delivered at a much higher frequency of 40–100 Hz in MST to produce a seizure in patients similar to ECT. Like ECT, it is also given under general anesthesia and muscle relaxant.

MST is proposed to retain the effectiveness of ECT with a better cognitive side effect profile. It is currently in the early stages of testing in depression. The side effect profile of MST is almost similar to that of ECT. It is not yet approved by the FDA for the treatment of any psychiatric disorder.

TRANSCRANIAL DIRECT CURRENT STIMULATION

In transcranial direct current stimulation (tDCS), a tiny current of 1–3 mA is applied over the scalp via two saline-soaked sponge electrodes to polarize the brain tissue. The electric field applied in tDCS is produced using direct current, unlike alternating current used in ECT, VNS, or DBS.

Mechanism of Action

tDCS does not produce action potentials like rTMS or other stimulation modalities, but rather increases or decreases the rate of firing of neurons by altering their resting membrane potential. Anodal tDCS is hypothesized to produce depolarization and is excitatory, whereas cathodal tDCS leads to hyperpolarization and is inhibitory.

Clinical Applications

The tDCS is safer, cheaper, and delivered by a small portable machine in contrast to rTMS. The maximum evidence exists for the efficacy of tDCS in the treatment of depression. It is not yet approved by the FDA for the treatment of any psychiatric disorder.

Side Effects

There are no known serious adverse effects associated with tDCS and it is usually well tolerated. Localized skin irritation and tingling sensation at the site of stimulation, headache, and nausea are few of the commonly reported side effects with tDCS.

KEY POINTS

Electroconvulsive Therapy (ECT)

- There are several neurobiological changes associated with ECT such as normalization of dexamethasone suppression test, optimization of neurotransmitter levels in different areas of the brain, and neuroplasticity The exact mechanism of its action is not established.
- Presence of space-occupying lesion is no longer considered an absolute contraindication to ECT.
- ECT is usually used for the management of treatment-resistant cases of depression, mania, and schizophrenia. It is also used in situations where other treatments are not tolerated or a quicker response is required clinically, such as patients with high suicidality or catatonia.
- ECT is particularly effective in treating patients with psychotic depression, with response rates ranging around 90%.

Repetitive Transcranial Magnetic Stimulation (rTMS)

- rTMS is a novel, noninvasive, and neuromodulation technique, in which intense, intermittent magnetic field is applied over different areas of the brain by placing an electromagnetic coil over the scalp of the patients.
- The low-frequency rTMS (≤1 Hz) inhibits, whereas the high-frequency rTMS (≥5 Hz) stimulates the underlying brain area. The rTMS is thought to act at the level of synapses, causing long-term potentiation or depression (LTP/LTD) of synapses depending on the frequency of stimulation used.
- rTMS is FDA approved for the treatment of patients with depression, who had failed to respond with at least one adequate antidepressant medication trial during the current episode.
- The FDA-approved protocol for depression consists of 10 Hz rTMS delivered at a stimulation intensity of 120% motor threshold (magnetic strength necessary to produce activation of the motor cortex in an individual) and a total of 3,000 pulses per session. The recommended target for stimulation is the left dorsolateral prefrontal cortex (DLPFC).
- rTMS is well tolerated by most patients; there is a potential risk for occurrence of seizure with rTMS, especially in vulnerable individuals.

Vagus Nerve Stimulation (VNS)

- VNS involves intermittent electrical stimulation of left cervical vagus nerve via two electrodes directly placed over it surgically and connected to a pacemaker-like pulse generator placed subcutaneously in the left upper chest wall.
- The right vagus nerve is not used as it provides parasympathetic innervation to the heart, and its stimulation is associated with an increased risk of developing bradycardia and cardiac arrest.
- The VNS is FDA approved for adjunctive treatment of depression, which had failed to respond with at least four antidepressant medication trials or ECT.

Deep Brain Stimulation (DBS)

- DBS is a type of functional neurosurgical procedure in which two electrodes are implanted in a specifically targeted region of the brain through stereotactic-guided surgery under general anesthesia.
- It has been shown to improve symptoms of various psychiatric disorders such as Tourette syndrome, depression, and obsessive-compulsive disorder (OCD).
- The FDA approved DBS under the humanitarian device exemption category for treatment of disabling OCD not responding with other less invasive treatments.

Magnetic Seizure Therapy (MST)

- MST involves the use of magnetic pulses to stimulate a focal brain area. However, in contrast to rTMS, the magnetic pulses are delivered at a much higher frequency of 40–100 Hz in MST to produce a seizure in patients similar to ECT. Like ECT, it is also given under general anesthesia and muscle relaxant.
- MST is currently in the early stages of testing in depression.
- It is not yet approved by the FDA for the treatment of any psychiatric disorder.

Transcranial Direct Current Stimulation (tDCS)

- In tDCS, a tiny current of 1–3 mA is applied over the scalp via two saline-soaked sponge electrodes to polarize the brain tissue.
- The electric field applied in tDCS is produced using direct current, unlike alternating current used in ECT, vagus nerve stimulation, or deep brain stimulation.
- The maximum evidence exists for the efficacy of tDCS in the treatment of depression. It is not yet approved by the FDA for the treatment of any psychiatric disorder.

SELF-ASSESSMENT

1. Write short notes on:
   a. Enumerate various neuromodulation techniques
   b. Electroconvulsive therapy (ECT)
   c. Repetitive transcranial magnetic stimulation (rTMS)
   d. Vagus nerve stimulation (VNS)
   e. Deep brain stimulation (DBS)

Chapter 34

Emergency Psychiatry

Om Prakash Singh · Sandeep Kumar Goyal · Samta Goyal

A psychiatric emergency is an acute disturbance of behavior, thought, or mood of a patient which if untreated may cause harm to the patient or others and for which immediate intervention is required.

Various emergencies are as follows:

- Suicidal patients
- Violent patients
- **Medical emergencies**
  - Delirium
  - Acute dystonia
  - Akathisia
  - Neuroleptic malignant syndrome
  - Lithium toxicity
  - Serotonin syndrome
  - Overdose of psychiatric or other medication
  - Overdose and withdrawal of substance of addiction

In this chapter, we will discuss common psychiatric emergencies. Some conditions are discussed in related chapters; serotonin syndrome is discussed in Chapter 30 (*Psychopharmacology I: Antidepressants and Antianxiety Drugs*), acute dystonia, akathisia, and neuroleptic malignant syndrome are discussed in Chapter 31 (*Psychopharmacology II: Antipsychotics*), and lithium toxicity in Chapter 32 (*Psychopharmacology III: Mood Stabilizers*).

DELIBERATE SELF-HARM/ SUICIDAL PATIENTS

Suicide is derived from the Latin word for "self-murder." Some people plan for many days before attempting suicide and some attempt suicide impulsively. Suicide is a primary psychiatric emergency. Suicide is impossible to predict, but many clues can be seen. Following a generally accepted standard of care reduces the risk of suicide.

More than 90% of the individuals who commit suicide have at least one psychiatric disorder. Depression accounts for 80% of the individuals with mental illness who commit suicide while schizophrenia accounts for 10%. Approximately 25% of total individuals with mental illness also have alcohol dependence (dual diagnosis). A previous suicide attempt is the best indicator of a patient's risk for suicide. Risk factors can be divided into high risk and low risk. Male gender, age more than 45 years, unemployment, divorced, separated or single marital status, conflictual interpersonal relationship, chronic physical illness, alcohol dependence, severe depression, psychosis or personality disorder, and hopelessness are high-risk factors.

Management

Most of the suicides are preventable. Suicide risk evaluation in OPD includes a complete history and mental status examination. All patients should be asked about suicidal ideation or intent. Suicide Intent Scale (SIS) or Columbia Suicide Severity Rating Scale can be used for assessing the risk of suicide.

Box 34.1 Indications of hospitalization in OPD patient with suicidal ideation

- Suicidal intent with a specific plan with high lethality
- In a psychotic patient
- Past history of suicidal attempt
- Limited family or social support
- With comorbid medical illness
- Patients not responding to outpatient treatment

Box 34.2 Indications of hospitalization in a patient presenting with suicidal attempt

- Psychotic patient
- Patients in which suicide attempt was near lethal or premeditated
- Precautions were taken to avoid rescue
- Patient regrets surviving
- Still has a persistent plan or intent
- Male patient, age more than 45 with a poor social support system
- Agitated patient refusing help

For a patient presenting to the casualty with suicidal attempt, psychiatric assessment should be done as soon as the patient is medically stabilized. The first task is to decide whether to admit the patient or to treat as OPD patient. Boxes 34.1 and 34.2 enlist the indications of hospitalization in OPD patients with suicidal ideation and a patient presenting with suicidal attempt, respectively.

In severe cases, admission of the patient provides security if proper safety measures are followed in the hospital. In the hospital, it is important to restrict access to the means of suicide. Family members should be alerted about the increased risk of suicide and the precautions needed to be followed in the hospital and at home. Proper documentation of communication with family members is important.

Lithium has an anti-suicidal effect which is independent of its effect on mood. In a suicidal patient with depression, antidepressants with a sedative property are preferred. Electroconvulsive therapy (ECT) is the treatment of choice in depressive patients with suicidal intent. Suicidal patients with schizophrenia require atypical antipsychotics along with medications to control anxiety and agitation. Sedating antipsychotics are preferred.

Psychotherapy can help in the development of new cognitive or interpersonal skills.

AGGRESSIVE AND VIOLENT PATIENTS

Violence in the emergency room is quite frequent. The risk of serious violence against healthcare workers exceeds the risk of workplace violence of all the industries combined.

Various psychiatric and medical illnesses are associated with violent behavior (Table 34.1).

Management

The emergency physician must ensure the patient's safety as well as the safety of himself and others if the patient is aggressive and violent. He should be trained in performing quick screening assessment to rule out any underlying medical condition which may be the cause of psychiatric symptoms. Suicidal or homicidal ideation should also be checked. He should recognize the early warning signs of impending violence so that chances of injury to staff and patients are reduced. **Early warning signs of impending violence** include threatening statements, clenched fists, loud vocalizations, staring eyes, flared nostrils, agitated movements, striking inanimate objects, and pacing in the room.

Maintain a safe distance from the patient. Easy access to the door should be available. Do not touch a violent person. Security staff should be available. Watch for escalating agitation. Verbal de-escalation of the situation which is a noncoercive approach should be tried before using physical or chemical restraints. For verbal de-escalation, a three-step approach is used: first, the patient is verbally engaged, then a collaborative relationship is established, and last, the patient is verbally de-escalated out of the agitated state. Avoid punitive or judgmental statements. Use good listening skills. If necessary, use physical or chemical restraint.

The most commonly used drug is haloperidol given as an intramuscular injection. Lorazepam is equally effective and can be used when alcohol withdrawal is associated with agitation and violence.

Physical restraints are used when other methods cannot control patients. When patients are restrained, vitals should be checked frequently. Restraints can be used temporarily to administer drugs or for long periods if medications cannot be used.

Once the agitation is controlled, general physical examination, systemic examination, and laboratory testing should be done to rule out the medical causes of the violence. Diagnosis can be usually made by history from family members (if available). Some features point to the medical cause of a mental disorder (Box 34.3).

Table 34.1 Psychiatric and medical disorders associated with violence

Psychiatric disorders associated with violence	Medical disorders associated with violence
• Paranoid schizophrenia • Antisocial personality disorder • Mania • Alcohol intoxication and withdrawal • Substance intoxication and withdrawal, (e.g., cocaine, amphetamine, phencyclidine) • Dementia • Delirium	• Head injury • Encephalitis • Seizure disorder (postictal confusion or temporal lobe epilepsy) • Hepatic encephalopathy • Metabolic disorders • AIDS • Endocrinopathies

In law, fitness to stand trial deals with the mental capacity of an individual to participate in legal proceedings.

To establish fitness to stand trial, one should assess regarding:

1. The ability of the person to understand and to respond rationally.
2. Awareness of the charge and the consequences of the charge if proven guilty.
3. Ability in assisting the lawyer to defend the case.
4. Understanding the procedure of the court.
5. Understanding the expected behavior in the court.

As a legal maxim, every person has the right to defend his case. A person with mental illness may not be in a position to defend his case. If a person has a mental illness and is not in a position to defend his case, the court postpones the proceedings of the case and the person is referred to treatment. Once he becomes all right, the proceedings of the case are restarted. Thus, the principle of natural justice is upheld by giving a chance to a person with mental illness to get treated and the opportunity to defend the case in a fair manner.

CRIMINAL LAWS DEALING WITH OFFENDERS SUFFERING FROM MENTAL ILLNESS

1. **Section 84 IPC:** Criminal responsibility (as discussed earlier).
2. **Section 309 IPC:** Section 309 of the IPC states that if anyone attempts to commit suicide or does any act toward the commission of such offense, he shall be punished with simple imprisonment for a term which may extend to 1 year or with fine or with both. This section was inhuman and against the spirit of providing support to the person attempting or contemplating suicide. Mental Healthcare Act (MHCA), 2017, decriminalizes suicide by repealing the Section 309 of the IPC.

   The Mental Healthcare Act, 2017, clearly states that a person who attempts suicide should be referred for evaluation and treatment. Now, the state government shall have a duty to provide care, treatment, and rehabilitation to a person, who attempted suicide, to reduce the risk of recurrence of a suicide attempt.

CIVIL LAW AND PSYCHIATRY

Various civil laws tend to protect the civil rights of the person with mental illness, for instance, as per the Indian Contract Act a person with mental illness who is incapable of understanding what he/she is doing is right or wrong cannot enter into any contract.

The ability of a person to make an informed choice concerning the specific decision is called capacity.

Civil Laws Dealing with Persons with Mental Illness

1. Testamentary capacity: Indian Succession Act 1925, Section 59.
2. Marriage and divorce.

Testamentary Capacity

Testamentary capacity is a legal term to describe a person's legal and mental ability to make or alter a valid will.

Assessment requires that the testator must be able to understand:

1. The nature and effect of making a will.
2. The extent and value of their property.
3. Natural beneficiaries.
4. Rationale for distribution.

Finally, for the will to be valid, the symptoms of the mental illness should not come in the way of writing the will. Often, a psychiatrist or a medical officer is called to assess the testamentary capacity of the person executing the will. It has to be specifically stated in the will that the testator possesses a sound mind.

Marriage and Divorce

Various acts govern marriage and divorce in India depending on the religion of practice.

1. **Hindu Marriage Act**: Marriage between two Hindus is solemnized only if at the time of the marriage the following conditions are fulfilled:
   i. Neither party has a spouse living at the time of the marriage.
   ii. At the time of the marriage, neither party:
      (a) is incapable of giving a valid consent of it in consequence of unsoundness of mind; or
      (b) though capable of giving a valid consent has been suffering from mental disorder of such a kind or to such an extent as to be unfit for marriage and the procreation of children; or
      (c) has been subject to recurrent attacks of insanity or epilepsy.
   iii. The bridegroom has completed the age of 21 years and the bride the age of 18 years at the time of the marriage.

Divorce can be sought only if a person has a mental illness to such an extent that he or she is not able to fulfill the obligation of the marriage for 2 or more years.

2. **Muslim Marriage Act:** For a marriage to be solemnized, both parties must be legally competent, that is, they must be sane and adult.

3. **Parsi Law:** Under this law, mental illness is not a ground for nullity of the marriage, but is ground for divorce. It is similar to the Hindu Marriage Act.

MENTAL HEALTH LEGISLATION IN INDIA

Legislations that come under the purview of mental health include the following:

1. The Mental Healthcare Act, 2017 (MHCA, 2017)
2. Narcotic Drugs and Psychotropic Substances Act, 1985 (NDPS, 1985)
3. Rights of Persons with Disabilities Act, 2016 (RPWD, 2016)

The Mental Healthcare Act, 2017

The MHCA, 2017, received the assent of the president on April 7, 2017, which superseded the previously existing Mental Health Act, 1987. The MHCA has been described as "an act to provide for mental healthcare and services for persons with mental illness and to protect, promote and fulfill the rights of such persons during delivery of mental healthcare and services and for matters connected therewith or incidental thereto." The Act seeks to fulfill India's international obligation under the Convention on Rights to Persons with Disabilities and Its Optional Protocol.

- Overdose with tricyclic antidepressants or carbamazepine requires cardiac monitoring.
- Antipsychotic drug overdose can cause acute extrapyramidal adverse effects, and immediate relief may be provided with a parenteral antihistaminic such as promethazine 25 mg IM.

Overdose and Withdrawal of Substance of Addiction

- Benzodiazepine, sedative, or hypnotic intoxication presents with slurred speech, unsteady gait, lateral nystagmus, areflexia, muscle hypotonicity, hypotension, and hypothermia.
- Benzodiazepine intoxication is treated with benzodiazepine antagonist flumazenil.
- Symptoms of opioid intoxication include drowsiness, slurred speech, coma, decreased respiration, blue lips, pinpoint pupils, pulmonary edema, cardiac arrhythmias, and seizure.
- Naloxone rapidly reverses coma and respiratory depression caused by an overdose of opioids.
- Treatment of cannabis intoxication includes reassurance and a calm environment. A benzodiazepine can be used for severe anxiety.
- Urinary screening tests for various drugs should be done, as the patient may be using more than one substance.

SELF-ASSESSMENT

1. Define psychiatric emergency and enumerate common psychiatric emergencies.
2. How will you manage a suicidal patient in an emergency department?
3. How will you manage a violent patient in an emergency department?
4. Discuss the management of a patient presenting with an overdose of medication in general.
5. Write short notes on:
   a. Benzodiazepine intoxication
   b. Opioid intoxication
   c. Cannabis intoxication

Chapter 35

Forensic Psychiatry

Vinay B · Shashidhara HN · Suresh Bada Math

Forensic Psychiatry is the branch of psychiatry that deals with issues arising in the interface between psychiatry and the law and with the flow of mentally disordered offenders along with a continuum of social systems.

The interface between persons with mental illness and law can be classified into:

a. Criminal responsibility
b. Civil responsibility
c. Issues related to curtailing of their liberty during admission and treatment

CRIMINAL LAW AND PSYCHIATRY

Insanity plea (criminal responsibility) and fitness to stand trial are two important aspects related to the persons with psychiatric illness implicated under criminal law.

A. Insanity plea: The insanity plea is a defense in a criminal case, arguing that the offender is not responsible for his or her actions due to an episodic or persistent psychiatric disease at the time of the criminal act.

In 1843, a Scotsman named Daniel McNaughton under his delusional experience shot Edward Drummond, secretary to then British PM Sir Robert Peel, whom he mistook for Sir Robert Peel and was declared not guilty by reasons of insanity. Following which the authority formed a 15-judge panel under the House of Lords, which put forward **McNaughton rules**.

In India, **Section 84** of the Indian Penal Code (IPC) states that "nothing is an offense, which is done by a person, who at the time of doing it, by reason of unsoundness of mind, is incapable of knowing the nature of his act or that he is doing what is either wrong or contrary to law."

To establish an insanity plea under Section 84, the burden of proof lies with the person with mental illness. It should be proved that:

1. The person had a mental illness.
2. The person had a mental illness during the commission of the crime.
3. The person was not aware of the nature of the act.
4. The person was not aware of the consequence of the act.
5. The person was not aware that the act was wrong or contrary to the law.

Thus, insanity, in order to be a defense, must be such that it disables an accused person from knowing the nature and consequences of his act at the time of commission of the offence.

B. Fitness to stand trial: The question of sanity of a person is relevant at the time of commission of crime. The accused may be quite sane when he did the act charged, but he may be insane to stand trial. That is, he may be insane at the time of trial and may therefore claim that he is "unfit to plead."

hemoperfusion can clear barbiturates and carbamazepine).

Multiple doses of activated charcoal increase poison elimination and decrease the serum drug levels, and this phenomenon is referred to as **GI dialysis**.

Specific precautions Overdose with tricyclic antidepressants or carbamazepine requires cardiac monitoring. Antipsychotic drug overdose can cause acute extrapyramidal adverse effects, and immediate relief may be provided with a parenteral antihistaminic such as promethazine 25 mg IM.

OVERDOSE OF SUBSTANCE OF ADDICTION

Basic management of an overdose of the substance of addiction remains the same, as discussed in medication overdose.

Benzodiazepine, sedative, or hypnotic intoxication presents with slurred speech, unsteady gait, lateral nystagmus, areflexia, muscle hypotonicity, hypotension, and hypothermia. Benzodiazepine intoxication is treated with benzodiazepine antagonist flumazenil. The recommended initial dose of flumazenil is 0.2 mg (2 mL) IV over 30 s. A further 0.3 mg (3 mL) dose can be administered over 30 s if the desired clinical effect is not seen within 30 s. Additional 0.5 mg doses can be administered over 30 s at 1 min intervals as needed to a total dose of 3 mg.

Symptoms of opioid intoxication include drowsiness, slurred speech, coma, decreased respiration, blue lips, pinpoint pupils, pulmonary edema, cardiac arrhythmias, and seizure. Opioid intoxication is treated with opioid antagonist naloxone.

Cannabis intoxication presents with incoordination, euphoria, anxiety, the feeling of slowed time, impaired judgment, and social withdrawal. These symptoms may be associated with conjunctival injection, increased appetite, dry mouth, and tachycardia. Treatment includes reassurance and a calm environment. A benzodiazepine can be used for severe anxiety.

Urinary screening tests for various drugs should be done, as the patient may be using more than one substance.

KEY POINTS

- A psychiatric emergency is an acute disturbance of behavior, thought, or mood of a patient which if untreated may lead to harm to the patient or others and for which immediate intervention is required.
- Suicidal or violent patients, an overdose of psychiatric medication, and overdose or withdrawal of substance of addiction are common psychiatric emergencies.

Suicide

- Mental illness is found in more than 90% of the persons who commit or attempt suicide. Depression accounts for 80% of the persons with mental illness who commit suicide.
- A previous suicide attempt is the best indicator of a patient's risk of suicide.
- Male gender, age more than 45 years, unemployment, divorced, separated or single marital status. conflictual interpersonal relationship, chronic physical illness, alcohol dependence, severe depression, psychosis or personality disorder, and hopelessness are high-risk factors.

- Suicidal intent with a specific plan with high lethality, psychotic patient, past history of suicidal attempt, limited family or social support, comorbid medical illness, and no response to outpatient treatment are the indications of hospitalization in an OPD patient with suicidal ideation.
- Psychotic patient; patients in which suicide attempt was near-lethal or premeditated; patient who took precautions to avoid rescue, regrets surviving, or still has a persistent plan or intent; male patients, age more than 45 with a poor social support system; and agitated patients refusing help are the indications of hospitalization in a patient presenting with suicidal attempt.
- Lithium has an anti-suicidal effect which is independent of its effect on mood. In a suicidal patient with depression, antidepressants with a sedative property are preferred. Electroconvulsive therapy is the treatment of choice in depressive patients with suicidal intent.
- Suicidal patients with schizophrenia require atypical antipsychotics along with medications to control anxiety and agitation. Sedating antipsychotics are preferred.

Aggressive and Violent Patients

- The emergency physician should recognize the early warning signs of impending violence so that chances of injury to staff and patients are reduced.
- **Early warning signs of impending violence** include threatening statements, clenched fists, loud vocalizations, staring eyes, flared nostrils, agitated movements, striking inanimate objects, and pacing in the room.
- Maintain a safe distance from the patient. Easy access to the door should be available. Do not touch a violent person. Security staff should be available. Watch for escalating agitation.
- Verbal de-escalation of the situation which is a noncoercive approach should be tried before using physical or chemical restraints.
- The most commonly used drug is haloperidol given as an intramuscular injection. Lorazepam is equally effective and can be used when alcohol withdrawal is associated with agitation and violence.
- Physical restraints are used when other methods cannot control patients.

Delirium

- Chemical restraints may be required in hyperactive delirium to perform examination, vital tests, or procedures. Haloperidol or risperidone in low doses (0.5–2 mg) are frequently used.
- Lorazepam 0.5–2 mg can reduce agitation and is preferable when delirium is caused by alcohol withdrawal.

Overdose of Psychiatric or Other Medication

- A high index of suspicion is required for the diagnosis and management of intoxication. History may not be reliable or complete, so a good knowledge of the clinical signs and symptoms is required.
- The patient should be managed in collaboration with a physician or critical care specialist.
- Immediately after establishing the IV access, a coma cocktail of dextrose, thiamine, and naloxone can be given in a comatose patient with unknown poisoning.
- Ipecac-induced emesis is indicated in fully alert patients only.
- The American Academy of Toxicology recommends gastric lavage if the patient has ingested a life-threatening amount of poison and if gastric lavage can be done within 60 minutes of ingestion.
- Charcoal can be administered after Ipecac-induced vomiting or gastric lavage. Multiple doses of activated charcoal decrease the serum drug levels, and this phenomenon is referred to as GI dialysis.

Box 34.3 Features indicating the medical cause of psychiatric illness

- Acute onset
- Current medical illness or injury
- Nonauditory hallucinations
- Significant substance abuse
- Neurological symptoms (e.g., unconsciousness, seizure, head injury)
- Disorientation
- Constructional apraxia
- Speech, movement, or gait disorder

DELIRIUM

Emergency management of delirium starts with the standard assessment of airway, breathing, and circulation; it also includes simultaneous screening for readily reversible causes such as hypoglycemia, hypoxia, electrolyte imbalance, and excessive opioid use. Chemical restraints may be required in hyperactive delirium to perform examination, vital tests, or procedures. Haloperidol or risperidone in low doses (0.5–2 mg) are frequently used. Lorazepam 0.5–2 mg can reduce agitation and is preferable when delirium is caused by alcohol withdrawal. Delirium is discussed in detail in Chapter 25, *Neurocognitive Disorder I: Delirium*.

OVERDOSE OF PSYCHIATRIC OR OTHER MEDICATIONS

A high index of suspicion is required for the diagnosis and management of intoxication. History may not be reliable or complete, so a good knowledge of the clinical signs and symptoms is required. The patient should be managed in collaboration with a physician or critical care specialist.

Supportive measures, including the **"ABC" (airway, breathing, and circulation)**, are required before confirmation of the intoxication. Endotracheal intubation is indicated in cases of acute respiratory failure and poor sensorium. Endotracheal intubation decreases the risk of aspiration.

The detailed history from family members is important in making the diagnosis of overdose. The history should include type, amount, and route of medication or substance of addiction taken in overdose. A basic metabolic panel, including complete blood count, serum electrolytes, blood urea, serum creatinine, blood glucose, liver function test, arterial blood gases, and ECG, should be obtained in all suicidal poisoned patients. Sample for urine toxicology screening for common drugs/substances of addiction should be sent.

The indications of admission to an intensive care unit are given in Box 34.4.

Immediately after establishing the IV access, a **coma cocktail** of dextrose, naloxone, and thiamine can be given in a comatose patient with unknown poisoning. A comatose patient should receive dextrose as the normal value of blood sugar by dipstick test does not rule out low blood sugar levels, and if value by blood dipstick method is high,

Box 34.4 Features indicating admission to ICU

- Respiratory depression ($PaCO_2$ > 45 mmHg)
- Emergency intubation
- Seizure episodes
- Tricyclic or phenothiazine overdose manifesting as anticholinergic signs
- Neurologic abnormalities
- QRS duration >0.12 s or QT >0.5 s
- Hypothermia or hyperthermia including neuroleptic malignant syndrome
- Cardiac arrhythmia (second- or third-degree atrioventricular block)
- Systolic BP < 80 mmHg
- Glasgow coma scale score <12
- Need for emergency dialysis, hemoperfusion, or extracorporeal membrane oxygenation (ECMO)
- Increasing metabolic acidosis
- Pulmonary edema

it should be confirmed by testing venous sample and dextrose should not be given. Naloxone rapidly reverses coma and respiratory depression caused by an overdose of opioids. Thiamine is effective in alcoholics.

Decontamination Gastric lavage (GL), ipecac-induced vomiting, activated charcoal, and whole bowel irrigation are common decontamination methods for ingested poison, which includes drug overdose.

GL can be done in patients who are alert and have intact pharyngeal or laryngeal reflexes. Stomach contents should be sent for analysis. GL should not be performed in patients who have ingested a nontoxic substance, a nontoxic amount of a toxic substance, or when the toxin is no longer expected to be present in the stomach. The American Academy of Toxicology recommends GL if the patient has ingested a life-threatening amount of poison or medication and if GL can be done within 60 minutes of ingestion.

Ipecac-induced emesis is indicated in fully alert patients only. **Activated charcoal** can be administered after Ipecac-induced vomiting or GL. Charcoal aspiration is associated with high mortality, so charcoal should be used only after securing the airway. Activated charcoal can adsorb poison in the stomach and reduce absorption. Charcoal administration is contraindicated in elemental metals (e.g., lithium, iron).

Catharsis with sorbitol decreases constipation caused by the charcoal, and **whole bowel irrigation** is used to push tablets through the GI tract.

Enhanced elimination Alkalinization of the urine may help in excretion of the drug in urine in poisonings such as salicylates and phenobarbital.

Hemodialysis, hemoperfusion, or hemofiltration can be used in patients with specific drug overdose not responding to the supportive measures. For example, hemodialysis can be used in barbiturates, alcohol, and lithium overdose, whereas

to the most vulnerable and underprivileged sections of the population.
2. To encourage the application of mental health knowledge, in general healthcare and social development.
3. To promote **community participation** in the mental health service development and to stimulate efforts toward self-help in the community.

The altruistic goals of NMHP were not immediately perceived to be doable, and the Government wanted a via media to implement the program. Hence, as a pilot project, **District Mental Health Programme** (DMHP) model was developed by the National Institute of Mental Health and Neurosciences (NIMHANS), Bangalore, during the eighth five-year plan in Bellary District of Karnataka and then Trichy District of Tamil Nadu. With the experience gained by these models, the DMHP was implemented in 1996, to begin with only four districts across the entire nation. Today, DMHP spans across more than 500 districts all over the country (508 districts as of 2018).

Apart from DMHP, which is the backbone of the program, NMHP also has other components. The salient points of NMHP are as follows:

1. **District Mental Health Programme:** The key activities of DMHP are as follows:
   - Provision of outpatient and inpatient mental health services with a 10-bedded inpatient facility at least at the district level.
   - Four **satellite clinics** per month at CHCs/PHCs by the DMHP team.
   - **Sensitization and training** of health personnel at the district and subdistrict levels.
   - **Awareness camps** for the dissemination of awareness regarding mental illnesses and related stigma through the involvement of local Panchayati Raj Institutions (PRIs), faith healers, teachers, and leaders.
   - **Community participation** through linkages with self-help groups, family and caregiver groups, and NGOs working in the field of mental health.
2. **Public–private partnership model activities:** There is a provision for the state governments to execute activities related to mental health in partnership with nongovernmental organizations as per the guidelines of the NRHM.
3. **Day care center:**
   - It provides rehabilitation and recovery services to persons with mental illness to prevent relapse.
   - It helps in enhancing the skills of the family/caregiver in providing better support and care.
   - It enables people recovering from a mental illness for successful community living.
4. **Residential/long-term continuing care center** for shifting chronically mentally ill individuals, who have achieved stability for their symptoms and have not been able to return to their families and are currently residents of the mental hospitals.
5. **Mental health helpline:** A countrywide 24 hours dedicated helpline to provide information to the public on mental health resources, emergency and crisis management, information pertaining to destitute mentally ill patients, registration of complaints on Human Rights Violation of mentally ill, and assistance on medico-legal issues.
6. **Tertiary-level activities focused on manpower development schemes**

(Center of excellence or Scheme A and Scheme B):

- **Scheme A: Centers of Excellence in Mental Health**—Upgradation of existing mental hospitals/institutes/medical colleges to start/strengthen courses in psychiatry, clinical psychology, psychiatric social work, and psychiatric nursing.
- **Scheme B: PG Training Departments of Mental Health Facilities**—Government medical colleges/mental hospitals will be supported for starting/increasing intake of PG courses in mental health.

Thus, the NMHP has the objective of improving mental health services at all levels of healthcare (primary, secondary, and tertiary) for early recognition, adequate treatment, and rehabilitation of the patients with mental health problems within the community and in the hospitals.

KEY POINTS

- **Community psychiatry** can be defined as a branch of psychiatry concerned with the detection, prevention, and treatment of mental disorders in a designated geographical area, with emphasis on environmental factors.
- The principle of community psychiatry is to treat people with mental disorders in a domiciliary setting instead of a psychiatric hospital (asylum).
- It refers to a system of care in which the patient's community is the primary provider of care for people with mental illness.
- Some of the common approaches of community care practiced worldwide are assertive community treatment (ACT), case management, satellite clinics, therapeutic community, and community-based rehabilitation (CBR).
- The Government of India implemented the **National Mental Health Programme (NMHP)** in **1982**.
- National Mental Health Programme has the objective of improving mental health services at all levels of healthcare (primary, secondary, and tertiary) for early recognition, adequate treatment, and rehabilitation of the patients with mental health problems within the community and in the hospitals.
- Apart from DMHP, which is the backbone of the program, the salient points of NMHP are public-private partnership model activities, day care center, residential/long-term continuing care center, mental health helpline, and tertiary-level activities focusing on manpower development schemes.

SELF-ASSESSMENT

1. Define community psychiatry and enumerate various community mental healthcare approaches.
2. Write short notes on:
   a. Assertive community treatment (ACT)
   b. Community-based rehabilitation (CBR)
   c. National Mental Health Programme (NMHP)

Chapter 36

Community Psychiatry

Shashidhara HN · Vinay B · Suresh Bada Math

Community psychiatry can be defined as a branch of psychiatry concerned with the detection, prevention, and treatment of mental disorders in a designated geographical area, with emphasis on environmental factors. The scope of community mental healthcare has extended way beyond mere outpatient care of mentally ill persons to holistic promotive, preventive, curative, and rehabilitative care of the people in the community through active community participation. Community mental healthcare comprises the principles and practices needed to promote mental health for a local population by:

1. Responsibility to a population for delivery of mental health care services
2. Treatment close to the patient's home
3. Multidisciplinary team approach
4. Continuity of care in the community
5. Emphasis on preventive aspects along with treatment
6. Comprehensive services at the doorstep

Community-based mental healthcare offers early diagnosis, initiation of culturally appropriate treatment, rehabilitation, and a higher quality of life. The principle of community psychiatry is to treat people with mental disorders in a domiciliary setting instead of a psychiatric hospital (asylum). It refers to a system of care in which the patient's community is the primary provider of care for people with mental illness.

APPROACHES OF COMMUNITY MENTAL HEALTHCARE

Some of the common approaches of community care practiced worldwide are given below.

1. **Assertive community treatment (ACT):** It is an intensive and highly integrated community mental health service delivery model that provides comprehensive, locally based treatment to people with serious and persistent mental illnesses. ACT recipients receive multidisciplinary, round-the-clock staffing of a psychiatric unit, but within the comfort of their own home and community. ACT model has a *low client-staff ratio* of approximately 10 clients per ACT practitioner. In addition, ACT teams provide *continuous coverage*, and emergency services, 24 hours per day, 7 days per week.
2. **Case management:** Case management is a model of care that is customized according to the individual's needs and limitations, delivered by a team of mental health professionals within the community from where the individual comes from. Several models of the case management system have been described. The key principles of any case management system include the following:
   I. Outreach or identification of clients
   II. Assessment of individual needs

III. Service or care planning
IV. Plan implementation
V. Progress monitoring
VI. Regular review and termination

3. **Satellite clinics:** These are often practiced in low- and middle-income countries like India, where tertiary care hospitals send a team of experts to remote areas. Here the team, usually with the collaboration of local community resources, delivers clinical services to the population of that remote area. Satellite clinics assure delivery of expert care to the needy people in their vicinity with minimal cost to the patients. However, the continuity of care cannot be ascertained, and they do not help in strengthening or empowering the local health resources. Hence, it may not sustain in the long run, unless there is a strong political motive.
4. **Therapeutic community:** The therapeutic community model is a system of care where persons with similar problems are brought together and live in common residential care, along with the therapists. The therapeutic community is based on the principle that clients modify their behavior by peer pressure. Group therapy is the mainstay of the therapeutic approach. This model is commonly used for patients with substance use disorders.
5. **Community-based rehabilitation (CBR):** It was initiated by the World Health Organization (WHO) in an effort to enhance the quality of life for people with disabilities and their families, meet their basic needs, and ensure their inclusion and participation. Initially, CBR was a strategy to increase access to rehabilitation services in resource-constrained settings.

   This strategy was intended to enhance the quality of life for people with disabilities through community initiatives. The intention was to promote the concept of the "inclusive community"—local resources being used to support the rehabilitation of people with disabilities in their communities.

COMMUNITY MENTAL HEALTHCARE IN INDIA

Over the last four decades or so, community psychiatry in India has made significant progress. The mental health services in India progressed almost parallel with the global movement, but the pace was limited by the availability of resources. When mental hospitals were found inadequate, a number of initiatives to improve mental healthcare were started, mainly by the government and government-run institutes. However, several nongovernment organizations and private institutes also took the initiative. There have been some long-standing, well-known community-based projects in India; the two most important among them were the Raipur Rani Project in Haryana and the Sakalawara Project in the peripheries of Bangalore, Karnataka. Both centers were based on the objective of establishing mental health services through primary/peripheral care centers and the principle of integrating mental healthcare into general healthcare.

National Mental Health Programme

The Government of India implemented the **National Mental Health Programme** (NMHP) in 1982 with the following objectives:

1. To ensure the **availability** and **accessibility** of minimum mental healthcare for all in the foreseeable future, particularly

The disability legislation prescribes punishment for fraudulently availing any benefit meant for persons with benchmark disabilities under Section 91, which states that whoever fraudulently avails or attempts to avail any benefit meant for persons with benchmark disabilities shall be punishable with imprisonment for a term which may extend to 2 years or with fine which may extend to INR 100,000 or both.

RPWD make provision of reservation in education and employment for persons with benchmark disabilities in government institutions. Person with **benchmark disability** means a person with not less than 40% of a specified disability as certified by the certifying authority. It speaks of inclusive education and penalties for offenses against persons with disabilities (PWDs). The Act also specifies provisions for special courts (to speed up the trial of cases of said offenses) and a national fund and a state fund for PWDs.

KEY POINTS

- **Forensic psychiatry** is "the branch of psychiatry that deals with issues arising in the interface between psychiatry and the law, and with the flow of mentally disordered offenders along with a continuum of social systems."
- The **insanity plea** is a defense in a criminal case, arguing that the offender is not responsible for his or her actions due to an episodic or persistent psychiatric disease at the time of the criminal act.
- In India, Section 84 of the IPC states that "nothing is an offense, which is done by a person, who at the time of doing it, by reason of unsoundness of mind, is incapable of knowing the nature of his or her act or that he is doing what is either wrong or contrary to law."
- **Fitness to stand trial** deals with the mental capacity of an individual to participate in legal proceedings.
- **Testamentary capacity** is a person's legal and mental ability to make or alter a valid will.
- Marriage between two Hindus is solemnized, only if at the time of the marriage neither party:
  a. is incapable of giving a valid consent of it in consequence of unsoundness of mind; or
  b. though capable of giving a valid consent has been suffering from mental disorder of such a kind or to such an extent as to be unfit for marriage and the procreation of children; or
  c. has been subject to recurrent attacks of insanity or epilepsy.
- The Mental Healthcare Act, 2017 (MHCA, 2017) prohibits certain procedures such as seclusion and chaining of persons with mental illness, electroconvulsive therapy without muscle relaxant, and anesthesia and electroconvulsive therapy of minors. MHCA decriminalizes suicide by repealing the Section 309 of the IPC.
- Amended NDPS Act, 2014 prepared a list of **essential narcotic drugs** (opioids identified for medical use approved by the drug controller general of India). The essential narcotic drugs include morphine, methadone, codeine, hydrocodone, oxycodone, tramadol, and fentanyl.
- Rights of Persons with Disabilities Act, 2016 (RPWD, 2016) makes provision of reservation in education and employment for persons with benchmark disabilities in government institutions. It speaks of inclusive education and penalties for offenses against persons with disabilities (PWDs).

SELF-ASSESSMENT

1. Write short notes on:
   a. Insanity plea
   b. Fitness to stand trial
   c. Testamentary capacity
   d. Mental Healthcare Act (MHCA), 2017
   e. Narcotic Drugs and Psychotropic Substances Act (NDPS), 2014
   f. Rights of Persons with Disabilities Act (RPWD), 2016

Salient Features of the Act

1. It protects the right of persons with mental illness.
2. In the case of future care, the individuals can make an **advance directive**, regarding how they want themselves to be taken care of, if decision capacity is impaired by mental illness.
3. It prescribes the minimum standards for establishing, registering, and controlling mental health establishments for mentally ill persons.
4. The act regulates the procedure of admission and discharge of mentally ill persons to mental health establishments either voluntarily or involuntary.
5. It provides every person the right to access mental healthcare and treatment from mental health services run or funded by the Government.
6. It enables mentally ill persons by providing free legal aid services.
7. The act restricts a mental health professional or medical practitioner to discharge any duty or perform any function not authorized by this Act.
8. It establishes duties and responsibilities for police in respect of persons with mental illness.
9. It provides provisions for the use of the ambulance services in the same manner, extent, and quality as provided to persons with physical illness.
10. It prohibits certain procedures such as:
    a. Sterilization of men or women, when intended as a treatment for mental illness
    b. Chaining of person with mental illness in any manner or form whatsoever
    c. Seclusion of persons with mental illness
    d. Electroconvulsive therapy without the use of muscle relaxant and anesthesia.
    e. Electroconvulsive therapy for minors: If in the opinion of psychiatrist, in charge of a minor's treatment, electroconvulsive therapy is required, then, such treatment shall be done with the informed consent of the guardian and prior permission of the concerned board.
11. It enables person who has attempted suicide by the decriminalization of such an attempt and making provision for support and treatment.

NARCOTIC DRUGS AND PSYCHOTROPIC SUBSTANCE ACT (AMENDMENT), 2014

Drug abuse has become a major social, economic, health, crime, and terrorism-related issue. To combat this problem, the Indian Government took the first step by enacting the Narcotic Drugs and Psychotropic Substances (NDPS) Act, 1985. Under the NDPS Act, the cultivation, production, manufacture, possession, sale, purchase, transportation, warehousing, consumption, interstate movement, transshipment, and import and export of NDPS is prohibited, except for medical or scientific purposes. The Act has been amended thrice—in 1988, 2001, and 2014. The Act covers the whole of India, and applies to all Indian citizens outside India and to all persons on ships and aircraft registered in India.

The NDPS Act focuses on three different categories of persons liable for prosecution. They are:

a. Drugs manufacturers/cultivators
b. Dealers/traffickers/transporters
c. Consumers (substance users/addicts)

The first two groups (manufacturers and traffickers) have monetary motives, whereas the third group (consumers) is a drug-dependent group, which does not have any profit-making motive but requires treatment. Research has proven beyond doubt that substance dependence is an illness and requires treatment for a long duration. However, the Act does not differentiate between these offender groups.

Section 27 of the NDPS Act states that individuals found to be in illegal possession of drugs in a small quantity for personal use are liable to punishment up to 6 months of imprisonment or fine or both, which in case of hard drugs like heroin would be up to 1 year's imprisonment or fine or both.

To tackle the menace of drug abuse and facilitate the treatment, NDPS amended the rules of 2014 and brought in paradigm shifts in the perspective of the legislation. Amended NDPS Act, 2014, prepared a list of **essential narcotic drugs** (opioids identified for medical use approved by the Drug Controller General of India). The essential narcotic drugs include morphine, methadone, codeine, hydrocodone, oxycodone, tramadol, and fentanyl. It defined registered medical institutions with criteria for stocking and dispensing opioids for medical use.

THE RIGHTS OF PERSONS WITH DISABILITIES ACT, 2016

India ratified the United Nations Convention on the Rights to Persons with Disability on the 1st day of October 2007. To align the national law, RPWD was enacted, which received the assent of the president on December 27, 2016.

The RPWD defines a "person with a disability" as a person with long-term physical, mental, intellectual, or sensory impairment which, in interaction with barriers, hinders his full and effective participation in society equally with others.

The specified disabilities under the Act are specified in the Schedule are as follows:

1. Physical disability
   a. Locomotor disability, leprosy-cured person (but is suffering from loss of sensation in hands or feet as well as loss of sensation and paresis in the eye and eyelid with or without deformity), cerebral palsy, muscular dystrophy, acid attack victims, and dwarfism
   b. Visual impairment
   c. Hearing impairment
   d. Speech and language disability
2. Intellectual disability including
   a. Specific learning disabilities
   b. Autism spectrum disorder
3. Mental behavior: "Mental illness" means a substantial disorder of thinking, mood, perception, orientation, or memory that grossly impairs judgment, behavior, capacity to recognize reality, or ability to meet the ordinary demands of life, but does not include retardation which is a condition of arrested or incomplete development of mind of a person, specially characterized by subnormality of intelligence.
4. Disability caused due to
   a. Chronic neurological conditions such as multiple sclerosis, Parkinson disease, and so on
   b. Blood disorders are hemophilia, sickle cell diseases, and thalassemia
5. Multiple disabilities
6. Any other category as may be notified by the central government

15. **Gilhari syndrome** is also known as the "**squirrel or lizard syndrome**" and is highly prevalent among the regions of West Rajasthan. **Gilhari syndrome** is characterized by patients complaining of small swelling on the body changing its position from time to time as if a gilhari (squirrel) is traveling in the body.
16. **Jhinjhinia**: In vernacular, "Jhin-Jhini" means tingling and numbness. As tingling and numbness are the presenting symptoms of the strange disease, it was called "Jhin-Jhini." This is prevalent in West Bengal. The disease strikes an individual unexpectedly with the sensation of tingling and numbness in the legs which spreads upward throughout the body.
17. **Suchi-bai syndrome**: Suchi-bai is found in Bengal, especially in Hindu widows. Common symptoms of these patients include washing too often; not eating anywhere outside; changing of street clothes (own and sometime compulsorily for all family members); washing of money (including currency notes); bathing for four hours twice a day; hanging out street clothes outside on a tree and entering house naked; hopping while walking (to avoid touching anything dirty in the streets); sprinkling of cow dung water on all visitors, etc.

Cultural concepts are important to avoid misdiagnosis. A clinician not tuned with cultural concepts may make the wrong diagnosis or misjudge the severity of illness (e.g., spiritual explanation of an illness may be misdiagnosed as psychosis). In conclusion, understanding that the presentation of mental distress can vary in different cultures in unique ways can help in better mental health screening and avoiding misdiagnosis.

KEY POINTS

- Psychiatric syndromes, which are thought to be limited and unique to a certain cultural group or geographic region with similar cultural groups, are called culture-specific or culture-bound syndromes.
- In **Dhat syndrome**, the patient complains of a whitish discharge during urination or defecation and he considers this whitish discharge as dhatu (semen). Dhat syndrome is characterized by anxiety, fatigue, weakness, weight loss, impotence, depressive mood, and the patient attributes his symptoms to semen loss.
- In **possession**, affected persons assert that they are possessed by a spirit which may be a God or a demon. It is more common in females and is precipitated by stressful life conditions.
- In **koro**, the patient has a morbid concern that his penis is shrinking and will disappear into the abdominal wall and may cause his death.
- **Amok** is an acute outburst of unrestrained violence associated with indiscriminate homicidal attack. The affected person usually has amnesia for the event.
- **Pibloktoq** (arctic/polar hysteria) is a hysterical attack among polar Eskimos, usually females. Sudden onset of loss of consciousness and various abnormal behaviors such as tearing off his/her clothes, glossolalia, fleeing (nude or clothed), rolling in the snow, and throwing whatever comes in hand are common symptoms.

- In **Latah**, a person gets startled by external stimuli (e.g., being tickled) and experiences dissociative state.
- **Whitigo** (wendigo) occurs especially during periods of starvation. The affected person experiences distaste for food. The person interprets his distaste for food as a belief that he has been transformed into a wendigo or a cannibal monster.
- Latin American people use **Susto** to define the loss of soul. People believe that certain conditions (e.g., being frightened or startled) cause the soul to leave the body and can be treated by recapturing the soul through certain rituals.
- Cambodians people have morbid concerns that **khyal** (a wind-like substance) rises in the body along with blood and causes symptoms.
- **Maladi moun** ("sent sickness" or "humanly caused illness"): It is based on the assumption that illness can be produced by others. Interpersonal envy and malice cause people to send illness to a victim who is attractive, intelligent, or wealthy.
- **Taijin kyofusho** (interpersonal fear disorder): It is a cultural syndrome found in Japan that is characterized by anxiety about and avoidance of interpersonal situations due to the thought that one's actions and appearance in social interactions are inadequate or offensive to others.
- **Ascetic syndrome** is characterized by social withdrawal, severe sexual abstinence, the practice of religious austerities, lack of concern with physical appearance, and considerable loss of weight.
- **Suudu**: It is a culture-specific syndrome of painful urination and pelvic "heat" found in South India.
- **Gilhari syndrome** is characterized by patients complaining of small swelling on the body changing its position from time to time as if a gilhari (squirrel) is traveling in the body.
- **Jhinjhinia** strikes an individual unexpectedly with the sensation of tingling and numbness in the legs which spreads upward throughout the body.
- Common symptoms of **Suchi-bai syndrome** include washing too often; not eating anywhere outside; washing of money (including currency notes); hanging out street clothes outside on a tree and entering house naked; hopping while walking (to avoid touching anything dirty in the streets); sprinkling of cow dung water on all visitors, etc.

SELF-ASSESSMENT

1. Define culture-bound syndromes. Enumerate various culture-bound syndromes.
2. Describe various culture-bound syndromes prevalent in India.
3. Write short notes on:
   a. Dhat syndrome
   b. Koro

the patient attributes his symptoms to semen loss.

Concerns about white vaginal discharge (leucorrhea) are a variant of dhat syndrome in females. This syndrome is prevalent in India, Nepal, Bangladesh, and Pakistan. In Sri Lanka, it is called **Prameha disease**.

3. **Possession syndrome:** In possession, affected persons assert that they are possessed by a spirit which may be a God or a demon, and make dramatic movements such as head bobbing, bodily shaking, or gyrating, or falling to the ground accompanied by verbalizations. It is more common in females and is precipitated by stressful life conditions.
4. **Koro:** Koro is a Malay term, which means the head of the turtle (symbolizes the male sexual organ which can shrink). In koro, the patient has a morbid concern that his penis is shrinking and will disappear into the abdominal wall and may cause his death. The symptom may be a simple excessive concern or obsessive/hypochondriacal concern or panic condition related to the shrinkage of the penis. It affects mainly young males. Any protruding part of the body may be involved in koro (e.g., nose or ear) in prepubertal children and nipples or labia in females. This culture-bound syndrome is seen in Asian countries such as China, Malaysia, Thailand, Indonesia, and India.
5. **Amok:** Amok is a Malay term which means to engage furiously in battle. Amok is an acute outburst of unrestrained violence associated with the indiscriminate homicidal attack. The affected person usually has amnesia for the event. It is reported in South Asia such as Thailand, Philippines, Indonesia, and Malaysia. Loss of social standing by way of insult, loss of employment, or financial loss are the precipitating events.
6. **Pibloktoq (arctic/polar hysteria):** It is a hysterical attack among polar Eskimos, usually females. Sudden onset of loss of consciousness and various abnormal behaviors such as tearing off his/her clothes, glossolalia, fleeing (nude or clothed), rolling in the snow, and throwing whatever comes in hand are common symptoms. Generally, it is due to some underlying anxiety triggered by severe culture-specific stress such as fear of impending situations, fear of loss, or fear of losing emotional support.
7. **Latah (startle reaction):** In Latah, a person gets startled by external stimuli (e.g., being tickled) and experiences dissociative state characterized by unusual behavior such as echolalia, echopraxia, or command automatism—explosive verbal outbursts usually of erotic words. This syndrome has been reported from Malaysia. It is known by different names in different countries, Burma (**Yaun**), Thailand (**bah-tsche**), Philippines (**mali-mali**), and Japan (**imu**). It predominantly affects women. Usually, a stressful event occurs shortly before the first Latah reaction, after that it becomes habitual and any immediate stimulus (hearing a sudden noise or being touched by others) may cause Latah. A person usually has amnesia after the dissociation reaction is over. The patient feels embarrassed about the inappropriate behavior during the attack (e.g., saying dirty words or touching men). Latah is socially accepted as a female attention-seeking response.

8. **Whitigo (wendigo):** This syndrome is seen in Native Americans of Cree, Ojibway, and Salteaux tribes, who experience severe winter and scarcity of food. It occurs especially during periods of starvation. The affected person experiences distaste for food. When this condition continues, he becomes anxious and interprets his distaste for food as a belief that he has been transformed into a wendigo or a cannibal monster.
9. **Susto (soul loss):** Susto is a Spanish word meaning fright. Latin American people use Susto to define the loss of soul. People believe that certain conditions (e.g., being frightened or startled) cause the soul to leave the body and can be treated by recapturing the soul through certain rituals. The victim may have sleep and appetite disturbance, absent mindedness, reduced strength, headache, dizziness, somatic symptoms or emotional symptoms of depression, anxiety, and irritability.
10. **Khyal cap**: Khyal attacks, also known as wind attacks, are found in Cambodia. People have morbid concerns that khyal (a wind-like substance) rises in the body along with blood and causes symptoms. Attacks resemble panic attacks, with usual symptoms like dizziness, palpitations, shortness of breath, cold extremities, tinnitus, and neck soreness. They believe that shortness of breath is caused by compression of lungs by khyal, and tinnitus, blurring of vision, and dizziness are caused by khyal in the cranium.
11. **Maladi moun ("sent sickness" or "humanly caused illness"):** It is prevalent in the Haitian community. It is based on the assumption that illness can be produced by others. Interpersonal envy and malice cause people to send illness to a victim who is attractive, intelligent, or wealthy. The acute onset of the symptoms or sudden behavioral change raises suspicion of a spiritual attack. The label of Maladi moun depends on the mode of onset and social status rather than presenting complaints.
12. **Taijin kyofusho (interpersonal fear disorder):** It is a cultural syndrome found in Japan that is characterized by anxiety about and avoidance of interpersonal situations due to the thought that one's actions and appearance in social interactions are inadequate or offensive to others. There are concerns about facial blushing (**erythrophobia**), having offensive body order (**olfactory reference syndrome**), too much or too little eye contact, body deformity, awkward facial expression, or bodily movements. **Taein Kong Po** is a related condition in Korea.
13. **Ascetic syndrome:** First described by Dr Neki in 1972 in India, it appears in adolescents and young adults and is characterized by social withdrawal, severe sexual abstinence, the practice of religious austerities, lack of concern with physical appearance, and considerable loss of weight.
14. **Suudu:** It is a culture-specific syndrome of painful urination and pelvic "heat" found in South India. It occurs in both males and females. It is attributed to an increase in the "inner heat" of the body, often due to dehydration.

KEY POINTS

- Consultation-liaison psychiatry (CLP) is the subspecialty of psychiatry, which deals with the understanding of "the interplay of biological and psychosocial factors in the development, course, and outcome of all disease(s)."
- Lipowski in 1967 defined CLP as a subspecialty of psychiatry that involves providing clinical service, teaching, and carrying out research at the borderland of psychiatry and medicine.
- In terms of work, a CL psychiatrist is expected to carry out the responsibilities of providing clinical care, teaching, administration, and research.
- CLP has demonstrated the role of communication skills, empathy, therapeutic alliance, and the doctor–patient relationship in the management of various physical disorders.
- The CLP has played an important role in breaking bad news.

SELF-ASSESSMENT

1. What are the contributions of consultation-liaison psychiatry to the practice of medicine?
2. Write a short note on consultation-liaison psychiatry.

Chapter 38

Culture-Bound Syndromes

Sandeep Kumar Goyal · Nimmi A Jose · Rajeev Gupta

Psychiatric syndromes, which are thought to be limited and unique to a certain cultural group or geographic region with similar cultural groups, are called culture-specific or culture-bound syndromes.

In the late 1950s, **Raymond Prince** described "**Brain fag**," a culture-bound syndrome characterized by mental fatigue, difficulty in concentration, and heat in head. The term culture-bound syndrome was introduced by **Yap** in 1969. The ICD-10 uses the term "**culture-specific disorders**."

COMPARATIVE NOSOLOGY

In the DSM-IV-TR, **culture-bound syndromes** were described as recurrent, locality-specific patterns of aberrant behavior and troubling experience that may or may not be linked to a particular DSM-IV diagnostic category.

The DSM-5 replaced the term culture-bound syndromes with "**cultural concepts of distress**."The ways by which cultural groups experience, understand, and communicate suffering, behavioral problems, or troubling thoughts and emotions are referred to as cultural concepts of distress. They are considered socially acceptable ways to express distress in the wake of a traumatic event.

Cultural syndromes, cultural idioms of distress, and **cultural explanations or perceived causes** are **three types** of cultural concepts of distress.

More than 200 culture-bound syndromes have been reported from different parts of the world, many of which have exotic names. In India, common culture-bound syndromes are possession syndrome, dhat syndrome, koro, gilhari syndrome, suchi-bai syndrome, Jhinjhinia, ascetic syndrome, and so forth. A few of the common ones are as follows:

1. **Ataque de nervios (attack of nerves):** It has been reported in individuals of Latino descent, and is characterized by intense emotional upset (anxiety, anger, grief), screaming and shouting uncontrollably, crying spells, trembling, heat rising into the head from chest, aggression, depersonalization, derealization, amnesia, suicidal gestures, and sense of being out of control. It usually occurs after some stressful event in the family (e.g., death of a family member).
2. **Dhat syndrome:** The term dhat syndrome was first used by Dr N.N. Wig. Patient complaints of a whitish discharge during urination or defecation and he considers this whitish discharge as dhatu (semen). According to Ayurveda, semen is one of the essential body fluids and myths about the harmful effects of semen loss are widespread in South Asia. The patient attributes the passage of semen in urine to his excessive indulgence in masturbation. Dhat syndrome is characterized by anxiety, fatigue, weakness, weight loss, impotence, depressive mood, and

Chapter 37

Consultation-Liaison Psychiatry

Sandeep Grover

Consultation-liaison psychiatry (CLP) and "psychosomatic medicine" are used interchangeably to describe the subspecialty of psychiatry, which deals with the understanding of "the interplay of biological and psychosocial factors in the development, course, and outcome of all diseases."

HISTORY OF CLP/ PSYCHOSOMATIC MEDICINE

The clinical aspect of psychosomatic medicine, that is, CLP, came into existence in the beginning of 20th century, with the setting up of first-ever viable general hospital psychiatric unit (GHPU) at the Albany Hospital in 1902 by **JM Mosher**. The unit was set with the basic aim of bringing mental health professionals into close proximity with other specialists in medicine for the purpose of training and providing psychiatric care. After this beginning, the subspecialty of CLP made huge strides across the world with the opening of GHPUs across the world.

However, the first formal definition of the subspecialty of CLP was given by **Lipowski** in 1967, who defined CLP as a subspecialty of psychiatry that involves providing clinical services, teaching, and carrying out research at the borderland of psychiatry and medicine.

He described the two interrelated roles of the consultation-liaison (CL) psychiatrist. According to him, the term "**consultation**" implies giving an expert opinion about the diagnosis and advice on the management of a patient with medical or surgical illness on the request of the primary physician/surgeon of the patient. The term "**liaison**" implies linking up of groups of professionals for effective collaboration.

Over the last half century, the concept of liaison has been further broadened to involve interpretation and mediation. Accordingly, the mental health professional working as a CL psychiatrist is expected to mediate between patients, family members and members of the clinical team, and also between mental health and other health professionals.

ROLES AND FUNCTIONS OF CL PSYCHIATRIST

A good CL psychiatrist is expected to be a medical expert, a good communicator, a good collaborator, a manager, a supervisor, a health advocate, and a scholar. In terms of work, a CL psychiatrist is expected to carry out the responsibilities of providing clinical care, teaching, administration, and research. The clinical work includes facilitation of the medical treatment of the patients by addressing the needs of the patients, primary physicians, nursing staff, patients' families and friends, and the healthcare system. Concerning training, the CLP expert is required to further the knowledge of the trainees in psychiatry and other specialties and members of the medical and surgical teams for the mental health issues.

CONTRIBUTIONS OF CLP TO MEDICINE

CLP as a subspecialty is based on the concept of "interaction of mind and body" and emphasizes the role of psychological and social factors in the development, continuation, help-seeking, following the advice, and overall outcome of various physical illnesses. Some of the most important contributions of CLP to medicine are shown in Box 37. 1.

CLP has helped in understanding the role of stress in the causation of various chronic physical illnesses. CLP has also contributed significantly to a better understanding of the role of psychological and social factors in the assessment and management of various physical conditions. Additionally, research in the area of CLP has demonstrated the role of communication skills, empathy, therapeutic alliance, and the doctor–patient relationship in the management of various physical disorders. The CLP has played an important role in breaking the bad news.

Box 37.1 Some important contributions of consultation-liaison psychiatry to the practice of medicine

- Guidance provided for communication skills of physicians
- Discussion about the diagnosis of cancer—a policy of "truth-telling" in medicine and individualization of information disclosure
- Pre- and post-operative evaluation of the recipient and potential donors
- Pre- and post-testing counseling for HIV/AIDS
- Psychiatric disorders as causative factors for various physical illnesses
- Contribution of psychiatric manifestations to the course and outcome of various medical illnesses
- Psychiatric sequelae of medical disorders
- Work-related stress among doctors
- Identification and appropriate management of delirium leading to a significant reduction in hospital morbidity and healthcare costs
- Evolution of psycho-oncology, transplant psychiatry, psychonephrology, and cardiac psychiatry

Index

T